TO TRICK A RAJA

MAJESTIC MIDLIFE WITCH BOOK 3

N. Z. NASSER

HANORA SKY PRESS

CHAPTER I

In the dead of the night, the tiger's rhythmic purr rattled the thin mattress beneath us. A heavy paw lay across my back, its warmth seeping through my skin. He'd been human when he'd drifted off to sleep, both of us spent with exhaustion from the day's dealings. Human, when he'd looped an arm round my waist and pulled me closer before he'd shifted into his beast in slumber.

Unexpectedly. Terrifyingly.

But I trusted him.

So much so that the rise and fall of his tiger's breath on my neck was hypnotic—a lullaby crooned into my tired mind. Even so, my knotty thoughts made sleep impossible. Round and round, the thoughts whirled, each one a jagged shard of glass in my mind. Whether we should turn our backs on the kingdom and make a small, happy life for ourselves like my parents had. Whether we were foolish to stay and fight for Jalapashu. Whether I could live up to the expectations of the rebels around me. Whether we would survive the coming days. Whether I had put Leena in unforgivable danger, just as Sitara had done with us. Whether I would ever sleep soundly again.

I counted the tiger's breaths, matching my breathing to his. As if mirroring him could bring me peace. As if our togetherness could drive away our enemies. Enemies that were already at our door.

There was a strange intimacy now between us that contrasted with the careful aloofness of our initial encounters. It would have been different in the bay when we could have dated on our own terms, choosing our schedule of meetings, taking it slowly, and playing the push and pull games of early relationships. But war made everything more urgent. The fortress meant we were in close proximity all hours of the day and night, like our relationship was unfolding back to front in the heat of fire before we had truly tested one another.

It was both frightening and exciting.

At least Deven was getting some rest in the scant few hours before duty called.

Taking care not to wake him, I shifted to face him, toppling closer into the mattress dip carved by his bulk. The air carried the scent of earth and rain, blending with the musk of the tiger. Moonlight spilt through window crevices, illuminating our room enough for me to make out the elongated lines of shadowed whiskers on his pillow. God, he was beautiful—almost enough to make me forget that I'd become the leader of the resistance entirely by accident.

A creature like this belonged in evergreen forests or mangrove swamps, not in bed with me. He was a study in feline grace: delicate whiskers extending from a rugged face, tufted ears, glinting teeth hidden behind his powerful jaw, and velvet pads that held claws. His graceful limbs sometimes jerked as if he ran across plains in his dreams. Even sleeping, he exuded cruelty and wildness.

But Deven wasn't cruel. I only had to hear the cycle of his breath or look in his eyes to know it.

I edged closer, my senses alive. Reaching out to touch the

dark pad of his nose, I wondered how many of his primal transformations he had endured and whether it hurt or whether he slid into his other self as easily as I put on a coat.

There hadn't been much time to talk. Not to each other. Not with war on our doorstep.

It had been three days since we'd freed Mahi and Menon from the labyrinth and broken the curse that had prevented Deven from embracing his full self. Three days since I'd wrenched a fortress from the earth, my magic heightened by our fledgling coven's spell. Three days of organising the resistance and plotting how to win the throne of Jalapashu while my gargoyles manned the ramparts in anticipation of Prem Kumar's army. Thanks to their loyalty to the general, half the raja's soldiers had abandoned the raja and joined the resistance instead. But the path ahead was wrought with danger.

My general.

I loved him. I felt the truth of it in the caverns of my being. I hadn't dared tell Deven, so the words thrummed inside me like a captured symphony. A hummingbird's wings inside my chest I didn't release. Admitting I'd fallen for him would make the coming days harder. It would tempt fate to destroy what we had found. So I made do with stolen glances, fleeting kisses and nights when my body pressed up against his.

I prayed we'd survive the days ahead, even as disquiet curled through my belly.

Even as another man's ring sat on my finger.

I loathed the shining honey-hued topaz that symbolised Prem's ownership of me. I'd wrenched it from my ring finger. Instead, it wrapped around my middle finger like a hellish shackle. Deven's attention lingered on it often—his colour rising, a shadow passing over his face—as if it mocked us. But I couldn't discard it.

Not in a kingdom where it elevated my magic.

Not at a time when I needed every ounce of power.

To hell with sleep. We needed the comfort of each other's touch as much as we needed rest. I raked my fingers through the dense fur of Deven's golden neck, tracing the intricate patterns of the geometric tattoo that blended with his stripes. The tattoo he had added to each year symbolised his resilience and his vow to break his cousin's curse. To be both man and tiger again.

He stretched his tiger neck, unconsciously opening himself to my touch.

Impatient for his attention, I brushed the ends of his whiskers.

The tiger twitched as a flicker of awareness penetrated the depths of his slumber. Beautiful beast. Primal energy charged the air as Deven transitioned from dream-heavy sleep to consciousness with a startling intensity. His midnight eyes snapped open in confusion, and an instinctive, guttural growl echoed around the room. He rolled up, pinning me beneath him, his breathing as ragged as mine, scanning my drawn face, the hair fanned across the pillow, the waves of fear that rippled off me despite me using every ounce of my will to stay calm. His ears lay flat against his head as he bared tombstone teeth. Teeth that could rip through the soft skin of my throat with frightening ease.

Panic seared through me.

There was no recognition in that savage face.

Grinding stone filled my mind as the gargoyles reacted to my alarm. They swerved their attention away from the barricades towards me, marking Deven as a threat. *We are coming.*

No. I directed their attention away from us and steadied my breath as the tiger's face loomed above me, adrenalin coursing through his quivering body.

Deven scanned the room, dark eyes alert, before baring his teeth at me in his vicious wildness.

I willed myself to control my breathing, even as his claws

dug into the soft flesh of my shoulder. My magic was strong and vibrant. It called to me in the night, willing me to use its unexplored depths. I had made this fortress; I could collapse part of it onto the general, but that would be like cleaving my heart in two. I wouldn't do it.

My lips barely moved to form the whisper. "It's me. It's Kiya."

Obsidian eyes narrowed on me. A heartbeat spanned between us, the tiger poised to strike.

I dared to caress him with tentative, trembling fingers, my heart rattling like a runaway train, wondering if this would be my last moment, if I had taken one risk too many in this brutal kingdom.

Then, mercifully, the tiger's eyes clouded with bewilderment. The tenseness in his muscles dissolved. With a mournful sound, the tiger leapt from the bed and thudded onto the floor. My body quaked with relief as his body contorted: bones elongating, tail shrinking, fur retreating, jaw transforming—a reassembly of flesh and bones into the man who was mine.

Moments later, Deven—naked as the day he was born—knelt on the bed and pulled me against the hard planes of his chest. Strong hands cupped my face with exquisite gentleness. When he spoke, his voice thrummed with horror. "I could have killed you, little witch."

I couldn't bear the anguish on his face. "I'm okay."

He examined me for injuries like he'd never forgive himself, even though I knew that some part of him must have known it was me underneath him to hold back his nature.

"I don't fear you, even with your teeth inches from my face."

His face twisted. "Maybe you should. I'm not fully in control of myself."

"You will be."

He dropped his hands, and the loss of his touch made me shiver. The ghosts of his past flitted across his face: the wife he was convinced he should have saved from Prem's murderous games. He had barely stitched himself back together after that. His quiet voice pulsed with fear. "What if..."

I shook my head, aching for him. The wounds of his past ran so deep. "That's not going to happen."

"I shifted inadvertently in my sleep and you're relaxed about it?"

It wasn't your typical relationship hiccup, but nothing about my life was normal anymore. My casual shrug belied the tiniest seed of worry. "So you still have kinks to work out."

"My senses are overwhelming. I can smell the bonfires that Prem has stacked with our belongings. I'm filing people I've known all my life under predator or prey. I'm distracted by your lingering scent all over the fortress."

"One of those doesn't sound so bad."

His smile lit a fire in my belly, but the stillness in his eyes revealed his worry. "I can't shake the restlessness in my bones. I yearn to be in my tiger form every second of the day. The only time I can bear to be human is when I am touching you."

Looping my arms around his neck, I dropped a kiss on his lips. He tasted of cool winds and distant fires. "Go ahead. I'm game."

He kissed me back hungrily, then pulled away. "You're not helping."

"Prem suppressed your animal nature for *years*. You're not going to find your way again overnight. It'll take a bit of time."

"We don't have time." A growl reverberated deep in his chest. "I need you to be safe."

"Then let's deal with our real enemies and not fight each other."

Footsteps skittered in the hallway outside. Somebody needed us.

I stole another kiss, and his tongue delved into my mouth as if he might never get another chance, as if only he and I were left in the world, and that was enough. That would be our heaven. A heaven of winter wilds, his lips on mine and a tiger tearing through forest ferns with me clinging to his back.

With a groan of protest, he relinquished his hold on me and reached for his clothes as Leena burst through the door.

Her mouth quirked at the sight of Deven's bare cheeks as he pulled on his trousers and buttoned up his shirt. "I'd apologise for waking you in the middle of the night, but I can see you didn't follow the advice you gave to your men. Did you get *any* rest?"

I rolled off the bed and searched her face. "Is everything okay?"

Her golden hair in a messy bun reminded me of when she'd come home from the hospital in her nursing days before we left Boundless Bay. Her fingertips were plummy from the fruit she had been magicking up for the resistance. "You're both needed in the hall."

Deven grunted. "We guessed as much."

She gave him a pointed look. "Yuvan told me you risked a run through the forest yesterday."

The air disappeared from the room. He'd promised me he'd be careful.

He kept his focus on my sister. "It's not Yuvan's job to keep track of my movements. He's not my servant anymore."

"If you're captured by Prem..."

"Then I'll make him pay." His face was unyielding. Like he wanted Prem to find him. "I can take care of myself, Leena."

"Fine. Then I'll worry about my sister." Her mouth turned downwards as she looked around. "I wish you weren't so determined to stay here. It's barely a room. There's not even a washbasin."

I swallowed my rising dread at the risks Deven was taking and deadpanned. "The spell didn't account for plumbing."

"That's not what I meant, and you know it." She huffed. "You should both be at home with us."

"What would the people think? We're no more important than anyone else. We can make do just like they can. And I like that you, Aanya, Grandfather and Nani are together. It makes me worry less."

"What about how much I worry? I've already lost one sister. Maybe I need the comfort of having my other sister close."

Leena wanted me close, but being near her was a reminder of losing Sitara. It made the grief pangs in my chest sharper. "You don't *need* to worry about me."

The comparison hung between us. How her magic was nurturing green witchcraft that allowed flowers and fruit to grow, although it could be wielded as vines and thorns. How mine pulsed with darkness—I could create, yes…vessels that contained spells, awaken sleeping gargoyles, raise walls and fortresses—but I could also rip trees from the earth, cause rockfalls and bore chasms in the earth where men walked. I could kill as easily as she grew. Maybe that is why fate had chosen me for this role.

A dark queen for a dark kingdom, if the seer was to be believed.

Leena's mouth opened like she wanted to protest, but her shoulders slumped in defeat at my stare.

"You have my promise. I won't let anything happen to her." Deven buttoned his borrowed civilian shirt. "Kiya's right. The people need to see that we're willing to suffer alongside them and fight for them."

Leena's shoulders slumped. "Well, that's that then. Get dressed. I'll wait for you in the corridor."

My throat was tight as I threw on a few layers, tidied my unruly hair and tucked one of Deven's sheathed daggers into my waistband. He no longer wore his belt of daggers; it had become another discarded part of his identity. Tigers had no need for daggers when they had razor-sharp teeth and ferocious claws. But I embraced the serrated steel. The tangible weight of it against my skin reassured me. I might have shown Leena bravado, but I was worried, too.

A blade between an enemy's ribs was more reliable than magic.

Old me would have been horrified that I carried a knife. Hell, old me would be incensed that I prioritised anything other than pottery. But it was impossible to live an ordinary life when the world was bigger than I had ever imagined.

Your anger makes you strong. Violence is the only way, said the chorus of gargoyles in my mind.

The night air vibrated with the promise of evil, and I blinked away its slithering embrace.

We followed my sister through the fortress. The scent of communal cooking—*aloo paratha, dosa and sambar*—filled my nose, as well as the lingering smell of sweat and fear rising out of pores. Those who remained had forgone regular hours to pitch in with chores. The fortress bustled with men and women building makeshift beds, frying dough and sharpening swords. But as we hurried past, our resistance fighters laid down their tools and woke their sleeping kin. Hushed conversations echoed through walls. Bleary faces spilt out of their beds and joined the footsteps towards the hall.

Dread ratcheted up in my chest. "Leena, what is it that couldn't wait until morning?"

She turned, her face bleak. "The factions are at each other's throats. They want you to settle it."

The gargoyle's breathing pulsed in my mind like the drumbeat of battalions trudging across a vast plain. They had chosen me as their leader, but I didn't even know if I could be a good one. If not—even if my knife stayed sheathed—there'd be more blood on my hands than I could ever hope to wash off.

CHAPTER 2

We made our way through the murky halls of the fortress, keeping close together. The general's arm sometimes brushed mine as though, even subconsciously, he wanted to close the distance between us. Strangers jostled for my attention, calling out my name with reverence and placing their hands on their chests in solidarity. Then there were those whose eyes flickered with unease or deceit, whose lips curled down or who retreated into the lingering darkness as we passed.

Deven's protective instincts flared. You could take away a man's standing, but his soldier's discipline remained. His hand settled in the small of my back, and his gaze swept our surroundings for threats, lips compressing at the unfamiliar terrain and the shadows that danced up uneven walls and stout columns.

The sacred banyan tree's sprawling roots intertwined with one fortress wall, its body divided between the enemy's territory and ours, a symbol of the divisions in the kingdom. The people strung messages of grief and yearning on the portion of the sacred banyan tree that stood within the fortress. Fluttering notes of hope that hung on its branches like delicate ornaments in the moonlight. Each note told a story: a plea for safety, a remembrance of loved ones on the other side of the divide, dreams and prayers for the future, and expressions of gratitude to the stranger, the earth witch. To me. The woman they believed might be a turning page in Jalapashan history.

My hasty witchcraft hadn't allowed for great architectural feats.

I'd crafted a refuge for the resistance in the heat of urgency. The fortress stretched over half the houses in the kingdom, a black behemoth compared to the gleaming white of the raja's palace. It was rough around the edges, born of need, not cunning. Its walls consisted of large stones and clumps of soil melded together. Small window crevices punctuated the walls, allowing in only slivers of light and trickles of ventilation as if gloom blanketed the resistance. Harya, the lion-maned gargoyle leader, was pleased about the defensive advantages of the narrow apertures that allowed us to survey the raja's army without being overlooked. But there was no doubt that the fortress was a monstrosity, devoid of embellishments to soften its hard edges.

It made me fear my own potential for darkness.

Even so, the fortress had become a beacon of hope for some. A small stream of citizens sought sanctuary amongst us, but I worried about those left behind. People like *Lokesh Saheb*, the royal tailor, who had been kind to me, but who had built a life too comfortable to leave behind. The gargoyles I sent to guarantee the safety of those fleeing encountered only minor skirmishes. Reeling from the desertion of key members of his court, Prem had taken a few days to regroup. But we knew the respite wouldn't last. That every desertion was an insult that would only fuel his bloodlust.

Others—loyal to the raja or fearful of incurring his wrath—abandoned their homes within the fortress, their curses rattling in my ears. I watched them leave with a stone in my chest, knowing I had fractured the foundations of their lives. *This isn't your fault,* Deven had said yesterday. *They'll be thankful when all is said and done.* But he couldn't hide the pulse of worry in his midnight eyes. Neither his kisses nor sombre words of counsel washed away the taste of bitter regret on my lips.

Sitara wouldn't have fumbled in this situation. She would have known what to do.

Her magic had been clever and intentional; mine was raw, instinctive, unbridled.

I missed her so damn much.

We'd been blessed with a long goodbye. It was more than we'd ever got with our parents, and I was grateful. But suspending grief didn't make it easier to bear. We'd been each other's comfort blankets for so long. Her absence magnified my lack. Without her—especially in this magical world she had fought so hard for us to be a part of—I was a lonely satellite nudged out of orbit, drifting out into the cold. Small, petty things were impossible to achieve, and meaty problems were utterly hopeless without her counsel.

That same desolation haunted Leena's eyes, although it irked me that she'd admitted in the labyrinth that she was ready to let Sitara go. Sisters belonged together. Sitara's death was as disorienting as finding a star missing from a familiar constellation. I'd give anything for one last meal together as a three, one last peal of laughter, one searing argument even— a tumble of words that ended in making up over cake— because the world was always imperfect, but having sisters was a balm against its storms.

Sitara's not done with you yet, Mahi had said, the way an old auntie sidestepped the painful truth and chose hollow comfort instead. I wanted to believe the beautiful lie. I really did. I wanted to sleep all day and glimpse Sitara in my dreams. I wanted to go home to Boundless Bay, rummage in her closet, and bury my nose in the lingering scent of her orange and magnolia perfume before it faded.

But war was coming, and the resistance was counting on me.

The skies above Jalapashu were dark, but one thing was crystal clear: the coven's wards would only hold for so long. Then the raja would be at our door, teeth and claws bared.

My sister grimaced outside the hall. "Brace yourself. It's intense in there."

"If it's too much…" Deven held my gaze, aware of every flicker of my emotions.

We both knew that from the moment we'd opposed the raja, there was no turning back the clock. There was no mercy for us or those loyal to us unless we saw this through. Defiance was like that. One disobedient act snowballed into another until you were too far changed to slip into the mould that had once been you.

I sucked in a ragged breath. "Let's get this over with."

We entered the hall to voices surging like a river in monsoon. This part of the fortress had formed over a central junction in Jalapashu. Remnants of the streets were discernible underfoot: potholes, gullies, the edges of pavements and gloop from where old men had spat tobacco. Candlelit lanterns swung from open rafters that revealed a patchwork of the night sky and a restricted view of stars. Through here, the gargoyles launched themselves into the air and up onto the barricades.

Half the resistance had shunned sleep to be here. Sixty-odd men and women milled in small groups. They sat on improvised seating made of wooden crates, salvaged planks and assorted cushions. Maps of the kingdom had been secured by rocks against gusts of wintery wind. We were a melting pot of those thrown together by circumstance: the young and old, the poor and powerful, the magical and non-magical, merchants and artisans, soldiers loyal to Deven and a few lowly members of the raja's court. The gargoyles, stern and vigilant, invoked jittering awe and horror from those unused to their breathing stone forms. I recognised familiar faces amongst the strangers: Deven's sister and her family; Nitin, the court poet; Jilu and Radha, the chefs from Biryani Junction; Farida, our neighbour who had taken the emergence of the resistance to leave her husband; and the prisoners and one guard that Leena had befriended when the raja had jailed her. Beneath my feet, the earth hummed from the residual energy of my magic.

"Over there." Leena pointed towards our inner circle.

We plucked away towards them, and I realised that this group of people—however dysfunctional— had become my lifeline: our friends, our allies, our family.

Mahi looked worse for wear. She'd given herself a hacked pixie cut after emerging from the labyrinth. Both her face and her harem trousers were in desperate need of a wash. Her twin stood at her side, his skin smooth and his temples only sprinkled with grey, in contrast to her silver locks and deep wrinkles. They had been inseparable since his return from the time-warped labyrinth. My grandparents were awake too, their faces tired and drawn. Merlin, who avoided large crowds, peeked out from behind Aanya's legs, his whiskers still drooping from the ignominy of being turfed out of our bedroom.

The seer's dour face brightened when she spotted us. She rolled her eyes as we approached, and her parrot familiar mimicked her. "It started in the kitchens. A rumble of discontent. You'd think the ungrateful sods could have waited until morning. Instead, they pull me out of bed smelling like a skunk."

Deven's mouth quirked. "We're here now."

Assuaging the people's fears wasn't Mahi's forte, but she'd already given us the gift of a vision: that the Amber Hollows were empty, at least for now, until whatever endemic magic in those caves produced more over the millennia. So Prem's greed for more topaz, or his taking the fight to Boundless Bay, was one thing we didn't have to worry about. Fighting the battle on our doorstep was hard enough. I bent down to caress Merlin's sooty ears, then stood, steeling myself for the onslaught of opinions.

The voices came at us thick and fast from rebels huddled together to ward off the chill.

"We can't just stay here, praying that the wards won't fail."

"Our food stores are already low. What will we eat?"

"The earth witch should invoke the duel. Why wait?"

"What if the raja's powers grow? What will we do then?"

"Prem Kumar's wrath won't fizzle out. Unleash the gargoyles on him."

A few lone voices spoke up in favour of patience. Farida. The chef, Jilu. One of Leena's cellmates.

My chest tightened at their desperation. Not everyone had been lucky enough to have their homes on our side of the divide when the fortress was erected. Some displaced citizens had been forced to share quarters. Already, there had been sparks of temper and barbed words that couldn't be unsaid, however regrettable. Winning the throne was our dream, but the basic needs of the resistance had to be our priority. If we couldn't meet their needs for food, water, warmth and hygiene, we were worse than Prem.

A farmer spoke, his weathered face mottled with capillaries, a landscape etched with the scars of honest labour. "We've taken in six people. Not everyone here is so generous."

"Tell that wife of yours to stop whispering in your ear," came the prickly response from Lata, once the raja's courtesan and now part of the resistance. "You have your home. Many of us aren't as lucky. The raja's men have already looted my apartment as punishment. The scouts tell me my keepsakes have been tossed into fires. Photographs of my beloved father. My mother's jewellery. And you're worried about sharing your armchair."

"Your opinion isn't wanted here, whore. Last week, you warmed the raja's bed."

A scuffle broke out between the farmer and an enamoured young man defending Lata's honour. Violence of volcanic proportions bubbled beneath the surface of us all, a primal force fuelled by the potent blend of fear and scarcity. Rebels jeered. Even in the quiet ones, excitement bubbled beneath the appearance of civility. Prem had primed them to act this way, to enjoy spectacles and gain release from violence. A shiver crawled up my spine.

He could have been my husband.

"Enough." The rich blue of Menon's wizard's robes had once mirrored the night sky. Now, they had surrendered to a washed-out grey. Hints of mossy green peeked through patches where repairs had been attempted, and arcane symbols hinted at his knowledge of the mystical arts. He was handsome once you got past his brown eyes clouded with guilt. Slim and elegant, with a noble brow and sensual lips. "This is what the raja wants. He wants you fighting each other and not him. Will you let him win before the war has even begun?"

The bearded farmer shook off the men who held him back. "I want to hear from the earth witch. How long are we expected to endure? What will we eat? Where will we wash and shit when household appliances fail, and we don't have access to the outside world and our supply chains? When the raja holds access to our fields and our livestock dies?"

Harya, the lion-maned gargoyle leader, swung his ridged tail with its pointed arrow tip. He unfolded wings that were as sharp as scythes and turned them towards the people in a show of force. *I will silence the rabble for you without you uttering a word.*

"The witch can't even control them," shouted someone amidst the rising terror. "What's to stop history repeating itself? What's to stop them killing us?"

My commands lashed out like a whip. *No! We protect the people. We never side against them.* The gargoyles' instincts had been shaped over centuries, and though they answered to me, they were not easily remoulded.

Sindhuja, always the outlier amongst the gargoyles and sometimes vilified for it, filled our bond with a rush of warmth as Harya retracted his wings, grumbling.

Satisfied that I had made my point, I insulated them both from my mind, grateful for Mahi's insistence that I work on my gargoyle sound-proofing skills to maintain some semblance of thinking space. Even though I had asserted control, doubt swirled in the rebels' faces, and they skittered away from the gargoyles interspersed in the hall.

How could I blame them? It wasn't easy for the people to trust the gargoyles in their midst. They remembered the warnings whispered to babes in cradles. The stories revisited in the kingdom's school about ancestors slain by these very same otherworldly creatures on the instructions of a barbaric rani. Almost all, barring children who didn't know better, shrank from wings and tails and protruding teeth–once mere chiselled details–that were now as menacing as bayonets. Even though Sindhuja softened her stony edges by wearing a daisy headband conjured by Leena.

I saw it in their wild-eyed expressions that they weren't sure if they had leapt from one devil's bed into another's. That their fear clawed at them. That we had to offer them hope. And though I knew Deven was right by my side, that he commanded the respect of the people, he was still and quiet. He was prepared to put his body on the line to protect me, but he didn't offer his words. He didn't think it was his place. He thought it was mine.

But the vein that throbbed in his jaw and his imploring

eyes told me that he, too, sensed the tipping point: how this group of people brought together by scraps of hope, aspirations and loss might turn on each other. How we might lose control.

In private, he'd impressed on me over and again that wars were won and lost on moments like this. Either I kept the people's trust, or I didn't.

I raised my voice above the din. "The gargoyles won't hurt you. They'll protect you."

The rebels quietened, though I hadn't uttered a spell or threatened my magic.

Our previous sacrifices had bought us attention, if not loyalty.

A glimmer of a smile played on Mahi's lips as if she knew what I was capable of even before I began. I took in their expectant faces around me. There were over a hundred souls in the fortress and perhaps two hundred more loyal to Prem, all embroiled in this tussle for power. I trembled at the assumption that I had all the answers. I hated that they had made me the focal point of authority. The juxtaposition of potholes and open sky made me think we could just as easily soar as falter in the coming days.

God, I had no idea what I was doing.

My throat was clogged with ash. "None of us chose this path expecting it to be easy. We need to be everything that the raja isn't. We need to stay kind despite our fears. We need to pull together so everyone carries part of the burden, and no one person carries it all." I crumbled inside as my inadequate words tumbled out.

The farmer huffed in disdain. He spun towards Mahi, and the mood of the crowd blackened further. "This is your *queen-in-waiting*, seer? How is talk of togetherness going to protect us from a violent foe? She controls the gargoyles. If she is so powerful, why doesn't she end it all now? She could be our queen. But she's too frightened to duel the raja and settle this matter once and for all. Even though the old laws demand it."

I trembled in the glare of their attention, and Deven drew imperceptibly closer. Two nights ago, I had ridden through the starry night on his striped tiger back. When he had returned to his human form, we had caught our breath under a weeping willow. Shadows flittered over the sharp cut of his cheekbones, and I smoothed back the wayward curl of his black hair as he told me I'd have to become accustomed to the discomfort of not always being liked in the crucible of leadership.

I wanted to be queen. The labyrinth had coaxed that murky truth from me.

But wanting something wasn't the same as being capable of it.

"It should be him," called out a stranger. "The general should duel his cousin. He has the right to the throne. He has defeated him once before but refused to land a killing blow."

My grandfather furrowed his bushy brows. "Show some respect, or I'll teach you some."

A shout from the crowd. "You're no longer the raja's enforcer, Prakash."

"It's not my path to wear the crown," said Deven with quiet resolve. "It's Kiya's. I will do everything to make that day a reality."

"The general would be a good and fair raja," said Mahi. "But my visions have never mapped a path for him to take the throne. We have one chance to defeat the raja, and she stands here. She has courage and strength, and her instincts haven't failed us yet. She and her sisters mined the last jewels from the Amber Hollows. The ancient gargoyles breathe again because of her. My brother is freed from the labyrinth because of her. Prem Kumar is weakened because of her. And yet, you fools require more proof."

Years of conditioning meant that Jalapashans respected

strength above all else. But I wanted to show empathy, too. After all, how were we to build a new world together if the foundations remained as rigid and unfeeling as before? "Prem Kumar oppressed you. He took your homes. He collected unjust taxes. He decided who has the right to magic and who deserves Jalapashu's riches." My grandfather shifted uncomfortably, but the hum of approval spurred me on. "Like me, some of you have lost loved ones. Perhaps you want justice. Or revenge. Perhaps you dream of a better world. Perhaps you crave freedom. Or perhaps you live under the fear that you might anger the raja in some innocuous way and find claws at your necks. Maybe you just want to be safe. I understand your motivations because they are my own. Prem Kumar can't be allowed to remain on the throne."

Faint murmurs of assent punctuated each of my statements.

Pride glimmered in the seer's eyes at the change in mood. She unleashed Babbu from his perch on her shoulder in celebration. He spun overhead in a dazzling whirl of emerald green feathers as if heralding the new shoots of our movement. *You carry destruction and creation within your soul,* Mahi said when we found her in the labyrinth.

I wondered how much of this she had foreseen, how much she kept secret from me, how much these decisions were my own or twists of fate. I could paint our resistance in the vibrant hues of defiance, but the obstacles before us were too mountainous to chisel away.

Could I really be the queen Jalapashu had been waiting for?

Or was I the spark of hope that the raja would snuff out?

I opened my mouth before I could second-guess my instincts and fixed the farmer with a stare. "You wanted answers. Well, this is what I can tell you. You're right. The fortress and our wards won't protect us forever. Violence will come to our door, and we will be ready. The gargoyles have been on scouting missions. They are our eyes and ears beyond these walls. We won't be caught off guard, and Mahi's visions will help guide our way." My tone hardened. "But you're mistaken if you think I'll share our strategy here. There are those here tonight who wish us harm or failure. Those who are loyal and lend their skills to the resistance will be richly rewarded when the time comes. But if you harbour *any* intention of stirring up trouble, leave freely now or suffer the consequences."

Tension hung thick in the air as the resistance absorbed my ultimatum. My mind pulsed with a command for the gargoyles to step forward. Their movements synchronised eerily: stony candlelit flesh rippled with corded muscle, eyes like voids absorbed all light, spiked tails that resembled a scorpion's barbs slashed. A shiver traced up my spine as I used fear as a tool for respect, and I wondered if Prem had started this way: with good intentions but too much power.

"Now you've done it," Deven's glinting eyes warmed me like the flames in a hearth.

I gave a grim nod, satisfied that I had solidified a fragile allegiance.

I should have known better. I should have known how swiftly danger materialised in this kingdom, how alliances dissolved as quickly as they formed. That a stranger couldn't simply wrestle control in a stranglehold of power, however well-meaning. That the complex dynamics of Jalapashu would take a lifetime to learn, even though this had been our mother's birthplace. That authority and respect were currencies with a steep price, and sometimes, that price was blood.

I didn't hear the serrated dagger whistling through the air towards my throat.

I didn't sense its lethal trajectory.

I heard only Deven's furious bestial roar.

CHAPTER 3

Somewhere, Leena cried out an anguished warning.

I pivoted as the dagger shot through the air, carving a line through the air towards my throat. At that moment, I forgot my training. Forgot the lightness in my feet that Deven had encouraged me to practice, the instinctive dance of battle, to duck and weave and protect my body. I froze as the blade glinted, seconds from winning new blood. My blood.

Deven's breath went still. I didn't see him move, but suddenly, he was there, intercepting the trajectory of the blade. His fist flashed with claws, and his coal-black eyes deepened in intensity as though he might shift there and then, before all the people. He was all coiled rage and primal instinct, as though he'd devour my assailant until there was nothing left. Wild eyes flickered to me, and then he pushed into the crowd, seeking my attacker.

Then all hell broke loose: a wall of noise, grasping hands and surging feet.

At Mahi's bidding, Babbu swooped down to secure the dagger. Shock, astonishment and subtle satisfaction played on the faces around me. I didn't stop to identify friend from foe. Didn't stop to mark out whose eyes gleamed with perverse delight. The gargoyles pulsed in my mind, frustrated at how I'd muted our connection, how they were most effective as war machines. There was no time to pacify them. Men—Deven and my grandfather amongst them—already surrounded my attacker.

I pushed through the crowd, my fingers splaying against my own sheathed dagger. At my feet, Merlin stayed close, oh so close, ears flat against his sleek body. Deven had careened ahead of us, hauling my attacker off the ground by the scruff of his neck. He'd retracted his claws through sheer force of will, lips tight with effort.

The breath in my lungs thinned. It couldn't be.

A child. My attacker was a child of no more than ten or eleven years old.

A child with piercing blue eyes and a pinched mouth. I studied him, heart clanging against my ribcage. He had a steely belligerence that was at odds with his tender age. Despite his violent act, despite the witnesses, he wasn't scared. His hands hung loose, and his feet dangled, almost relaxed, as if he had determined he might get caught and didn't care. He didn't tussle with Deven, didn't try to escape or flinch when men rapped his head with their knuckles. His embroidered clothing suggested he came from a well-off family. He had an edge to him, as though he was accustomed to navigating a harsh world. As though he'd long since lost his innocence.

A shiver of unease swept through me. Others lurked within the resistance, wishing me harm. But it was a child who had taken it upon himself to act. "Put him down, General."

Deven's obsidian eyes darkened to the hue of the deepest night. His voice was a rasp of pain, laced with a growl, like the life he had built had been taken. "That title isn't mine anymore."

The tiger waited just beneath the surface, still. "Of course. All the same, put him down."

Passion sparked from his eyes, volatile and unquenchable. "He tried to kill you."

My mouth was like sandpaper. "Deven, he's unarmed. He's a *child*."

With a curse, Deven released his grip and motioned for the men to block any escape routes. The boy slid to the floor and regained his footing. His icy eyes widened at the hare, whose whiskers quivered in anxiety, and then—as if shaking off any childlike affinity to animals—squared his shoulders.

I squatted to face him and he didn't show a lick of fear. "What's your name?"

Cobalt eyes found mine as he ground out the words. "Like you care."

Merlin nudged around me, liquid gold eyes fixated on the boy. Broken children had always called to me, but this boy's flaws and hurts didn't seem small enough to patch up, even with time. There was a gaping chasm where naivety and faith in the goodness of the world had once been.

I kept my voice soft, though my heartbeat clattered. "Why do you want to kill me?"

The boy flexed his hands as if he lamented his missing dagger, as if he wished he had it still so he could bury it in my neck. "You're nothing. But you act like you're everything."

"That's not an answer."

A smirk lifted the corner of his mouth. "If you die, we can go back to how things were."

What made a child so bleak, so damaged? "Where are your parents?"

Nothing. Nothing except venom in the boy's eyes and a tight mouth.

This wasn't getting us anywhere. I glanced around. "Does anyone know him?" There was a communal holding of breath. A silence pregnant with uncertainty and mistrust. No one came forward, even though the kingdom was small enough for everyone's intimate affairs to be common knowledge. Even though someone must have cared for him. "Mahi?"

The seer snorted. "Don't ask me. I barely tolerate adults."

"Your face. I know it." My grandfather rubbed his temple as if trying to solve a knotty problem. As if he was mentally ruffling through the filing cabinet in his office. The raja's enforcer, guarder of secrets, master manipulator. "Tanay. Your name is Tanay. You're one of Prem Kumar's strays."

"Prakash–" Nani wrung her hands. "No need to hurt the boy's feelings."

Grandfather lowered his voice a notch, but it still carried as he turned to me in explanation. Perhaps the mark of his lingering authority or an old man's failing ears. "Prem has sown wild oats over the years. He pays the mothers a monthly sum, enough to keep the children well clothed and fed. But he shows no interest in being a father to illegitimate children. Against my counsel, I might add."

Behind me, Deven unleashed a growl.

My eyebrows snapped together. So we had the raja's son.

The boy's flushed cheeks told me the explanation stung. "Shut it, old man."

Grandfather gave a disgruntled harrumph, but Nani put a hand on his arm, saying to the boy with infinite gentleness, "I know your mother. Sunita is a kind, humble woman. A seamstress, isn't she? She's chopping okra in the communal kitchen. She'll be ashamed to find out what you did here today. Let's hope your little brother doesn't follow in your footsteps."

Limp locks framed Tanay's face. For a moment, he looked stricken, like Nani's tenderness had pierced his armoured heart. Glacial eyes thawed, too, when they flickered to Merlin's twitching whiskers and drooping ears. But by the third breath, Tanay toughened up. Eyes so like his father's—full of loathing—narrowed on me where I still crouched before him. "My mother hasn't made a good decision since she fell into the raja's bed." He sprang for my neck, his wiry hands reaching out with unexpected strength.

But this time, I was ready.

I repelled the surge of gargoyles in my mind offering aid and crushing retribution, shifted to avoid Tanay's grasp, and Merlin tripped him up with one long sooty foot for good measure.

The boy sprawled on the hard ground with a grunt.

A witch, a witch, a witch, intoned the gargoyles. *A queen-in-waiting and a witch.*

Yes, Deven had trained me. But I had so much more. I tuned in to the cycle of my breath to fuel my magic. The hum of the earth sounded in my ears like a musical score. I sensed the living canvas beneath the leather soles of my shoes: cracked concrete imprinted with the footfalls of long-departed citizens; damp soil teeming with beetles in iridescent armour; the subtle tug of gnarled tree roots; earthworms carving sinuous tunnels; ants erecting miniature cities; deeper and deeper still to decay and rot, rock and lava. With my hare familiar and the coven beside me, I had no fear that my hands wouldn't do their work or that the spell wouldn't come. The incantation wove itself in the loops of my imagination and fizzed on my tongue, a communion of vowels and consonants spilling through the air like ephemeral silk. Like an axe. Like a promise. *Taṃ grāhaya.* I spread my fingers into a tulip shape, lifted them and brought them down. Restraint warring with retribution.

The concrete peeled up, and the earth roped around the boy's feet, even as he tried to stand. It solidified there, around his feet and ankles.

Tanay froze in horror, though he did not cry out.

He was a child. Just a child.

The rebels gawped at my show of power. Even those who had grown to care for me baulked at my actions. Their expressions wavered as they considered whether I was friend or foe. If they could take a chance on me. If power would go to my head. In that suspended moment, thoughts flitted across their faces, speculation about how I channelled potent magic without a topaz jewel, unaware that Mahi's witchcraft had implanted one in my body.

So my legend grew through choices and circumstances.

My breath hitched in my chest at Ishaan's puckered face as Deven's sister led him away. The words I had uttered before, of solidarity and compassion, suddenly felt false on my tongue, curdling like old milk.

Even my sister looked at me like I was a stranger.

Deven's charcoal gaze met mine, his lips compressed.

But we both knew I had to make an example of Tanay, however young. I had to show my strength and backbone, even though it sickened me that Prem Kumar also used punishment as a tool of control.

How else could we navigate the coming days? How else could I cement control?

"Go to bed, all of you. But not before you surrender every weapon to my gargoyles," I called out over the biting wind. I didn't let the mask of my resolve slip. "The boy stays here until morning. No one touches him. No one speaks to him."

Tanay's shoulders slumped, his steely will broken at last.

Leena implored me in the candlelight. "Kiya, he's just a child."

A murderous child. I avoided my sister's doe eyes. "Even a child can be a weapon." I turned to the fishtail gargoyle, whose daisy crown fell in crushed petals from her fist. Her rubbery lips turned downwards as I spoke. "Sindhuja, inform his mother, then return here to guard him."

He was just a child, whirled the merry-go-round of my thoughts. *He was Prem's son.*

A sheen of perspiration dotted Mahi's upper lip. Her gaze shifted uneasily as she interlocked her arm through her brother's. "You're right to be wary. There are threats inside the fortress as well as outside it. We'd do well to remember it."

Then why did I feel like I was losing myself before the war had even begun?

CHAPTER 4

With dawn so close and my gnawing conscience offering no hope of sleep, our inner circle gathered at Mahi's tall, narrow house. While the hall formed the meeting point for the resistance as a whole, the seer had offered her shadowy, leaning home as our command centre.

We accepted, and Grandfather named us the Council of Rebels, as though some hidden part of him still hankered after grand titles and palatial rooms.

In Mahi's house, secrets lingered like ghosts. I could sense them in the dust that coated my skin, in the heavy clouds of incense and the brittle leaves of neglected plants, withering in corners. With its sealed-shut, chapel-like windows, mystical objects and decades-old spellcraft to keep out prying eyes, it was the perfect venue for our discussions.

The seer had cleared a room on the ground floor of the house for our use. Although the door required us to pass through one by one, in a sideways fashion, she had managed to fit oversized furniture inside. A weathered table for ten people dominated the interior, ancient symbols scratched into its surface, together with frayed, upholstered chairs in autumn colours. A tarnished brass orb lit the room with a hazy light as if the room existed outside the normal flow of time. Even the dust particles stood still in the stagnant air.

We had spent endless hours securing the fortress in the past few days. Then, endless hours again in this room, debating the path forward. Each time, before we had the green light to begin, Nani sprinkled salt around the perimeter of the room, lit incense and placed a fresh bunch of dried rosemary in the middle of the table.

Her fussing caused a visible swell of annoyance in Mahi every time. In fact, the seer had taken to carrying a canister of tea around with her that seemed to act as a pacifying tonic against the swell of people she now was forced into close proximity with.

We had sketched out working plans for the first few days. Our first point of order was erecting wards and issuing outlook posts to the gargoyles. The gargoyles also took to the skies over the kingdom to spy on the raja and to scoop up any deserters from the kingdom.

We each had a role.

Mahi focussed on piecing together her visions. Menon assessed the strategic usefulness of magical abilities amongst us. They were few and far between, given the majority of those with power opted to back the raja. Grandfather organised the division of labour between rebels in the fortress, overseeing a roster of carpenters, metalworkers, cooks and carers. He also used his knowledge of secret histories to map out who amongst the resistance we could trust and who we should beware. Leena tended to ailments, as she always had, and maintained our food supply with green witch magic, but it wasn't enough to meet our full nutritional needs. Nani oversaw the cooking, together with Jilu and Radha, whose restaurant had become a sort of mess hall, though the number of mouths to feed was so great that food preparation spilt out of the kitchens at Biryani Junction into assorted homes. Aanya's singing kept the children and the most anxious among the rebels calm, but her magic depleted quickly.

She and Leena had already fought a thousand times about how pulling too much on Aanya's magic was too dangerous and that she should hold back to allow herself to replenish. That wise witches maintained balance or burned out.

Harya and Sindhuja kept a close eye on simmering tensions, though they needed my say-so to quell any flare-ups. Just in case. Just in case they went a step too far.

As for Deven, he trained any adults willing to hold a blade and pored every other waking second into war gaming. How to protect our people. The plains a war might be fought on. How the raja might strike.

Deven pushed me so hard in the training room that I thought I might break. When my magic raged through my veins, and I thought my vessels might overflow, there'd be nothing more left of me than a vessel, a conduit, an empty husk.

That was my job, Deven said, when sweat gleamed on his skin, and I knew that his muscles burned as much as mine did. When we were so spent that my legs buckled and he brought salve to our room at night to soothe my bruised body. My job was to become strong enough to withstand what was coming.

Beyond those tasks, everything else stopped.

Schooling. Trading. Crafting. Market days. Religious rituals. Celebrations.

Everything ground to a halt except survival, strategising and stemming the rising anxiety.

So far, our discussions hadn't yet yielded a consensus of strategy beyond our day-to-day survival. But the status quo of the resistance holed up in the fortress wouldn't last. We all knew it; our anxious tells were written into our body language of drawn and shadowed faces, pallid skin, jerky movements and shallow breath. Even Menon looked afraid. Menon, who had survived bleak decades alone in the shadowy labyrinth. Or maybe it was Deven he feared. Deven, who had neither forgiven the returning sorcerer's crimes against him nor forgotten his part in establishing his curse.

I glanced at our inner circle through wafts of cedar smoke. Of our allies, only Sindhuja—who guarded the boy— remained absent. A shiver of vulnerability crawled up my spine at what I had done to Tanay and what they might think of me.

Leena spoke first, loosening her too-tight bun. "What you did out there–"

My fingernails dug crescents in my palms. "What I did was hard. I didn't do it lightly."

At my prickly tone, Merlin ceased his hopping at my feet and stretched out to appear at table height with a mournful chirp. "Please, both of you. Remember, we're a family." His primary goal had always been to be the tether between us all, however frayed our connections became.

Empathy beamed from my sister's eyes, making it easier to breathe. "I don't want to fight. What I was going to say is that I don't envy you."

Across the table from me, Deven had schooled his expression into neutrality, but his leg shifted under the table, leaning against mine, its warmth a caress. Absolving me of guilt. Understanding.

My eyes stung as I gave my sister a grateful look, but even in this room full of allies, I couldn't show my real emotions. I didn't know if I'd done the right thing. Didn't know how to steady myself against the shifting ground beneath my feet. Didn't know if I could be the leader they needed. There were too many things that felt impossible. Too many things that could go wrong. If we failed, the forthcoming horrors would be my fault. I had bound a child to the earth. I had done that. Even my thoughts were too messy, too messy to be of use to anyone. I lifted my eyes to Deven, and my heart ricocheted in its cage. "That farmer was right. It should be you. You should take the throne."

It was nothing I hadn't said before.

Deven had a claim to the throne, too. What if he didn't want to play second fiddle again?

Shadows danced in his inky eyes. "I'm not interested in power for its own sake. I only duelled last time because I was concerned about Prem's nature. My place is at your side. Not on the throne."

Good leaders don't doubt, mistress. They set a course and maintain it, grizzled Harya, diagonally across from me, his stony flesh contrasting deeply with the saffron chair he filled.

Sindhuja's voice came to the fore in my choppy mind despite her being a few hundred metres away guarding Tanay. *Your history needs brushing up, Sir. A lack of doubt has been the downfall of many world leaders.*

Merlin nuzzled my hand. "Mahi said you're Jalapashu's only hope."

She'd been so quiet these past days, preoccupied, scheming. A face of experience but also cunning. "But you don't see everything, do you, Mahi?"

Her forehead rippled, and I tried not to recoil. "That is true. But I'm not wrong, Kiya. I have pieced together enough to be sure."

"Perhaps we've been too quick to assume Prem will tumble into the default of violence. Perhaps half the kingdom deserting him will mean he gives up the throne. If not, we try diplomacy or appeasement. We offer him riches. We weaken his credibility and win over those who remain in his camp, so he has no choice but to yield. So we avoid violence." The futility of my ideas soured the words on my tongue.

Menon thumbed the medallion around his neck. "Negotiating is not an option. Prem understands no other language but violence." The truth rang out like a temple bell.

I met Deven's eyes across the table, white specks hazing my eyes.

According to Jalapashan laws, only descendants of the founding families could inherit the crown. The line of succession could be interrupted if the crown was won in a duel.

His gaze swept across my face, and I thought maybe he'd tell me what I wanted to hear. That it wouldn't be hard. That we'd find a way. But instead, he said quietly, "From every angle I look at it, I end up with the same answer. Prem will allow a duel for the throne only when he thinks he can win it. But he has no idea how strong you are. Just like we have no idea how strong he is."

Grandfather grunted. "It won't be a fair fight. He'll attempt to tilt everything in his favour."

Deven fisted his hands on the table. "That's why Kiya should nominate me as her champion."

I jerked my gaze to him, sliding my leg away from the warmth of his, noting in the set of his jaw how serious he was. How he had planned this all along. Despite our long training hours. Despite insisting I put everything into getting stronger. "You can't be serious."

"I've never been more serious in my life."

Typical of him to want to shield us all. Typical of him to want to take the brunt of it.

I exchanged glances with Mahi. Despite her curmudgeonly personality and Dev's serious one, there was a respect between them, a bond that sometimes veered into the maternal. She was a kind of sourpuss woman who had carved out a corner of her steely heart for the general. If anyone could talk sense into him, it would be the seer. But her eyes shuttered.

"It's within the rules. But it's never been done before," said Menon carefully. He pursed his sensual lips and slid an assessing look over Deven. "Not once in Jalapashu's history. Because of the risk of the champion claiming the throne himself. But if you trust your champion to remain loyal, I see no reason why it can't be done."

My sister bit her lip. "The last time... Why was Prem convinced he would beat you in a duel?"

Devastation flashed across Deven's face. "Because he knew I didn't have it in me to kill my own kin. It will be different this time. I won't fail."

"Of that, I have no doubt. We're writing a new story." My grandfather's moustached face grew ruddy as he fixed his stare on me. "When all is said and done, I'll gladly kneel to you as my queen."

A shiver ran up my spine, and I wondered if this was his penance for how he'd acted with Mum. If he had traversed the gap from prideful, demanding love to a humble, gentler love.

Nani patted his veined hand. "Prakash and I will do everything in our power to support you."

My grandfather nodded, and I knew it was true. It didn't have to be about the past or even about his granddaughters. He would do anything Nani asked of him, anything to keep his beloved wife safe, anything not to sink in her eyes after the years she had quietly endured. Anything to keep the joy that had ignited in her eyes when she realised that her granddaughters walked on Jalapashan soil.

And when his eyes lingered on Leena and me, I dared to think he loved us in his own clumsy way or that someday he would. That someday he would support us because his heart willed it as much as hers did.

Glass shards lined my throat when I finally spoke. "How much longer can we last? How much more time can we buy to figure out his strengths and be sure of what we will face?"

My grandfather's belly no longer strained against his shirt, and we hadn't even begun rations yet. That time would come. Not once had he complained about his fall from grace. "By my calculations, we have enough stores for two weeks without additional supplies."

My fingers were a tight knot in my lap. "What if the wards fail? We have to assume that, even now, Prem is finding ways to unravel them. I scanned their faces, my insides knotting. "Can we be sure Prem will limit his wrath to a duel, or will he seek to punish us all? Maybe we should move the people somewhere else. Somewhere further afield, just until it is all over." I couldn't bear to think of them in the firing line. I couldn't bear to be responsible for the death of innocents.

"We could send them to Boundless Bay," said Leena. "They could sneak out under the cover of night. With the ratio of gargoyles to rebels, they'd have to make the journey three or four times, perhaps, unless they were strong enough to carry more than one at a time."

Harya's snort trumpeted his disgust at being used as transportation, but he didn't object.

My sister's eyes shone as her idea gathered steam. "We can stitch harnesses from old saris for safety."

Aanya squeezed my sister's hand and shook her head, knowing that it was a pipe dream that we could spirit away the people from the only land they had known. "It won't work, darling. They won't go."

My tired brain skirted over strategies we'd considered and discarded a dozen times over—impossibility after impossibility. "I wish we could do that. I really do," I said gently. There was no way in hell the people would trust the gargoyles enough to step into their stony embrace. Not overnight. We had no time to break down the clawing fear, and I was the fool who had made it worse tonight by angling the gargoyles towards them as a weapon. "You saw the fear tonight. They're more prone to believe the gargoyles will drop them from a great height."

"On purpose," cawed Babbu, with a gleeful sparkle in his beady eye. "Splat."

Deven didn't deign to give the parrot a kernel of attention. "My soldiers and I would lay down our lives to get the people out. But there are too many people and too few gargoyles to escape by flight. Even if the gargoyles agreed to play stork, and we get the children out first, Prem will have planned for this. He will have laid traps at the veil to the outer world. Where would the children be without their caregivers?" His eyes darkened as though he was thinking of his nephew.

As if there were pitfalls and pain ahead, whichever path we chose.

Grandfather harrumphed, his cynicism a counterweight to Leena's idealism, even though we all would prefer to live in her version of the world. "Where would we even place them? There are other kingdoms of magic, but none are our allies. The rajas and ranis of Jalapashu have always been isolationists. Careful to protect their power."

I filed away that information. There was still so much I hadn't learned about this world of shadows and magic, so much history that had been cloaked by the sands of time or by the walls around this place. So much that even Merlin hadn't been able to tell me, given his focus on our family at the expense of all else. Maybe one day, my grandfather or Deven would sit me down and tell me all they knew.

Maybe one day, I'd be able to walk into the library in the white-washed palace of Jalapashu and devour all the knowledge I desired.

Nani hadn't noticed that her henna-coloured beehive had begun to unravel. "None of the *hows* and *what ifs* matter. Jalapashans won't abandon this kingdom. It goes against our nature." Pride sparked in her eyes, and I knew she was thinking of Mother and the courage it had taken to uproot and pursue the life she wanted. But I knew what family separation had cost her, and I wouldn't wish it on anyone. "Jala-pashans cling to familiarity like moss to a stone, fearful of foreign places, wary of a technological, industrialised world full of strange scents and even stranger customs. And maybe that's what the rajas and ranis of this kingdom always intended. To keep us dependent on them. Fearful. Controlled. Either way, Kiya, whatever plans we make, it will be with the rebels here. Here with us."

"So it's settled. We keep the wards up." Deven's eyes met mine. "And I duel Prem as your champion."

Aanya trembled. "The raja will sacrifice everything not to lose. Are we prepared to do the same?"

Maybe Merlin sensed her vulnerability, or maybe he wanted to hear her soothing tones crooning in his ear, but he scuppered across the table and tumbled into her lap. I couldn't help noticing my sister's longing looks in her lover's direction. Like she knew what was on the horizon. That some of us would be hurt. Some of us would end up completely changed. Some of us might not make it.

Exhaustion lines spidered on Grandfather's rumpled skin, and in his voice, I heard the experience of a man who knew the colours of the raja's heart. A man who had experienced other men and women who strove for power and who didn't care who they trampled beneath their feet or whose blood stained their hands. "Maybe we don't have to play this with honour."

Nani sighed, and I realised this was a conversation they'd had many times before and that they'd had quiet disagreements or fierce ones, that even though she was mild-mannered and wise, there were certain things she couldn't stomach, and maybe I was the same.

Or maybe I wasn't. I didn't know anymore.

My chest was tight with anxiety. "This is a holding pattern, that's all. Mahi has been deciphering her visions. They will be instrumental in capturing the throne without bloodshed." I turned to the seer, suddenly realising how quiet she'd been when this was all she had ever wanted. When she'd wanted to bring about the end to Prem Kumar's reign for decades. "Your vision about the Amber Hollows being empty was pivotal, Mahi, but you must have something else for us by now. A path forward. Anything." *Please, don't let it all be bad news. Let it be something we can work with.*

Menon brushed a fleck of dust from the ruched shoulder of his tatty robes and averted his gaze from his twin, discomforted somehow.

I swept my gaze over Deven. The stoic set of his shoulders. The clarity and pain in his eyes. The hands that he unconsciously opened and closed, as if he still wore his belt of knives and needed to feel the comfort of his weapon. I didn't want him to duel Prem for me.

Every cell and bone in my body cried out against it.

And I realised that, like my grandfather, maybe I'd be prepared to act dishonourably to win. There were countless paths we could take: steal the raja's vaults of topaz, rendering him harmless without his magic; commandeer and throttle the supply chains into the kingdom, so he suffered rather than us; convince those loyal to him to withdraw their backing; find a loophole to avoid the duel and instead murder him in the middle of the night by virtue of one of the dark passageways that led into the palace; or we could use his son as leverage. I silenced the thoughts as soon as they buoyed into my mind to a soundtrack of Harya's chortle of admiration.

I didn't want to venture down any of these paths without Mahi's say-so. Without a guarantee that we would come out on top. That sullying my soul would be worth it. That my loved ones would live and this future would be worth the pain. This metamorphosis into a new identity.

Thief. Killer. Queen.

"Mahi?" I prompted again, seesawing between gloomy despair and bright hope.

Babbu flapped on Mahi's shoulder as if fending off my attention.

The seer's kohl-painted brows furrowed. She flipped over Tanay's dagger in her gnarled hands, over and over. Its gleaming silver hilt spun as if Mahi was embroiled in a chance gambit—a coin toss—and didn't know which side to fall on.

She'd been my compass and my guide since I arrived in Jalapashu. But she was multi-faceted, capable of great kindness but also Machiavellian moves. She didn't always share her visions in a timely fashion; she was often cryptic. Could it be that even though we stood at the precipice of war—for the future she had persuaded us to create—she was holding back the truth?

She placed Tanay's dagger on the table with unusually clumsy fingers. It skittered away. A storm brewed in her dark eyes, eclipsing the usual clarity of her gaze. There was guilt there. Mahi was usually unapologetic, her personality forged with strength not shame.

I frowned, realisation dawning. "You *knew*. You knew the boy would do that tonight."

Mahi could be self-serving. She could be dangerous.

"It was a single path in a kaleidoscope of possibilities."

Babbu bobbed up and down. "Oh, oh. Trouble. Here it comes."

My blood turned cold. "What if he had met his target?"

Heads ping-ponged between us, and Deven loosed a snarl.

Mahi shushed Babbu, her eyes never leaving mine. "It was a chance I had to take."

The light buzzed about our heads. My heartbeat clamoured in my ears: a ticking clock. Prem could attack at any moment, and the seer was hiding pieces of the jigsaw from us.

"There's more you're hiding." It wasn't a question; it was a statement.

Her violet eye opened, a chasm in her forehead. "Yes, Kiya. There is."

I wanted to coax every detail from her pinched mouth.

CHAPTER 5

I sprang up, my trust splintering like fine porcelain meeting the ground. In my peripheral vision, Harya's wings jutted out with malign intent. "Why, Mahi? Why would you leave my safety to chance?"

Deven's obsidian eyes narrowed with a predatory glint, watching for one false word. One false move. Without his intervention, I would have just been a blip in the story of Prem Kumar's reign.

"Answer her," Nani stumbled over her words. Hard to imagine how a vital piece of information could be withheld when her own nature was so open. "You demand blind faith, but this reeks of betrayal."

Mahi's mouth opened and shut like a fish. Her brown eyes flashed to Menon. Their telepathic connection was part of Jalapashan legend. I couldn't be sure if the connection was magical or biological, a residual gift from when they had shared their mother's womb.

Under the table, Babbu—in a fury of crimson beak and emerald feathers—hen-pecked Merlin in a pre-emptive attack that made a mockery of their hard-earned friendship. I released a curl of my power. A spell that I had uttered mere months ago, or a lifetime ago, unspooling in my mind like a ribbon. *Abhayam.* Be fearless. My spell struck Merlin. He overcame the parrot and puffed out his chest in glory.

I might be the queen-in-waiting, but the seer was the queen of masks, the queen of guile and duping, the queen of ruses. But I was no longer an ingenue to be led unwittingly into battle. She owed me more than that. "Why wouldn't you warn me of a threat to my life?"

I fought to keep calm. Mahi could have inspired the resistance with visions of the future. She could have rooted out traitors and helped us navigate traps. But instead of setting us on a foolproof path to victory, she'd sabotaged us.

I was no stranger to her manipulation, but I didn't know if I could forgive her this time.

My anger rose to a fever pitch as a silent conversation flickered between the seer and her twin. They shut the rest of us out, and my cells tingled with earth magic at their audacity. Their body language synchronised in an unspoken choreography: the rise and fall of breath, a narrowing of their gazes, quirks of the mouth and subtle hand gestures. They reminded me of a duo in a silent film. I understood why they'd been a formidable pair at court, why Prem had sought to drive a wedge between them.

Right now, I wanted to do the same.

Maybe if I hadn't been so intent on deciphering their interaction, I might have been alert to how the separation between my mind and the gargoyles had become porous. How their fury leaked into and fuelled my own. A cacophony of grinding stone, laboured breaths and the echoes of ancient oaths filled my mind. *The wards have fallen, mistress. He comes. The raja comes. He is here. He stands at the wall, saying he will enter. Unless the traitors come. Unless you come.*

Harya scrambled up from his chair in response to the

missives down the gargoyle bond, a thunderous growl ripping from his throat as he stomped to the door.

My breath hitched, and my blood ran cold. *Do what you can. Don't let him inside. Tell him I am coming.*

Mahi's forehead yawned with the violet eye. "He's here?"

Eyes jerked to me. The drumming of their rebel hearts gave away their alarm. Or my own.

I gave a curt nod, bones quaking, chill rising, stone grinding in my mind, my grip on the table the only thing keeping my knees from buckling from the sheer horror. I wanted to be anywhere but in the fortress. For a moment, it crossed my mind that Mahi might not be on our side. That perhaps she enjoyed playing games, that Prem had promised her a reward in return for toying with us, or that she cared for nothing now that her beloved Menon was back at her side.

But there was no time for recriminations, not when the tiger was at our door.

Foolish—unforgivable—to think I could so easily take an evil king's throne.

WE LEFT THE CRACKLING TENSION OF THE SEER'S HOUSE, heading into the fire. Heading towards tombstone teeth, jutting claws and seething power. Power that Prem Kumar had undoubtedly tried to amplify.

Out. Out into the breaking light, wearing not a scrap of armour, with only my wits and magic as my defence. Out, out into the throngs of the petrified resistance, cowering from the raja. Out under the dawn-kissed rafters, over the speckled pavement outside Biryani Junction, where Prem and I had dined together. Where he'd plotted our grand future, and I'd brewed a plan to escape his clutches. Out to the broken wards and mud-caked walls where the raja waited.

My old life looked rosy from this perspective.

Maybe we had been foolish to let the twins accompany us, but one nod from Deven and we had let them come all the same. The raja had demanded the traitors meet him by the broken wards. So we offered four of us up, hoping to keep him from the sleeping people. Hoping to prevent the need to put my family in the firing line. Hoping that Mahi and Menon might still be on our side. That we could trust them, and their magic would, with ours, weigh against whatever waited for us.

Dreamers and fools, that's what we were.

Not an inch separated Deven from my left side. Mahi and Menon flanked me on my right. A flash of emerald plumage told me that Babbu remained close. Merlin, too. He hopped from one pool of shadow to another in the dawning light. Loyal, devoted creature. Friend and conduit for my spell casting.

We ploughed on through the fortress towards Prem Kumar, gathering our courage. All the while, spitfire reports barrelled into my consciousness from the gargoyles. I counselled them against escalation but warned them to guard our boundaries. To be ready for shadows and fire and claws. Tanay's face floated into my mind. I visualised the hard earth keeping him captive and spun my fingers like I worked a loom, loosening the soil's hold. *Let the boy go unharmed, Sindhuja. Let him go back to his mother.* He was just a child, I told myself on repeat as if my integrity was fraying.

As if another decision were possible.

As if I might actually have been capable of harming him.

Deven had his faction to organise. He barked out orders to his former manservant Yuvan to wake a small contingent of deserting soldiers to guard the sleeping people. The gargoyles would have enough to do protecting the walls. The soldiers to prepare for a possible confrontation. No visible weapons. Keep the people calm. If the raja entered, they were to prioritise the safety of women, children and the elderly. Secure vital resources. Hold back the strongest magical assets. Await further orders.

With every command, the nightmare became more monstrous, more real.

Behind us, the seer and her sorcerer twin bickered.

"You'd have done better to heed my advice. Time is of the essence, as you well know, dear sister."

Her restraint snapped like a rubber band despite having been overjoyed to be reunited with him mere days ago. "It was your disloyalty that taught me to hold my cards close to my chest, brother. And you know as well as I do that it isn't as simple as that."

He responded with more ice than fire. "You push yourself too hard."

I inhaled deeply to centre myself. "The gargoyles say he comes without an army," I said to Deven.

Deven didn't so much as walk but stalk, claws on the cusp of unsheathing at the tips of his fingers. "He won't be waging war, then. Not today. His main goal will be to gauge the terrain and our setup."

"They say he is composed and that he prayed at the sacred tree." The banyan tree now split half and half between our territories. "They say power rolls off him in waves. That he wears rocks of topaz, but there is some lurking in his flesh, too. That he glows with it. With the power he has accessed."

The revelation hung between the four of us, too late to be of use. If Mahi had known, she was a more gifted actress than I'd given her credit for. But then, she'd survived decades in Prem's court, been elevated to the position of a close ally, and hadn't been bound by the decrees determining dress code and residence. All because he had trusted her and never suspected her tenacious plot to free Menon.

Menon pinched the bridge of his nose. "Against unknown power, our magic is little more than a throw of the dice."

"We need better intelligence." Deven's steely gaze remained fixed ahead, scanning the terrain.

I nodded. Neither the seer nor the gargoyle scouts had been warning enough. My thoughts whirled like a dervish as I gamed potential scenarios. "I'll summon a wall of earth to fend him off if he tries to enter the fortress. That has to be the line we can't cross."

"A temporary solution. He'll find a way in. Today, tomorrow, or the next day," said Menon.

I ran my fingers over my sheathed knife. My voice was a ripple on a forgotten lake. "We could kill him while we have the chance." But I didn't know myself anymore; didn't know what words signalled intention and which were simply playing at war. Like this was a board game, not visceral reality. Would Deven love me if I allowed the dark violence of my shadow self to consume me?

Obsidian eyes locked onto mine. "We don't attempt anything until we grasp how powerful he is."

I curled my palms into fists. "Okay. That's our primary goal."

"Let him think he has the upper hand," Mahi didn't look well, and the red-hot blaze of my anger thawed a little at the thought that our argument had wounded her as much as it had me. "He'll wrap himself in knots, given enough rope. He'll boast, and he'll preen. He won't be able to resist telling us what he can now do. He has always been that way, ever since he was a boy."

Dawn illuminated the dark flesh of the gargoyles on the ramparts. Twenty, perhaps thirty, on the ramparts and more on the ground, their stances alert, tails whipping, the odd growl of warning tearing through the air. We were mere seconds away from seeing the raja's preening, self-assured, hated face.

I braced myself. "What if it all goes to hell, and he forces his way into the fortress despite our efforts?"

Menon gave me a grim look as though I was weak for even thinking it. As though pure belief had accompanied him through the solitary years of imprisonment in the labyrinth and that to even question our odds was tantamount to blasphemy.

It was easier to be brave when only your own life hung in the balance.

Sweat beaded his sister's face from the exertion of keeping up. "You will turf him out, earth witch."

"But if. If he makes it inside. If we aren't enough. If the gargoyles and the soldiers aren't enough. Will he spare lives if we surrender?" Surrender. The word was poison on my tongue.

The gargoyle queen does not surrender, chided the chorus in my skull.

Deven's laugh was as bitter as soured whiskey. "He'd throw us a feast, then send in soldiers and sorcerers to kill us before we'd swallowed a mouthful of *roti*. Out of spite. Even after our deaths, he'd stop at nothing until he commands the gargoyles."

"Any future rebellion would be dead in the water." There was a grey tinge to the seer's skin.

My hackles rose. Could we overcome the raja together, or would Mahi twist a knife in my back?

The seer, as complex and devious as the labyrinth, caught my glance. "You can trust me."

The words whistled through my gritted teeth. "Can I?"

"Yes," she said simply. Concern and something softer sprouted in her eyes. Love maybe.

Or perhaps my imagination fooled me. "Our argument isn't over. This is a temporary truce."

"I wouldn't expect any less." She stroked her medallion as though she had more tricks up her sleeve.

"Don't say a word in there. You don't speak for us until I determine if we can trust you."

She huffed out a breath but clamped down her mouth on any sour words she'd been tempted to utter.

Part of me wanted to end this battle with the raja now, regardless of the cost. Regardless of the ethics. But then I'd be no better than him. I'd be the queen who began her reign with murder. The queen who cared not a jot about initiating violence, though the people slept mere yards away.

All my talk of a better world would amount to nothing.

A tick in his jaw betrayed Deven's nervousness. Even Menon glanced his way as though he sensed I was the chink in the celebrated general's armour. "He can't harm you. If there's no other play, invoke the ancient right to duel for the throne," he said, almost to convince himself that I would be safe. "He'll say yes. He won't want to be seen as a coward. He can't harm you if you elect me as your champion."

My blood thickened. "Okay."

But I didn't understand this archaic place and its archaic laws. Not really. I just knew that I was too far along this path to back out. That I loved its people too much not to try. That above anything else, I had to keep my sister safe.

Deven's words were as clipped as our footfalls towards the raja. "He'll try and get on the front foot. He'll weasel and worm. He'll try to get a rise. He'll paint you as incapable of leading." He spoke with such venom that it was hard to remember they had loved each other before the bonds of family broke under the strain of Prem's ambition. Before Prem killed Deven's wife and cursed him to lose his tiger self. "He's a predator by nature, Kiya. Promise me you won't show fear. It will just excite him. Don't let him sense it."

"I won't." I wouldn't let Prem smell the blood.

Then why did the world spin?

Resolve lined his face. He'd counselled me to be calm, but his own eyes carried a quiet rage as if he might be on the verge of detonation. "We'll get through this. I won't let him hurt you. I promise."

When I looked at him, I almost believed it.

His voice had the fervency of a prayer. "Just stay alive, dammit."

My insides twisted, blooming with love and shrivelling with foreboding.

I wondered if Prem would shift in front of the people. It wasn't the cultural norm for the rajas and ranis of this kingdom to show their beast or dazzle with their magical gifts. Such a display was deemed uncouth: a lowly deed suitable for performers and the military but not for rajas. They preferred lounging on gilded thrones. They preferred others to do their dirty work. Be that as it may, I didn't put it past him to shift. I didn't need the seer to tell me that he'd revel in taking his vengeance in a show of pounding muscle and bloodied gore. He thirsted for it.

A simple wave of my magic heaved open the stone door I'd conjured. Outside, the fallen wards glimmered like beer bottles crushed beneath a clumsy drunk's feet. As if Prem had taken them down with utter ease.

I saw him then: the raja who had stolen Sitara from us and caused such pain, who treated the people unjustly, like they were worth less than the floss he cleaned his pearly teeth with.

Teeth that became a beast's bite.

He rode an elephant painted in pink and orange mandalas, the colour of the rising sun, and wore a turban of shimmering gold and a snowy white *sherwani* as though he was the embodiment of purity. I discerned Lokesh *Saheb*'s handiwork in every stitch. He carried no weapons, but a tiger had no use for steel when its very body was an arsenal. And yes, he glowed. Not overtly, but I could sense his power. How he had amplified it. How it writhed inside him. A saintly expression graced his face. We all knew better than to trust him, down to the baby bawling in her mother's arms somewhere deep in the fortress.

Eyes of the cerulean sea glittered with amusement as he looked down from the wrinkled grey of the elephant. "You didn't think your wards would hold forever? Against me? Oh, my poor Kiya. You *did*."

CHAPTER 6

I was a rabbit caught in the sightline of a hunter. Craning my neck to meet the Prem's piercing gaze atop the elephant, I prayed he couldn't tell how my gut churned. My need for revenge made it almost impossible to think. One way or another, we'd make him pay for his countless cruelties.

For Sitara. For Deven's curse. For his greed. For his killing.

A shiver traced up my spine as I opened my bond to the gargoyles. *Be vigilant. Don't let him enter the fortress.* With a twist of my hand, the stone door swung shut, prompting a snort of derision from the raja. As if my magic paled in comparison to his own power. I tried, tried not to show my fear. Tried to school my face into an expression that oozed disdain, the haughtiness of a usurping queen.

What had his preparation uncovered? What new skills or allies had he armed himself with? Spells swirled in my mind, letters and consonants in a tornado's grip. *Tvamapaśya* and *vismar* and *mohitah bhava*. Wild, harsher ones, too. Spells that demanded his blood, that demanded he bend to me, that urged me to break him. I bit down on my lip, tasting salt and iron. Willing myself to maintain control. Willing myself to find a permanent solution to his corrupt rule, not a temporary one.

He'd come alone, on the most imposing beast in the kingdom: not a horse, but an elephant. Presumably to impress upon us that we were gnats in comparison to him. His eyes glimmered with vanity and the patience of a crocodile, noting how quickly we had barricaded ourselves out.

As if our compassion for the people made us more vulnerable.

As if our belief that they were worth protecting made us weaker.

Deven stiffened beside me, his power coiled and ready to strike. Mahi and Menon stood further back with the parrot and hare, letting us take the first heat. Two gargoyles flanked us, and Harya watched from the ramparts, ready to fly to our aid.

The raja turned a hard, ravenously curious gaze on the gargoyles, creatures of legend he had only ever witnessed as weathered statues on the rooftops of the kingdom's houses and dotted along palace walls.

Then Prem curled his lip and turned the entirety of his focus on me.

He took in my dishevelled state—mussed dark hair, crescent shadows beneath my eyes, ragged fingernails and the jumper and leggings that he wouldn't be seen dead in—and contempt sharpened the planes of his face. As if there was nothing rani-like about me. As if I was filth on his shoe.

Once, his attraction to me had warmed his frigid gaze. Now, all that remained was chilling clarity. "I should be calling you betrothed. Or wife. Not the leader of a band of traitors."

The insult slipped off my skin as easily as water. I had been called worse things.

Women were used to name-calling. *Bimbo* when men

wanted to make us feel small. *Liar* when our story didn't match theirs. *Slut* if we said yes to sexual pleasure. *Sweetie* in the boardroom, although her knowledge rivalled theirs. *Angry* if we spoke up for ourselves. *Old maid* if we stayed single. *Damaged goods* when we'd suffered. *Bitch* when we dared tell the truth. *Hag* when we aged. *Cougar, gold digger, cock tease, welfare queen.* The list went on as if we had to be monsters or saints, and there was no in-between.

I didn't care what he called me as long as I was his undoing. Prem had no idea what a woman's rage could achieve. He underestimated me even now. I longed to teach him a lesson he'd never forget.

But Deven couldn't bear to hear me insulted. He loosed a snarl. "It's you who's the traitor."

Prem's expression didn't even register a flicker of acknowledgement. It was a calculated choice: he wanted to make Deven feel small. He wanted to stir up trouble.

I chose my words with a potter's feel for where the clay had a weakness and where a crack might form. "The people stand with me because you demand loyalty without showing them any yourself."

His eyes ensnared me. "I could have given you the world."

Revulsion snaked up my spine. "You want to rule over a kingdom of puppets."

Secrets lurked in the oceanic abyss of his eyes. "You could have ruled alongside me."

I clenched my fists and could have sworn that the earth beneath our feet rumbled in answer. "A silent voice. A doll. A tool. You have no respect for individual dreams."

"You broke your promise. You agreed to be my wife."

"I had no choice but to make and break that promise. You said you'd kill Leena."

Prem shrugged like his coercion was a technicality. Like promises only mattered if they were made to him, not by him. He slid down from the back of the elephant, untroubled by how the animal's painted body stained his white clothing. After all, his servants in the palace did his grunt work.

The elephant—presumably more used to royal parades—soaked up the anxious thrum of energy in front of the gates and beyond them. It shifted from foot to foot, ears flapping against its wrinkled sides, as first, Prem turned his attention to the twins.

Still ignoring Dev. Still making me smart at the arrogance of it.

He swept his lazy gaze across Mahi and Menon, the familiars and the strange stone gargoyles that had once pledged their allegiance to another ruler of Jalapashu, his voice silken with malice. "You'd bow to her?"

"I would," said Mahi without hesitation.

Although I'd told her to stay silent. Although I doubted her.

Menon shrugged as if he were a sell-sword. As if true allegiance didn't matter and it was instead a matter of the odds or rewards or which side his sister landed. "I will when the time comes."

Prem harrumphed, but he looked at Menon with brazen interest.

"Don't you look at him," Mahi blazed with defiance, her parrot tutting on her shoulder.

"You're worried he'll betray you."

"You merrily sew discord. You needed more building blocks and fewer hammers as a child."

Prem raised a perfect eyebrow. "Be sure to tell my parents that when you meet them in the afterlife, seer. It will be soon, I promise."

Menon followed their interaction, a nervous twitch dancing along his jawline.

I wondered if he missed the dark magic he had practised at Prem's behest, wondered if he regretted standing here with us and not with Prem. My heartbeat thundered. I prayed I could trust them.

Pressure grew to a roar in my eardrums as Prem drew closer until only a metre separated him from Deven and me. Still, his eyes were for me, his gait loose and easy.

As though he didn't care that I could defend myself with a whispered spell and a swell of earth and rock and sediment that could shatter his bones.

As though the general was a speck of dust, an irrelevance, and his snarl was a lamb's bleating.

As though the gargoyles didn't litter my mind with missives, demanding permission to attack.

Prem drew closer still until he was a dark silhouette against the backdrop of the rising sun, and tentacles of hidden power grasped at my mind.

Kill him, demanded Harya's voice in my head. *Kill him and be done with it. Unleash me. Unleash the gargoyles.*

Deven barked a warning, his voice reaching me through the fog of my mind. "Something's different."

My hand had already gone instinctively to the hilt of my dagger. Prem smiled as the world around me slowed, and an insidious force washed over me. I staggered back, a strange compulsion to lower my guard coming over me. As if I could trust the raja standing before us despite every instinct screaming otherwise. Despite Deven recoiling just as I did. Despite him dragging me roughly towards him.

Prem smiled, making no attempt to advance further. Instead, he drew his sword and turned it in the earth, three times forwards and five backwards, and he muttered words under his breath that I could barely make out. With a jolt, I realised this was new. He had no skill in spell casting. I wasn't even sure that shifters could do spellwork. His words didn't sound like they were English or Hindi or Urdu. Words that were perhaps Sanskrit or some other language of magic and spells, syllables that stung, runes and glyphs that slid into my mind but evaded my reach.

Somewhere, Merlin and Mahi were casting their own spells, shielding us. I thanked the stars for their magic. Nobody fell among our number. No bodies broke. No harm was done. When I looked at the raja, it was as if the darkness had passed. His steel dragged at the earth, reflecting the dawn sky, but his face was relaxed, as though he had done his worst. As though his strike of magic was a test we had passed with flying colours.

As my mind cleared, I held my ground. The general's advice over the past few days cut through the haze of my apprehension. This was foreplay and not the real battle. Though Deven's tense stillness cautioned against getting any closer, he waited for me to call the shots: a vote of confidence not just in the magic flaring in my cells but in my intellect.

If Prem wanted to get a rise out of us, I could do the same. I could play cat and mouse just as well as he could. This was a man who revelled in his power over other people. I just had to show him his impotence. I had to show him how his control was slipping, not only as a king but as a man.

His hated face hovered before us. I could have reached out and slapped it if I dared.

Still, he ignored the general. As if it was part of his game.

I brushed aside how fear and exhaustion wiped me out and how perspiration pooled on my skin and curled the tendrils of hair on my nape. I let a small smile play on my lips, which I knew would get under his skin and willed my voice to be level. Willed myself to flush out his intentions and the full extent of his new magic. "This isn't where I thought we'd end up. But it has its upsides."

Prem took the bait. "Oh?"

"I don't have to be pawed by literally the worst love match the universe has ever subjected me to. And I get to knock the crown off your head. Best of all, I met Deven."

I locked eyes with the general and smiled slowly like he was the damn moon. Because he was.

Then I slipped my hand into his—not robotically, but sensually—tangling our fingers together, even as the seer's delighted cackle reached my ears.

The general stiffened in surprise. Switching lanes between his public and private persona didn't come naturally to him. I'd only ever seen him do it with his nephew. In this kingdom, burying vulnerabilities was a matter of survival.

A heartbeat passed. A heartbeat in which the elephant's trunk swung, the dawn washed the distant palace in shades of blushing pink, then Deven returned the pressure of my fingers, circling his calloused thumb in my palm.

At last, the raja looked at us both fully. Utter loathing turned the raja's face into a hellscape as he tracked every flicker of movement. A twisted laugh flowed from his lips. "I've known since our engagement party that you're a woman of loose morals…but then you were brought up in a different culture." He addressed Deven. He was like a viper in the grass, calculating where best to strike. "Kiya's an outsider. Just a potter. A common whore. Nothing more."

Merlin hopped from one spot to another, willing me to unleash a spell, the earth, the gargoyles.

My thoughts whirred like cogs in a broken clock. Think. I had to think. Prem could have set his terms without risking his skin: via emissaries, on neutral territory, or accompanied by his army. Yet he was here, content to trade insults. Mahi taught me over and over again that this game was about sleight of hand. He seemed to have some sort of mind powers in addition to his shifter ones. We needed him to reveal his strength without succumbing to it.

Deven's growl sent a shiver up my spine. "Take her name out of your mouth."

Prem's eyes were cold, a relentless avalanche on an arctic

landscape as they flicked to the ring I wore on my middle finger. He smirked. "It's funny you say that. I've had a lucky escape, cousin. Don't you think? Although, she still wears my ring. When she sighs in your arms, is it my name on her lips?"

I should have known the general couldn't stomach the taunts.

It was one thing to have me wear another man's ring, but for Prem to lord it over him. When he'd already taken Roshni from Deven, the wife Dev hadn't loved romantically but had cared deeply for. Prem had used her. Discarded her. Killed her.

Deven would have shifted there and then—to golden fur, jagged claws and dagger-like teeth—had I not pressed my hand to his chest, where his heart pounded like a herd stampeding across a savannah.

He'd told me that my touch grounded him, and it was true.

His beast dipped under the surface once more, but his self-control hung by a thread. His words steely. They were violence leashed. "You've lived in Jalapashu a lifetime, and the people loathe you. Kiya has been here mere months, and they love her. Because she fights for them, not herself."

Prem huffed out a cynical laugh, idly turning his sword in the dust. "Love her? Then why do I smell fear, not hope?"

Claws glinted under Deven's knuckles. "Drop that weapon and state your terms before I finish what we started all those years ago. I should have ended you then."

The raja's eyebrows jackknifed as he poured salt on the wounds of the past. "In our tussle for your wife's loyalty or in our tussle for the crown?"

The elephant trumpeted against the candy sky.

Deven fought to contain his beast. Sweat beads formed on his forehead, and muscles rippled beneath his skin as he restrained the primal instincts of his shifter nature. His breathing became laboured, while his usually focused coal-black eyes appeared wild, betraying the internal battle raging within him.

The rubber band of his restraint was so close to snapping that even the seer huffed a curse.

A warning. A warning about honour and rules.

Of crowns won and lost. Of the timing of battles and bloodshed.

But Deven—Deven didn't seem to hear anything but the call of his own power.

CHAPTER 7

As the raja watched the general from under hooded eyes, I understood his play at last.

Deven warred with himself after years of that damn curse. Prem had known the curse would lead to this. He'd known that Deven would not find happiness without his whole identity and that even if the curse on his submerged identity could be lifted, finding balance again would be an impossible task. A task that required super-human strength as he struggled to realign the two parts of himself.

The brute had known. Just as he had known the high standards Deven held himself to.

It didn't matter that the people weren't here to witness it. Prem had known Deven since childhood. He knew the core that ran through Dev's centre: a faithful nature, shaped by his nuclear family and love for the kingdom, tempered into steel by his military training. Despite trauma and heartbreak. Despite the humiliating, heartless curse that Prem had imposed. A curse intended not only to neutralise the threat of a powerful adversary for the throne but to break him.

Through it all, honour was the one thing that Deven hadn't lost. That he prized.

Every move Prem had made under the dawn sky had been to get under the general's skin. He wanted to shatter his self-control. If Deven unleashed his tiger nature without being under the aegis of the duel, without being under the banner of my champion, he'd show himself to be no better than his cousin. And that would kill him.

The raja's lips curled as though he had already won. He didn't need an army to defeat us. I might be the queen some had been waiting for, but Deven was integral to our ambitions for Jalapashu.

He was the glue that held us together.

Just as, for a long time, he'd been the glue that had held the kingdom together under Prem's rule, softening his cousin's baser instincts. He'd helped the people, ate with them, protected them, counselled restraint, overseen those damn gladiatorial spectacles, and sated the raja's cruelty with his suffering. Bore the weight of it gladly if it meant protecting the weak.

Those glacial eyes flickered with the knowledge as if Prem could taste the victory that edged closer with every taunt—a sadist salting a wound. "I saw the life drain from Roshni's eyes, you know. She was always so naive. She begged me to leave you alone with her dying breath."

I sucked in a breath at the low blow, even as Deven's pupils dilated. If Prem sullied his belief in himself, our house of cards would tumble down despite the walls I had built. Despite the gargoyles that guarded them. A fist tightened around my heart.

Deven held himself to such high standards that if his control slipped, he would leave the resistance of his own accord. He would leave me.

"No!" My voice was a strangled warning. A warning

against his loss of self. A warning against Prem's mind trickery, whether borne of learned manipulation or new magic.

Deven closed the distance between the two of them and seized the hilt of the sword. Coal-black eyes met azure blue ones. Then, with a deft twist of his wrist, claws glinting, Deven wrenched the sword from the raja's grasp. His face hovered against his cousin's, his dark locks slipping onto Prem's golden turban.

Merlin bounded to my feet. "Kiya, the ba–"

But I was too concerned with Deven's plight to lend my ear to the hare, even when he reached up and pawed at my thighs.

"I warned you, cousin." Deven held the blade within slashing distance of the raja's throat.

Prem didn't flinch. "My, my. How far the honourable general has already fallen."

"Don't," I pleaded with Deven. "He wants you to lose control."

A brittle laugh spilt from the raja's lips. "My dear cousin, give it your best shot. I took a leaf out of the seer's book. My body has become home to a dazzling array of topaz jewels, and my power claws at me. I'd hate to hurt the witch before the appointed time."

I raked my eyes over him for further signs of the power lurking there. His body remained still, almost eerily so, as if frozen in place. However, his piercing eyes flickered with an intense concentration, darting from between us with a predatory focus. And in my body, in my mind, I felt a tug that made me recoil, made my power surge within my veins and almost, almost had me call for the gargoyles. Call for them to rain down hell upon him and damn it all. Deven felt a tug, too, because a growl spilt from him as if battles raged that I couldn't even see.

Prem's honeyed voice was steeped in cruelty. "Judging by

your pallor and the claws you can barely control, you aren't quite the tiger you once were, cousin."

"We shall see," said Deven quietly as he extricated himself. He took the sword with him, flipping it with an ease that spoke volumes about his superior skill. Still, there was a glimmer of relief on his face when he moved back to my side as if the net of the raja's power lessened when he stepped away.

Prem had a tongue like a whip. "For decades, you were my lapdog. Now you're someone else's."

Deven's answering growl masked the scurrying of Tanay over the fortress walls, but I caught the boy's scampering in my peripheral vision. Tanay must have been a slippery eel to escape Harya's careful vigil. Nonetheless, I instructed the gargoyles to keep that pawn piece on the board, knowing he could be of use even as I loathed myself for it.

I curled my fingers into my palms. "Enough. State your terms."

Prem smoothed down his clothes, ruffled from Deven's grasp, and adopted the tone of a reluctant executioner as though there had been no crack in his authority. As if I hadn't cleaved his kingdom in two. A wisp of a smile played on his lips as he surveyed first me and Deven, then Mahi and Menon. "I sentence the four of you to death on the grounds of treason. Before death, Kiya Marlowe will transfer authority of the gargoyles to me. Should you submit, my subjects may return to the fold and be forgiven. After they have repented, of course."

It was nothing we hadn't expected. Nothing that hadn't played out in my nightmares before.

An offer that Grandfather had anticipated and advised we needn't even extend to the people. Because whatever Prem Kumar promised, history had shown him never to uphold his side of the bargain. He was always more cruel, more barbaric than his silken promises.

I didn't miss a beat, and I felt the power of standing there with my friends despite our differences and obstacles. He was alone, and we were not. "No."

A caustic laugh fell from his lips. "It was worth a try. You refuse?"

Mahi raged. "Is it too much to ask you to show a sliver of self-knowledge and slink off into the afterlife?"

The raja didn't think I had the guts to call the duel. He was wrong.

My voice was as smooth as the polished surface of a river stone. As if the words had been written by fate. "I'm descended from the founders of Jalapashu, who first discovered the Amber Hollows. I invoke the right of a duel to decide who wears the crown." The gargoyles roared in my head as if they had been waiting centuries for this moment. Somewhere behind me, the seer gave a sigh of pleasure.

Prem smiled like the tiger he was. "Delicious. I was hoping you would. I accept."

His eagerness made me think we'd done it all wrong, that we'd been played, but I met his gaze and didn't falter. I met his gaze even though we couldn't be sure what plans he had for us, and I couldn't even be sure that the seer would shed light on it, that she was completely with us, or that Deven could hold it together as he always had. And I couldn't be sure if I had been too eager or naive or foolish to think I could best the raja, even if my host of friends and family stood by me.

I swallowed the ashes in my throat, turning away from the raja's crowing to lift my face to the dawn rays, there, right there before his malign presence. Right there in front of the general, and the seer and her sorcerer brother, the parrot that seemed to be plucking his feathers out again in anxiety, my murmuring Merlin and the boy Tanay, pinned against a gargoyle and squirming against its thin humanoid arms.

I couldn't help but think of Sitara and whether this was

what she had wanted for us all those months ago when she had uncovered the truth of our roots in this kingdom and the possibility of our witchcraft. For a bitter moment, I yearned for my pottery studio and the quiet life we had left behind in Boundless Bay: three sisters living in a ramshackle house, the childhood friends, the lapping ocean, bracing swims, gliding seagulls, vinegary chips and the sooty hare that had been a family pet rather than a familiar.

A life that didn't involve such danger. A life that was simple and good.

The nostalgia hit me like a wave I wanted to consume me. But there was no turning back.

"Nominate me as your champion, Kiya," the general thundered.

The raja's blue chip eyes gleamed. "How quaint."

I bit my lip. "I have no demands other than to settle this matter cleanly without involving the people."

Deven's voice was dangerously soft. "Kiya…"

I ignored the confusion in Deven's searing gaze. But what woman would send the man she loved to fight her battles? What queen didn't want to win her throne by her own hand, intellect or merits?

Prem's cobalt eyes twinkled like shards of ice on a frozen lake. "Let the earth witch fight. We want to be remembered, don't we, dearest?"

My throat was dry. "Where?"

"That's for the incumbent to decide."

Hostility seeped out of Deven's pores.

I didn't dare look at him. "When?"

"The law says within a month. We will take the full month," ground out Deven.

He was trying to win me more time to prepare, even in his anger.

Prem smiled with malice. "I'm raring to settle the matter and to get back to the business of ruling."

Foreboding prickled in my belly as he focused over my shoulder. A coy smile twisted Prem's lips as he fixed his gaze on the banyan tree split between our territories.

A sickening sensation came over me.

Somewhere, the seer cried out.

I ran, Deven cursing at my heels.

It took mere seconds to reach the exposed half, the half not shielded inside the fortress.

Perhaps it had been a spell, after all. I had seen his lips move, and there hadn't been time for poison. It shouldn't have been possible, but the magic in the kingdom was fluid and full of trickery and unexpected growth, and more than anything, it was hoarded by a few.

Too late. Already, white threads of glowing magic cobwebbed the half of the tree visible from outside the fortress. The once verdant, leathery leaves of the banyan tree had browned at the edges. Its aerial roots withered even as we watched. The sacred tree—in existence since the founding of the kingdom—groaned as if in agony, its branches twisting and contorting in protest. An entire clump of the evergreen tree crumbled to dust.

"What have you done? You selfish fool," said Mahi.

Menon was quiet. Oh-so-quiet.

The sacred banyan tree had meaning. It was part of rituals and celebrations, a symbol of protection and renewal. It was tied to the fortunes of the kingdom, and now, it was dying. And with it, perhaps the magic of this place. The jewels. The veil. The possibility of creating a just kingdom.

"The games have begun," said Prem cooly. "I've had years to think about how I would handle a usurper of *my* throne. It's not in my best interests to wait a month."

The smugness on his face told me he had achieved all he set out to do.

Mahi's third eye flashed open, intense violet in colour, like the sky during the deepest storm. When she spoke, her voice rang out like a spectral ballet, words unfurling like flags of an unseen nation. The words clawed at me from the edge of reality, slinking into the air with a disquieting energy that lingered in the spaces between breaths. "If the fate of the crown is not decided by the time the sacred tree turns to dust, the kingdom and its magic will fall."

"You bastard," spat Deven, and his teeth and claws were just a breath away.

"Now, now, cousin. Play nicely. I did give you an out. You didn't take it. It's becoming quite a habit for women to lay down their life for you, isn't it? Yes. Get angry, Deven. Show everyone your true beast. We'll see each other soon, Kiya." Prem turned on his heel like he didn't have a care in the world. With a click of his tongue, the elephant meandered after him, its trunk and rump swinging haphazardly.

We let him go. We let him go even though a dagger in his back would have been a comfort.

Only one person wanted Prem Kumar to stay.

At my nod, the humanoid gargoyle released Tanay.

Mouth dry, I observed the world spiralling, the sacred tree glimmering. Part of me wanted Prem to witness my benevolence. Part of me wanted him to take Tanay and his mother back under his wing so that the dark, writhing, angry portion of my soul wouldn't be tempted to use the boy as leverage.

"Father," Tanay fell to his knees in front of the raja, looking younger than his ten years, his blue eyes the mirror image of his father's, his face pinched with ragged hope. "Take me with you. I'll serve you loyally. I know the earth witch's weaknesses. I can be of help."

Prem stepped over him, no hint of magic—or humanity— flaring. When Tanay grabbed his leg, his kick connected with the boy's shin and the child arced a few feet away with a thump. "I don't know you, boy, and I don't need your help. Move or be trampled."

The boy scrambled to his feet as the trumpeting elephant approached, a rope ladder swinging from its saddle. Prem climbed deftly up without the slightest hint of curiosity or care for the child and ambled away on the wrinkled grey back without giving Tanay a second glance.

Then he was gone, leaving the dying banyan tree in his wake.

CHAPTER 8

Deven turned over Prem's sword in his hands, his expression cold and shuttered.

Silence hung between us like a storm cloud until the raja and his elephant disappeared over the horizon. Only then did we deem it safe to return inside. We'd convened with the raja for a little over a quarter of an hour, yet I was entirely drained. Throat tight, I opened the great door to the fortress with a curl of my power and led the way through like I was the leader of a delegation. The gargoyles guarded our backs, and in my peripheral view, Menon hauled Tanay back to his mother by the scruff of his neck. The seer fussed over the familiars with staccato praise and gnarled hands.

But it was the general I was aware of.

His inky eyes didn't drift to me to check in, as had become his habit at council meetings and across crowded rooms. His body didn't brush against mine as we walked.

The golden rays of the new day settled into harsh winter light.

I reached out a hand but let it fall midair. "Can we talk? I know you're angry."

"You have *no* idea." He spun to Mahi. "I thought it was a

myth that incumbent rajas and ranis challenged for the throne to gain new powers. I thought it was a fucking myth."

The seer nodded, sombre as a funeral. "So did I."

Deven paused only to take in the crumbling branches of the sacred tree inside the fortress, then stalked past towards the armoury without a second glance.

The scent of decay and corruption hung heavy in the air as I watched his stiff, retreating back.

My pulse hammered in my throat. Had Prem Kumar really gained new magic from the kingdom to help him keep the throne? Was this whole thing rigged against us?

"Don't," said Mahi.

"Don't what?"

"Allow him to frighten you. It's one of his greatest weapons."

I tried not to sound scared. "How did he get that mind magic? What myth was Deven talking about?"

Mahi's kohl-painted brows drew together. "Just stories passed down the generations about rajas and ranis anointed, so that in their time of need when challenged for power, they became more powerful. Overnight."

My heart drummed. "And crushed their enemies?"

"Yes." She hesitated. "I've never believed those stories. People in power write their own histories. It's far more likely that Prem found a way to channel a new jewel or struck a bargain for new magic."

I searched her face, praying for honesty. "Have you heard of that happening before? Or seen it in your visions?"

"No. I haven't." She sighed. "We can't let this knock the wind out of our sails. Not when we've come so far."

I didn't respond. Instead, we took in the ruins of the sacred tree together with our familiars. Though the sickly white web of magic had evaporated, it was a husk of its former self. Its once majestic branches hung limply. Its smooth bark was now rough and cracked, marred by lesions that wept a sickly ichor. Roots that had once anchored deep into the earth with vigour had become feeble. Patches of moss and fungus clung to the surface of its gaunt trunk like a shroud. Charred notes, broken lanterns and torn ribbons that had adorned the banyan tree now littered the ground. As if whatever magic Prem had wielded against the tree had rejected any baubles of faith or goodness.

Worse still—perhaps due to my earth magic—I gleaned how the sacred tree's death was not gentle.

It was agonising—the death of a kingdom itself.

We had seen him mouth the spell and yet had been helpless against him.

The people would soon wake. I dreaded to think how they would react to the desecration. How it would gut them. How it might shatter their belief in the resistance.

Soldiers already gawked, their horror held in check only by the restraint they practised professionally. The seer sank to her knees at the roots of the tree.

Merlin's liquid gold eyes held profound grief. He spoke in a voice that had witnessed the rise and fall of civilisations. "I tried to warn you as soon as I realised."

My gut wrenched. "I was distracted." I scooped him up and held him close in apology as he trembled in my arms. "Maybe Leena and Nani can find some way to halt the deterioration or reverse it."

Somewhere, Aanya sang a song of such timeless beauty that it dulled the thorns of our anxiety. I didn't care that her song was a sticking plaster, not a cure. I didn't care that I was suspending logical thought and choosing ease for a few moments or that the sweet notes pirouetting through the air brought us an unearned sense of healing. I didn't even care that Deven had probably escaped the song to hold onto the spikes of his anger. I only knew that I was tired and fighting with my friends when I usually would have stopped to understand why a woman wholly devoted to our mutual goals had chosen to pull the wool over my eyes.

"It was a spell. Or perhaps a poison? A curse?" The seer dragged a hand across her wan face. "It was one of a myriad of possibilities, but I didn't think he'd stoop this low. That he'd risk so much."

"You're not to blame." My anger at her was hollowed out, either by my own choice or Aanya's song. Deven wouldn't have left me with her if he considered her a threat. She'd shielded us from Prem's spell casting or whatever new magic he now wrought damage with. I didn't want to fight my friends as well as our enemies.

"We must halt the poisoning of the tree to give you time to become strong enough to challenge him. We'll all have to work on our shielding."

I hoped she couldn't read the terror in my eyes. "One day at a time."

She slumped, and I realised that a seer could rarely take things one day at a time. That she was forced to focus on the nebulous future. That she had been trying to wrangle it into a version we could all live with. "About before...not sharing my vision of the boy–"

"It's okay." And when I said it out loud, I realised maybe it was. Maybe I could let it go.

In my arms, Merlin chirped with approval.

"No, it's not. I owe you an explanation." She heaved herself to her feet.

I blinked at her rare humility. "Yes, I think perhaps you do."

The seer opened her hip flask of tea and drank deeply of the foul concoction before screwing the lid shut as though she needed time to formulate her words. "You're one of the only people in this kingdom who isn't scared of me, who tolerates my moods, who maybe even likes me."

Pity flared in my chest, but I masked it with teasing. "I wouldn't go that far."

Mahi snorted, then grew sombre. "My visions started as a teen. All those hormones, all those feelings of womanhood and the future, and suddenly, a tap opened, and images flooded in. Unsettling, painful, sometimes beautiful images just poured into my mind at all hours of the day and night. I hated them. I hated them for interrupting my life. For their relentlessness when I was doing ordinary things. Friendships were destroyed because how could I explain everything that was in my head? Dreams, set aside. Sleep disrupted. My first kiss, ruined."

"No child should have that burden." I smoothed the hare's velveteen ears between my fingers.

"It took me years to recalibrate. To slow them down. To learn how to breathe through them, to sieve through the knowledge. Instead of providing clarity, they made me second-guess every decision I made. A dozen versions of one future disorienting me. Futures that sometimes involve me and often do not. How could I act on such unspecific magic? What use were all those warnings if I was paralysed on how to act? It took decades to learn how to track them over years and how delicately I had to tread about sharing my information and with whom." She went quiet as she wrestled with her demons.

My arms were sore from carrying Merlin. "Do you write them down?" I asked her gently.

The hare hopped away when I released him, though his inky ears were still turned in our direction.

Mahi tapped her head. "It's all in here, and that makes it even worse." Flat brown eyes turned to the dying banyan tree, and I realised she had seen some version of this future, and her failure would always haunt her, that such failures were perhaps the reason for her prickly, demanding nature.

"How much blame do I bear for horrors I foretold but didn't prevent?"

"I've always thought it's the person who perpetrates the horrors who is to blame, not the person who tries and fails to stop them." My breath bottled. "Unless that person sits on crucial information."

She sighed, accepting my criticism. "Sometimes, I can plot a path through. Not a foolproof one—never one that gives me peace of mind—but a messy one. One that is enough of an edge. But I never know if it'll be enough." A crack of vulnerability. "So now you know."

I frowned. "Know what?"

"That your faith in me is misplaced. My visions have been coming thick and fast since I left the labyrinth. But they are unreliable. Unfinished. Unshareable." Mahi shuddered and looked down at her gnarled fingers. "I make mistakes. I'm just muddling through. I can't give you the guarantees you want."

I sucked in my breath. I'd been relying on her with the faith a child has in their parents. I'd been blind to the reality I should have confronted from the moment Sitara slumped on our kitchen floor.

Nothing came without risks. Especially not in Jalapashu.

"I haven't been fair to you. You're only human. Not the hand of destiny."

She didn't register my words. Maybe she hadn't ever spoken as frankly about the burden of her magic before. "You know what the worst thing has been? Not the deadened emotions. Not the sweat-drenched nights. Not the sense that suppressing my visions to *live* is a dereliction of duty. Not even the preventable losses." Mahi gave a wry smile. "Oh yes, I have a mental tally of them… The worst thing about my visions is what *knowing* steals from living. I knew how my great love ended before the relationship even began. I knew my twin would one day do something so heinous that even I might not be able to forgive him. I knew that I would become the raja's trusted seer, and I would have to mask my disgust for him. How I fretted over that one. So many moments lived, not with the presence of mind, but as if in retrospect. Each relived moment is like an echo, a pale shadow of itself, that imitates human interaction."

"I still don't understand why you didn't tell me Tanay would attempt to take my life."

Her lips compressed, and I thought she might deny me the truth, but in the end, she blew out her breath. "In every pathway I have pieced together, you and Tanay meeting in a gentle way ended in our defeat. So I kept quiet. Even though I wanted to tell you."

I lifted my chin. "Did you know I'd survive?"

"I hoped you would."

"Have you kept other things from me?"

"From you. And from others… I didn't tell the general that he would fall in love with a grieving woman from Boundless Bay. There are no shortcuts to authentic connection. To healing and redemption."

"You knew we'd fall in love."

"I suspected." The seer's violet eye peeled open from amongst the wrinkles on her forehead. "I could tell you the points on the map it will take to reach our destination, but if those individual points are unearned and we are just going through the motions, we will fail. And that man, that despicable man who sits on the throne of our great kingdom, he'll remain there until he is old and fat and surrounded by sycophants." The spectre of the sacred tree loomed behind her.

My tone was careful. Her barriers remained high despite it all. "Would you give up your magic?"

A wistful smile played on her lips. "Not my witchcraft. But maybe my seer's ability."

"You're no longer alone. We're a coven now. We'll find a way through."

"Perhaps." The parrot flew to her shoulder, sensing our conversation coming to a close, and she caressed his emerald body as he preened against her hand. "There is something I *can* tell you. You need to get back to making pottery. It's key to your wholeness. Key to your magic."

"We're at war, Mahi. There's no time for pottery."

"Beauty is needed even more at times of war. Beauty sustains us. It heals us."

It was true; I felt broken inside. Creativity had always been my go-to remedy when my emotional equilibrium went off-kilter. Apart from minor fixes I had made to the injured gargoyles—tending to cracks and chips—I hadn't crafted any pottery in days.

The seer looked into the distance to where the general had cut a path to the armoury. "He's angry you didn't nominate him as your champion. He wanted to take the brunt of this fight."

I met her tired brown eyes. "I know."

"I love him like a son."

"I know." It was a warning of sorts: to take care of his fragile heart.

"Don't let him simmer too long. He'll build walls you'll find impossible to scale. And the vision I have for Jalapashu requires you to work in step with each other."

CHAPTER 9

I slipped past the hordes gathering at the sacred tree, past the rhythmic chopping of mangos and pickles for breakfast and subdued conversations, and found the general in a room adjacent to the armoury. There, he practised his skills against his brother-in-law Ashwin.

The sparring room was unlike the standards to which Deven had been accustomed at the vast training warehouse, now off-limits to him in the raja's domain. Shafts of murky light streamed through narrow, mud-caked windows, casting irregular patterns of light and shadow on the ground. The room was meagre and damp, with a worn wooden floor with markings that hinted at its past as a grain storage room. The scent of sweat mingled with the earthy aroma of the fortress. There were no carefully arranged sections to train various fighting techniques. There were no gleaming racks of weapons, pock-marked training dummies, mirrored walls or slick gym machinery. No scuff marks or splinters or memories of triumphs in training. Instead, there was a random assortment of mats, a jug of water, a pile of wooden swords fashioned by carpenters within the resistance and a collection of makeshift weights crafted from rocks wrapped in thick cloth.

I'd spent hours in here over the past days while Deven took me through my paces.

Yet, he didn't want me to face danger. He preferred to put himself in harm's way instead.

Leaning against the door frame, I paused to watch him spar in the subdued light. Whatever familial respect existed between the men had been set aside. Here, it was man against man, a level playing field, torsos bare and slick with sweat, muscles rippling as they circled each other. Ashwin was shorter, stockier and less lean than Deven, but the physicality of rearing horses and regular training bouts with the general over the years meant he was a worthy opponent. They didn't use the wooden swords. Neither did they use weapons from the armoury next door—blunt swords, battered shields and rusty spears—salvaged by the gargoyles under the cover of night. Stashes left unguarded by the raja given their inferiority. Instead, the two men had strapped their knuckles for safety and fought hand to hand. I hovered at the sidelines encased in shadows. Clipped conversation punctuated their combat.

"Stop fretting." Ashwin threw a punch.

Deven dodged it. "She has to survive the duel."

"She will." Ashwin threw another punch, but it missed its mark again.

Deven advanced with a jab, then a cross. "It can't come to war. The lack of external threats has made us soft."

Ashwin blocked and retaliated with a hook to the chin. "Nonsense. You've trained your men well."

Deven ducked. "Thirty soldiers deserted with us. I'm grateful. I am. But there have been no more arriving under the cover of night."

"Prem's locked the kingdom down?"

"Yeah. We'll have to use guerrilla tactics to stand a chance."

"Nisha always wondered why you gave Prem the time of day."

A growl of exertion accompanied Deven's next punch. "Leave the past where it belongs."

Every passing moment made me feel more uncomfortable, and I knew I should leave or announce myself. But I didn't. Instead, I stayed rooted to the spot.

"You could tear up the battlefield yourself if you shift." Ashwin threw a left and right hook in quick succession.

The general easily blocked them. "Controlling my gifts isn't as easy as it used to be."

"Can't be as hard as controlling Ishaan. He keeps getting into trouble."

"Want me to talk to him?"

"Nah. We're already laying it on thick."

Deven huffed a laugh. "I tossed him out of here the other day and told him to grow a beard before he took up fighting. He was shadowboxing in the corner."

"See? If this situation goes on much longer, the children will need more structure."

The general landed a punch on his brother-in-law's abdomen. "He's a good kid."

Ashwin panted. "Easy. You know what an earful we both got from Nisha after our last bout."

Deven's mouth quirked, his footwork light. "What? You can't handle my sister's nagging?"

Ashwin struck Deven's side. "She's not the sort to kiss it better."

The general absorbed the punch, barely a blip in his footwork. "I prefer talking shop to your bedroom antics with my sister."

Beads of sweat dotted Ashwin's bald head. "Most of the

new recruits aren't like me. They have no knowledge of combat."

"You have no idea. Yesterday, someone dropped an axe on his own foot during training. Nothing a few stitches couldn't fix, mind." He circled his brother-in-law. His coal-black eyes gleamed, and I could see him weighing up whether to go hard or not.

"Kiya and her gargoyles are a huge advantage," said Ashwin carefully.

Deven slammed him with an uppercut to the torso that sent Ashwin momentarily reeling back.

His brother-in-law cocked an eyebrow. "I touched a nerve. Feeling protective? Or do you doubt the earth witch?"

My breath caught in my throat at the turn in conversation. This was too private a conversation for eavesdroppers, an intimate conversation between family. And that's precisely why I stayed.

Deven's balled fists hovered in the air, waiting to strike. He paused too long for comfort. "It's not about doubt, Ash. It's about preparation. Prem has already amplified his magic. He'll break into every vault, arm every man, woman and child, commandeer all the topaz at his disposal to crush this rebellion."

"You really care for her. It's nice to see you drop your armour, brother."

Midnight eyes narrowed. "That woman just won't listen."

A chuckle. "Oh, she definitely got under your skin."

I froze, wanting to sink into the ground. Shame—and desire—made my cheeks heat, but I couldn't tear myself away. I hung onto every word.

"It's not that. That bastard doesn't give a shit who he hurts."

"And you don't want her hurt." A pause. "Your history doesn't determine your future, Dev."

"I don't know what you're talking about."

"Yes, you do," said Ashwin. "You know, it's funny. The family is used to seeing you put yourself in danger and come out unscathed. Why do you think Ishaan thinks you're invincible? But Nisha…Nisha worries about your heart, and I do too, brother."

Deven's face darkened. His biceps flexed as he lunged with a flurry of punches. "Leave the psychology to someone else, Ash. Stick to mucking out horses."

"I'll stick to kicking your arse, *General*."

The sparring became even more brutal. A jab. A swift hook. A block. With lightning reflexes, the men traded strikes, each blow delivered with controlled precision. Grunts and the thud of fists meeting flesh echoed off the stone walls. Each strike was met with a swift counter as the men sought openings in each other's defences. It was like a dance I couldn't tear my eyes from. They weren't evenly matched in skill or build, but even if they were, there was a predatory gleam in Deven's eye and an aggression and speed that would have left Ashwin in the dust regardless. Deven maintained his energy, whereas Ashwin's stamina couldn't hold out against Deven unleashing a series of calculated blows. He drove his opponent back with each strike, the muscles in his tattooed back working with every movement. A feint to the left, then a quick step to the right, allowed him to catch Ashwin's jaw. The crack made me wince. Nisha wouldn't be happy. Ashwin jerked backwards, and for a moment, I thought the general might take advantage of the lapse and deploy the agile footwork he had shown me. That he would send his brother-in-law to the ground.

A glimmer of mischief filled Ashwin's eyes as he glimpsed me. "Kiya, what a nice surprise," he muttered through his bleeding lip.

My voice cut through the maleness of the environment. "I didn't mean to disturb."

Deven spun, midnight eyes narrowing a split second

before his brother-in-law dealt him a mirror blow on his jaw. Ashwin wasn't finished. With a chuckle and a calculated strike behind the knees, he sent the general sprawling to the mat. Deven rubbed his jaw ruefully before standing up and shaking his brother-in-law's hand.

Brotherly respect radiated between them. "Well played, Ash. It won't be so easy next time."

"Easy? I thought you would drive me into the wall for a second." A grin. "I think that's the first time I've handed you your arse. I'm going to relish giving Nisha a blow-by-blow account. Maybe Ishaan will hero-worship *me* for a change instead of you." Ashwin thumped the general on the shoulder. He tipped an imaginary hat to me and called out over his shoulder as he headed in the direction of the armoury. "I'll give you the time and place of our next tussle, Kiya."

I turned to the general, my heartbeat fluttering within my ribcage.

CHAPTER 10

The warmth drained from Deven's face as he poured himself a glass of water and drank half its contents. He eyed me warily, face tight. "What do you want, Kiya?"

"Don't be like that." I handed him a towel, trying not to take in the planes of his torso, the tattoo stretching across his back that took my breath away. "Don't push me away."

He accepted the towel, dried off his sweat-drenched hair and chest, and pulled on a T-shirt. Deep grooves lined his mouth. "What are you playing at? We had a plan."

"*You* had a plan."

"Just tell me why."

"I've spent so long hearing everyone say that I'm the change Jalapashu has been waiting for that I want to earn it." I dragged in a breath. "And I don't want you to go up against Prem any more than you want that for me."

The general glowered. "I'm *trained* to do it. He's the viper *I* let into the den."

"It's not your job to protect me."

He cursed. "Of course it is. That's precisely my role."

"You're infuriating."

A growl. "So are you."

The air between us fizzed with animosity or something more vital. More intoxicating.

"I can protect myself." My hands fisted at my sides. "You know I can."

"Not from him. He doesn't play by the rules."

"What use is my training if you don't want me in the ring?"

His gaze narrowed, and there was a fire in those inky eyes. "Get on the mat."

"Excuse me?" I huffed.

A growl as he came closer. "If you're so convinced you can protect yourself, then prove it."

I turned away. "I'll give you some time to cool down."

He grabbed my elbow. "Get on the mat."

"No." I frowned and wriggled free.

"What are you scared of?" He'd never baited me before.

"I'm not scared," I shot back.

"Get on the mat. No magic. No weapons. Come at me with your strength, agility and intellect."

He'd been courteous when we'd sparred before, generous with his knowledge and gentlemanly when it came to using his full strength. Our sparring had been performative, a sharing of technique rather that a real bout. "You've got decades of training on me."

He folded his arms across his chest. "So has Prem."

"I'll never win without my magic."

"You think Prem will play fair? The minute you're alone with him, you'll be at his mercy. Who knows how long the banyan tree will hold out. We could have hours. Days. You might be forced to call this duel *tomorrow*."

"Fine." I clenched my fists, as angry at him suddenly as he was at me.

"I won't go easy on you."

I lifted my chin. "Do your worst." A pause. "Are you

going to take your T-Shirt off?" It was a fair question. He had fought bare-chested with Ashwin, after all. I didn't want additional distractions.

He cocked an eyebrow. "Are you?"

Glaring at him, I made my way to the mat, set aside my dagger, slipped off my shoes so we were both barefoot and tied my dark tresses into a high ponytail.

Deven followed, a cruel smile playing on his lips as he noticed my nervous fumbling, how I nearly snapped my hairband, how my breath was shallow. "Do you want to warm up, little witch?"

I twisted Prem's topaz ring in my palm to protect it and to rile him. My heart quickened. "Make your move, General."

"I told you not to call me that." He lunged in my direction, not with closed fists but with open hands, seeking to pin me down, to humiliate me, to prove that I could never match up to a man of his size or Prem's. To prove that I needed him to be my saviour.

He tried to overpower me and assert his dominance. He was taller and stronger by far, with a body honed to perfection and all the predatory instincts of his shifter nature. I sidestepped his advance, despite our proximity—using my smallness to my advantage—and slipped out of his grasp with a grace that had him grunting in approval. Our bodies brushed against each other, igniting a spark of awareness that crackled between us. He grabbed my arm, but I twisted away with the finesse of a dancer, regained my balance and kicked at his groin.

"That was a low blow," he said darkly as he caught my foot and kneaded the ball of my foot with a lover's touch. "Is that all you've got?"

A red mist of fury descended over me. I wrenched my foot away. "Oh, I've got so much more."

We went at it again, and this time, I sharpened my focus and went on the attack. We circled each other, my mind racing with strategies he had taught me. He'd drilled it into me to use every advantage at my disposal. To figure out if agility, speed or strength would tip the odds in my favour. To use my best weapon and everyday objects if necessary. To use trickery and distraction. To destabilise a challenger by striking the knees as Ashwin had done. That combat wasn't always honourable. Sometimes, it was filthy and humiliating and made you sick to the stomach with what you'd been forced to do or what was done to you. To not think twice before targeting an opponent's throat or kidneys with a punch or poking the eyes. To do what it took to survive.

To never go into a fight alone. In the worst case, to run, to live.

When Deven lunged again, I met his advance head-on, my balled fists ready to strike. A quick feint to the left baited him into exposing his side. With my thumb protected, just as he had taught me to do, and the forward thrust of my body lending me power, I drove my fist into the soft spot beneath his ribcage. A sharp exhale escaped him as the blow landed, but he recovered quickly, his eyes twinkling as if it were child's play. He countered with a swift jab aimed at my shoulder that made me yelp. That would certainly bruise.

"Bastard," I panted, beads of sweat pooling on my brow and between my breasts.

"You have no idea." Our eyes locked in a silent battle of wills.

I pointed at his ribs, where his skin was mottled. "I'm not the only one who's going to bruise."

"So fucking what." His breathing was barely out of sync, and he'd gone a whole round with Ashwin before we started. Maybe even more. "Are we just going to dance all day?"

Despite the fact that he said he wasn't going easy on me, it made me furious that he *was*. We weren't using weapons that he wielded with breathtaking skill, he hadn't shifted into his tiger, and his movements lacked their usual intensity. He was holding back. I wanted no part of his pity. I wanted to prove that I was deserving of all the gifts that had been given to me: my magic, the people's trust, the time and experiences that Sitara hadn't had.

Determination thrummed in the air between us. Deven's midnight eyes widened as I ran at him, my body a coiled spring, the mat groaning beneath my feet, fingers loose. He shifted his stance, preparing to block my attack. With a fluid motion, I leapt and shoved his shoulder with all my might. With my free hand, I called the rocks waiting for me. The rocks wrapped as weights that had sung to me from the moment I stepped into the room. My earth magic fizzed through me. I called them, and they came, sweeping Deven's feet from under him. Deven stumbled backwards, his arms windmilling as he fought to regain his footing.

He crashed onto his back with a satisfying thud, with me on top of him. For a moment, we lay entwined on the ground, locked in a tangle of limbs, our breaths mingling in the dim light. When I looked at him, his gaze was raw and primal.

I gave him a triumphant grin. "I bested you."

His hands closed around my waist. "You didn't play by the rules."

"Neither will he."

A rueful smile. "Touché."

"You're lucky I didn't call the gargoyles on you."

Heat pulsed between us. "That would have been *very* naughty."

All I could concentrate on was the small circles he was drawing on the damp skin beneath my T-shirt. "You're not angry anymore."

He pressed a kiss to the shoulder he had struck and sighed. "I am, a little."

"Your ego was hurt," I murmured.

"Wrong, little witch. I can't bear the thought of him

hurting you…and I want him to know we're united. I want us to *be* united. He'll be sniggering now at the thought he divided us."

I stroked a hand across one pectoral muscle, then the other. "We're hardly divided."

His lip quirked. "It doesn't look like it. But you're not ready to take him on alone."

"I will be. I have to do this myself."

His eyes darkened. "You felt the tug on our minds, Kiya. He has new magic."

"It sounds stupid to say it, but I heard you before about the myth. Do you think this land somehow gave him new magic, that the kingdom itself wants him to keep the throne?"

"That our gods or our soil or the universe rewarded him with more power at precisely the time he risks being toppled?" He gave a mirthless chuckle. "No, Kiya. I don't think the universe would reward that bastard with a single damn thing. I think he fights tooth and nail to claw every advantage to himself."

I swallowed hard. "At least we know. Mahi said we'd need to work on our shielding."

"You've forgiven her?"

"Yes. Have you?"

"She's a complicated woman." His arms tightened around me, and he shuddered. "We have to make the next few days count. I'm not sending you to your death."

My stomach pitted. "Then help me get ready."

"We'll have to train hard."

"Yes." I dared to kiss him.

His hard body and stubborn mind yielded, letting me in so that the first tentative brushes of my lips clinging to his deepened, opening to deep caverns, sweeping tongues and longing. A passion that washed all logic from my mind until there was only him. His mouth, his hands, his salty, sweaty skin, his strong thighs against my soft ones. My wet core and his pulsing one.

At that moment, it didn't matter that the door to the sparring room was slightly ajar. It didn't matter that our problems were larger than either of us could solve. All that mattered was the need we had for each other and the comfort we took from one another.

We pushed aside the weights, and he growled at being separated from me and pulled me right back to him. When he peeled off my shirt and unhooked my bra, I gave myself freely, letting my breasts spill onto his chest. Groaning as he kneaded them, his eyes dark with desire as he took one tight nipple into his mouth, sucking it, biting it, making me moan with pleasure before turning his sweet, tortuous attention to the other nipple. I tangled my fingers in his damp hair, melting into the pleasure, straddling him, rocking against the thick length of him. A brazen hussy.

"We shouldn't. Not in here," I muttered, even though I was so desperate for him that I thought I might lose all thought. All decorum. A queen-in-waiting and her general.

He dragged his head back, breath ragged. "I need you."

There was more than need in his eyes. There were whole worlds. Worlds of pleasure and pain, of promise and sacrifice. He kissed me, ravaging me with such fire that I couldn't do anything but submit and moan and accept what he offered me. When he smoothed down my leggings and my knickers, trailing his lips down my thighs and calves, throwing aside the garments before working his way up again to my apex, I closed my eyes and fell into my bliss.

He eased me apart, hooking my legs over his shoulders, and slipped his fingers into my wetness, where I was ready for him. Then he lowered his head to the softest part of me, and I writhed on his tongue when he dipped it in and stroked me with it, up and down and around until I saw stars. Until all I could think of was his name. He let out a soft laugh at my arousal, at how I was putty in his hands. He teased my pleasure, using me as his plaything, working me to heights that had me biting down on his fingers with my scent still on them.

When his hands raked over my breasts, flicking my nipples, I couldn't stand the clothing between us anymore. A millimetre of distance was too much. I needed to feel him, to have him in me.

I clawed at his trousers. "Take them off. Now."

His arrogant smile was my undoing, but underneath, there was a vulnerability, like he couldn't quite fathom how I needed him so much. Even though he drew female eyes— and male ones—wherever he went with his looks, his stoicism and his damn honour. "You're in a hurry."

But I could see his own need despite his flippant words. The way he couldn't keep his hands off me. The outline of his arousal against his trousers. The catch in his breath when I freed him and pushed him back on the mat for the third time that day. This time he didn't complain about being laid on his arse. He didn't complain when I guided him into me, my eyes widening as my body accommodated his size, and I began to rock.

Shadows danced across his face. "So beautiful, Kiya. Keep doing that."

I rode him as he held my waist and clenched my buttocks. The velvet length of him slipped in and out of my wetness, sending shooting pleasure so intense through me that I thought I'd lose my mind. When he grew impatient at my rhythm, he flipped us over, ramming so hard and fast that I could sense the untamed wildness of the tiger in him. But when he lifted my chin and kissed me deeply, I melted into the tenderness of his humanness, too. We came, me first, then him, stars in our eyes, our minds a whiteout.

It was a dance as old as time and a dance that was ours

alone. With no one else in the cosmos but him and me. And our ragged breath and fragile, aching hearts.

Afterwards, sprawled in his arms, I looked up into his handsome face. "You know he wants to drive you from us. He wants to make you believe that you're worthless. Or dangerous to us. Or a liability. Because you are struggling to control your shifter side."

He stiffened, halting the flow of his breath. "He's an arsehole, but I'd say that was a true strike."

Pain speared through my chest. I took his face in my hands and tumbled into the dark pools of his eyes. "You don't believe you're worthy of happiness, and it's bullshit. Just because bad stuff happened to you, just because you were there…your wife, Jalapashu, Prem's shitty trajectory…none of it is your fault, Deven. You don't have to sacrifice yourself to find redemption. You can choose to let go of the weight of your past. You can choose to fight for yourself as well as others."

He turned his head away like he couldn't fathom the thought of fighting for himself. "If Prem loses the duel and lives, he'll declare war regardless of any promises made."

"I know."

"I'm done underestimating you," he whispered. "You're not Roshni."

I breathed in the musky scent of him. "No, I'm not."

"We'll have to use more spies, wring advantages from our allies, and you'll have to dig deeper into your magic than you are comfortable with. It won't be pretty."

"So be it. We'll end his reign. We'll beat him." The bravado made my voice uneven.

Him. I wanted to be rid of him so badly. Even now, I could feel the topaz ring in my palm.

"I was so close to losing my tether altogether this morning."

"I want you to let Leena take a look at you."

The general's whiskey-deep voice reverberated in my ears. "You make fixing things sound so easy."

"I'm a potter. Broken things don't phase me."

"Sometimes I think you could be everything I've been missing. That I've waited a lifetime for." He caught my palm and kissed it. "I lov—"

I pressed my fingers to his lips, hot tears pricking behind the nebulous pink of my eyelids. "No, don't say it. Don't say it until this is over. Until we are safe."

It was too much. It was all too much.

Hurt flashed in his eyes, but he pressed a kiss to my forehead. "Okay."

I wanted to save those three words until I could savour them. When the time came, I wanted to sit with them in a quiet room, turn them over and over in my mind, to hear him say them when we could tangle all day in bed and talk about the future. Hearing them now amidst the chaos and crises of our lives washed away their power.

The door to the sparring room was thrown open, and his nephew stood there, gawking at us through the shadows. "Uncle Dev, mummy told me to tell you to come to breakfast. She says you've been working too hard to eat." His eyes were as wide as saucers. "It doesn't *look* like you're working. Why aren't you wearing any clothes?"

"Turn around, Ishaan." Deven cursed and chucked me my clothes. "We'll be right there."

We scrambled to our feet, the spell broken. Minutes later, we sat at separate tables to eat a breakfast of *puri* and mango chutney, the memory of our tussle lingering between us.

CHAPTER 11

N ani entered Mahi's house in a crumpled *salwar kameez*, soiled with mud like she'd been kneeling in the dirt. "Your sister has been at it for hours now. Even with our combined efforts, it doesn't look like what Prem Kumar did to the sacred tree can be easily undone. It's shedding leaves at an alarming rate."

That meant I'd have to call the duel soon. Too soon.

I kneaded my temples. "Is Leena still there?"

Nani gave the snoring hare a fond glance as if, even amidst our strife, they'd begun to mend historic hurts. "Your sister's worn out by her attempts. Fishtail gargoyle flew her out of the fortress for a burst of nature."

Harya would never have let Leena's need for nature supersede his defensive concerns, but that was what made Sindhuja different. Her infatuation with Leena made her both attentive to my sister's every need and mindful of her safety. She knew my sister suffered without an open view of the landscape and would sooner die than let anything happen to her.

"And the people? Have they calmed somewhat?"

Even with silver roots coming into her henna-coloured

hair and the muddied clothing that hung off her bird-like bones, she had a quiet dignity that stemmed not from how polished she was but from the shining kindness in her eyes. "They're beside themselves. Poor Aanya's vocal cords are nearly wrung out with trying to bring them ease."

Mahi's bosom quivered with passion. "Those fools would rather spend all their time mourning than doing something."

Nani smoothed her dishevelled beehive, unfazed by Mahi's surliness. "According to our history, the sacred tree's health has declined only once before…when the rani instructed the gargoyles to kill civilians. It's a bad omen."

"It's not just a bad omen, Kavita. It's happening." Mahi's violet eye yawned in its search for fragments of truth and closed once more. She swallowed a gulp from her flask of tea and slammed it back down on the kitchen counter. "I need more visions."

"We must keep our heads. And you must rest," said Nani. "If only for a few hours."

Babbu flopped from his perch, squawked a few snores that might have mimicked his mistress, and promptly shut his beak when the seer sent him a venomous glare.

There was an otherworldly timbre to her voice, as though she'd been combing through her visions even as we sat there. "You want me to sleep now? By my gleanings, in four to five days, the kingdom will fall." Mahi had been using more ambiguous language around her visions since our talk. Insights. Reveries. Illuminations. As if she was already caveating what she might share. Underlining their uncertain foothold. As if she was shirking the leadership that had always been hers around usurping the throne from Prem. "Something's wrong. I just can't see it. It's there. Shielded. I have to break through."

"You said it yourself. You can't force the timing of your visions," I said. "Let Leena make you a sleep remedy. Just to take the edge off your exhaustion. Then you can try again."

"I'm perfectly capable of concocting my own sleeping draught, as you well know." Her sour expression relented at my sigh. A pillar candle—her kitchen was more for mystic spells than gourmet cooking—illuminated the haggard grooves on her face and the wan pallor of her skin. "Perhaps a short nap when Menon returns from mending the wards."

Intuiting the implicit command, Babbu soared out of the house in search of her sorcerer brother, his emerald wings a welcome splash of vibrant colour in the dusty light.

Unease rippled in my belly. Like Deven, I didn't trust Menon fully. The seer fervently desired his rehabilitation, and I hoped she wouldn't be disappointed. To be on the safe side, Grandfather had assigned Aanya to subtly check Menon's work on the wards.

If Nani was nettled about the squalor of Mahi's kitchen, given her own kitchen witchery, she didn't let it show. Instead, she pulled a balm from her bra and applied it to the seer's temples. "Just a little…that's it, let me rub it in. It'll bring you a little comfort on a difficult day. Then we can put our old heads together and get on with our task of teaching Kiya how to shield until Menon is here."

I frowned. "But this lesson is vital to everyone in the resistance."

Notes of menthol and lemongrass dispersed into the kitchen as Nani opened the balm. "That's true, but who will Prem concentrate his fire on?" The seer grumbled but melted into her touch.

"Prakash will educate the rest of the rebels," said Mahi. "It's his chance to ingratiate himself after the raids he led and taxes he demanded as the raja's Enforcer."

Nani finished up. "None of us are perfect."

Mahi had the grace to look chastised and brushed aside an assortment of witchy objects from the counter—a gloopy mortar and pestle, a well-thumbed spell book, luminous potion bottles and sticky tarot cards—to make space for our studies.

"Can everyone learn to control their minds? Even the non-magically inclined?"

"It's not a magical skill. It's a human one. Experienced magic users have more of an edge, but I'll tell you something I haven't allowed myself to think in many years." Nani ran her papery fingers over the bracelet that held her topaz jewel. "Everyone in Jalapashu has a smidgeon of magic. The blood-lines of the founders have long merged with the common people."

Mahi snorted. "The dating pool could be bigger."

Nani pursed her lips. "I think the soil in this kingdom feeds the magic as much as the jewels. I've been convinced for a long time that if every person in the kingdom had access to a topaz stone, their magic would be amplified."

Mahi chuckled. "You've been a secret member of the resistance all along, Kavita. Better late than never. Did it take you this long to realise that our rulers have controlled the population by dividing us into haves and have-nots?"

"I'm not judgemental or pessimistic." The *unlike you* hung in the air between them, but Nani was too polite to say it. "I like to think it was the limited supply of topaz in the Amber Hollows that forced their hand."

"No need to throw daggers." I nudged the curled hare awake on my lap. "You're much better at peace-making than I am, Merlin. Tell them to simmer down."

"Oh no." The hare stretched. "I know how to pick my battles."

"You should have seen us at school," said Mahi. "And there's always a reason to throw daggers. And as for being pessimistic, do you think I would have embarked on this whole journey if I didn't think we would succeed? I'm the sunniest optimist I know."

It was my turn to snort. "No, you're not. That would be Leena."

There was a catch in Nani's voice. "If you want me to admit it, I will."

"There's no need to admit anything, Kavita."

"I benefitted from our good fortune rather than speaking up for others. In that way, I'm like Prakash."

"I'd never expect you to be a saint. I'm not one either."

My gaze ping-ponged between the two of them. "Now that we've established that we all make mistakes, let's get back to the business at hand."

Nani set her bony shoulders back. "As I was saying, all Jalapashans should be capable of defensive mind techniques. This may be a difficult skill to learn, but I have full faith in you."

"Thank you." My heartbeat drummed in anticipation.

Nani blew out her breath softly as though reaching for a mental reset. "There are three steps to defensive mind techniques, and you'll need to master a combination of all three. First, you must clear your mind of distractions. Empty it of all the wayward thoughts we send out into the world. The thoughts that—particularly for those of us with an open nature—are ripe for the plucking. They orbit our mind like little messes waiting to be cleared up, and that's all well and good unless an enemy wants to enter your mind. Then those little messes become vulnerabilities. Access points to your innermost thoughts."

"Got it," I said, even as my stomach pitted.

I'd never faced such looming dangers. Working at the potter's wheel or handcrafting clay was similar to meditation in some ways—a sacred yielding, a harmony encased in the rhythm of the wheel's rotation, a communion with the divine —but I was out of practice. It was easier to empty my mind when my hands were busy. But on the battlefield, it would be me, my enemy and my thoughts. And right now, my thoughts overflowed like a river basin after heavy rains.

Nani continued. "Central to this ability is breath work, focus and mental agility. Imagine a corset or battening down the hatches. You want to pull in all those thoughts as tightly as possible and hold them in place until you are out of danger. Think of it as a type of armoured meditation."

I grimaced. "*Armoured* meditation? Meditation is supposed to be soft and pliable. A gentle release of thoughts. Not a steel-plated, bulletproof chamber."

"You sound resistant," said Merlin.

"I'm not resistant," I retorted.

"You sound like you did as a child when you didn't want to eat your carrots." A pause. "I would have killed for those carrots."

"Give me strength."

Nani's voice was like worn velvet over steel, and I understood how she didn't want to fail me. "We didn't say it would be easy. Seer, perhaps you'll enlighten my granddaughter on step two?"

Excitement glowed in Mahi's tired eyes. "With pleasure. The first step is about focus and control. The second step is about harnessing your particular brand of talents within your mind. Each of us has an inner landscape. You need to turn inwards and connect to the shape of yours. Mine is a cavernous house much like this one, with vintage light bulbs of assorted sizes all over the floor. Those light bulbs represent my thoughts. My visions. And if someone attempts to breach the inner sanctum of my mind, I snuff out those light bulbs one by one." She gave a dark chuckle. "Then I lock them in there with me."

My mouth went dry. "Yours sounds delightful."

"Mine is a sunny garden of herbs, so real the scents wash over me," said Nani. "There is chamomile, basil, lemon balm and mugwort. Rosemary, lavender, calendula and comfrey.

Science doesn't matter here. It doesn't matter which herbs I place alongside other ones. They grow in nutrient-rich soul, wildly magnificent, leaves shimmering. With each exhale, I plant another row of aromatic herbs. But if I am under threat, an equinox occurs, and my sunny garden turns into a shadowy realm. My herbs wilt and wither and turn monstrous. They grow teeth like ice picks, and their blood thirst knows no end until the threat has passed. Until the delicate bloom of my mind and my thoughts are safe again."

I looked at her with newfound respect. "I didn't know you could be violent."

"Violence is a part of all our natures, Kiya. At my age, I know my inner darkness well. The question is how far we are pushed before we embrace it." She lifted her eyes from the candle flame, and there was a challenge in them. "Enough explanation. It's your turn."

"Fine."

"What are you going to turn your inner landscape into?"

"The beach at Boundless Bay."

Nani smiled with approval. "Perhaps one day I will see it. Now get to work, Kiya."

I stilled the whirlwind of doubt in my mind and turned inwards. At first, I was only aware of the weight of their expectations and the empty blackness of my mind, but I persisted—one breath, a trio of breaths, a dozen more—and my awareness deepened. The Amber Hollows with their glittering topaz jewels and the beach at Boundless Bay sprang to mind. The curtained landscape of my mind began to shift and change. It became the beach that I missed so much. The beach that had been my happy place through childhood and into adolescence and adulthood. Where I'd learned to swim, built sandcastles with my sisters and spent pocket money on vinegary chips. Where I'd had my first fumbling kisses with boys and taken the first few heady sips from a bottle of fizz we'd stolen from the newsagents. Where I walked to clear the fog in my mind and mined for inspiration for my pottery. I pictured the beach so vividly that it became real in my mind: the golden sands under a cloudless aquamarine sky, the swooping seagulls, the cliffs in the distance. I tasted the salt-water on my chapped lips and wiggled my toes in the sand.

"Do your worst," I murmured.

I imagined myself rooted to the earth, my feet sinking into the rich sand, drawing strength from the ancient rhythms of the land. With each breath, I felt the shifting of the sand beneath the soles of my feet, grounding me in its nurturing embrace.

Mahi folded her arms across her chest. "Time for you to shine, Merlin…"

Without a mind sorcerer embedded in the resistance, it was Merlin's job to simulate the technique by casting spells to make me loose-lipped. He hopped onto the counter, liquid gold eyes shining with mischief, as he unleashed magic that reeked of ancient knowledge and dormant spells. I closed my eyes, furrowing my brow in concentration, and imagined encasing myself in a shimmering barrier, resilient against any onslaught.

His first spell unfurled like a resplendent flag on a blood-drenched field, demanding unrestricted access over my mind. *"Tvayi manaḥ svatantraṃ dadātu."*

It skirted past the walls in my mind, dipping into memory vaults I'd long since slammed shut. I divulged secrets like I was a drunk in a tavern or a teenager that was high. Long-buried secrets spilt off my tongue, and Merlin collected them with glee. How my father had brought me bluebells every spring, and I had never told him how I disliked them. How my mother and I had clashed painfully, far too often because we were too alike, and I was too stubborn to admit it.

The seer chuckled. "Maybe it's a good thing you missed her childhood, Kavita."

Nani tutted. "You must assert dominance over your thoughts, or they'll leave you vulnerable."

A wave of frustration crashed over me. "How am I supposed to do that?"

"Make peace with whatever is bothering you," said Nani. "We can't control everything. We can only do our best."

I huffed a sigh. The loss of Sitara. The madman at our gates. Leena's safety. The banyan tree. The child I had cruelly punished. The gargoyles I commanded but, somehow, feared. The people's future. The man I wanted to spend all day and night with, to hell with duty. The list went on and on.

Merlin scuffled against the counter. "Would some tap dancing help you focus?"

"No," said Nani and Mahi in unison.

I adjusted my position on the stool, glared at Merlin and tried again. My brow furrowed in concentration, and the Amber Hollows bobbed up in my mind like a buoy. I built the inner landscape in my mind, one step at a time. The chambers within, the glistening surfaces, the sound of the crashing waves outside, the thick darkness, the rocks I could so easily collapse to keep out intruders. I was barely ready when Merlin directed his magic.

The hare didn't show me any mercy. His second spell landed like a Molotov cocktail, commanding me to tell him my fears. *"Tvayi bhayāni vada."*

It penetrated my defences with humiliating ease, making me a fool, making me unfit to be queen. The secrets spilt out, even though I clamped my hand over my mouth. How I hated elements of Sitara's personality even though I loved her. How I had stayed longer with Tommy than I should have because I didn't want the sassy redhead circling him to have him, even though I no longer wanted him myself. And I knew I'd utterly failed in my attempt to shield.

Merlin hadn't even broken a sweat.

"I'm impressed, Merlin." The seer arched a kohl-painted eyebrow.

The hare hopped over to me. His cheek against mine was soft and warm, and his rumbling voice conjured images of forgotten woodlands and nomadic beasts. "That brought me no joy."

"Liar," I whispered, my doubts sending darkness to devour me, the Hollows to trap me until I was skeletal bone and rotted flesh. I didn't know how to master this skill with enough speed and depth to sustain the integrity of my mind against the raja. He'd do more than steal secrets from my childhood.

He'd covet my innermost thoughts and vulnerabilities.

He'd bend me to his will, and I'd be powerless to stop him.

Merlin thumped his foot, and I didn't know if it was a tantrum or whether he was going to break into dance. "You're an artist, Kiya. It's merely visualisation."

I knitted my fingers together, my body as tight as my mind. "The beach and the Hollows didn't work."

Mahi sank her head into her hands. "Of course, that didn't work. Since when are the Amber Hollows somewhere you feel safe. It can't be a place *you* find threatening."

"Your manner of instruction is a little disheartening, seer," said Nani.

Mahi kissed her teeth. "If you want good manners, I'm not the right pick."

The hare's liquid gold eyes bored into mine. "Try something else, Kiya."

The seer grunted in agreement. "So what if your first attempts at fortifying your inner landscape are not successful? As a young witch, I first tried imagining a vast cosmos swirling with stars and constellations in my mind. Each star represented a thought or revelation. I thought I was so clever. My cosmos shimmered with layers of protection. It felt to me like I'd woven a veil of starlight into not just my mind but the very fabric of space and time."

Nani patted her dishevelled beehive. "Oh, the arrogance of youth."

"The point is that my inner landscape was penetrated again and again until I struck upon the idea of the house and the light bulbs. No one has ever succeeded in infiltrating my mind again."

"The seer is right. Construct a landscape that brings you peace and contentment. One that feels true to you," said Nani. "Once you've established the parameters, build traps that can hold up against even a sorcerer's probing."

I shot them all a harangued look but gave it another go all the same. Focusing on my breathing, I drowned out Nani's worry, the seer's heaving breath and the creaks in her leaning house. It was just visualisation. So, the beach hadn't been a good fit. Better that I discovered that now, rather than when I was at Prem's mercy. If Nani's inner landscape was a garden and Mahi's was a house filled with lightbulbs, what could mine be?

This time, I pictured our home in Boundless Bay. Not the ramshackle house itself, too painful for me and swamped with the memory of Sitara's death. Instead, I pictured the fields just beyond. Fields where Mum—Dad had a bad back after years of working on his cars—had taught us to ride our bikes. Fields with memories of jelly sandwiches and choco-late finger picnics with my sisters. The memories came rushing back. Of hide and seek, lemonade stands and ant races up plump arms. Of windswept high grasses, daisy chains and buzzing bees that made us shriek. Of rounders with Mum and Dad and board games at twilight underneath the apple tree. Of pretending to be asleep out there, under the rising moon, so Dad would have to carry eight-year-old me back to the house. Of pebbles collected on the beach and stacked into towers by three sisters.

Sacred memories. Happy, safe memories.

I took a deep breath, and eyed the pebble towers on my inner landscape, the ocean-washed pebbles that made up the essence of me. "I'm ready."

Merlin's third spell landed like a grenade, insisting I share all my secrets. *Cittaṃ prakaṭam kara.* Round vowels and sharp consonants, lyrical turns of phrase that made the air fizz with magic. A spell repeated and chanted with such reverence that it couldn't fail to reach its mark.

But it didn't.

I found that once I stumbled across a fitting landscape, my mind gymnastics with the gargoyles—turning down the rabble of voices in my mind, isolating individual ones or sometimes tuning them out altogether, as well as preventing the leech of my thoughts into their minds unless a two-way radio was necessary—had laid a good foundation.

Soaring snowcapped mountains encircled my childhood field of pebbles and memories, rising to protect my thoughts from invaders. From Merlin. From whoever was foolish enough to venture there. I imagined them growing taller and stronger with each breath. I made them into an impenetrable fortress, a bastion of my will. Their peaks reached up to the sky in a protective barrier around my mind. The ease of manipulating my inner landscape, now I'd found the right one, astonished me. And when the hare's spells scratched against my mind, demanding entry with force, I rained down rocks, and I was not sorry.

"Well done," said Nani.

"She must practice," said Mahi. "But for now, it is enough."

Slumping with relief, I coaxed the mountain range in my mind into submission until their peaks were flat and no ominous presence lurked around the grassy fields. I opened my eyes, only to find Merlin small and cowering on the counter, his sooty fur damp. "Thank you for putting yourself in harm's way for me. So that I can learn."

"I'll give whatever you need," said Merlin. "Whenever you need it."

The residue of the rockfalls I'd crashed down on him lingered like sticky tar clumping on pristine sands.

I prayed that wouldn't be necessary. Standing on legs like jelly, I washed out a grubby bowl in the seer's sink and fetched him some water, only half-noticing that Babbu returned from his errand in a swoop of emerald feathers. When Merlin had drunk his fill and recovered somewhat, and the light had entered his eyes again, I gathered him to me.

The seer unravelled a rolled note in Babbu's beak while Nani coaxed her to rest for a few hours.

"You won't like it," squawked the parrot over and over. "You won't like it at all."

Mahi stretched the note between her gnarled fingers, peering at it in the dusty light—red ink on parchment—for a few seconds before letting it fall to the ground. The violet third eye on her forehead yawned open. Shifting, searching, finally closing. Broken, beaten, a look of utter desolation washed over her face.

She pulled at her hacked pixie hair, at the tender old skin of her cheeks, until she drew welts there.

Her wounded, animal wails pierced the heavy quiet of her house.

CHAPTER 12

R ed ink on parchment.

I am sorry, sister.

That's all it said. Four short words, sorrowful in nature, without explanation or context.

Four words that caused such grief.

Mahi connected the dots immediately. Her walls went up, and she didn't even speak of her loss to Aanya, whose ability to comfort exceeded even Merlin's and whom she trusted after their years of service together. I heard her say only to Nani, "Why couldn't I see it?"

Nani replied, "Maybe you willed his malevolence into being by not believing he could be good."

Mahi didn't specifically voice out loud that Menon had betrayed her. Neither did we speak of her twin's betrayal in her presence. It seemed cruel to talk of it after all the seer had weathered and risked to be reunited with him. We didn't mention that the gargoyle spies had sighted him at the raja's side. We didn't mention the gargoyle reports that Menon had returned to the sprawling quarters in the white-washed royal palace: the ones he'd once enjoyed as the raja's right hand. We didn't mention that he'd been responsible for assessing the nature of magic harboured within the resistance and that, most likely, the price of his return had been divulging intelligence to our enemy. We didn't mention that he knew our plans, weaknesses and the cracks in our not-so-united front.

We reined in our tongues and our anger.

But the seer knew, and she suffered with all her brother had done. She suffered from the bruising to her own heart and the knowledge that she had conspired to enable his return.

Though she looked broken, and her back curved like a question mark, though circles of sweat marred the armpits on her eighties pop culture T-shirts, she threw herself into her work. She didn't stop to eat or even sleep. She existed only to slurp from the putrid tea she seemed to like so much, her violet eye perpetually yawning, her body jerking with endless visions, her gaze cloudy when she found one of us to share her gleanings.

EVERY HOUR, THE SACRED BANYAN TREE GREW SICKER.

Not even our best efforts could hold that gloopy, cobwebbing, crumbling sickness at bay.

We trained until our bones ached. Magic and minds and weapons and fists. We kept our cards close to our chests. Although we weren't upfront about Menon's absence— chalking it up to diplomatic talks with the raja— we were honest about Prem's mind magic as justification for Grandfather's shielding lessons. We plotted until our thoughts collided. We sent gargoyle spies into the skies over Jalapashu. We found that a common enemy is helpful in knitting together quarrelling groups. We didn't expect harmony, but we demanded loyalty. After my stunt with Tanay, there was little pushback and a smidgeon of fear. We pored over gleanings like a crow picks at the dead. We waited for the hour my skills reached their zenith so I could challenge the raja, but I didn't beat the general again. Though I tried with grim determination until my knees were scarred, my knuckles raw, and my chest tight with rasping breath. We rarely slept. Though I yearned for the comfort of Deven's touch and to uncover ordinary things about him—his favourite foods and books and films, what made him laugh out loud and his buried dreams—our snatched moments were few and far between.

I mulled over our situation as I ate amongst the resistance in the hall, my mind a beehive. The air was thick with the aroma of communal meals being prepared and eaten. Yet I didn't make an attempt to seek out company. I barely remembered to lift my spoon and take the next bite of my *daal*, served on its bed of saffron rice.

"Penny for your thoughts." Leena nudged me over on the bench with her backside. In her hands, she nursed a steaming mug of *chai* with a crushed cardamom pod bobbing on its surface.

"There aren't any pennies in Jalapashu."

"It was a turn of phrase, you pedant."

"I know." I stole a sip of her tea. "How did the mind-shielding lessons go?"

"Grandfather is a mean taskmaster. At least everyone else can escape him when class is over. Living with him means he's been going on and on at me. Aanya said she'd teach me, but he isn't having any of it."

"Probably assumed he'd do a better job."

Leena helped herself to a heaped spoonful of my *daal* and rice. "Right? He said he'd serve you as queen. That was pretty sweet."

"Yeah, it was." A pause. "What does your internal landscape look like?"

"I weave vines and thorny stems together into a protective tapestry. How about yours?"

"Mountain ranges."

"Like the Scottish Highlands?"

I laughed. "More like the Himalayas."

"Show off. Just for the record, you're annoyingly accomplished in your midlife."

A bitter tang in my mouth. I pushed away my food. "Sitara was the achiever, wasn't she? The one who wanted to conquer the world."

"Yeah, Kiya. She was."

"My grief is so heavy. Does yours sit on your chest, making it hard to breathe?"

Doe-brown eyes found mine. "I don't think it'll ever go away. There's always a scent, a colour, a joke, a memory that pulls you back into the vortex of it."

"That sounds about right." I clawed my way out of the past and into the present. "Deven told me he'd been to see you. He said you didn't have the answers."

My sister frowned. "I had plenty of answers, but he was looking for a quick fix. Medicine, herbs, a spell, anything but doing the work. You should ask him about it, though. It's confidential."

"Leena, you're no longer in Boundless Bay. There's no hospital contract. Just spill the beans."

"Fine. He's bottling up his emotions. Reining himself too tightly. He needs to release the pressure valve, or he'll end up losing control when he least expects it. I told him the training sessions weren't enough. His body needs real outlets, not pretence. He needs to run in his tiger form, indulge his predator's need for danger and express his emotions."

My eyes flickered to him. "The other day, he started to tell me he loved me."

"Started?"

"I stopped him. I said it's best to wait until this is all over."

"Why on earth would you do that? This could all be over tomorrow, or...worse. Sitara's death taught us that. You should have told him." Exasperated, Leena turned her face away for a moment. "You two are just as bad as each other. Control only goes so far before trust has to come into play."

A vice tightened around my ribcage. "What do you expect? I'm so worried about everything. I'm worried about you, dammit. I can feel the threads about to snap–"

Leena bristled. "Oh, so it's okay when *you're* worried about my safety, but not the other way round?"

I threw her a sharp glance. "Keep your voice down."

She shoved away her *chai* in frustration. "You're insufferable. Just because you're my older sister, just because a tragedy happened to us, just because you're *queen-in-waiting*, doesn't mean you get to call all the shots."

"Leena–"

"Listen to me. Being in Jalapashu is a choice *I* made for myself. When are you going to get that? I love Aanya. I love getting to know our grandparents. I want to be here, in your corner. And I sure as hell want to explore my magic. You think you're the only one that senses your magic is an untapped well? I'm powerful in my own right."

I sighed. "I know you are."

"Then stop trying to protect me and support me instead. If Mahi and Menon had supported each other all those years ago, maybe he wouldn't have betrayed her."

"Don't do that. Don't put us in the same camp as that man."

Leena winced. "I didn't mean that. I meant that you have to trust us all to do our part. Look around the mess hall, Kiya. *Really* look. Yes, times are hard. But can't you see the resilience around us? I mean, you and Deven are remarkable, and Mahi's very stubbornness is extraordinary. It makes her soldier on."

"Even when every atom in her body wills her to give up."

"Yeah, well, Aanya has been taking the edge off with her song whenever that stubborn mare sleeps. I've got my eye on her, too… But look at what we've achieved here even in a few days. Look at how *together* everyone is."

I followed her gaze. When we blocked out the threat that loomed over us, life wasn't bad. The resistance had found a way to live. Trickles of laughter became a defiant counterpoint to the uncertainty. Leena's flare for green witchcraft kept the immediate concerns about food supplies at bay. Jilu, Radha and their battalion of helpers cooked up a storm with meagre ingredients. They presented their creations with muted fanfare but unrivalled expertise. Their fragrant vegetable curries, infused with fewer spices and aromatic herbs, offered a burst of flavour that belied the simple ingredients. Tangy tomato soups, simmered with garlic and onions and finished with a squeeze of lemon, provided warmth and comfort on even the most wintery days. *Biryanis* cooked with carefully rationed rice and garnished with toasted nuts and dried fruits, turned out to be a gargoyle favourite. Spicy potato and pea *samosas*, fried until crispy, provided a satisfying treat for weary rebels training with Deven.

I almost believed I could be a good, kind queen.

I even considered the half-truths we told and the high walls as a mercy.

I blew out a breath. "Okay, so we've given the people a sense of security. But it's a false sense of security. The tiger's at our door. He could prowl right in here if he wanted."

"Maybe he'd get more than he bargained for. Look at the rest of our inner circle, Kiya. Look around at even ordinary members of the resistance showing steel." She prodded me with her elbow.

I huffed a sigh. The hum of the communal hall washed over me as I located familiar faces. Unlike Prem's court, whose potential was suppressed under fear and corruption, my court glittered with bright lights. In one corner, Deven, stern and straight-backed, shared *roti* and a plate of *daal* with his former manservant Yuvan. Women fussed around him, approaching with swaying hips and leaning close, bringing him food and *lassi*. Though he was unfailingly polite, they couldn't pierce his shell.

My stomach tumbled as he caught my eye and smiled, knowing that he bestowed the gift of his attention on precious few people. He'd been carving out pockets of time for Yuvan because he believed that in a reformed Jalapashu, the boy could have a brighter future. A future of equals. The first scratchings of a moustache on the boy's upper lip had become thicker as if his increased confidence had somehow invigorated him.

There was the court poet, Nitin, in full flow of verse and holding his enraptured listeners in the palm of his hand. Then there was Farida, who had given her abusive husband the boot before coming to the fortress. She cleared plates and washed dishes, her demeanour unshackled and hopeful. There were Leena and Aanya, unafraid of showing their love despite the rigid mindset of some Jalapashans. And there was Merlin, hopping from one group of children to another, braving his dislike of crowds to buoy their spirits.

"I've been looking at the big picture for so long, I've been missing the smaller details."

"Yeah, I think maybe you have." Leena jerked her head to the closest quadrant of the hall, where our grandmother sat in a circle with gargoyles and listened intently to their stories. "She knows that food is about community as much as it is about eating."

"I underestimated her. Her example of interacting with

the gargoyles is more effective than my grumblings about not fearing them."

Nani had been quickly satisfied that the owners of Biryani Junction had more than enough experience and gumption to tend to the needs of the resistance. They neither needed her help in the kitchen nor to craft menus. As a formidable hostess in her own right, a homemaker, a woman with a deep well of experience and empathy, Nani worked her magic by fluttering across the communal hall like a butterfly, tending to hurt egos, placing a kind word in someone's ear and a stern one elsewhere, and listening to the flock of those who sensed her lack of judgement and her gentle, supportive manner. Her keen eye and understanding of human nature allowed her to intuit where trouble might arise and who might not deserve our trust.

Leena pursed her lips. "You know, I think you underestimated Grandfather as much as Nani."

I baulked. "What do you mean?"

"He's a big softie underneath the cunning. And underneath the softness, she is more cunning than we gave her credit for. None of those are bad things, only sometimes we see the world the way we are primed to see it."

"You're obviously trying to get at something. Just come out and say it, Leena."

My sister shrugged. "You've been hesitant in loving Grandfather because of his past, perhaps you've been quick to forgive Nani's part in his actions. But I reckon she ferreted out little kernels of information and offered them up to Grandfather. That she played a huge part in his success as the raja's Enforcer."

I frowned. "What makes you think that?"

"Take the gargoyles. When they spill into your thoughts, it's all spy knowledge and battle goals, right? They are close-lipped about personal dreams?"

"Yeah." I tapped my forehead. "They're all business and no pleasure in here, thankfully."

"I thought as much. Apart from Sindhuja, of course. Something went wrong in her making. I'm glad it did. I love her."

"Leena…"

"Well, Nani's been so lost without her kitchen, so determined to help you, that she's been like a heat-seeking missile about making herself useful. As part of that, she founded a therapy circle for gargoyles. Her first session was a great success. This is the second."

"What?" I turned to stare at Nani. Stone faces cracked smiles. The gargoyles took their turns speaking, and when I tuned into the conversation using our bond, I was astonished to find Leena was right.

"I want to bash their heads in," said Harya.

"Hmm," said Nani, mildly. "And you, Sindhuja?"

"I prefer to smell the flowers than watch over people. Apart from Leena."

"My tail looks like a baby's rattle," ground out a third gargoyle.

My brow furrowed. For all the decades Grandfather had been Prem's Enforcer, for all the formidable locks on his filing cabinet in his study, she'd played a part in his success. Because her well-being had always been intricately tied to his. Because she loved him. A wife always knows her husband's flaws, even if they don't admit it to themselves. Sometimes, they protect them; sometimes, they enable them.

None of us were saints. We were all trying our damn best.

Leena squeezed my leg, and I tugged my attention back to her with difficulty. "So you see. If we're going to win this thing, then maybe it's time to take off the blinders and see everyone with all their glories and flaws. All the talents that can shift the dial our way. Maybe those we haven't trusted need a little more faith. Maybe the ones we thought harmless aren't harmless at all." She leaned her golden head on my shoulder. "Maybe Grandfather deserves just as much love as Nani."

"Point made." I laid my hand on her mussed hair and dropped a kiss at the top of her head. "I'll make amends with him."

"Good. Because you, Deven and Mahi are as bad as each other. You've got to stop competing to take the whole world on your shoulders. You have to trust the team." She lifted her head and scanned the mess hall, which by now had thinned out. "And I've got a proposal for you."

CHAPTER 13

"This is unthinkable. A woman heading behind enemy lines when we have dozens of soldiers that can attempt the same mission." Grandfather bristled as he paced the tiny living quarters of what had once been the weaver's cottage before Prem had commandeered it for our use. "Let the general take a fellow soldier."

I sighed. When this was all over, I'd track down the weaver and his family and give them their home back.

For now, we had enough to deal with. Grandfather clearly believed a) both career and novice soldiers in the fortress were expendable and b) a woman couldn't deal intelligently or pose the same level of threat to the enemy even when she had formidable magic.

"Thank you for your counsel, but it's been decided, Grandfather."

"You've read the gargoyle reports. Bustling streets now eerily deserted. Scorched farmland. Acrid smoke in the air. Market stalls left unattended. Overturned carts blocking routes. Children's toys left abandoned outside. Armed patrols on the streets. Does that sound normal to you?"

Nothing sounded normal to me, but I didn't tell him that.

He reddened. "I know better than most how easy it is to be enticed to Prem Kumar's side. It's dangerous to assume Menon is anything other than compromised."

I'd learned by now to let my grandfather's passions burn themselves out. He was a robust voice on my council, but he wouldn't agree with everything I decided. If we came out of this smelling of roses, I'd earn his respect. If not, I'd simply have to weather his disappointment.

Granted, every cell in my body also flooded with panic at the thought of Leena going into Prem's territory, but after her insistence that I treat the team as equals, I could hardly overrule her. Instead, I fussed around her as she packed a belt pouch with her kit: food, water, First Aid and a spare pair of knickers—a habit from her nursing days in case she needed to stay for another shift. She carefully stashed three freshly fired vessels brimming with simple spells: *āmram naya*, *vismar* and *tyāga*. I hoped the welcoming, forgetting and leaving spells would be enough to get her out of any scrape and to break the wards around the palace, but they weren't the sole elements of the safety net I'd devised.

"I can't believe you insisted on Deven accompanying me."

"I would have preferred a gargoyle escort. At least they would have been able to fly you out of there, but you were the one who insisted on a ground approach."

She wore a lightweight tunic in earth tones paired with loose trousers for ease of movement. A belt equipped with small pouches sat snugly around her waist. Her feet were clad in sturdy ankle boots, and she had plaited her golden hair. A hooded cloak from natural materials hung around her shoulders to protect her from the frosty air and to conceal her face if necessary.

Leena zipped up the last pouch on her belt. "Well, duh. My green magic won't camouflage me in the sky, will it? Do you want Prem Kumar to see us coming? I'll be more stealthy alone, you know."

"You'll be more fleet-footed with Deven. You're the one who said he's been all cooped up. That he needs the thrill of danger. If anything goes wrong, you can climb on his back, and he can race you both into the fortress."

Arms folded, Deven lounged against the bedroom wall in a grey T-shirt and joggers, chosen because he'd be conducting this mission in tiger form. "I *am* here, you know."

"I know," I huffed, trying to keep my eyes from the strip of skin exposed by his low-slung joggers. I trusted him with my sister's life—of course, I did—but his magic was still so unbalanced. "You two won't do anything stupid?"

Grandfather spluttered. "More stupid than attempting to break into palace grounds? Why aren't you saying anything, Kavita?"

"It's not news to me that women are capable, Prakash." She was furiously burning sprigs of heather and holly.

"Then why, woman, are you knee-deep in protection rituals?" he shouted.

She gave him the look a mother gives her toddler. "Because they are an expression of love."

"I give up." He glared at us and stalked out into my pottery studio with Nani hot on his heels.

I sat on the bed next to my sister. "Are you sure about this?"

"I told you. I trust Aanya. She was one of Mahi's only confidantes through the later years of the Menon saga. She says Mahi's too stubborn and hurt to see it, but there's no way he'd make the same mistake again. She's convinced we're missing something. She's convinced that Mahi's hopelessness is clouding her visions."

"Gleanings. She calls them gleanings now."

"Whatever. Even that shows her doubt. Since when does Mahi care about language? Her style is more on the nose."

She adjusted her cloak. "It got me thinking…if I had messed up with you or Sitara as badly as Menon did with Mahi, I'd do anything to set things right. Even put myself in enemy territory."

"A hunch is not proof, Leena."

Her face shone with conviction. "It's been two days since Menon's been gone, and the gargoyles' reports have matched both days. Menon walks in the gardens every twilight at the same hour, ending at the yellow rose bush Mum loved so much. Why that rose bush when it's not even in bloom this time of year?"

"You can't think it's a message to us."

"Damn right, I do." She was in full flow now, and it was a joy to behold, even though there was no besting my sister in this mood. Her enthusiasm could flatten mountains. "Why did he choose twilight? Or the same hour? He wants us to reach out to him."

"If he had grand plans, he should have just told his plans. Or at least left more details on his note."

Deven's whiskey voice cut through. "But we all have our reservations about him. I wouldn't have backed him. If it had come down to a strategic vote, most of the court, except for Mahi, would have voted him down. Look, I don't like it either, but the fact is, we're on the back foot. The sacred tree has only deteriorated further. And we need better spies. If Menon is an ally, we owe it to ourselves to find out."

I nodded, curling my fists into my palm. "So we go on the attack. Let me come."

Deven's obsidian eyes glinted. "It would be a mistake to surrender our queen. You stay here."

Leena gave me a hug. "We'll be fine."

"Take this then. Don't be scared to use it if you have to." I pressed my sheathed dagger into her hands and sent prayers into the universe that she wouldn't have to use it on Deven. Or anyone.

There must have been some strange osmosis of thought between us as he eyed the dagger and told my sister evenly, "You know what is happening with me. That my control sometimes slips. If I'm not myself, I give you permission to use that blade on me."

When he darted a glance at me, I understood he'd said it as much for my benefit as hers, so I would be assured that he would be her protector, whatever it took. Even against himself.

Her lips compressed, but she took it and stashed it in her ankle boot. "Aanya's waiting for me in the garden to wish me luck. See you outside, Deven."

"Don't let Prem capture you."

"Stop worrying, sis." Her brown eyes twinkled as she made a bluebell stem, Sitara's favourite flower. A lump burned my throat as she slipped it carefully into my ponytail. "I'll be back before it wilts. One more thing—don't tell Mahi where we are until we are back. Her heart can't take any more." With that, she went out into the garden.

The back door swung shut, and I watched her through the window, making a spray of colourful palm flowers for Aanya under the grey skies. Their breaths escaped in wisps of mist as they faced each other. With trembling hands, Aanya—shadows smudged beneath her eyes—reached for my sister's face. Their breaths mingled as they leaned into each other. There was tender longing and acceptance in how their lips met, a gentle pressure that made my heart ache.

I turned away from their private moment to find Deven reading my expression.

"They can be themselves here," he said quietly. "Aanya never would have dared that before you and Leena came to Jalapashu... It's the same for me."

My breath caught in my throat. Openness and freedom were so innate to my sisters and me that accepting the shackles of Prem Kumar's oppression would have been impossible. Maybe it took someone with a foot in both worlds to demand change. Maybe, in a way, that was a gift my parents had given to us.

His gaze was intense. "I like that you're close to your family."

"You're close to your sister, too."

"Family is the most important thing in the world."

"I've always envied Leena's ability to be happy despite the storms around us."

"Siblings aren't always built the same way."

"Oh, you definitely aren't built like Nisha."

He gave a low laugh that loosened the tight coil of my worry. When he held out his calloused hands, I reached out and let him tug me towards him. He spun me at the last second, and my back collided with his chest. Strong fingers splayed my hips, and he dipped his head to murmur to me. His breath danced off the sensitive skin of my ear. "You know *exactly* how I'm built."

I closed my eyes and leaned into him, resisting the urge to rub my body against his.

Yet I felt every hard sculpted part of him through the barrier of our clothes.

I needed him as much as he needed me.

His hands skirted my hips as I turned slowly, my heart pounding with anticipation. Just like his. Our eyes met, and I shivered at how his dilated with desire. Time stilled. He scooped me up, hands on my tush as I hooked my legs around his waist. Then he crushed my body against his and met my lips in a punishing kiss that demanded commitment. Demanded my everything. The kiss was electric, tearing a moan from me. He tasted of untamed forests and moonlit nights, of earthy musk and days spent in the heat of battle. His hands slipped under my tunic, and tingles of pleasure darted across the skin of my back.

One day, we'd be able to stroll through the kingdom

together, to sit by a crackling fireplace and talk about books, to nestle under a blanket under a glowing moon, to race—my thighs clenching his tiger back—through sun-dappled meadows, to cook each other's favourite meals, to devour each other's bodies until we were sated, to begin anew at dawn and discuss all the hidden crevices of our souls.

But today wasn't that day.

For now, it was enough to have learned the sound of his heartbeat and the pattern of his tousled hair. To know that he was honest and true and brave.

He pulled away, his voice almost angry, rasping, but when he adjusted the bluebell in my hair, his hands were gentle. "I'll look after her."

"I know you will." I stepped out of his embrace and smoothed down my clothes, reaching sanity, grasping for anything to say. "I didn't think leaders were supposed to be scared."

The general's night-dark eyes locked onto mine. "Whoever told you that is a fool. I've cared about every man I've ever led. Even when they're arseholes, they're family."

My breath bottled. He had already become family to me.

"I'll get Harya to drop us near the other side of the fortress walls so you don't have to open the door magically." He ran his thumbs over my cheek, the slightest caress. "We'll be back before you know it."

I clamped my mouth shut to prevent myself from begging them to stay, and stood statue-like until long after they had departed. Then I gathered the pieces of myself together and, with a shuddering breath, went to find solace in the one place I knew I would unearth it.

Miniature droplets of clay splattered my apron as the potter's wheel spun. My fingers caressed the moist pyramid of clay as I shaped it with practised precision. The studio at the front of the house had once been a place of vibrant energy, filled with natural light. But now, encased within the fortress walls, heaviness and shadows had crept into it. Once, I would have filled the studio with the sounds of jazz or acoustic guitar, but silence was a better fit in sombre times.

I'd missed the simplicity of practising my craft. In training, I'd commanded the earth to swallow footsteps, masking my presence. I'd summoned pillars of rock to shield and shelter allies. I'd made waves in the earth, causing walls of soil to rise and crash. I'd broken apart stone and even knitted it together again.

But that felt like destruction. Whereas this was creation.

The gentle whirring of the pottery wheel couldn't quite lull me into a state of tranquil focus, but it was a comforting backdrop to my nagging worries about Leena and Deven's safety and the success of their mission. With the gargoyles back within the fortress perimeter, even tuning into the bond couldn't provide the reassurances I craved.

So I continued to work as time inched past, immersing myself in the sensory experience: the earth scent of the clay, the slip of its texture beneath my fingers, the sound of the wheel spinning, the growth of the clay towards its final form. As my fingers gently slipped against the clay, my magic hummed softly in the air, infusing the vessel with love and energy. I felt a sense of connection to Sitara as if her spirit hovered nearby. I could almost smell her sweet orange and magnolia perfume, though I knew she was long gone. With each turn of the wheel, my body released tension, catharsis washing over me, and I rued how long it had taken me to find my way back here.

Merlin had intuitively sensed my turmoil and had made his way to the weaver's house only to shoo my fretting grandparents out of the studio. He now napped at my feet, his soft fur rising and falling with each peaceful breath, his small body brushing against my leg. Every inhale-exhale seemed calibrated to take the edge off my anxiety. He occasionally grumbled as my foot worked the pedal and threw a mind spell at me to test my shielding. His cunning spells ricochetted off the mountains I erected in my internal landscape, causing powdery sprays of snowfall but no real damage.

Meanwhile, my hands shaped the clay subconsciously. Smooth, rounded contours flowed seamlessly from its broad base to a slender neck. When I had stretched and spun the clay into its finished form, I made another and two snug lids. Then, I dotted designs on the outer surface with a stylus.

Only then did I admit to myself what I had created: two new urns, almost exact replicas of the one which held Sitara's ashes. A trickle of cold air chased goosebumps up my arms. I stared at their perfect symmetry and the careful motifs on the clay. Sitara's urn had been etched with swirls of water. These two featured twisting vines and soaring mountains.

The hare rose on his hind legs beside me to take a look. "Freud would have a field day with you."

I stood as dread filled me like a chilling fog. Why had I done that? What did it mean? Suddenly, Nani's therapy circle didn't seem like such a farfetched idea. "It doesn't mean anything. I'm worried, that's all."

"Well, those are two creations I don't want you firing the kiln up for." He harrumphed. "All three of you sisters were practical, even as children: an archaeologist, a potter and a nurse. But Leena is the one who puts the two sides of her humanness together most naturally. She doesn't bottle up her emotions. She understands cause and effect more than you and Sitara ever did. Maybe it's nursing that taught her that." His voice echoed with wild magic. "What are you so afraid of?"

"Failure. I'm afraid of failing them all."

"That's the price of trying." The hare's sweet face shone with wisdom.

I washed the caked clay from my skin and cleaned my tools and work surfaces.

Merlin hopped after me from one workstation to the next. "I failed you all the years I kept your heritage from you. But we got there in the end, didn't we?"

"Did we?" In my mind's eye, Sitara fought a swarm of the raja's soldiers in the kitchen of our house. Then she fell to the kitchen floor, her mossy green eyes lifeless. My chest constricted as I dried my stylus and replaced it in the rack before hanging the dish cloth from a hook on the wall.

"Nobody gets through life unscathed, Kiya. We all flail through stormy seas."

I'd missed his odd metaphors. His kindness made my eyes prick with tears.

I rummaged near the base of my ponytail and eased out the bluebell Leena had made. Its delicate stem was flattened, but I cupped the vivid sapphire bell at its head before crouching at a recessed alcove in the studio, out of the sight-line of customers.

Not that anyone frequented the studio or any other shop during the heat of rebellion.

My shoulders bowed at the sight of Sitara's urn with its blue and grey glaze and firmly fastened lid. There hadn't been time to think about where to scatter her ashes yet and to be honest, letting her go entirely was more than I could handle. I laid Leena's bluebell in the alcove and adjusted the placement of the urn, swivelling it so its motif of the waves stood front and centre.

Only to pull my hands back with an astonished gasp, like they had been scorched in a fire.

The urn was warm. As warm as grass heated by the sun on a summer's day. But the air in the studio was cool. Frowning, I considered the possibilities. The weaver's house was simply made. There were no radiators in the studio to maximise display and workspace. No pools of light on the wintry day directed into the alcove. No sources of heat that could explain the unexpected warmth.

Perhaps it was imagination. My head was all over the place. I stood to mention my finding to Merlin but was interrupted by the studio door jangling open.

Nisha and Ashwin stood there, their eyes wild with panic. They didn't bother with formalities.

"He's gone." Nisha trembled, and Ashwin's state of mind was no better. "He went into Jalapashu."

"It's a mission, Nisha," I said gently. "I'll let you know when he's back. Trust him."

"Not Deven. *Ishaan*." Ashwin's olive skin was pale. "Ishaan, the rascal. When I get my hands on him… I think he squeezed through the gap that has opened in the wall by the withering sacred tree."

"Shit." My heartbeat accelerated. Why hadn't we thought of that before? Had the tree decayed so fast to breach the perimeter? The wards had been cast not to let people enter the fortress. We hadn't thought about those trying to escape. "How long has he been gone?"

A wail ripped from Nisha's throat. She wrung her hands on the front of her plaid shirt. "It's my fault. I told him it was fine to play but to stay close by, and when I looked up…"

"Focus, Nisha." He wrapped his arm around his wife, dampening the sharpness of his words. "If I know my son, he's following his uncle."

Merlin's sooty ears drooped. "An hour then."

"If Prem gets his hands on our son…" Nisha's almond eyes were red-veined with horror. "You *know* what he did to Roshni. We're rebels now. We deserted. He has a reason to hurt him. Please…"

I met Nisha's desolate eyes. She was kind and good and didn't deserve this pain. My mind whirred with the dangers

—the rising dark, the raja's roaming brutes, Ishaan's innocent belief in heroics—but my mouth gave her the platitudes she craved. "That's not going to happen."

Ashwin rubbed a hand over his face. "We came to you because, with the gargoyles, you can…"

"You don't need to explain." I took off my apron, my magic waking to my call. I tore my gaze away from their anguished faces, took a deep breath, and stalked to the sideboard that held the new urns. The ones marked with motifs that represented Leena and me. Closing my fingers around the freshly made urns, I applied a surplus of pressure. The malleable clay surrendered to my touch. I crushed the forms into shapeless mounds beneath my palms. "No one is getting hurt today."

The hare murmured his approval.

"I'll bring him home." I squeezed Nisha's clammy hands. "What's he wearing?"

"A red pyjama set," she said.

I nodded and made my way to the door. "Merlin, don't let Sitara's urn out of your sight."

He recognised my urgency enough not to question me.

"You're going alone? Let me come," pleaded Ashwin.

"Stay with Nisha."

"He's our son. I'd die for him." He held his hand to his chest in an old-fashioned gesture of allegiance that made me shiver. "For you."

"I won't be alone. Look to the skies." I ran, opening my bond to the gargoyles as I went.

CHAPTER 14

Word had spread of Ishaan's misjudged adventure. Words like wildfire, driving people from their homes and chores and training. The crowd gathered under a gunmetal sky that dusted snowflakes over us. Men already wedged the gap in the fortress wall with planks of wood, but a flick of my hands sealed it with a flinty substance that surprised even me.

I didn't have time to marvel or even to think.

If Deven had been here, he'd tear the world down to bring his nephew home. I'd never forgive myself if I failed Ishaan, never be able to look Deven or his family in the eyes again.

Seven years old and in a world of trouble for leaving the fortress.

Better that than in a grave.

Somewhere, the seer cried out, and when I spun in the direction of her voice, she hurtled towards me, grim determination on her face. "I had a gleaning. You can't go. Menon is part of the raja's plan." She lunged for me, but she wasn't agile or fast, and her old limbs protested too much to keep after me.

I didn't stop to cajole or persuade, nor did I feel guilty. Her visions had hardly been as sound as the North Star guiding sailors through the night.

Hurry. I called for Harya and Sindhuja as I pressed on, not stopping for a coat or a cloak or a weapon. Leena had my dagger, but I didn't waste time stopping at the armoury. Every minute counted. Thanks to Deven, I was confident I could handle myself without a weapon in hand. I could use the terrain itself to my advantage. Vision or no vision, I had to do this.

I was the weapon, and—even without a crown or throne —I was the witch queen they had chosen.

Harya and Sindhuja came as commanded with a grace belying their stumpy forms, their wings cutting through the deepening skies. The quiet menace in their eyes was jarring, a reminder of the violence they were capable of unleashing. A rescue mission reflected their abilities, whereas I'd assigned them to guarding the fortress and quelling the odd flare-up of trouble within the resistance.

But there was a brazenness in Harya's eyes, too.

I braced myself as he grasped my shoulders with his talons. He lifted me clean off the ground, though he was half my height. Within seconds, we were airborne again, soaring over the fortress walls, the people mere ants beneath us. I winced as Harya wound his ridged tail around me for safety. The chill wind tugged at my clothes, whipping up my ponytail and his lion's mane, and the chatter of the gargoyles was like a static radio station in my mind.

I tuned out everyone but my two companions. *We need to find the boy, Ishaan. He went after the general.*

It was not my error. Neither I nor my gargoyles made a mistake. Harya tightened his grip on my shoulders as we traced the outline of a grove of trees to avoid detection. The leathery membranes of his wings whooshed with every beat.

I frowned. It wasn't important whose mistake it was. It

mattered only that we fixed it, and it didn't happen again. *Now's not the time to discuss this. Eyes to the ground.* Lifting my knees to avoid being spiked on a branch, I concentrated on avoiding obstacles. He clearly thought I'd survive a hit with smaller ones.

Beneath us, the kingdom sprawled out in a patchwork of shadowy meadows, dense copses and dusky red rooftops where once the gargoyles had perched. Sooty patches of ground glowed with embers doused by the falling snow. It was unfeasible for Ishaan to have kept pace with his uncle in tiger form, even with Deven travelling with Leena's extra weight. Though Deven had a superior sense of smell in tiger form, the direction of the wind tonight carried Ishaan's scent in the opposite direction. A small mercy given that Prem's camp, by our count, included twenty-odd shifters, only too eager to win his favour.

I prayed that the snowfall had covered Ishaan's tracks.

Scanning the terrain with accuracy was impossible given our height, the punishing wind stinging my eyes and the jerking flight path adopted by Harya to maintain cover. My stomach roiled with every sharp manoeuvre. So I bided my time, steeling myself against the harsh wind, trusting the gargoyles to do their job. They had a wider field of vision than me, a trait developed over the centuries from their fixed position on rooftops. Even in the dark, they could see for miles. Long, unbearably fraught minutes passed in which they split the terrain into quadrants and combed through each section with care.

Each quadrant we cleared brought us closer to the raja's white-washed palace.

My brain flooded with grainy images of Ishaan afraid and alone, his uncle nowhere to be found. Of him falling and breaking a bone, or worse. Of his young body splayed on an icy mound.

I shook the poisonous thoughts out of my head, choosing

instead to game happier scenarios: a clean getaway with Sindhuja carrying Ishaan, an unfortunate sighting that didn't matter because we were airborne and the shifters were not, or even a short scuffle on the ground that we'd decisively win.

We were a hundred metres from the palace. My heart pounded to a frantic rhythm.

Sindhuja was smaller in stature than the gargoyle leader, but she'd easily manage a child's weight and would be patient if Ishaan was wriggly or frightened. She'd been the natural choice to come along, as I trusted her above all other gargoyles.

Fifty metres from the palace. A cold knot of dread in my stomach.

Harya's voice rumbled like thunder through my mind. *Your thoughts are making my flight more erratic.*

I focused on the cycle of my breath, not that it helped, and ignored the scrape of debris against my face. It would be okay. Even if Ishaan was in trouble, I could cause tumult on the ground from the air whilst still in Harya's grip. Sure, the gargoyles would most likely be peeved not to be involved, but I'd soothe their egos later with praise, a special dish cooked up by Jilu and Radha, or the promise of later action.

Sindhuja yanked me from my plotting with a staccato call that cut through my mind. *Over there.* Her pale yellow eyes bulged even more than usual as she stared through the twilight. She adjusted course by a few degrees, her fishtail pointing in the direction of her discovery. Her rubbery lips fluttered in the wind, and the tattered banner of her parchment-like wings cut a determined path through the air.

Well done, Fishtail. Harya's guttural voice throbbed with grudging approval.

I almost expelled the contents of my stomach as he swung me around at full pelt and lurched after her. It took a moment for my stomach to stop heaving and my eyes to adjust, but I spotted unusual colours bleeding together just outside the palace compound: red cotton and luminous yellow.

We had found him. Thank the heavens.

Nisha and Ashwin would have their son back in their arms within the hour.

Now, to get him home, I said to the gargoyles, giddy with relief.

When we were almost above Ishaan, Harya bobbed in our vantage point in the dusky sky. *We risk discovery as soon as we emerge from this line of trees. The command is yours to give.*

Scan the perimeter and the grounds. We might only have a small window to retrieve him, I said.

Long shadows stretched over the opulent palace with its series of domes, turrets and balconies, untouched by the tumult across the rest of the kingdom. The symmetrical gardens—with their multitude of trees and elegant stone benches, bubbling fountains and rows of oil lamps— remained a slice of heaven. Elephants roamed near what had once been the general's apartment.

My bleary eyes focused on interpreting the antics of the red pyjamas.

Even from the air, his movements were animated, gestures bold and eager as he darted about. Each springy step exuded an air of adventure. His head swivelled around, taking in every detail of the surroundings—though he didn't look up—and his arms swung wildly as if he mimicked a military parade. His body practically vibrated with excitement. There was such innocence and joy at being part of this unfolding escapade that I wanted to shake some sense into him.

In fact, Deven's nephew or not, I'd give Ishaan an earful myself when we rescued him.

He'd located the very juncture of the gates where Deven and Leena had—presumably using my spell vials—bowed apart the iron bars near the rose bush my mother had adored.

The blob of red darted through the opening.

Shit, I said. *We'll have to time our rescue between guard patrols and pray he keeps quiet and still.*

He has more courage than sense to get that close, said Harya.

Our trouble quota just multiplied. Resolve mingled with a hint of fondness in Sindhuja's voice.

My gaze narrowed at a blob of luminous yellow that I had mistaken for winter jasmine or a burst of camouflaging greenery conjured by my sister on her mission. But the blob moved, and my heart almost stopped altogether.

I shouted into the air in frustration. "Dammit. Damn it all. They are in *so* much trouble."

Below us, I made out Ishaan in his red pyjamas. But he wasn't alone.

Tanay, the raja's unwanted son, was with him.

I balled my fists. First, we'd rescue them. Then, I'd assign them potato peeling duties for the week.

Actually, I wasn't even sure I'd trust them with a potato.

What the hell was Sindhuja even thinking with her note of *fondness*? She'd been in the firing range of Tanay's foul-mouthed wit when she had watched over him following the example I had made of him. Following his *dagger throw* at me. Not only did Tanay clearly have a chip on his shoulder, he had now been a bad influence on a child four years his junior. Ishaan may have wanted adventure, but Tanay was cut from an entirely different cloth. His luminous yellow tracksuit appeared to have been chosen precisely because he *wanted* to be discovered by his father's men.

I quashed the tiny seed of sympathy in me.

Anger made me stronger, and this was still a rescue mission, one more complicated than I'd envisaged. Tanay would need a gargoyle of his own to hitch a ride back to the fortress with.

As a ferocious growl rolled through the evening air,

horror tightened my belly. *We need a better vantage point now. Leave the tree line.*

As you wish, intoned Harya.

The gargoyles flew clear of the trees, opening a view of the palace gardens. Against all odds, the rascals had achieved what they set out to do. In fact, *their* mission had been a blinding success. The boys had stumbled upon the original mission *and* attracted the attention of Prem's men.

My blood ran cold at the sight of Deven in his primal power: golden, tattooed, teeth bared, paws grounded in a dusting of snow. He stood his ground at the rose bush, obsidian eyes tracking every threat, every innocent, lingering on the nephew he loved like a son. He used his body as a shield, placing himself between my sister and the children and a battalion of guards armed with spears, daggers and bows.

At the battalion's centre stood Menon in a new set of wizard's robes. It was impossible to tell whether they had managed to speak to him. The sorcerer was as still as a serpent about to strike. He made no attempt to slip from the soldiers' control or to lend his powers to our aid. My gut twisted at the realisation that we'd fallen for a trap. Not for the first time, I asked myself if he'd always been black-hearted, if his twin's love had been a way to wash his sins, only to hurt her all over again.

Devastating our dreams in the process.

Breathe. I willed myself to breathe. To focus.

To be more than a potter. More than myself.

To be a queen.

Deven's determination radiated from his body language as the guards advanced, weapons readied. He'd take on a sorcerer and over a dozen men on his own. He would hold off our enemies for as long as necessary for my sister and the children to escape. Even if it meant his death.

Bloody-minded, honourable man. Even in beast form.

And my sister. My sister was already extending her hands.

High above them, the raja watched the unfolding scene from the comfort and safety of a palace balcony. He could rot there for all I cared, as long as his mind magic didn't interfere with us. I hoped Mahi was right about the distance restrictions, but I slammed my shields up all the same and braced myself. At the moment, the immediate safety of our people was more important to me than anything else, Prem and Menon be damned.

Get down there now, I relayed to the gargoyles.

You could be captured, said Harya.

We'll cross that bridge if we come to it. They need us.

Then we will help them, said Sindhuja.

We swooped, the speed of our decent so quick that even the general didn't catch our scent until we were nearly upon him. The gargoyle leader swept me awkwardly into his arms to execute his landing before placing me on my feet.

Deven registered my presence and risked a swift look in our direction, his nostrils flaring with my scent. He emitted a low, rumbling purr deep in his throat. A purr of welcome and rekindled hope.

"Harya and I will take the right flank. Sindhuja, protect the children with your life." Already, my magic fizzed and sputtered in my veins, craving an outlet. "Everyone, mental shields up!"

"What, no hello?" Leena gritted her teeth as her vine rolled under the earth and ensnared her first victim. "I'm glad you're here, sis."

Deven gave a roar of approval that made my very bones shudder.

"Where else would I be?" I quipped. The smile I flashed them cooled when I turned my attention to the children. "Stay back with Fishtail, and you'll be fine. Do *not* get involved. You hear me?"

Ishaan had the audacity to look crestfallen as Sindhuja henpecked them to a safer spot.

"It was all going well until all hell broke loose," said Leena.

Sitara's urn is warm, I wanted to tell her, but now wasn't the time. I no longer felt the cold, despite the crackle of thin snow underfoot and the flakes that still fell. "We'll have a natter later. First, we've got work to do."

"Spoilsport." My sister sent more vines roping towards a foe, choking him into a slumber.

We battled as a team. Grunts and shouts and roars filled the air, human and bestial. We paid no heed to accusations of trespassing, threats of arrest or promises of safe passage if we surrendered.

Not when there was murder in the guards' eyes.

Not when the raja stood above it all like an executioner.

Not when Nisha had begged me to bring her son home and Tanay's mother had worked her fingers to the bone to bring her son up alone.

Not when I'd already lost one sister and had found a man who I could build a life with.

Harya stayed knitted to my side, small and mighty, protecting me as his priority. His stony flesh meant that blows glanced off his battle-hardened skin. He pounded our adversaries with bone-crushing blows, and his feet kicked with the force of a battering ram. At times, he rose into the air, his wings beating furiously, only to come down hard again on a man's neck or spine.

My magic sparked in my core, and the air crackled with the sound of stones hewn from the earth. They levitated, and I sent them shooting towards our enemy with tiny flicks of my wrist or a curl of my fingers. I decimated the terrain, causing the gardens to rise and fall like waves at sea, creating barriers that towered like ancient sentinels or trapping the guards within earthen prisons, their cries muffled by the damp soil. Never packed tightly enough to kill, but enough to trap them and perhaps even maim them, but I wouldn't, couldn't dwell on that.

The metallic tang of blood from the battlefield seeped into my nostrils. The faint glow of moonlight illuminated the fallen bodies of the raja's troops. Cuts and lacerations marked the skin. Bruises darkened once unblemished flesh. Soldiers gagged on soil or shook it from clogged nostrils. Fractured limbs twisted at unnatural angles.

And I wondered whether this was really what we wanted. What we intended.

Leena took the left flank. At her coaxing, branches twisted and writhed as if possessed. She directed the vines with precision. Thick, sticky stems snaked towards two guards, restricting their limbs and binding them. She moved onto her next victim, lashing out at him with thorns as sharp as daggers. A nurse turned warrior. Her victim cried out hoarsely, his attempts to free himself resulting in deeper cuts and scratches. Leena didn't kill them, though. The thought of killing was anathema to her.

But Deven's predatory nature and military training meant he didn't have such qualms.

He tore through the middle first and then began picking off whoever was foolish enough to stand against him with calculated precision, prioritising those who shifted. With lightning-fast reflexes, he swiped at his adversaries, delivering swift and powerful blows that left them gouged and staggering. That brought them to their knees or left big cats whimpering and seeping with wounds. His fluidity and grace were infused with deadly efficiency, a marriage of instinct and training. His intent was deepened even further by his sense of duty and the threat to his loved ones.

The threat to Ishaan and me.

I read it in the wild fury of his midnight gaze, the prowling power he unleashed, and the flesh he ripped with his powerful jaw and gouged with his claws. Men that once stood under his command, that he gutted without a second's thought because they no longer stood with him, even though we would have opened the fortress gates, even though he would have forgiven anything perhaps—stupidity, cowardice, greed—except daggers turned on those he loved in the service of the raja.

His roars echoed across the palace gardens, making even the raja flinch.

Blood seeped into the palace gardens, feeding the thorny yellow rose bush.

Their blood and ours.

Leena had sustained a deep gash to her arm, and I couldn't be sure anymore if the blood on Deven's golden fur was our enemies' or his own. I sustained a gash on my shoulder from a glancing blow of a sword and bruised ribs from a blunt force impact. And all the while, Menon didn't lift a finger to help us. I wanted to shake him into action if only to flush out his allegiance.

When only a few guards were left standing, more entered the courtyard from a sly, hidden angle to target Ishaan and Tanay, death and malice in their faces. Desperation was writ large on their faces, but their movements were strangely robotic. Even if they survived, the raja would punish them for their failures. After all, we had broken into the palace compound. If they couldn't protect the raja in his own home, if they couldn't fulfil his orders, what were they for?

Sindhuja held off the attackers valiantly, keeping the boys shielded behind her wingspan, though it hurt her to keep her wings open while fighting. She delivered head butts and tore through flesh with her claws until the general, Harya, Leena, and I fought our way towards her. Deven's growl and flash of teeth made one man release his bladder. I knew it by the stink and the spread of wet across his muddied ivory trousers.

Ishaan whooped with joy, drinking up the heroics of his uncle—of us all—still blissfully untroubled by the danger he had courted. Only a mild cuff across the ear from Deven chastened him.

But Tanay's spirits had nosedived. At last, I read regret in his face. The older boy was pale, drained, and slack with spent excitement that had ended in bitter disappointment. It was one thing for your father to ignore your pleas to show you care or interest, quite another for that father to command your death or be ambivalent about it. Especially when you had given him a second chance and a third and fourth. How many times had Prem let the child down?

Perhaps Tanay might have respected his father had he joined the fray.

But Prem didn't. He remained safely encased on his balcony.

By this time, everything was a blur. I looked around. Blood. Fallen bodies. Buried men. Not just buried men. Men I had buried. The curtain of night fell on men who would never see another dawn. I didn't know how long had passed —minutes, hours—only that Prem had instructed Menon to be brought to him. The sorcerer went gladly, weaselling his way out of the danger zone. There were orders from Prem for more guards. I sensed it from his body language rather than catching the words, from the defiance in his stare and his twitching gaze to the palace exits, even though he remained grimly silent. From the claws of his magic against my mental shields.

I reinforced them, fury spiking. My heart galloped like a thousand horses, as much as from urgency as from the tattooed tiger that brushed against my side, a slight tremor in his magnificent body. "We have to go. He's called for rein-forcements."

Leena peered at her gouged arm and retched. "No way I can make it through another round."

Neither would I, I thought, though I didn't burden her with the knowledge of my exhaustion. Not when I had to send her on without me. I opened my bond to the gargoyles. *Take my sister and the children by air. I'll ride with the general.*

Harya's gravel tone scraped against my mind. *I will not abandon you, gargoyle queen.*

A shiver ran up my spine at the title he'd given me. *The commands are mine to give, not yours.*

His face flickered a moment before it returned to its stony smoothness. Then he bowed, his lion's mane rippling in the wind, and helped Sindhuja find a position to carry the children.

"Uncle?" Ishaan suddenly looked uncertain.

"We're too heavy," cried Tanay.

"Not a word, you two," I snapped.

Deven emitted a low growl, not at me, but at the guards and soldiers who flooded into the ruined gardens, boots and bare feet running at pace towards us, grim faces illuminated by the flickering light of torches. The barefoot ones wore loose-fitting clothes for ease of shifting. The booted ones carried steel blades and tightly strung bows, promising retaliation. They didn't pause at the general, though they must have recognised him, must have served under him. They moved with mechanical precision, devoid of natural fluidity, except for the occasional momentary freeze, as if conflicted.

I frowned, but there wasn't time to overthink. Not when Harya finished arranging the children and smacked Sindhuja on the shoulder, signalling a green light. Not when, as expected, we were heavily outnumbered.

I won't let you down, said Sindhuja, though she was already worn out by the battle. She launched herself into the sky and barely managed to get off the ground. Only with a second Herculean burst of effort did she gain altitude, rising slowly into the night sky with Ishaan clinging desperately to her back and Tanay suspended from her fishtail.

The children were clean away. Relief flooded through me.

"Go with Harya," I said to my sister. "Deven and I are right behind you."

Leena baulked. Not because she would have been more comfortable with Sindhuja—although that was true—but because sisters didn't leave each other behind. "I'll ride with Deven."

Fear twisted in my gut. My shoulder stung and oozed, and the rush of soldiers was almost upon us. "There's no way you can cling on with your arm like that. I'll be okay."

She paled as the gargoyle leader lost patience, plucked her from the gardens and took to the skies. But Leena was still fixated on helping us. She pivoted in the air, her face scrunched with determination. Quick as a whippet, she grabbed my dagger from where it was strapped to her thigh and flung it at a reed-like soldier on a panther's back, riding fifty or so metres ahead of the battalion. It hit the soldier just about his hip, but he doubled down, snarling like the jungle cat beneath him.

But my sister wasn't done.

Magic flared, sparking in the night as she refocused her efforts, just as the soldier threw a spear at us. The spear skittered from the soldier's hand harmlessly as my sister's magic transmuted him into a sapling. A sapling that tipped from the panther's back, roots and all.

Horror twisted Leena's face as she disappeared deeper into the night.

Oh god, oh god, oh god. Were those my thoughts or her words?

She'd never forgive herself.

Our magic was as terrible as it was magnificent. I stared at her handiwork, awestruck, searching for the reed-like soldier whose clothes were now on a mound on the ground. Alarm rang through me as my eyes raked the ground, even as the battalion pounded towards us. There was a slim trunk with a jumble of roots and wiry branches, my dagger tangled within it like an unholy bauble.

Oh god, oh god. She'd never done that before. She'd never cope.

Deven lunged at the panther's neck, making short work of him in a display that left me trembling. When he was done, Deven roared and laid on the ground—an urgent plea for me to clamber onto his back—as more soldiers discarded their clothes and shifted into jungle cats, some lither, faster, more muscular than him.

Without thinking, I grabbed the sapling with the dagger, trying not to look into the dead panther's eyes, then leapt onto Deven. The raja's men were too close for comfort, and I didn't know if we'd make it. If we should give up and be done with it. But I loved Leena, and I loved Deven, and I loved the kingdom, and the children were safe, and maybe it would be okay. I tried desperately to find purchase for the rough ride ahead as Deven launched himself forward, deciding that a low centre of gravity would help him stay aerodynamic and me to stay seated. He raced away with me clinging to him, my thighs clenching hard, my chest flat against his back, fingers threaded into his lustrous coat.

My ribs hurt so much, but I gritted my teeth, riding the pain, riding Deven.

On the balcony, the raja roared at his men to salvage the evening.

Behind us, the thorny stems of my mother's favourite rose bush reached out like skeletal fingers against the pale dusting of snow. Tiny buds, tightly closed against the cold, nestled amidst the thorns, promising eventual renewal.

CHAPTER 15

I thought Sindhuja was clean away.

I was wrong; Mahi had been right.

Even over the short distance back to the fortress, the gargoyle's tattered wings couldn't easily bear the weight of Ishaan and Tanay. Her flight had always been haphazard, but more so now when she had already expended energy and had precious cargo to carry. She zigzagged through the air above us, overtaken by the gargoyle leader, flying sidewards more often than forward.

I could barely bring myself to track her progress through the starry sky.

I'd made a tactical error. I should have opened my bond to the gargoyles and called more to our aid. At the very least, another gargoyle to bear the weight of Tanay. Because Sindhuja was precious to me, and it was clear from her flight path that I had put her and the boys in great danger.

Perhaps more danger than Deven and I faced on the ground, with tigers and panthers tearing after us, their paws pounding the earth, seeking purchase on the icy ground even as my magic tore it out from under them. With vehicles revving up in the grounds.

But Deven was fast as if the energy he had stored up through the years of his curse had lain dormant in his body for this very moment. As if his feelings for me made it inconceivable that he would give up. The growls and furore behind us, the terrain that rolled and ejected bulwarks at my command, didn't even give him pause. A bulkier tiger that attempted to outflank us bit the dust when he didn't account for Deven's soaring leap. Another drew blood from his haunch before I loosed one hand to fold him into the earth in a fury, my thighs aching with the feat of clinging on, of not being thrown to oblivion.

Deven kept on, breathing hard. Single-minded, bullish, heroic.

I couldn't look up. I just had to hold on.

But I opened the bond to all my gargoyles. *Sindhuja needs help.*

Silence. Silence for the sister who was an oddity among them. Who they sometimes resented.

Muscles rippled beneath me as Deven flew forward, inky eyes focused on the fortress winking in the distance. His paws barely made a sound as they connected with the icy ground, leaving only fleeting impressions in the powdery snow. The frost-laden air whipped around us, carrying the scent of pine and winter's chill as we raced forward, a blur of gold and black against the landscape.

Only when there was a gasp of distance between us and our pursuers did I look to the sky.

Sindhuja's flight was erratic, but she was still aloft, inching valiantly towards the fortress. The children were mute as they clenched her. She had perhaps thirty metres to go before they reached safety. I believed her promise that she'd complete her task, believed she would give everything of herself to get it done. Her wings wilted, on the verge of collapse, quivering unnaturally as she wrung every bit of motion from them.

She didn't see the arrow slicing through the darkness until it was too late or the four that followed.

But she heard my scream reverberate through the night.

She felt the arrows tear through her poor, wilted wing and sink into one malformed leg. She felt one drive into her back, and another hit her shoulder with such force that it spun her around in the air.

I wanted to close my eyes, but she was my gargoyle. She was my friend. And those boys were mine to protect. They shouted in terror, calling for their mothers, death spinning shadows across their faces. My heart cracked in my chest. Sindhuja lost altitude, plummeting towards the ground, and the boys were thrown into impossible positions, hanging off one claw, sliding from her back, tumbling with her.

Bawling. Yelling. Scrambling for a foothold in the sky.

Seven and eleven years old. This end too horrible to fathom.

One, the raja's son. The other, his cousin's child.

Time slowed to a crawl as I reached out with my magic to soften the impact. I couldn't help it. I blinked my eyes shut, praying that they would survive the fall as Deven raced us forward, unleashing a mighty roar. As if he might catch his nephew himself, impossible though it was.

Our enemy pounded the ground behind us, paws and tyres and vengeance.

A whoosh of gargoyle voices in my head— *protect the gargoyle queen, the gargoyle queen*—forced my eyes open. I cried out with joy as their otherworldly forms flocked through the night sky, grey flesh cutting through the deep blue expanse, catching Sindhuja and the boys like they were falling stars.

Four more came for us, casting eerie shadows across the landscape.

Swooping, piercing, stirring an unnatural wind. The beat of their wings was a haunting symphony.

I pulsed gratitude down the gargoyle bond as they wrapped me in their stony embrace and finally, thankfully, dropped my mental shields.

The tiger hung limp with exhaustion as my gargoyles flew us home, leaving our enemies in the dust.

~

I EMERGED SLOWLY FROM THE DEPTHS OF SLEEP AND FOUND myself in the bedroom I shared with the general. Snowflakes drifted lazily outside, and the kingdom slumbered beneath a blanket of stars. The air was cool and crisp, carrying the scent of frost-kissed grass and a tiger's musk.

Beside me, a glass of water sat on the bedside table, its surface shimmering faintly in the dim light. My shoulder throbbed as I reached trembling fingers for it and lifted it to my lips. The cool liquid went some way to neutralising the bitterness on my tongue.

Hushed voices drifted to me from the bedroom door. I listened, my senses still clouded by sleep.

"I deserved to know you were going after him."

"Says the seer whose very currency is secrets," said a voice with smooth whiskey notes that was unmistakably Deven. "My apologies. It's not nice being on the receiving end. Just ask Kiya."

My cheeks heated at his mention of me. I propped myself up on my elbow to get a better look, my shoulder protesting. Deven stood barefoot in joggers, his tattooed back illuminated by a sliver of moonlight, his arm leaning against the door jamb. The seer's hacked pixie haircut and a flash of emerald green feathers were just visible through his armpit.

"I apologised to her for that."

"That's something at least."

Mahi grunted. "Tell me again what he said. Don't leave anything out."

"He said we were asking the wrong question," said Deven. "That it was not about *what* magic Prem has obtained, it was about *how*. His tip-off about the pr–"

She snorted. "It's a trap. Prem promised him a reward to lure us in. My vision stopped just short of confirming it. I don't see why you're defending him. You're hardly his greatest fan."

A harsh laugh. "I haven't forgotten the curse or his part in it, if that's what you mean."

Bitterness swelled in her voice. "I wonder what it took. More topaz, more magic, more riches? Or just a place at his side."

"My instincts tell me you're wrong."

"Then you're a fool. How convenient that the guards arrived when they did."

"Maybe Prem trusts him as little as we do."

Sadness bloomed, swamping Mahi's anger. She sounded wrung out by emotion as if she would have given anything for Menon to be worthy of her love. "I wash my hands of him. You'd be wise to do the same."

"You know how proud he is, how reluctant to show vulnerability."

"Sounds like a typical Jalapashan man to me."

"His expression gave me pause. It was odd. For a second, I almost thought he was concerned."

The seer scoffed. "Concerned about his own skin, you mean. That note he left...Pah! What use is *sorry* when you repeatedly twist the knife in the people you love?"

"I know betrayal. It eats away at you. I also know the reason you've been drinking that putrid tea."

"You know nothing, General." Her tone warned him not to push past her prickles, to let things be.

"It's not only to help the resistance. You think I haven't noticed that the tea is sending you into deeper and deeper trances? You've been forcing *gleanings* to see whether he'll betray you again."

"I have not."

"You've been doing it to skip the pain of building your relationship from the foundations again. It's cowardly, Mahi. For the love of the stars, stop drinking that tea. Forcing magic never did anyone any good. You taught me that."

She stuttered like an exhaust pipe. "Okay, maybe that was one of my motives. So sue me. It didn't work, did it? I didn't foretell Menon hurting me all over again."

A voice as soft as a tiger's underbelly. "Are you sure? Has it occurred to you that he might not have betrayed you? That he's trying to help us?"

But she didn't hear him. "He didn't learn anything from being alone in the labyrinth. All the scheming I did. All the risks I took to free him. None of it mattered. I don't matter."

Deven changed tack. "I won't tell you how to feel, but we can't let your feelings cloud our judgment. What if Menon is right? If we don't act on his information, we're forfeiting the chance to get the upper hand. Think strategy."

"It's all I think about! We already have the upper hand," said the seer. "We have Kiya. She's everything we need. She's Vikram-*ji*'s heir, as clear as day. Prem won't stand a chance once her full talents emerge. Your concerns about the size of our army will be for the birds."

"Your gleanings have been all over the place, or have you forgotten?"

Babbu squawked at the insult, flapping his wings and threatening to turn his crimson beak into a battering ram until the seer's wizened fingers found his body and calmed him.

Mahi took an extra long slurp of her tea to spite the general. "I'm not wrong about this."

"She can't save us all," Deven's whiskey voice rasped. "I know that pressure. It breaks you."

"She's *not* you though, is she? She can put broken things together. Even us."

A growl. "Then we give her what she needs to succeed. That includes following every vital piece of information. Even if it's from Menon."

"The council meets as soon as she wakes. We put it to a vote."

I shifted in an attempt to join the conversation, and the bed groaned.

They must have heard me, because there was a tussle at the door like Mahi tried to slip past, and the next thing I knew, Deven had closed the door on the seer. There was a tired droop in his usually proud shoulders as he approached, and his walk had none of his usual feline grace as if his injury pained him.

Relief glimmered in his inky eyes, and his hair was damp from a shower. "You're awake."

I stretched to return the glass to the bedside table, but he peeled it from me. My tongue was like parchment when I spoke. "How long have I been sleeping?"

"About five hours. How do you feel?"

"Fine." My body ached, and my mind was a whiteout from spent magic. I suspected it would take days of rest and a dozen salt baths to feel human again.

"I cleaned you up before I tucked you in. I hope you don't mind."

I peeked under the cotton sheets. Warmth tinged my cheeks as I noted my ensemble of a T-shirt and knickers. He'd seen me naked often, but the intimacy of undressing me when I was unconscious belonged to a more seasoned relationship. Someone had applied a salve and gauze to my shoulder. Even my hair was neat and tidy, the telltale signs of battle gone.

When I saw the tenderness and worry in his face, I found that I didn't mind.

I found that my body softened at his nearness instead.

Deven's eyes darkened as he noticed, but he didn't bridge the gap between us. Instead, he focused on my well-being as if I was fragile. As if together we hadn't felled two dozen men, beasts amongst them. "Your grandmother gave you a healing elixir. It made you drowsy, but your wound will heal faster."

That explained my wooziness and the sour taste in my mouth. I studied him, taking in the grooves that bracketed his mouth and the slackness of his bones. The memory of a tattooed tiger rampaging through our enemies flashed in my mind. "The way you moved and fought out there..."

The bed dipped with his weight. "You didn't think I'd let you have all the fun, did you?"

"You were hurt."

"I heal quickly."

"You seemed in control."

A tremor ran through his body. "I wasn't. Not when I saw Ishaan and you out there. But it felt good to release that energy out there."

I nodded. Dread churned in my body. "My sister... Is everyone okay?"

"Leena will have a nasty scar, but she's fine. The evolution of her magic is scaring her, though. It's a small mercy that the boys weren't harmed at all." He took my hands, night-dark eyes swirling with emotion. "I can't thank you enough. If you hadn't come..."

I swallowed hard. "I thought we'd lost them when they fell through the sky."

A vein throbbed in his cheek. His fingers kneaded mine where they were sore from my vice-like grip on his fur during our escape. "They're safe. Back with their parents and in a mountain of trouble."

My mud-caked nails from the battlefield were pristine again, and there was no dirt on my skin. It roused a faint memory of his calloused hands cleaning me with a wash-cloth. "They'll need a list of chores as long as their bodies as punishment."

"Oh, I am on exactly the same page."

I bit my lip. "Prem didn't care that they were on the battlefield. He didn't care about his soldiers. He wouldn't have minded if the boys had ended up as collateral damage or if he'd killed his own son."

His eyes blazed like smouldering coals. "I know."

Prem's ring shone on my finger. How it must have cost him to leave it there.

"Have we ruined everything with what happened tonight? All semblance of civility and rules?"

A bitter laugh fell from him. "Civility? Rules? They've been nonexistent since Prem's reign began. What's left to ruin when everything was built on deceit?"

"Tonight won't go unanswered. He's going to make us pay."

His eyes glinted. "Maybe. But I think we learned something vital tonight."

"I heard." When he frowned, I added, "Not the whole conversation."

"Mahi wants to hold a meeting of the council. After last night, I think it's time to ask ordinary women of the resistance to take up arms, as well as the men. Just in case the worst happens. To give them a chance to defend themselves."

I nodded, thinking they weren't ordinary at all. "You've updated me on everyone but Sindhuja." I should have asked about the gargoyle first, but I'd been scared of the answer. When I reached down the gargoyle bond for her, I found only silence. A snapshot of Sindhuja—wearing the daisy head-band Leena had conjured—darted into my mind. And then her falling, falling, pierced by arrows. "How is she?"

His Adam's apple bobbed in his throat. "She's in a bad way."

My stomach knotted as I pushed back the covers, testing my balance. "Take me to her."

He steadied me, a strong hand on my hip when I rocked, and then he looped his fingers around my wrist as I tried to move away. "I know you love her. But maybe you can't save her."

I slipped free to pull on my trousers, socks and boots. "Excuse me?"

"Soldiers die in war." Deven looked away, jaw clenched tight. "It's what happens."

"You don't have faith in me," I said slowly when it was me who doubted if I could save her.

Dark brows rose. "Of course, I have faith in you. I saw you *crush* our enemies tonight. I wanted to rush to your side to protect you, but I didn't. Because you could handle yourself."

The cool air, the intoxicating air I had experienced when I woke, had grown denser. I couldn't breathe. I couldn't stay in our bedroom. Sindhuja was dying. "I have to help her."

"Why won't you let me love you?" he said quietly.

That isn't it, I wanted to scream. That wasn't it at all. Tension coiled in my chest, squeezing tighter with every passing moment. Death snapped at our heels wherever we went. He knew that as well as I did. He'd lost Roshni, and I'd lost Sitara. He'd seen the bloodied gardens. He'd seen the falling boys. He'd tasted bile in his throat when Prem's men and beasts had given chase, just like I had. In Jalapashu itself. In the fortress. When we slept and when we woke.

I forced myself to meet Deven's bleak gaze, searching for comfort there.

Instead, I found my fears mirrored back at me.

I lifted my chin. "I have to do this."

He gave a curt nod. "Would you like me to stay with you while you tend to her?"

Maybe if he'd been less formal or more hopeful, I might have said yes.

I chose my words to wound. "No. It's Merlin I need this time. Where is she?"

"In your studio at the weaver's house. Your grandfather made a bed for her there."

We left the bedroom before he finished his sentence. He held the door open for me, and I avoided touching him because I was angry. I should have swallowed my pride and held his hand as we walked through the dark passages of the fortress, past houses where the resistance slept and others where mothers were watching the sleeping babes they had almost lost. We should have taken a moment to celebrate the wins of that night—because there had been many—and I should have told him how I understood that he wanted to protect me, that it was in his nature.

But I didn't.

The raja didn't take care of his people, but we did. It didn't matter that the gargoyles weren't human, that they were more stone than flesh, more of the otherworld than of the earth. They were family.

Silence stretched between us as he escorted me to the weaver's house. The general watched me out of the corner of his eye to make sure I was steady on my feet. Against my better instincts, I pretended not to notice, knowing I'd regret my stubbornness later.

Only when he had gone did I remember that I had forgotten to ask him what vital information he and Leena had uncovered from Mahi's duplicitous brother.

CHAPTER 16

The door jangled as I stormed through and pushed my way past gargoyles standing vigil in stacked semi-circles around Sindhuja's makeshift bed. It was dark in there—low light and grey flesh—squeezed into what floor space remained free around my potter's wheel, workspaces and cabinetry. By my count, only a few gargoyles had remained at their guard posts. The others had been drawn here, including Harya, in a show of solidarity or humanity.

Sindhuja would like that, I decided.

To be part of a family after feeling like an outsider for centuries.

Someone—presumably Nani—had lit incense and candles. Notes of frankincense and eucalyptus drifted through the room, mingling with the scent of Sindhuja's blood. It was faintly mineral-like, with undertones of damp earth and moss. When I reached the patient, I found only Grandfather and Merlin were doing anything at all. The gargoyle was lying on her front, with her head turned to one side. Grandfather held a damp cloth to Sindhuja's head, but it wasn't her head that oozed a dark, viscous liquid that shimmered like polished stone and clumps of stony dust.

Merlin's body was hunched over the gargoyle. The faraway gleam in his eyes told me he recounted ancient stories into her ear in an attempt to distract her, but he brightened when he saw me. "I knew you would come. The seer did, too."

Mistress. Sindhuja tried to right herself and failed miserably.

Stay still, I told her gently. *You saved them. I have come to save you.*

It's okay, she said. *Even if you can't. I wouldn't change a thing. Even stone crumbles.*

But it took centuries for jagged cliffs and sea-struck boulders to succumb to the caress of the wind and the assault of the waves. It took centuries for etched patterns to deepen into cracks. It wasn't yet her time. I wanted her to endure.

I wanted her to be a part of what came next.

Grandfather, who only showed softness to Nani, was on his doddery old knees to mop the patient's brow. He wrung out his cloth and looked up at me. "Your sister did her best, but this is more your area of expertise. She ripped open her stitches trying to help, so your grandmother and Aanya took her to the infirmary to fix her up again. We can't find anything to help Fishtail. Not painkillers. Not tourniquets. Neither elevation nor coagulants. We couldn't even get the damn arrows out."

I noted Leena's presence in the discarded medical equipment around Sindhuja and the pink thistle clutched in the gargoyle's hand.

Merlin's liquid gold eyes glimmered. "That's when they turned out the lights and lit the candles."

The hare didn't say the quiet part out loud: that's when they had given up.

But I wouldn't give up on her. It wouldn't be fair. She hadn't given up on us.

I dared to look at the injured gargoyle, *really* look at her, sucking in my breath as I did so. Her broken body rested on a low bed of woven reeds and blankets. She had been struck in her wing, her right leg, her right shoulder and the centre of her back. It was normal for the gargoyles to retract their wings when not in use, but hers were stretched out still, with a gaping hole at the centre of the left one. It was a small mercy that the arrow had exited the wing, but three others protruded from her, their arrowheads buried deep in her grey flesh. Her lips stretched over her teeth in a grimace, and her breathing was shallow. A sickly blue hue crept across her skin even as we stood there. Jagged tears had become impossibly deep cracks. Scales flaked from her fishtail as if her body was disintegrating and in its final throes. Despite her injuries, she exuded a quiet strength, her yellow eyes fixed on a flickering flame dancing in the corner.

I turned to Harya first and then cast a glance around the sombre vigil. Stoic forms cast elongated shadows against the plain walls, their wings folded tightly against their backs. Candlelight danced across their solemn faces, and their grinding breath flowed around the room almost in unison. An otherworldly coldness emanated from the mass of their bodies.

Go. I have work to do, I said. *Go.*

Anger flashed across Harya's face, but I could have been mistaken.

It's easy to assume we don't have our own heart or will, he said. *We would like to watch over her.*

I shook my head. *I must do this alone.*

His stony face hardened. *You have no need of us.*

Frustration spiked. *I won't let her down, I promise.*

Perhaps you already have. He spoke for them all. *You will take care of her?*

I'll do what I can, I replied. This wasn't the time for promises I might not be able to keep. I muted their voices in a chamber in my mind before they had even walked into the night, letting only Sindhuja's laboured breathing filter through.

"You heard her." Grandfather's moustache bristled as he heaved himself up and eyed the gargoyle throng. "It's oppressive in here. Hardly conducive to healing with all that gargoyle glowering. It seems my wife's therapy sessions have been less useful than she imagined." He ushered them out, muttering under his breath about the depths he had stooped to, about how his knees couldn't take the strain, much less his heart. But the softness in his gaze told me that he didn't mind at all, and his good wishes for Sindhuja warmed the lingering look he gave her and me. His departing words were, "I trusted you with my daughter once, hare. My granddaughter is no different."

The hare quivered with responsibility. "You can trust me."

Men and their posturing, I said to brighten the mood, to coax Sindhuja to ease.

A meagre ball of light floated down the gargoyle bond.

"Candles out, Merlin. Lights on." I put my apron on. "Let's get to work."

WE TOILED FEVERISHLY TO SAVE HER IN THE QUIET SOLITUDE OF the studio. Leena had tried medicine to heal our friend; now it was time to try art. The floor beside her bed became our work surface, and soon, it was littered with tools, pastes and jars of murky water. When well-wishers came knocking, Merlin shooed them away without niceties and returned to my side, his presence a balm and a conduit to greater magic.

The minor cracks and chips I'd mended for the gargoyles after previous skirmishes were nothing compared to what faced us. Sindhuja's injuries were too severe. This time, I couldn't use clay paste to reinforce weakened areas, crushed stone and sand to provide stability, sealants, or even the Japanese art of *kintsugi*. Neither could I restore her with a steady hand and clever bonding processes. However meticulously I wielded my potter's rib or wire clay cutter, however much I attempted to mend contours made into ribbons by arrows, death hovered. It taunted us.

I'd already decided that losing her was not an option.

So, I threw caution to the wind.

Would you change anything about yourself? I asked the gargoyle, eyeing wings frayed and worn through countless storms, the limbs disproportionate to her squarish body that gave her a crab-like appearance, and the fishtail that dragged along the floor. As if the great pottery master had made her first and had made countless mistakes.

Her yellow eyes fluttered open, where she lay panting. Behind the pain, there was clarity, and I realised that she was no longer the painfully shy gargoyle I'd first met. Every word was an effort, with gaps stretching between the fragments of her thoughts. *Harya's wings would grant me the freedom to soar high above the world...to see it from a perspective I've never known... A sinuous, spiked tail would help in battle... Longer limbs would give me more ground speed and strength... than my pitiful ones. But in the end, I like who I am... Your arrival here helped me accept myself. But there are others who would change who they are.* Her eyelids drooped. *I'm more than the sum of my parts.*

I stroked her clammy forehead. *Yes, you are. Those boys would have died without you.*

I let her rest a few seconds, then helped her rise, a lump in my throat. We took it slowly. Her limbs had grown leaden, and her muscles protested against the strain of every movement. Flames danced in her amber eyes, and her skin was no longer clammy but cold, as if her body knew what I would ask her to do. As if nature already had the answers.

I prayed she wouldn't be afraid. *Now I know how you wish to be made, I need you to turn yourself to stone.*

Her eyes rested on me for a moment, faithful like a puppy's. *As you wish, mistress.*

Panic coursed through me. *Wait. I want you to know that yours is my favourite name of all the gargoyles, and I will never forget it as long as I live.* It sounded like a goodbye, and I kicked myself for it.

Parched lips stretched into a smile before she let Leena's pink thistle fall from her hands.

Steely grit settled over her features as she focused her waning energy on a singular purpose: to turn herself to stone. Slowly, almost imperceptibly, a transformation took place. First, her features became more defined. Next, stone crept up her limbs like ivy until her sickly blue flesh became grey again. Until it lost all pliancy and suppleness. Until not a trace of softness remained, even in the wisps of her hair and her bulbous lips. With a final rush of breath, she surrendered to the ancient power in her veins and stilled completely.

Icy fear engulfed me. My friend's once-beating heart was silent within her chest, her body a statue, and the night felt too close for comfort. "What have I done?"

Merlin's gold eyes glimmered like he was already crafting spells of power like he had the faith of a thousand men when he was only a hare. "You've given her a chance. Touch her, and you'll see."

I laid a hand against her frigid stone body. Even in her petrified state, a pulse of magic thrummed beneath the surface of the stone, a faint echo of the life and dreams within. My lungs expanded, breath whooshing in. Centring me. Grounding me.

With the inky hare beside me, I summoned my courage.

Silence and magic swirled around me as I sank into my work. My fingertips grazed the smooth stone form before me, acutely aware of the fragile balance between helping Sindhuja and causing more harm. Dread rising, I inspected the areas where the arrows were embedded, tracing their outlines with a feather-light touch. With painstaking care, I took a chisel and chipped away at the stone with careful strokes. My usually steady hands trembled. I buttressed my thoughts against the doubts that sang that I could cause irreparable harm with each blow of my chisel or might sever vessels or damage vital sinews or organs.

Soon, there were tools scattered around me: rolling pins to flatten and smooth out the clay, rulers for precision, cutters and carving knives for clarity and meticulousness of form, bowls of water, sponges to add and remove moisture, burnishing tools to smooth, and rollers to add texture.

Only the work mattered, the here and now, one step after another.

Until the bitter end or revival.

All the while, I chanted incantations of renewal and healing. Consonants and vowels knitted together on the tip of my tongue, arriving there effortlessly through the strength of my connection with Merlin, with the coven. The words flowed from my lips like a prayer. Like sparks of energy waiting to ignite—*navīkrtya svayaṁ* and *punarjīvana prāṇa* and *prākṛtikī navīkaraṇa*—as if we had tapped into a wellspring of cosmic power.

Small chips of stone skittered across the floor, eventually revealing the arrows buried underneath. I dislodged arrows from their stone prison—from her shoulder and back—placing them aside in turn like grim trophies. Then, I moulded great lumps of clay into the gaping holes I had left behind. Her leg and wing were trickier still. I carved off injured sections from her body, a sickening whirl in my stomach, and hunched over slabs of clay as I moulded it, matching it to the sad, broken pieces of her body. I grappled with the challenge of crafting a left wing to replace her ravaged one, trialling various tools to mirror the exact form and pattern of her right one.

The image of Sindhuja's classic zig-zag flight path swept across my mind.

I worked until my neck craned and my back ached.

Until my fingers grew stiff and my eyes bleary.

And the spells, they were powerful. Endless spells flooding into my mind, as powerful as my intent. *Patthar cikitsā. Patthar cikitsā. Māṃsāni rūpāntara. Māṃsāni rūpāntara.* Over and over, till my mouth was dry and my voice a rasp. Every chant wove potent magic in the air, building in intensity. The spells coursed through the fibre of our bodies, first like subtle tingles, then like surges of electricity. They sank into my soul and Merlin's and the gargoyle's stony skin, each word a promise of vitality, transformation and rebirth. We chanted until the shadows slunk away, the night dissipated, and the first dawn rays spiralled across the sky.

We chanted until I made final fixes to her scales and her body.

Until she was whole again.

The spells infused the air with sacred energy. With each syllable we uttered, the world held its breath, and the boundaries between the physical and the metaphysical blurred as our magic took hold. I could feel it in the rising buzz at a cellular level in my own body, in the fine hairs standing on end on my nape and my arms. Most of all, in the soft glow that enveloped Sindhuja. A magic borne of history and art, of deep-seated determination and the karma that this particular gargoyle—this kind, unique gargoyle—had put out into the world.

When we finished, I heaved her into the kiln with utmost care, perspiration pearling on my skin. Praying that I wouldn't be clumsy. That I could bear her weight. She was small, and the kiln was cavernous, but it wasn't made for the likes of gargoyles. Constructed with fire-resistant bricks, a heavy metal door, and lined with glowing red-hot coils, it was made primarily for flowerpots, dinnerware, mugs, tiles and figurines.

Sindhuja barely fitted. It didn't seem right to put her in there, this living, breathing, otherworldly creature. It didn't seem right to lock her inside, where the air was hot and dry, where the smell of scorched clay lingered from previous firings.

A chill ran down my spine as I closed the kiln door, sealing my friend inside. The robust door clanged shut with a finality that echoed in the silent studio. I programmed the kiln, heart in mouth, scared, so scared. I didn't let myself dwell on the flames that danced on her petrified skin, the chemical processes that changed her at a molecular level, or whether the oxygen needed for combustion would make it impossible for her to breathe.

Merlin and I tried to think of anything else as the kiln hummed, heat radiating into the wintery studio in shimmering waves. We spoke of Sitara's warm urn, of Leena's soldier-turned-sapling, of the chastised boys and the gargoyle's sacrifice. We spoke of the acceptance he had finally found again with my grandparents, who had shunned him, and how that felt. We spoke of a tattooed tiger and stubborn hearts and how the world stopped when a loved one was hurt. We spoke of family.

We didn't speak of what we had attempted and whether we would succeed.

No, that we left aside, though the spectre of our attempts loomed over us.

The kiln roared as it reached its peak temperature, and I didn't know if I'd done enough or if I had signed her death warrant. Her voice in my head was silent, and its absence gutted me. The occasional pops and clicks as the stone expanded and contracted made me wince. Once the flames died away, maybe Sindhuja would emerge from the smouldering embers and ash and find a new beginning—alchemy and magic and heat and hope.

All we could do was wait.

"You'll watch over her?" I laid my cheek against Merlin.

He nodded, and we stayed entwined for a cycle of breath. "Of course."

Then I curled my tired, bruised body onto the makeshift bed of reeds and blankets, where Sindhuja's viscous blood had oozed, and slept.

Perhaps a regent wasn't someone who sat on a throne or stood on a balcony.

Perhaps they were someone who slept on the floor, their heart cracked into a thousand pieces.

Meanwhile, the kiln blazed.

CHAPTER 17

Nightmares like molasses, like treacle.

I couldn't find my way out of the suffocating darkness.

Tendrils of shadow coiled and writhed, shrouding my way. The terrain warped, and it wasn't my doing. Deep in the distance, the sacred banyan tree thrived, but I couldn't reach it. My body was sluggish, with none of the strength and power I had grown to love in my physicality and my magic. Dark figures danced around me, an unnatural ballet of unsettling grace. Shapes flitted in and out of focus in my peripheral vision, grotesque caricatures I recognised but couldn't place. Shadows so sinister that my breath turned to ice in my throat. Twisted strings dangled from above, tugging me to their will. I thrashed against their malevolent influence, but when I looked around, I couldn't make them out. They choked me. Immobilised me. Ensnared me.

I couldn't escape them.

This land wouldn't ever be mine. I knew who it belonged to. I heard his cruel laugh.

My own voice ripped from my throat, but no sound came out.

A CALLOUSED PALM HELD MY CHEEK. HE WAS SO CLOSE THAT HIS breath fanned my face. He was rocking me like he might console his nephew. Rocking me against the hard planes of his chest, stroking damp hair back from my face. "It's a nightmare. Just a nightmare. Wake up, Kiya. Come on, love."

I jolted up, my throat raw, my breath coming in ragged gasps. The remnants of the nightmare clung to my skin like a cold sweat. I leaned into Deven's chest, taking a moment to orient myself. Strong arms enveloped me like we hadn't fought. Like being near to him was the most natural thing in the world.

The drone of the furnace brought it all home.

I jerked my eyes to the kiln, my pulse racing still. Recalling the disagreement with Deven made me stiffen in his arms. Awkwardness entered our embrace, our contours suddenly no longer moulding together but resisting. "Has the cycle finished yet?"

"No," said the hare. "We must be patient."

Patience had always been part of the potter's process. I sent a rush of love to the gargoyle encased within the kiln. God, I hoped she made it.

The hare's gold eyes glimmered. "You were thrashing in your sleep. I couldn't wake you."

"So he called for me," the general murmured, disentangling himself from me.

The withdrawal of his body contact felt like a snub.

He stood up from his crouch and scanned the room as if he'd been distracted by me and was taking in the mess in the studio for the first time: the tools and lumps of clay, the broken, discarded parts of Sindhuja's body. Then he walked over to the kiln, but there was no peephole to see the progress—or my failure—no way of telling the outcome at all until the timer rang.

My bones were stiff from sleeping on the floor, and the blankets knotted around my legs. I extricated myself from the blankets and smoothed down my clothes. My fickle body craved the comfort of his touch, but I held firm, the softness leeching from my voice. "Merlin can't stand discord. I suppose he saw my nightmare as an opportunity for us to kiss and make up."

Deven's eyes glittered. "Is that what you want? To kiss and make up?"

My traitorous eyes dropped to his lips, and he definitely noticed. "It's a turn of phrase."

"Bringing people together is one of my best qualities," said the hare. "As well as tap dancing and knowing when to dip out of a situation. Speaking of which…"

I knelt beside the hare and caressed his sooty ears. "Stay with her, Merlin. We're leaving anyway." I met the general's eyes. "Leena and my grandparents didn't come back here last night… I assume that's Mahi's doing, and you're here to hurry me to a council meeting?"

"The seer and your grandmother are working with Leena on the sapling. And the council meeting is not until seven." His mild voice confused me when I thought we were raring to fight again, when war was all around us and left no room for quiet consideration.

"Good. I need a quick wash and a change of clothes. Are you coming?" I kept my voice cool though my heart thrummed. Picking up the pink thistle, I placed it for Sindhuja at the base of the kiln, then walked out into the misty light of a new day.

He fell into lockstep with me, shortening his stride to match mine.

My head was still woozy. I hadn't yet allowed the gargoyles to enter my head again for fear of Sindhuja's silenced voice within the chorus, or worse. Somewhere in the fortress, Leena was fighting her own battle with her evolving magic. We were all fighting in one way or another. For what we believed in or what we could be, for the relationships we valued, the power we craved or for justice we deserved.

The sounds of the resistance waking met us: the faint shuffling of feet, the hum of voices, the clatter of plates being stacked. Somewhere in the distance, someone—Simeon perhaps, Deven's second-in-command, or Yuvan—rallied an early training session. The metallic clang of swords and the dull thud of wood floated on the wind towards us. Goose-bumps chased up my arms.

Deven's footsteps were clipped, but his voice was gentle. "Do you want my coat?"

His attentiveness erased the sharp edges of my haughtiness after our argument. "I'm okay."

"I should have explained last night. I hadn't imagined that she could be saved."

"Loving someone is staying."

"I know that. I wanted to spare you from witnessing her death." There was a slight catch in his resonant voice. "Soldiers deal in harsh realities. You're better at hope than me."

"My worry got the better of me. I'm sorry I was sharp." I snuck a look at him. Silvery light smoothed the sharp angles of his face, and here in the fresh air, by ourselves, away from the furnace, he didn't look angry or stern or disappointed. He looked unchained as if he was learning a new way.

We walked in an easier silence, keeping our heads down, past all the houses under the awning of the fortress, both conscious of how easy it would be to be overheard, how important our privacy was and how quickly the first bricks of a new relationship could erode when exposed to too much scrutiny or rumours or meddling.

War had sped up the pace of our relationship, making implosions more likely.

I was so very glad that we hadn't hit pause or pretended we were nothing to each other. That we'd decided to muddle along, even though neither of us was practised at navigating the seas of romantic relationships. Even though it might have been easier or more sensible to focus on the kingdom and lock away the possibility of what we could be.

We weren't primed to communicate well. We didn't yet know each other's foibles or sore points. I didn't know what would make him laugh or melt or how he took his *chai*. We'd missed all the usual trials of early relationships: disagreements over who had raised their voice or left the kitchen window open, who should cook or empty the bins, or who had stolen the duvet at night. We hadn't yet had enough time to figure out who preferred which side of the bed, to lazily play with each other's bodies or spend a day curled in each other's arms. We'd skipped tussles over religion and routine, which social events to brave and whose family to visit for holidays.

The intricate dance of personalities that made up a couple was a foreign land to us.

So when it came to life and death decisions, we didn't know how to fight.

I didn't know whether we should feel our way with careful words like you do with strangers, let things simmer and wait for the hurts to blow over, or ride the wild storm of our anger and strike with sharpened tongues, trusting that the sun would follow. We had to work harder to find common ground because it wasn't easy to mould our convictions or soften our instincts in established adulthood.

We had different histories, different expectations, different patterns of behaviour.

But I found none of that mattered when we slipped inside our bedroom door. None of it mattered when I closed the door, pressed my back up against it, and he looked around at me with questioning obsidian eyes. A small whoosh of breath escaped me as he turned to face me, leaning his forearm on one side of the door, so close that the scent of wintery woods and worn leather enveloped me.

A lock of his hair skimmed his forehead, and crescent shadows pooled beneath his eyes. "I don't get close to people. Maybe it's the soldier's way. Seeing injury and death. Seeing friends slip away like smoke on the wind. Even without war, it's been like that in Jalapashu. Those fucking gladiatorial battles. The choices I had to make." His voice vibrated against my ear. "Limiting who I get close to is how I've survived."

I bit my lip. "You got close to me."

"I couldn't help it." He tracked the sweep of my lashes, the curve of my mouth. "I tried to avoid it."

The air prickled with tension and something else that was new: a dropping of shields, a peeling back, a new layer of openness, and a delicious tingling of heat that had nothing to do with the wintery day and was made by the nearness of our bodies.

I wanted him to kiss me. "Why?"

Shadows danced across his face. "I don't care about myself. A soldier knows death is on the cards. But I don't cope well when people I care about get hurt. It's the thought of…" His brow furrowed, and I resisted the urge to smooth away the frown lines. "I get nightmares. Flashbacks. The guilt…it's paralysing. That's why I overreacted earlier."

"You're not made of stone. It's human to feel that way." I let my body soften against him, dipping my head beneath his chin. A delicious shiver ran up my spine as he rested his hands on my waist.

"I should have backed you when you helped Sindhuja. I knew it the minute I tried to stop you. I want you to know I'm working on not getting in your way." Somehow, our legs had entwined, and my pelvis was against his strong thighs. "I like what we have, Kiya. And I'm willing to grow to keep it."

I reached up to dust kisses over his jawline. "Me, too."

His laugh reverberated through me. "I'm glad because this is new. For me, it's new."

I looped my arms around his neck. "What's new?"

He pulled me snugly against him like there wasn't any hiding anymore. "You turn me inside out in a good way. You make me think. You make me feel. I can see how hard it is for you to breathe sometimes after Sitara, but you keep on. You're strong in ways I'm not."

A lump formed in my throat. I whispered against him, "I'm not strong."

His voice was oh so gentle. "You are. Even hurting, you are. You're strong and brave and kind and fucking beautiful." He traced my bottom lip with his thumb and lifted my chin to kiss the corner of my mouth. When my tears started to fall, he licked their sweet, salty pathways and returned to my mouth, a gentle exploration that melted me. That didn't try to hold the broken parts of me together but honoured them, worshipped them.

Something about his tenderness broke the dam of my grief.

The barriers I'd erected since Sitara's death crumbled. My tears carved rivulets through the landscape of my grief. I buried my face in my hands, my shoulders shaking with sobs. Deven became an anchor amidst the torrent of my grief. He stroked my hair and pressed his lips to my temple, the warmth of his breath a whisper against my skin. His hand traced smooth circles over my back until my cries faded. Until the shattered parts of me had come together again.

I could have stayed like that for an eternity, but the weight of the world slid between my shoulder blades again, so I lifted my head. "I'm sorry."

The silver scar across his eyebrow glistened in the early light. "Don't ever be sorry. Not for that."

"She was our oldest sister. I shouldn't have to live without her."

"I'll help you find a new normal."

I kissed him, and beneath our feet, the earth stirred with life denser than I'd perceived before: rocks that formed the foundation for life to flourish, soil in a tapestry of colours and textures, creatures burrowing past knotted roots, nutrients, coarse grains and pockets of pooled water. The scent of freshly turned earth crept into my nostrils. When else did I feel such possibility apart from when I was in his arms?

I knew we could be everything to each other by how he brushed a damp lock of hair from my face, the warmth of his hand seeping into my back, and how he listened attentively and made good when he didn't. How he didn't stop me on the battlefield but was always aware of where I was and what I needed. How he had introduced me to his family like it was the most natural thing in the world, even before we were together. How his arms were the safest place. How his eyes shone with pride when he looked at me, even across a crowded room. How he was the stern soldier, but his eyes crinkled for me.

When the time was right, we'd tell each other those three little words I'd been keeping locked inside.

The scent of him, the feel of him, was driving me to distraction.

His hands were at my waistband. "Forgive me?"

"There's nothing to forgive." My stomach coiled with desire.

"We're in this together, every step of the way."

It was the most natural thing in the world for us to undress, slowly, taking care with our injuries, drinking in the sight of one another. For my hands to sweep over the planes of his hard chest and down lower to where the trail darkened and he strained against his trousers.

Our clothes heaped at our feet, and it was bliss, pure bliss, when he unclasped my bra and slipped my knickers over my hips, when his calloused hands lifted my heavy breasts, and he first took one peak in his mouth, nipping and sucking gently, before repeating the exquisite touches to the other peak. I arched my back to give him better access, wanting more, needing more. His leg, dusted with hair, provided torturous friction to the apex of my thighs, and his arm supported the small of my back as I released my hold around his neck and gave in to my need to hold him where he throbbed.

He sucked in a breath, said my name like a prayer, and I slid down his body, every part of me aching for him but needing to taste him, needing to give him pleasure. I cupped him first before licking the saltiness of his skin, taking him in my mouth and swirling my tongue over his tip in slow, excruciating circles that had him groaning for me, begging me to go deeper, to take him as far as I could. His hands settled into my hair, but he let me set the rhythm until he was a shuddering wreck, his eyes closed, eyelashes fanned, mouth partially open, tensing with every teasing, worshipping touch I offered him.

"I need you," he said, and I thought it was the most wonderful thing I'd ever heard.

Deven pulled me to my feet, and I thought he might take me then, against the door, but his night-dark eyes grew smoky, like the last embers of a bonfire, and when he dipped his fingers inside my wetness, I cried out. He dipped his tousled head to my breasts once more while he lazily, expertly, circled the nub of my pleasure, using two fingers then three, thumbing my core, brushing it, working me into a frenzy until I bit his shoulder to keep quiet, not to beg him to enter me.

He gave a husky laugh. "One day, we'll have time for me to dip more into you than my fingers."

I could barely think straight. "Oh?"

His smile was wicked. "We'll start with fruit and work our way to naughtier things from there."

I flushed. I hoped that day would come fast, but all thoughts of the future shrank to a point when he led me to the bed and climbed on top of me. It was the bed where we'd both had nightmares, where he'd struggled to contain his tiger, where we'd tossed and turned devising schemes to thwart the raja.

But we reclaimed it.

We made new memories there, as he found me slick and ready, as he pressed home, hooking my legs over his shoulders so he could drive deeper. His rhythm was punishing, first slow, until my ecstasy was a whisper away, then hard and fast. My nails made half-moons in his skin, and I dragged down his head for kisses that stole my breath.

"You're mine, little witch," said the general.

"I am," I gasped. My body told him what my mouth could not.

He plundered me as only a lover could, giving as much as he took. Until stars spun and galaxies ignited. Until my thoughts turned to smoke, and there was only him, him, him, filling my body and soul. Until his eyes locked with mine, and our release came in shuddering gasps, first me, then him.

As we lay resting, tangled in the sheets and each other's arms, he drew lazy circles on the small of my back and smoothed back my hair. My breathing regulated, and my heartbeat matched the drum of his.

"Long ago, when I was bent double with grief, the seer told me I would be happy again."

"Did you believe her?"

His voice was soft. "I didn't then."

It didn't seem unthinkable anymore that I could be happy again, either.

I sent a fevered prayer into the universe that Deven made it through the coming days.

CHAPTER 18

The hour was early when the Council of Rebels met, but it could have been midnight, judging by the bleak light and gaunt faces in the seer's mothball house. Nani had already conducted her rituals of a salt perimeter and lit incense by the time we arrived. The glowing tips of the sticks sent curls of smoke into the room as Deven and I took our seats.

"Are you okay?" I mouthed at my sister across the table.

She nodded yes. When I searched for traces of distress after her harrowing experience, I was astonished not to find any. Her arm was heavily bandaged, but joy radiated from her nonetheless: in the gentle sway of her torso and the palpable excitement that danced in her brown eyes and tugged at the corners of her lips. Her excitement was reflected in Aanya's gaze, too. The maid beamed with pride.

Once, our trio of sisters had been everything to each other, the first to know of slights or happiness. Now, Aanya had been the first to know Leena's news.

But our conversation had to wait.

"Start the meeting," squawked Babbu. "Or she'll hear him."

Mahi thumbed her medallion, lips turned downward. Her skin had the sickly tone of addiction, and I knew that Deven had been right about the tea. "Stop your fussing." On her shoulder, Babbu squawked in protest, either at the admonishment or because he didn't feature in the headcount. But begin she did. "Seven of us sit here today. We are fewer and fewer as the days go on. Our window for success is closing, and we have much to discuss."

Nani nodded. "The sacred tree is now a husk that has folded in on the weight of itself."

"It has three days at most," said Leena. "The half inside our walls is faring marginally better than the half outside that was exposed most closely to Prem's spell. The dispersed aerial roots mean it can hold up longer than oak or an elm, say, but it won't be long."

Grandfather's moustache vibrated with each word. "The good news is Aanya leads the people in singing songs of your heroics. They say you are forgiving and brave. That you help people who don't deserve it. That you are the kind of rani they have dreamed of."

Aanya's musical lilt was the polar opposite of Grandfather's bristles. "But they grow more scared with every passing day that the tree deteriorates. They might not always benefit from magic, but they can't imagine living without it."

"It is true that there remains a number of troublemakers amongst the resistance." A wrathful fierceness descended on Grandfather's features that reminded me how deeply ingrained the persona of the Enforcer was. "Needless to say, I'm keeping a close eye on them."

"There may be troublemakers, but there are also those who are simply afraid of the kingdom no longer existing," said Aanya. "They'd choose a broken Jalapashu over braving a life in England every time. The old way is all they know."

I hoped I sounded braver than I felt. "Whatever happens, it's time to find new ways of living."

Nani's hands made tiny butterfly movements. It unnerved me when usually she was as steadfast as the rising sun. "Then perhaps it's time to discuss how we operate. I think we should consider who we want to be before our next clash with enemy forces. People died in the rose garden. Soldiers who were just following orders. Soldiers who might, given the chance, leave peaceably under new rule..."

Grandfather stroked his shrinking belly. "I think what Kavita is trying to say is–"

"I am capable of speaking for myself," said Nani fondly. "But go ahead, husband."

He basked in her affection. "The council has not yet decided the parameters for violence. Prem decided that all on his own as judge, jury and executioner. Kavita has always said how easy it is to slip into the banality of evil. I have been party to that slide once before."

Deven's cheekbones looked carved under the light of the tarnished brass orb. His voice was steely. "The choices we made in the rose garden were not taken lightly. I saw both sisters go easy on those intent on harming them. The gargoyles and I fought ruthlessly, but that's the nature of the battlefield. Choices are dictated by the gravity of the situation. We survive. We adapt. We try to be measured, but we protect our side, even if that means using lethal force. I resent the implication that we took those choices lightly. I don't know how many I killed that night, but I remember their faces. And I'll grapple with the moral fallout from what I did long into the future. Maybe until I am felled myself."

Grandfather held up a hand. "Stop, son. No one is saying you should have acted differently, only that it is right that we discuss as a council where we draw the line in theory. I hope, by the grace of the gods, that we are at the birth of a new kingdom. Without agreed guidelines, we risk becoming as monstrous as Prem Kumar. Kavita and I only ask the question."

"I will never be him," growled Deven, and across the table, Aanya shrank back.

I laid a hand on his thigh, willing my touch to bring down the temperature in the room. I thought about my sister, who had been forced to fell a man in the heat of battle. "Then let me ask this question. What are the costs of nonviolence in the face of escalating brutality? Before I came here, I cringed from even killing a spider or a kitchen ant. But how can nonviolence deter someone as brutal as Prem? This is war, not a fairy tale. Violence is around every corner. You all feel it."

Beneath my fingers, the tenseness left Deven's body.

Nani twisted her fingers on the table. "Fairy tales are violent, Kiya. Didn't your mother tell you that? I read her enough as a child. I'm glad you came home safely. I'm glad that our side suffered fewer losses than the raja's. But we can't be the same as him."

"Kavita, my idealistic friend, I don't like that the mission to the palace took place, but I have no doubt that the violent action there, in defence of our rebels, was necessary. Have you ever thought we might need to be the same as him to escape him?" Grooves of sorrow bracketed the seer's mouth. "Prem Kumar won't be deterred by nonviolent resistance. He'll only interpret it as a weakness. It'll only embolden him to be more violent. He would slaughter every one of the people sheltered within this fortress if he thought it the only route to retain the throne. And if the people here return to his fold, that wicked man will double his suppression, his censorship, his crackdowns."

"You could have stayed in the air. With the gargoyles." Nani's eyes were red-rimmed.

Was this how ruling was? Did it amount to constant friction, a balancing of priorities, a locking of horns with those who stood by your side and those who stood locked outside the prisms of power? I shook my head. "No, Nani. We couldn't have. The boys were down there."

Babbu cocked his emerald head and sang. "I can hear him."

The seer and I both shot him an exasperated look.

"We finish this soon," said Deven quietly. "Because the losses we've chalked up will mean nothing if we give up or baulk at what is asked of us. I know my cousin. Violence will escalate, and it will be harder to maintain the support of the rebels when our losses mount. It's not just the rebels we need to worry about. Prem has increased taxes and sanctions in our absence. The kingdom is thrumming with fear on both sides of the divide. We have to hold our ground."

I locked eyes with everyone around the table in turn, quashing my instinct to comfort Nani. I was their *queen-in-waiting,* and this wasn't the time to be soft. "Leena?"

My sister bit her lip. "Violence isn't in my nature, but I can stomach what we did. Jalapashu is walled off from the world. There is no one who will intervene if it's not us."

"Aanya?" I prompted.

Doe eyes met mine. "We have made our bed. I'm not the bravest, but we shouldn't flinch now."

I nodded. "This is our chance. We defend ruthlessly and attack as necessity dictates. We mourn our enemies like we'd mourn our friends. Is everyone agreed? Speak now or hold your peace."

There were no dissenters. I knew that Grandfather, though he had voiced Nani's concerns, felt the same way by the way his chest puffed up with pride, even though his eyes flitted to his beloved wife.

"Good. Then we move on to the next order of business."

Beside me, Deven cast me a glance that was a mix of awe and unease, and I wondered if I was learning too quickly or not quickly enough for all that he and the kingdom needed me to be.

"Mahi? I believe you had something to raise?" I said.

The seer adopted a snippy tone reminiscent of a mother chiding her child. I tried to ignore the T-shirt of Elton John in enormous embellished glasses she wore though it did little to add to her credibility. "I won't waste precious time dwelling on how the general and Leena ventured to the palace to speak with my deserter brother at great risk to us all, not to mention how those damn children unwittingly lured Kiya straight into the mouth of the tiger." Her kohl-painted eyebrows jerked up at Deven's heavy sigh. She eyeballed him. "Perhaps you can illuminate for us the issue at hand."

Deven placed a hand on his chest and nodded with courtly courtesy. "Of course. In the brief moments that Leena and I were alone with Menon, he told us of Prem's visits to the deepest part of the dungeons. He hadn't been able to ascertain the nature of these visits, but Prem's caginess gave him cause to believe that uncovering the secret might be beneficial to the resistance."

My grandmother furrowed her sparse eyebrows. "Menon has an appetite for betrayal."

Mahi harrumphed. "Quite right, Kavita. It would be utter stupidity to give his information any credence. What cretin would trust the loyalty of a man who has repeatedly been disloyal?"

"What's the point in forgiving him if you repeatedly bring up his past?" said Aanya.

Mahi was as dour as a tombstone in a forgotten grave-yard. "I thought you, for one, would understand."

My sister squeezed Aanya's hand in comfort. "When I was imprisoned, the inmates told me stories about roars that echoed from the depths of the dungeons and one section where no new prisoners were ever sent. Where a reclusive guard delivered food once a day."

A shudder ran through me. I'd imagined Menon's tip would lead us to an inanimate object.

"The guard is a lumbering sort of fellow. He never said hello, and they didn't hear any strains of conversation," said my sister. "He simply kept his eyes down, delivered one tray, took away the previous day's one, and didn't carry a weapon."

"His name is Adil Shetty. I grew up with him. The man is mute and can't write. He has no magic or skills in combat. He was known as a simpleton. When the raja offered him a job as a guard, I wondered why." Grandfather paled. "The ancient plans of Jalapashu show that the northern-most chamber of the dungeons is clad in iron. Perhaps the reason for Adil's employment is because he cannot disclose the secret of what he sees down there."

Pulse racing, I leaned forward. "Who or what is Prem hiding down there? Why would the chamber be iron-clad?"

Grandfather bowed his head. "I'm sorry, *beta*. I learned not to ask questions I didn't want to know the answer to." His use of the endearment did not slip me by; neither did his cowardice.

"My brother is well aware that the most effective lies encompass some of the truth," said Mahi.

"Melon lies, lies, lies," sang the parrot with glee.

"There was a time when the prison was full of prisoners and monsters from previous reigns," said Nani carefully, almost as if she was reluctant to voice her wisdom after our clash of opinion. "So it might be that something exists down there that Prakash is not aware of. A monster made in the labyrinth or some poor soul that the raja wanted to belittle or tame or torture."

Mahi's third eye yawned in her forehead, glassy violet and blinking rapidly like she skimmed through reels of gleanings. "Whatever pathetic, beaten creature is down there is not our concern. A rat—and mark my words, that is what the raja considers each and every one of us to be—does not go into the cage unless it wishes to get caught."

Whereas Mahi had been scornful and cutting, Deven was calm and careful and all the more convincing for it. "You saw what Prem did outside these very walls. You saw how he gave the sacred tree a sickness, how he came alone and arrogant, full of new magic that we can't yet fathom. We can't win if we're behind the curve. We need to take this chance and follow this lead. If we're clever and prepared enough, we can confirm the validity of the intel and evade capture even if it is a trap."

"I understood you quite well when we spoke earlier," said Mahi, and I wondered if Menon's betrayal hit deeper given their twin's bond, whether she kicked herself for missing all the signals, not only as a seer but as his twin sister. "Tell me, why didn't my brother return to the fortress with you? Is it because he's too afraid to face me?"

Deven met her glare. "Have you considered that he's giving us a fighting chance to uncover the secret in the dungeons before Prem destroys all evidence of it?"

The seer glanced around the table. "The general is keen to explore every bit of information that might aid us. Even at the expense of lives."

Deven's jaw tightened. "I didn't say that, Mahi. I will go myself."

"No," I blurted out. "We'll go together. The skies will be heavily watched after our last escapade, but the raja is unlikely to anticipate us going underground. Between us, we have speed, strength and subterfuge. I can tunnel into the palace, and you have knowledge of the secret passageways that can take us to the prison. Leena and Grandfather can help with mapping the dungeons. We go together, Deven."

Mahi glowered. "Then let us vote. All those in favour of Kiya and Deven tunnelling to the prison to find out what lurks there?"

"Your wording is hardly neutral," said Deven, but he needn't have worried.

Leena, Aanya, Grandfather, Deven and I were in favour. Mahi voted against, and Nani abstained.

The seer rolled her eyes. "The vote carries. Does this generation of couples not vote against each other? The gods help us all."

Nani threw me a worried glance and tucked an errant strand back into her beehive. "Then we turn to the business of the sapling. It transpires I have many talented grand-daughters."

My sister's smile was pure sunshine as she palmed the table. The words sprouted from her lips like delicate shoots reaching for the light, thoughts spilling out unfiltered, the catharsis plainly evident. "The other night, I was horrified at what I'd done to that soldier. But I'd forgotten that a tree is a living organism. That soldier wasn't yet dead, at least, that's what Nani reminded me of."

Nani's eyes twinkled as if her joy for Leena had chased away the clouds of our disagreement. "Trees can survive without soil and water for a while. After I tended to the injured, I planted the sapling in rich soil and gave it water. By the time Leena and Aanya arrived, its leaves looked happier."

Aanya rubbed her undercut, her eyes full of wonder. "That's when the magic started happening."

My heartbeat thundered. From the glimmers of smiles around the table, it seemed everyone was in the know apart from Deven and me, although he remained deathly quiet. "He's alive? Did you use a spell? An elixir?"

"No, nothing like that. It had to do with my emotions. I think my powers surged as Harya flew me away because I was so scared for you, and that fear—I directed it at the nearest threat. I didn't even think about what I was doing. I just sort of released my pent-up fear. I don't know why I didn't produce a vine. I just, I directed my anger wholly at the soldier." Leena dragged in a breath, eyes full of wonder.

"And somehow, that anger died when I realised what I'd done. It kind of became love for a stranger. I'd robbed him of his essence, even in death. But his essence was still there, don't you see? When I saw the sapling again, I only had to touch him to sense him. He was like any other sick patient I've nursed. He was there, just in a different form."

My nails made crescent moons in my palms. We listened so intently that even Babbu stayed still.

"Somehow, I sensed the gentle thrum of life within the sapling, the way it was constructed, the veins and curl of its leaves. That it craved the sun, not the darkness of this house. I touched it, and my magic responded. The branches quivered in anticipation… It was a gift, Kiya… I envisioned the sapling's cells rearranging themselves, the slim trunk and leaves morphing to match the form of the soldier it once was. And it happened." She grinned. "The plant changed. Its form kind of elongated and broadened until it became the silhouette of a human that became more and more human and flesh again."

Nani shook her head in wonder. "The soldier was there, standing tall. Fully restored as himself."

The ear piercings on Aanya's cartilage chimed softly. "He's a little confused but entirely himself."

"Quite a sight to behold." Mahi folded her arms across her chest, but her eyes shone. "That young man is now locked deep in the bowels of my house. It seems there's no end to the strays I take in."

Babbu cackled in mirth. "I told you I could hear him. Lucky Yash. Not dead Yash."

I reached for my sister across the table, dazed. "I wish I'd seen it. I'm so happy for you. I'm so happy he's alive. That you're mastering your magic, and it reflects who you are."

"Leena's nature is bright and sunny, but some of us are made for darker work," intoned my grandfather. "Isn't that right, General?"

Deven's inky eyes narrowed. He looked only at the seer, although I willed him to look at me, and he had always felt a magnetic pull to my gaze. A vein in his jaw throbbed. "Where are you holding him?"

"The chamber of mirrors," said Mahi.

His mouth twisted. "Of course... Take me and Prakash to him."

My brow furrowed. He'd said we were in this together. "Deven?"

He kept his gaze fixed on the seer. "Don't let anyone in."

CHAPTER 19

The soldier who had been the sapling had been installed in an upstairs room in the seer's leaning, warren-like house, far away from where we would have been able to hear his clamouring. Leena and I exchanged a glance of mutual understanding and left Nani and Aanya in the council chamber. We followed the general and our grandfather up the narrow staircase behind the seer.

Every step took us closer to the howls of rage and despair.

We passed endless chambers. I glimpsed the library filled with book towers and strong-armed Leena past the green room with its withering plants. We passed the apothecary, meditation room, the heathen chapel with its ivy-draped altar, the room of open bird cages and another filled with curiosities from beyond the borders of the kingdom. The clamours and shouts made my heart seize. At the end of the long corridor, where the mothball air had grown oppressive, Mahi stepped aside with a grim nod, and the men strode past her into the chamber of cracked and whole mirrors.

Deven turned back. "Don't watch this, I beg you."

Then, the men went inside and locked the women out.

We were left standing in the narrow corridor, all sound blocked out, perhaps by the runes carved into the internal walls. We faced the polished obsidian door as if the glossy slip of its surface had been construed like Teflon to sanitise the monstrous actions within. A viewing panel of ruby stained glass was set into the door at eye level, but the seer muttered a spell that could have been *avarṇayāmi jyotiḥ* or *dhūmrīkṛta kara* or *andhakāra kara*. A spell that clouded the window. That tried to blind us to the transgressions happening within.

Fury cut through me, true as a winter storm. This wasn't who we were. We were better than this.

I glared at her. "No. Reverse that spell. We don't look away. Not when each of us has played a role in how that soldier came to be here."

"It is necessary," said Mahi, but she did as I asked.

They pummelled him with questions and their fists. When he didn't talk, they showed no mercy.

In the whole mirrors, the sapling soldier found reflections of his deepest fears, and the darkest corners of his soul laid bare. Shadows clung to the edges of the mirrors, whispering secrets of past traumas and future horrors, leaving him wide-eyed and slack-limbed with fear. Grandfather gripped him hard and refused to let him look away from the polished monstrosities. The fragmented mirrors showed him glimpses of alternate realities and distorted memories. Each shard, each macabre funhouse mirror, provided a piece of a disjointed narrative.

A kaleidoscope of confusion that led to madness. That led to the abyss.

We could make out some of it: the faces of fallen comrades, their accusing stares haunting him from beyond the grave; replays of bloody violence he had tried so hard to forget; an old woman—perhaps his mother—back bowed by her crippling loathing of him; a future scarred and hollow-eyed version of himself; a woman in the throes of rapture, riding a man who wasn't him.

Leena clutched my hand as his mouth contorted into pained shouts. We witnessed every silent scream and wordless plea. We read the shape of his agony in his expression and contortions and what they did to him. This eerie disconnect between sight and sound heightened our guilt. His head drooped from what they forced him to see in the mirrors and the turns they took grinding him down, bending his limbs in unnatural angles, dripping blood from him like he was on the chopping block at the butcher's and not somebody's son.

Even Mahi turned away then, as accustomed as she was to the brutality of the kingdom. Thin-lipped and miserable, she didn't explain why she had a torture chamber in her house or who had been held in it before and how often.

Grandfather let us see him from all angles, but Deven was careful to keep his back to the door. His posture was rigid, his shoulders squared, and though I searched for him in the mirror reflections, neither he nor my grandfather was featured there. I didn't know whether he was ashamed, feared me seeing him as a monster, or didn't want to lose standing in my eyes. I knew only that every fibre of my being warped, recoiled in horror at what unfolded before us, and that Deven teetered at the edge of a precipice I didn't know he could come back from.

"Why?" asked Leena. "Why did we keep him alive for this?"

Despair darkened Mahi's face. "All is fair in war. This is nothing compared to what some would do."

Leena vomited the undigested remnants of a clutch of cherries onto the floor. They looked so much like gore that she retched again. "Perhaps it might have been better if he had died after all."

I banged on the door. I could have opened it with a flick

of the wrist. I could have called a boulder or flint or an army of gargoyles. I could have dug in my mind for a spell or simply demanded entry from Deven and Grandfather. They loved me, and I would be their queen. They would have obeyed me.

But I didn't.

I hated that I didn't.

"His name is Yash Sharma," Mahi said quietly.

His eyes were grey like the morning mist. He couldn't have been more than twenty-two by the hollows in his reed-like frame, the pitiful, wispy moustache that was not yet a man's, and how he called for his father. That was the shape his mouth made—*father*—over and over.

They didn't take his fingers, his eyes, or his limbs. They didn't take his life, though they spilt his blood. But they took his peace of mind, his innocence and perhaps his sanity.

What broke me most of all was that when the general first walked into the room of mirrors, a smidgeon of trust bloomed on Yash's face. Like he had once served under him or admired him or heard tales of heroism. Like his saviour had come.

But it was the beast who had come instead.

My gut twisted with each claw Deven pushed into the sapling soldier, and I wondered if the general's genteel civility was a mask and if violence was his real face. If it was a worse crime to betray those we loved or ourselves.

EACH SECOND MUST HAVE SEEMED AN HOUR TO THE SAPLING soldier. When it was over, Leena took him to the apothecary, where she mopped his brow, cleaned his wounds and gave him a sleeping draught.

Then, the two of us walked outside to breathe in lungfuls of clean air. A winter mist lingered over the fortress like a forgotten dream. The wintry sun, its warmth feeble against the cold, struggled to penetrate the thick shroud. Within the fortress walls, the mist billowed like the breath of a slumbering giant.

Something didn't feel right out here, but why would it, after what we had seen?

Deven had gone straight from the chamber of mirrors to a meeting he'd called for women of the resistance in the courtyard. His shoulders sagged, but he tried his best to conceal his exhaustion, and there was a haunting bleakness in his eyes when they flicked to me.

But he had a job to do.

The women, especially, hung onto his every word as he spoke, not because of his handsome demeanour or his standing amongst them—though that was a factor—but because they were intrigued by what he had to say and why he had asked them to come dressed in comfortable clothing.

"Will you join the menfolk in taking up arms to protect our community?" said the general.

The women murmured amongst themselves, surprised by his request. For generations, they had been confined to traditional roles within the kingdom, tending to hearth and home while their husbands and grown sons carried out the physical labour. Their eyes widened as Ashwin and Yuvan carried out boxes of training equipment.

He continued. "We're facing a time of great peril, and I want you to be ready. I want us to be ready to stand together."

We watched, and I wondered if I should step forward and say something, even though my chest burned with what he and Grandfather had done to the sapling soldier. But it was enough when Lata stepped forward, whose agility and strength as a dancer would probably make her a more accomplished fighter than most men.

I remembered how she'd always wanted more for her life

than the box she'd been put in. She'd talked to me once about the constraints of courtly etiquette, about finding herself at court because her face was a flower, even though science was her passion. Looking at her now, she had taken off the mask of beauty, the diligent application of makeup that had made her the perfect rose. Instead, she was a wildflower and all the more beautiful for it.

Her smile was a jazz improvisation, an eruption of freedom and possibility. "I will join you."

Deven's sister and Tanay's mother stepped forward in quick succession, followed by Kavita, whose cackle of glee and waggling eyebrows I interpreted as an eagerness to sock it to her ex, who remained in the raja's camp.

Deven gave them a grateful nod and offered them a choice of weapons from the boxes. "Who else amongst you is willing to test yourself in new ways? To have the honour of protecting your children, your community, and your queen?" His words stirred the flicker of defiance that burned in the women. Defiance that had made them join the resistance in the first place and dream of a better world.

My heart cracked open as a significant majority stepped forward to accept his challenge.

Leena and I slipped past them, dipping our heads, hoping to go unnoticed. We passed another group that had gathered at the sorry branches of the sacred tree, chanting as if their prayers might hold back the rot, grieving like they might at a grave. Only then did I release my pent-up breath.

Leena hooked her arm through mine like she had done when we were carefree teenagers. A bubble of irony about the topsy-turvy nature of life made me pull a grotesque face before I closed my eyes, and hot tears welled behind the nebulous pink of my eyelids.

Neither of us talked. Neither of us could talk.

Eventually, I said, "Seeing the raja's cruelty is hard, but when it's us, it's unbearable."

"It wasn't us, though, was it?" Anguish painted her face. "I want to burn that chamber of damn mirrors out of my memory. That soldier… He flinched from me when I cleaned him up. Even after Grandfather and Deven, he was *trembling* because of what *my* magic did to him. But after a few seconds, he gave up. He was resigned to his fate, like a discarded rag doll. I was trying to help him."

"You did help him."

Deep breaths did nothing to cleanse the fire in my lungs. "Does it make you want to go home?"

"This is our home now. We weren't born into this ecosystem. We're the ones who can make it better. I have to believe that." She kept her voice neutral. "Does it change how you feel about him?"

We both knew she meant the general. After all, Grandfather's darker side was hardly a surprise.

"I don't know. Maybe."

"I like that he asked the women to fight."

"I do, too."

She sighed and leaned into my shoulder, and we walked like that for a while over cobblestone paths in labyrinthine corridors, through the cold and creeping mist, past dusky red rooftops shielded by the dingy overhanging fortress. Shafts of dim light filtered through ramparts, casting dappled patterns across the ground.

I gestured to the moss and ivy she had added to the earthen walls, softening and bringing colour to the original structure we had magicked. Vines snaked their way up the walls, their stems reaching towards the sky in a quest for more light. "When did you do those?"

She gave a soft smile. "At night, when Aanya and I need to be alone, we come out here and I make the building my canvas, and we look at the stars together, and I tell her about Boundless Bay. She says she wants to see it someday."

"You're making plans for the future. That's good."

"It's really good." A pause. "We're going to pull this off, aren't we?"

I nodded, swallowing hard. "I need to tell you something."

"Oh? Go ahead."

There was no couching it in less jarring terms. "Sitara's urn is still warm," I blurted out.

She spun to face me, eyes like saucers. "Sorry, what?"

"I adjusted it in the alcove when you went into Jalapashu, and it was warm. Not just lukewarm, warm like cocoa on a frosty morning. Like it was filled with embers instead of ashes."

"The studio can be stuffy, especially under the awning of the fortress. Maybe it was just the lingering warmth from your touch." Compassion filled her eyes. "You miss her so much. Maybe this is how your imagination is responding to your grief."

I bit my lip. "Leena, it was radiating its own heat from the inside out."

"Shit," she said. "Mahi said Sitara wasn't done with us yet, didn't she? We have to take this to her."

"Yeah, I guess we do."

"The urn's still at the studio?"

"Merlin's with it."

"Good... Promise me you won't get your hopes up. This could be anything. A trick of the mind or a weird trickle of sunlight into the alcove. I miss her too, but death is a natural part of life."

Her words left a bitter taste in my mouth. I'd buried the truth she'd unveiled in the labyrinth, but it bobbed up to the surface: she'd been ready to let Sitara go.

"I have to go." I hugged her goodbye.

"So do I." She clung to me for a second, and when she drew back, her face was serious. "You know, all three of us dealt with broken things in our own way. Sitara with archaeology, you with pottery, me with nursing. I always thought the perfectionist was Sitara, but maybe it's you. Only, people aren't perfect, Kiya, and this world is more cutthroat than ours ever was. Maybe you should forgive him."

My cheeks flushed red as she walked away to check on the sacred tree. Her parting shot stung, and I would have preferred comfort rather than honesty in that moment, but Leena had always told it straight.

Needing to be stronger to face the kiln and what awaited me there, I headed for the training room. The general showered before he came to me like he needed to wash away his sin or the evidence of it. He found me waiting to take out my frustrations on him, waiting to make him bleed, just a little, for what he had done to the sapling soldier.

For what he had done to us.

He approached the mat, where I was ready for him, my feet bare, a short sword in my grip.

Obsidian eyes glimmered. "Talk to me."

I shook my head. "No. Fight me."

"You've excelled at training. And on the battlefield. We don't need to do this, Kiya."

I lifted my sword, stubbornness flaring. "Yes, we do."

The general picked up a blade from the rack, choosing one smaller than mine, and I huffed with the audacity of it. "You're worried the line has blurred between man and beast."

"Yes." My blade met his, clanging like an unholy riot in my ears.

"The blurring is about control of the physical form, not about the emotions. I am myself, even in tiger form. Even then, I know right from wrong."

"It wasn't so long ago that you were being tortured by Prem, Qasim and Grandfather."

Sorrow flashed across his face, and something deeper-rooted: shame.

For a moment, I forgot my sword. "He served under you. I saw it in his eyes."

He cursed. "Mahi let you watch?"

"You said you cared about your men."

Deven winced, the expression so fleeting I might have missed it.

"Then why did you hurt him?"

"It doesn't sound pretty, little witch, even to my ears. He was an opportunity."

"Don't call me that," I said, though I liked it. Despite how it felt like an honour for a man as rigid as him to address me in that teasing way. My hands tightened around the hilt of the sword as a pearl of mirthless laughter fell from my lips. "Is it this kingdom that dehumanises you or its raja?"

His jaw tensed. "Prem would have enjoyed hurting him. You know I didn't want to do it."

I looked away. "Was it worth it?"

"For the information we got, yes."

He held my gaze, and we both knew he could have called me out for not intervening. But maybe he needed to believe in my innocence. Maybe I needed someone to be the monster for when I couldn't stomach the violence.

I didn't have any more words, so we got to work. He was so close I could smell the scent of his bergamot soap. Our swords clashed, and soon, I was covered in a film of sweat, though he wasn't. My muscles ached, but I didn't stop, and he didn't ask me to. He soaked up my anger, even when it continued to flow. When I nicked his arm with a sweep of my sword, beads of crimson dotted his forearm in a long line. The swell of remorse in me told me I still loved him.

Even though he was darker than I'd believed.

Even though his moral compass differed from mine.

We pretended normality when Deven's sister and brother-in-law peeked into the training room as if our sparring had naturally come to an end, even though we might have fought on. Deven took my sword from my hand, and I smiled politely at him. He replaced our weapons in the rack. Then he folded his arms and leaned against a mud-caked pillar, almost as if he was hiding the cut. Nisha held a spray of multi-coloured geraniums that couldn't have grown at the height of winter.

"I told her we'd find you here," said Ashwin. "Did she hand you your arse again?"

Deven arched a droll eyebrow. "Something like that."

Nisha didn't bother to greet her brother and kissed me on both cheeks, not caring that I was slick with sweat, and pressed the bouquet into my hands. "A thank you. For what you did for my little devil Ishaan. I love him so much. I don't know what I would have done…"

"How about my thank you? I *am* your brother," said Deven.

Nisha grinned. "I heard Kiya did all the hard work."

"Mahi thinks Ishaan should get a spanking," he replied. "I'm inclined to agree."

His sister rolled her eyes. "You see. That's why you're not getting any flowers."

Ashwin placed a hand over his heart and gave a slight bow. "We'll never forget what you did."

"It's okay," I said, despite the distance between Deven and me. "You're family."

Deven jerked his gaze to me but his expression was unreadable. At least to me.

Nisha gave us an assessing look. In their way, maybe she and Deven were like my sisters and I, or—to a lesser degree—like Mahi and Menon. As stoic and as careful as her brother was, she'd learned to read him like a book. She raked her eyes over the subtle shifts in his expression, the dullness in his inky eyes, the absence of the quirk in his sensual lips that was customary when he was with family. "Is everything okay between you two?"

Deven met her stare. "Why wouldn't it be?"

She shrugged. "You're tense." She bit back a whole lot more.

"Leave them be," chided Ashwin.

I buried my nose in the bouquet to cover up the awkward silence. "Where did you get the flowers?"

Ashwin's eyes crinkled. "Your sister made them."

I smiled. "Of course she did."

We said our goodbyes, and Deven refused my help with the nick on his arm, although his small smile told me he'd noticed I cared. The injury he'd sustained in the rose garden had healed so completely that I didn't fuss. My mind grasped for a conversation topic that didn't centre on us.

"Do you think I'm ready to face him?"

He stiffened. "I do. But I don't want you to."

"I know." My breath bottled in my chest. "It was good to see women take up arms."

Obsidian eyes glimmered. "Yes. It was… I could accompany you to the studio if you like. To check on Sindhuja."

"Okay." I cursed my traitorous heart. "You can fill me in on what you learned."

He bowed like I was already his queen. "With pleasure, little witch."

But when we walked out into the fortress, a deep foreboding gnawed at my insides. The heavy mist had mostly cleared, leaving only tendrils snaking in isolated pockets. I scanned the parapets and perimeter, my senses on high alert. The distant howl of the wind set my teeth on edge. My eyes darted from shadow to shadow, and Deven followed my gaze. The battlements were clear of their usual occupants. Emptiness stared back at me.

A shiver ran down my spine. "Deven? Where are the gargoyles?"

His jaw clenched. "Shit."

Questions swirled in my mind, each more unsettling than

the last. Even when attending Nani's therapy group, some gargoyles had manned the boundaries. Harya was meticulous in his planning. Their absence magnified the noon shadows that danced along the walls.

Heart thudding, I tuned into the gargoyle bond at last.

CHAPTER 20

The general gripped my hand. "Can you hear them?"

Closing my eyes, I heard her voice first in the landscape of my mind, like a solitary beacon in the sea of my thoughts. A guiding light in the night sky. *Mistress. Earth witch. Gargoyle queen.*

A sob escaped me, knowing she was well, that she'd survived her ordeal, the way I'd taken her apart piece by piece, that the kiln had released her at last. Her tone and voice were unchanged, and it gave me hope that her spirit and character had remained intact, even as her body had been constituted anew.

Our bond allowed her to track me. Not a second after her beloved voice had illuminated the corridor of my mind, she swept through a pocket of mist and landed in front of us.

Deven cursed softly. "Gods be with us."

"Sindhuja," I breathed.

I'd sketched her form a dozen times. I knew it as well as the lines on my palms. She had been short and squat, with her ridiculous fishtail, tiny limbs and parchment wings, and had crumbling teeth behind bulbous lips and bulging eyes that resembled polished citrine stones jutting from a weathered cliff face. Her eyelids were reminiscent of heavy stone slabs. She was awkward as a spider caught in its own web. But when she smiled, it was like a lighthouse in the misty gloom.

I have changed, she said as Deven looked between us in awe.

Indeed, she had.

She had undergone a subtle transformation. Her physique was marginally taller and more sculpted. Sinewy muscles rippled beneath the surface of her still-small limbs. The fish-tail retained its unique shape but now shimmered with a lustrous sheen as if it had been polished to perfection. Her parchment wings, once weathered and worn, now bore a slightly broader span and intricate patterns of ancient runes. Her diminutive frame was imbued with a newfound sense of presence. Gone was the pathos of her previous form: she now radiated a quiet confidence. She wore Leena's pink thistle in her hair.

Deven shook his head. "Incredible."

I reached down to hug her. "I was so worried."

She nodded. "That is why I fought my way through the flames back to you."

"Your gargoyle kin have fled the fortress, Sindhuja," I said.

She ground her teeth. "They are with Prem Kumar now."

"They have severed their link with me. I can't hear them."

"It is easier to sever a bond that is new than one which has lasted centuries."

"Why?" My chest constricted. "Why have they deserted us?"

"I told you once before, mistress. Gargoyles might be servile, but we have an internal world, too."

She had told me that, and I suppose Nani's therapy circle underlined that fact, but I hadn't thought it would come to this. Not when I most needed them. But then, that's the thing with internal worlds, they come to us like smoke on the wind, intangible and utterly ours, however inconvenient for other people, even queens. I had no right to ask the gargoyles to put their desires on hold for me. Just as I had no right to ask the people to do that either. They weren't here to serve or prostrate themselves before me; I was here to serve them.

Otherwise I had no business being their queen.

"So it's not my cousin's dark magic—his mind magic—that has enticed them to betray us?" asked Deven.

She moved her head slowly from side to side and even the once-grating sound of stone grinding against stone now seemed less abrasive, softer somehow. "The raja can't control the gargoyles with mind magic. That is the preserve of the gargoyle queen."

Deven's face was grim. "That means we have a fighting chance."

I bit my lip. "It means we have a day—perhaps two—to convince the gargoyles that if they serve me, there is no conflict between their duty and their desires. And we'll have to do it without being able to talk to them telepathically. When they're in the raja's territory."

Deven's eyes met mine. "I've always liked a challenge. And we have nowhere else to be."

I sighed. *Sindhuja, what about you? Are you with us?*

She flapped her stronger wings and rose into the sky, testing them and bounced back down to the ground with a vitality that belied her ancient origins. The imperfections of age had been erased. Where once cracks and fissures marred her surface, now there was smoothness and solidity. Every line and curve had been sculpted to perfection.

Rapture shone from her stony face. *Always. Can I show Leena now?*

Of course, I said. *Just promise me you won't let the gargoyles hear you. Let them think you are gone.*

DEVEN DIDN'T RETURN TO OUR QUARTERS THAT NIGHT, THOUGH he insisted that my job was to rest. Instead, he pored over strategy with Grandfather and ran through the night in his tiger form. He was the ghost of a whisper. The faint memory of a kiss dusted over my forehead at twilight or gentle hands tugging me against the hard, warm planes of his body as I slept. When I woke that morning, there was an imprint in the mattress where he had been, and I missed him.

After a brief talk with Grandfather, I wandered out into the courtyard, where a training session was in full swing, under the watchful eye of Deven, a handful of seasoned soldiers and reservists like Ashwin. Among those training were teachers, farmers, cooks, artists and traders—men and women—who had answered Deven's call to take up arms, their backgrounds as varied as the weapons they wielded.

Deven and his deputies demonstrated various combat techniques, and their movements were fluid and precise, guiding the novices through the intricacies of swordplay, archery and hand-to-hand combat. The sound of clashing swords and whistling arrows filled the courtyard, mingling with shouts of encouragement and instruction. The fighters drilled tirelessly, repeating the moves until they became second nature and their muscles burned with exertion.

Training together had achieved a marginal lift in their basic level of technical fighting skills. More importantly, their meekness had become steely resolve, and their sense of help-lessness had become a sense of unity.

In a corner of the courtyard, the children gathered, their faces alight with excitement as they watched the adults train. Though too young to join the ranks of the fighters, they weren't excluded from the preparations for the coming conflict. Though some, such as Ishaan and Tanay, yearned to join in the fight and were repeatedly caught shadowboxing and poking each other with wooden swords, Deven agreed only to survival lessons.

Sindhuja, Leena and Aanya taught the children how to disappear into the shadows and how to navigate the labyrinthine passages of the fortress if one avenue was blocked off. The children learned when to run away, when to hide and whose houses had the best hiding places. They learned how to work as a team and to watch each other's backs. They learned to stay warm, forage for food and tend to minor injuries. To the chagrin of the adults, they even invented a coded language to use between themselves.

Deven wasn't one to shout orders without getting his hands dirty. Clad in a grey T-shirt and a pair of well-worn sweatpants, his muscles gleamed with sweat as he wielded his sword. Its blade caught the winter light as he executed a swift parry and then another, deflecting the imaginary blows with practised ease. Then, in a seamless transition, he lunged forward, driving the point of his sword toward an imaginary foe. Spinning around, he performed a series of slashes and thrusts, first to the left, then to the right, each movement executed with a dancer's finesse.

He gave the novices a cocky smile. "If you can do half of that in a month, I'll be impressed."

He knew we didn't have a month, but he instructed the sword-carrying group to string together the first three moves and was patient when he was asked to demonstrate them again. Next, he called out instructions to the archers and made adjustments to the hold of one woman's bow, whose *dupatta* scarf was causing her trouble. Then, as if the universe had whispered in his ear that I was there, he paused midstride and locked eyes with me before coming to my side.

His lips twitched. "You could join us, you know."

"Next time, I promise." I flicked my eyes to the shadows beyond the courtyard.

A bead of sweat trickled down his brow. "You need me?"

My stomach clenched. "Yeah."

I filled him in then, and he understood at once, called a halt to the training and asked for the return of the weapons. Then I beckoned my court to my side. Leena and Sindhuja stood to the left of me, Merlin in Leena's arms, Deven and Mahi stood to my right. If anyone noticed the subtle differences in Sindhuja's appearance, they didn't mention it. The resistance gathered around, maintaining a respectful distance, a hint of reverence in their faces, as though we stood on a podium and not in the dust.

Grandfather and I had agreed to interrupt training in this manner to take advantage of when the bulk of the resistance had gathered in one place. It was best to deal with the matter openly, not because we craved a spectacle, but because transparency was important. I wanted the rebels to understand what had happened before we put the boot in.

Whispers swelled as Grandfather dragged the court poet to what remained of the sacred tree. The court poet was shorter and slighter than my grandfather, and it would have been easy to knock him to his feet, but instead, Grandfather allowed him to keep a smidgeon of dignity.

Grandfather's voice boomed across the courtyard. "I promised to root out troublemakers."

I kept my face blank like I had no knowledge of the matter.

The faces of the rebels gave me pause. There was something dark in their expressions, too: the thrill of the catch, barely hidden glee about the unsavoury turn fate had dealt Nitin.

"Nitin Gupta is a traitor," announced Grandfather. "The hole in our perimeter was his doing."

Jeers ripped through the courtyard like a tempest, voices gusting with indignation and contempt.

Pressure settled in my chest as I caught sight of Nisha and Ashwin's stony faces; Ishaan cocooned protectively between them. Tanay's mother stood next to them, whom the raja had bedded. Her arms were wrapped around her son's, and her trusting eyes never left my face.

It was a paradox that a poet could be capable of hurting us like this. Poets were supposed to be purveyors of beauty, sensitive souls, relentless in their pursuit of honesty and meaning. They were supposed to be champions of the underdog, challengers of the establishment, at the edges of society and not milking the fat of it. Artists fought with wordplay and wit, with canvases and colour, stages and performance, not with sabotage and trickery. Over the centuries, some had labelled them deviants, but only because they spoke truth to power and refused to conform to tradition. They weren't supposed to be deceitful, greedy, or hungry for conflict. But here Nitin was, clinging to the glimmering gold facade of Prem's corrupt reign like he was suckling his mother's teat.

It was a lesson that we all had dark impulses.

My sister nudged me, and Grandfather's quizzical look told me there was a rhythm to our exchange, like a song and dance, a question and riposte, a mirror and its reflection. I had a part to play.

I raised my hand to quiet the crowd's taunts and hisses. "What is the evidence?"

"The damage to the fortress wall through which the children escaped was not a natural occurrence. There was no inherent weakness in the wall, and it was not the result of forces applied by the sacred tree. On the night in question, in a matter of mere minutes, the court poet used a sledgehammer to breach our defences. I retrieved it from his quarters and have obtained signed eyewitness statements."

I exchanged glances with Leena in silent acknowledgement of how much he was enjoying this.

The crowd lapped up Grandfather's every syllable. At his nod, Yuvan dragged forward a sledgehammer. An older woman who worked in the kitchens and one of the black-smiths stepped forward next to him.

"Is this true?" I asked the kitchen help and the blacksmith.

"Yes," they responded in turn.

My lips tightened. This past week, the court poet had held my eyes for longer than was comfortable. I should have known better to mistake his arrogance for awkwardness. Known better than to misconstrue his presence amongst the rebels as the turning over of a new leaf. It's not like he'd been a natural fit for the resistance. He'd enjoyed the trappings of power and courtly life too much to fit in amongst everyday folk. He still wore his square-stone topaz necklace proudly, though, to many within the fortress, it marked him out as one of the elite, someone they couldn't trust.

But Nitin revelled in the differentiation.

"Have you anything to say for yourself?" I asked the poet, keeping my face expressionless.

Nitin gave me the sanguine smile of someone who rarely faced consequences. "For the old ways, my allegiance I declare. The new regime's allure I simply cannot bear."

"Dickhead," murmured Leena.

I'd once found his rhyming couplets mildly charming, if a little pretentious.

Now, they made me sick.

Fury made my body heat. The crowd was a sea of hostil-ity, and the air crackled with a desire for retribution. He'd put our safety at risk. Ishaan and Tanay could have been killed. Sindhuja had suffered, and I'd assumed the gargoyles had been derelict in their duty. All because of him.

Nitin stood defiantly before us. He didn't even have the grace to show remorse.

Not that it would have made a difference. I bit back the urge to cast a barrage of spells, to make the earth swallow him up, to rip regret from his smooth throat. It was so tempting to let my power smother my humanity. Especially when it was clear where his allegiance lay and that he'd been working for the raja. Instead, I simply said, "I take it that you're not denying the allegations?"

His chin lifted haughtily, dark eyes glinting with a cold indifference. Despite the anger swirling around him, he remained eerily calm. Anticipation gripped the crowd as they waited for the next verse to fall like a thunderclap. His words hung in the air like a gossamer veil, each syllable pregnant with the weight of magic. "In the embrace of tradition, my loyalty is bound. The rani's call is but an empty sound."

Not everyone was enthralled. Deven huffed out an impatient breath. "Give me strength."

But given long enough, his magic had the power to inspire, provoke thought, and persuade with the gift of a hundred orators. A tingling sensation danced along my skin.

"The poet is right. Where are the gargoyles?" someone called out.

"Gone to their master, Prem Kumar," said Nitin, and my mouth went dry.

The accusation held more power than the one against Nitin. It electrified the air like a live wire, sending alarm through the gathered rebels. Calls spiralled from certain pockets in the crowd, with the withered sacred tree as our backdrop: how we had misled the resistance about the chances of success, how the feat was impossible without the gargoyles, and we were doomed to fail, how I should hand myself over as a token of surrender so that the people of the resistance might be accepted back into the fold. Think of the children. Think of the old. Think of those who would continue to live under the cloud of the raja after the demise of the ringleaders. A calamitous loop of fear.

All I could think of was the pin-drop quiet in my mind without the intrusion of the whole gargoyle host. How I must have let them down somehow for them not to want to stay with me. How if the people found out the gargoyles were Prem's to command, they would fear a repeat of history. That those solemn, stone creatures would unleash themselves on the people. We would lose any chance of justice, any chance of renewal.

But the seer clapped her hands, and her parrot soared through the air, squawking for silence, before she said, "Then why is the Fishtail gargoyle here?"

It was enough to stem the flood of angst, but my heart drummed knowing the seer had bought us a temporary reprieve. It wouldn't last without the return of Sindhuja's ancient stone companions. I wondered how many within the resistance Nitin had already poisoned with his silver tongue.

A traitor couldn't remain in our midsts. We needed to make an example of him.

But I needed to be sure. I needed, for my own soul, to give him a way out, to try to understand.

"Did Prem Kumar make you do this with his mind magic?"

The poet's lips curled into a sneer as if he couldn't envisage anything I could say or do might leave him marked. As if his power and standing would always be his, regardless of what I did. "By my own volition, I chose my path. No spell nor charm led me to wrath." His gaze flicked to the banyan tree, and there was triumph there.

I thought back to our encounter with the raja outside the walls of the fortress, to his moving lips, to the calculating look in his glacial eyes. My eyes widened. "It was you. It wasn't Prem. Prem can't cast spells. He was distracting us from his proxy inside our walls. You. You poisoned the sacred tree. I bet my grandfather would find the evidence hidden in plain sight in your quarters."

Leena's usually soft brown eyes blazed. "What was it?

Nightshade? Hemlock? Belladonna? Arsenic? Some sort of chemical catalyst or biological agent to speed up the effect?"

He gave an affirmative blink, followed by a small smile.

Like he had nothing to lose. Like he wanted it to be known that he'd left his mark.

Like a damn dog pissing against a tree.

"Imbecilic fool," said Mahi.

His revelation lit the fuse of a powder keg. The crowd ignited, voicing their indignation in a cacophony of angry shouts. It had been a heinous act to harm their sacred tree. Cries of *traitor*, *blasphemer* and *sinner* echoed through the air, accompanied by curses and vows of retribution. The sanctity of their tree had been violated, and their fury knew no bounds. They demanded his penance, his punishment, his blood. The poet was unmoved by the barrage of censure, calls for his death and lamentations for the tree.

He only smiled. His pride and hubris still blinding him.

I met the general's inky gaze. It was unwavering, as if urging me that I was good and righteous, that I should trust myself. It bolstered my resolve.

We wanted—no, needed—the kingdom to be a haven of justice, but meting out punishments was not something I relished. But leaders didn't shirk their duty. Deven had offered to be the one to deliver the decision, as had Grandfather. I couldn't allow them to bear that burden. The responsibility was mine. Any backlash and reverberations were mine, too, otherwise, I didn't deserve to lead them.

I might not have a tiger's teeth, but I could bite.

"Let it be known that the breach in our defences was not the fault of the gargoyles. They are absolved of any blame." My words carried the weight of finality. "Nitin Gupta, you leave me no choice. Your words have incited unrest and sown seeds of discord amongst the resistance. Your artistry, once celebrated, is now a tool of chaos. You've betrayed your kin and put our children in harm's way. You're banished from this fortress, and should I win the throne, you won't be welcome on any inch of this soil."

I felt the crowd in the palm of my hand, and the power was dizzying.

Defiance flashed across his face. He rushed at me—and Deven moved to block me with his body—but Grandfather slapped the poet back like he was a street urchin, not a man who had dazzled the court his whole adult life. He reeled and spat his words, "I'll be welcomed back to Prem-*ji*'s side."

Deven's dark brow rose. "Will you? My cousin has very exacting standards, and I'm sure he expected you to cause more chaos than what you achieved." We had Aanya and Nani to thank for the community building and Grandfather and the gargoyles for enforcing the peace, or the damage Nitin had caused might have been much worse.

Nitin's eyes narrowed on the engagement ring on my middle finger. This time, he didn't speak in verse, and I thought maybe we'd breached his armour of indifference. "Tomorrow, you won't have a finger to wear his ring. He will take everything from you."

Mahi's forehead yawned to reveal her bright violet eye, sending my heartbeat into disarray. As if this was finally the green light we had been waiting for. As if she could guarantee our success. "Tomorrow, Kiya Marlowe will win the throne, and you'll have nowhere to hide."

The poet's smooth face crumpled, panic tinging it before it became an empty canvas once more. "Are you going to throw me out personally, rani? Do your worst." He craved validation and accolades, honour and prizes, pedestals and applause. Not the sting of humiliation.

I didn't deign him with an answer. My magic pulsed through every fibre of my being, calling for release. Calling for revenge. But there were others in Prem's camp who weren't loyalists but had stayed in Jalapashu proper for their own reasons, like the tailor Lokesh *Saheb*, who had been good to me and had trusted me with his secrets. I would want Prem to show restraint, were the tailor discovered, so how could I act any differently now?

For a moment, I allowed myself to revel in the hum of my magic before shushing it to rest. Then, I opened my bond to Sindhuja. *Transport him beyond our walls, where he can't trouble us. Do it swiftly but safely.* We wouldn't stoop to Prem Kumar's standards.

Yes, mistress. I will give him a ride he never forgets. Sindhuja's yellow fish-eyes sparked with malice as she stalked over to where Grandfather had collared Nitin.

The poet flinched as her wings began to beat in a furious rhythm. She needed less time to become airborne with the adjustments I had made. Just before she left the ground, she seized Nitin Gupta with her taloned claws. With a disdainful flick of her fishtail, she hoisted him into the air. He hung suspended, face contorted, finally wordless, an empty vessel devoid of purpose. As they ascended, Sindhuja's movements were jerky and ungraceful, as if she revelled in the opportunity to show her contempt. With a powerful thrust of her wings, she soared higher and higher still until she cleared the walls carrying her cargo of disgrace. A hundred pairs of awestruck eyes followed her progress. With a sudden and deliberate motion, she released her grip, sending the poet hurtling toward the ground below as if he were a mere plaything. Nitin's screams were lost in the rush of wind.

Babbu launched himself from Mahi's shoulder and spiralled into the sky for a bird's eye view.

I might not have seen what happened next, but something happened to the bond. Not only did Sindhuja's soft grinding voice sound in my mind—a solo voice now that the other gargoyles had severed their bond to me—I glimpsed the world through her eyes as Nitin Gupta hit the ground with a resounding thud and lay sprawled on the cold earth.

I blinked in surprise as Sindhuja returned to my side. *Our bond is stronger.*

Her stony facial flesh carved an adoring smile. *I told you I was changed.*

I don't think that particular talent was the pottery.

It is our friendship. We are friends.

Yes, we are, I told her and felt the glow through the bond, before arching an eyebrow at the slack-mouthed crowd. "Anyone else? Supporters of Nitin, please step forward."

"Go on," said Deven, mildly. "Make our day."

Was it fear, respect or hope that led them to stand statue-still and quiet their tongues?

"No one? Good," I said benignly. "You are forgiven."

But someone did speak up, after all. "My wife and I are no supporters of Prem Kumar or his acolytes," said a farmer who'd once complained about having to share his quarters with another family. "We had started to feel secure with the gargoyles' presence. Where are they, Kiya-*ji*?"

"They're risking their lives on a mission." The lie was effortless, like a dancer gliding across a stage. Because if the people believed we had lost the gargoyles, their fear, their knowledge of the gargoyles' bloody past would destroy every ounce of trust we had worked so hard to build. It would drive them back into Prem Kumar's arms.

Which was precisely what he no doubt intended.

"And you can't tell us of this mission?"

"No," I said. "No, I can't... Tell me, are you and your wife more satisfied with your living arrangements? I hear she continues to make *samosas* for your new friends."

His eyes widened like he hadn't expected me to remember what had bothered him or to care.

"Prakash Malini redistributed two of our guests the next day."

"He's quite the fixer." I paused. "I hope you can hold your trust a little longer."

Then I signalled Lata, who had been the raja's courtesan, and Kavita, who was a different woman without living under the shadow of her volatile husband. As agreed, they threaded through the rebels, embellishing facts, adding salt and pepper to stories about the escapades the gargoyles were embroiled in. They harnessed the power of rumours to lend credence to my lie.

To usurp the throne, I'd use the power of community in whichever way was necessary.

"Impressive," murmured Deven. He extended his hand. "Are you ready?"

I placed mine in his. "I am."

CHAPTER 21

The council gathered in the armoury as Deven and I made our final preparations for our mission to the kingdom's dungeons. We had rooted out and banished a traitor, but it was hardly time for euphoria. We were in deep trouble. The main host of the gargoyles had deserted us—that much was clear from their chatter through Sindhuja's link to them—and presumably, they now stood with Prem.

They tipped the balance of power wholly in Prem Kumar's favour.

Even if I managed to win the duel, he could attack the fortress. He had us in a pincer movement; we would be at his mercy. A coldness seeped into my bones. Unless I killed or maimed him. It was how the crown of Jalapashu traditionally changed heads, after all. Why would it be any different when it was my turn? It seemed impossible to escape the spiralling violence, to maintain any semblance of our humanity.

Oddly, every face around us was grave and pensive, apart from the seer's.

Leena and I had filled her in about the lingering warmth of Sitara's urn, and her eyes had lit up in a knowing way that terrified me, but she'd refused to tell us any more, saying only that some connections endured, even when space and time settled between them like an unbridgeable chasm. That some loves were so great that they stretched like taut wires across vast expanses.

Deven briefed the council, telling them what he'd already confided to me. "The soldier withstood our efforts out of some misguided sense of loyalty to Prem, but Prakash and I got it out of him in the end. The duel won't be behind closed doors as per tradition. It will take place at open court. At a ball."

I didn't take in the reactions around me but instead puzzled over the seer's mood. Deven had told me that Mahi's health didn't suffer when her gleanings came naturally. The consumption of the tea fuelled more of her magic, but it wrung her out. Nowadays, in the aftermath of her visions, she was like a balloon with all the puff gone out of her. As if all her bodily potential was funnelled to her mind at the expense of her general health. She suffered fierce migraines, and only Aanya's lilting singing could soothe her. But today, her eyes sparkled despite her slack body.

I wondered what insight the universe had entrusted to her when she'd said at the banishment that I'd win the throne tomorrow. I couldn't imagine how that could be true.

Her eyes kept darting to me as if she waited to confide in me. Maybe that was why she was harsh to Yuvan, who, though no longer Deven's manservant, insisted on preparing our armour for the mission.

"Leave, boy," she said. "You've no business being here."

Yuvan's head jerked up, a deer in headlights. He hadn't been listening anyway. He was too busy humming and buffing our armour to pay attention.

Deven paused his briefing, dark brows knitting together. "You speak out of turn, Mahi. Yuvan has my trust and backing. He's here out of friendship, not duty."

Within a heartbeat, Yuvan started up his humming again. He polished two lightweight breastplates designed to deflect blows and offer protection to vital organs without hindering movement. With a soft cloth in hand, he buffed away imperfections. Each stroke of the fabric brought out the lustre of the metal. For weapons, he prepared slender blades, chosen for swift strikes and easy concealment: short swords with sleek handles and keen edges, each one was polished to a gleaming sheen.

This was an intelligence-gathering mission. It required care and guile rather than speed or strength. As Deven would likely stay in human form, weapons were a necessity to be on the safe side, even though we'd be going to great lengths to avoid conflict. Merlin was accompanying us, and I was glad, not only for his talent with spells but for his keen senses. His acute hearing, sharp eyesight, and ability to blend into his environment and navigate tight spaces made him an invaluable ally.

"As I was saying, Prem's rewritten the rules." Deven's inky eyes darkened like shadows enveloping a midnight forest. "The duel won't be behind closed doors. It will be in front of the whole kingdom, the culmination of a night that begins with food and dancing."

"He really does excel himself at callous extravagance," I said drolly.

"What does he gain by having an audience for the duel?" said Aanya.

Nani sighed. "He'll parade the gargoyles. And that will be enough to turn the resistance against our cause."

"It's a message not to cross him. So no one challenges him in the future," said Mahi.

"He wants to humiliate Kiya and is certainly underestimating her," said Nani.

Grandfather grunted. "Or he intends to lure us out and quash us in one fell swoop."

"Prem enjoys subjugation too much to hurt his subjects en masse," said Deven. "Isolated acts of violence are more his modus operandi, especially as a form of control. It's far more likely that he's orchestrating a political manoeuvre to win back the favour of the people."

"Well, then we make sure the resistance doesn't waver in their support for what we're building together. While you're gone, we'll shore up relationships and figure out if there are any loose cannons," said Leena.

My chest tightened. "Either way, we can't attend open court without the gargoyles on our side. It's too dangerous."

"If serving you didn't make them happy, then who's to say Prem will be any more successful?" asked Nani.

"Perhaps they can be won back," said Leena.

"Perhaps," said Nani. "During the therapy sessions, they didn't have one common complaint."

The two of them were so hopeful when they looked at me that I tried to hide the rising pressure in my chest. The pressure that told me that dungeons were mine to infiltrate, the gargoyles were mine to win back, the throne was mine to take, the people were mine to save. When all I had ever been was a spoke in the wheel. Never the axle.

"You need to leave soon if you have any hope of returning before nightfall," said Leena.

"Your files had no further information about what we might find in the dungeons today?" I asked.

"I'm afraid not." Grandfather shook his head, then said to Deven, "May I have a private word?"

They moved away, and I gravitated to the seer, who sat in a corner, kneading her temples as if they throbbed like the relentless march of an army. She stood as I approached.

"You had a gleaning," I said.

She nodded. "I tried to block you from going, but maybe your faith will restore my own in Menon."

I had to ask. I had to hope. "Have you had confirmation

that it's not a trap? That I'll win the throne? That we'll survive, and the kingdom will prosper?"

Her face shuttered, and I regretted my spitfire questions. I should ask her one, or none at all, after all her warnings about the fallacies of visions and how there wasn't one fixed future. But vulnerability meant I couldn't just let it go. I needed reassurance.

It didn't come. I thought only of how she had toyed with me in the past. How she had manipulated the resistance into thinking I would win because belief—even empty belief—had its value, fuelling action for a time until a person was strong enough to accept the truth.

"Authenticity is everything. I can only tell you this." Mahi gripped my arm. "There'll come a painful choice for you today. You must take the path you're instinctively opposed to. It won't be easy, but there is no other way."

My heart raced, an anxious flutter beneath my ribcage. "A painful choice?"

"The sort that Prem Kumar would never make. A choice that serves the greater interests, not your own. Remember, Kiya, nothing worth building is ever easy."

I moved away when Deven beckoned me, saying only, "Ask Aanya to sing you to rest."

By now, Yuvan had made final adjustments to our gear. He carried it over to us and presented the items with a respectful nod and quiet pride. Deven and I had dressed in supple, matching black leathers. Our feet were clad in sturdy boots fitted with steel toe caps that offered reliable traction in rocky caverns or slick dungeon floors. We stood side by side as Yuvan helped dress Deven, checking the straps and buckles, ensuring a snug yet comfortable fit. Leena emulated him, fastening the breastplate to me. When she was finished, she handed me the dagger I'd loaned her and watched as I strapped it to my thigh.

She kissed my cheek. "I hope you don't have to use it."

Grandfather scowled to one side as though berating himself for not knowing what lurked in the dungeons.

Nani clutched me. "Come back to us."

We made a quiet exit from the fortress, leaving Sindhuja behind to guard it. It was easy enough to slip past groups of assembled rebels discussing the day's events with the help of a vanishing spell. *Adṛśyatāṁ dadātu. Adṛśyatāṁ dadātu. Adṛśyatāṁ dadātu.* I uttered the spell three times—once each for me, Deven and Merlin—and it built in power enough to make us disappear from plain sight. Its vowels were smooth and fluid. They carried a sense of openness, like the vast expanse of wintery sky stretching out above us. Its consonants were solid and defined, each one leaving a distinct imprint on my palate, like the rough edges of a stone worn smooth by the passage of time.

"I'll never get used to witchcraft," muttered Deven, and I thought how courageous it was for him to choose me when sorcery had for so long taken half his identity from him.

Mahi had warned us about the spell's effects. A tingling sensation prickled along my spine and spread out to my fingertips like a cool breeze sweeping my innards, and a strange feeling of detachment came over me that I didn't like at all. As if I was disconnected from my body. The world around me faded, colours becoming muted. We'd slipped through the cracks of reality and could only be seen by each other, but there was no telling how long it might last. Mahi thought perhaps six hours, which was why the spell had been unsuitable for Deven and Leena's foray into the rose garden to speak to Menon.

With any luck, it would last long enough to break into the dungeons and return to the fortress.

After what had transpired with Nitin, it was all the more important to keep our cards close to our chest. As agreed, Sindhuja soared around the perimeter of the fortress, executing sharp turns and sudden dives. Her aerial manoeuvres distracted from my opening of the fortress door, and we squeezed through the crack unnoticed before my magic sealed the entrance again.

Our trio crossed the terrain outside the fortress, hugging the tree line and talking in murmurs. We carried water but no food. We didn't plan on staying long enough for hunger to be a concern. The air was crisp and biting, each breath sending plumes of mist into the wintry landscape. The scent of pine needles mingled with the earthy aroma of decaying leaves. Branches creaked in the cold breeze, and occasionally, the soft thud as snow fell from boughs.

Merlin raced off, and in the delighted spring of his body, I recognised how much he'd sacrificed while he'd stayed at my side in the fortress. He hopped through the frost-kissed grass, full of the same boundless energy that marked his springtime romps. Each leap carried him further into open fields, and I didn't call for him, though he left a trail of footsteps. His ears twitched at the slightest sound, swivelling to catch the faintest rustle of leaves or the distant call of a bird. With each bound, his hind legs propelled him forward over pooled shadow and lemony light, sending him sailing over patches of icy ground. His whiskers quivered, sensitive to subtle changes in the air, and his nose twitched, drawn by hidden treasures beneath the snow or the scent of prey stirring in burrows.

I marvelled at how happy he could be amidst the chaos we endured.

Deven scouted ahead of me at times, serious and alert despite the invisibility spell. My eyes lingered on the snug fit of the leathers across his buttocks and thighs, the easy swing of stride and the open-palm hands never more than an inch away from the hilt of his short swords. Although we were a breath away from danger, I felt safe with him beside me. He'd mapped out where troops patrolled and where houses stood empty. For a time, it would be possible for us to stay above ground, but as we got closer, we'd be approaching the dungeons via tunnels of my making. The plan was for me to only tunnel if necessary, so I didn't overtire myself when every ounce of energy might count in the duel.

A few hundred yards from where we'd agreed it was safe to start, on the ranch belonging to his sister and brother-in-law, with the hare hopping across the meadow, he stopped at winter jasmine that stood out against the bleak tones of the winter landscape.

"I've always loved this bush." His warm breath clouded the cold air, and his brow furrowed.

I laid a hand on his chest. "What's wrong?"

He darted a glance at the delicate yellow blooms that defied the season's chill. He reached out to touch a flower as though marvelling at its resilience. "I guess I'm still smarting at the fact you didn't nominate me as your champion to fight the duel in your stead. Don't get me wrong. I respect your choice, but it's still hard... If he harms you–"

"He won't."

"–don't expect me to let it stand. To let him get away with it."

I breathed in deeply, taking in the faint scent of the jasmine mingled with the crisp winter air. "Those are the rules of the land. You're a soldier. You have to abide by them."

He tipped my chin up. "I couldn't give a flying fuck about the rules of the land when it comes to you."

For a man who used to follow orders, he was now ripping them all up.

I swallowed hard. "Come on."

We went the length of a field, where he said Ishaan had learnt to ride, and called Merlin to us at a spot between two tall oaks, where fallen leaves could mask the entrance to my tunnel.

"Whenever you're ready, little witch," said Deven.

The hare's liquid gold eyes willed me on. "She's an artist, not a performer."

I deepened my breathing, grounding myself to the earth, and it was as if the soles of my boots disappeared and my feet touched the earth. Magic brimmed as the ground yielded to my will, parting like a curtain to reveal hidden depths. With tulip movements of my hands, I shaped the soil and stone. The earth compacted and solidified to create sturdy passageways that stretched out like veins. That made Merlin chirp with pride. That made the general curse under his breath and made him murmur over and over again how magnificent I was.

We stepped in.

The work was slow and required patience, and I wasn't sure I could hold out. Perspiration pooled under my leathers, and even the lightweight breastplate was too restrictive, too warm, and the air too dense. But my discomfort was worth it.

Slowly, tunnels opened up before us as we walked, their walls smoothed by my magic and ceilings supported by sturdy pillars of rock. Deven traced our path with a torch, and Merlin leapt alongside us as I worked, but the earth's secrets were only for me. It revealed hidden passages and forgotten chambers to me. It relinquished its integrity so I might have temporary sanctuary in its embrace.

The general found that his maps of the kingdom and the palace were unnecessary when I sensed vibrations of footsteps above and echoes of voices carried through to the tunnels, disclosing whether we were beneath a family home, a temple, army barracks, a bedroom chamber or the palace kitchens. Finally, mercifully—once I'd bored a deeper avenue in the network of my tunnels—we found ourselves beneath the palace dungeons and, thereafter, at its iron-clad, northernmost chamber. The hare scuffled at our feet.

Deven switched off his torch, and for a moment, we stood in the darkness.

"This is it. Break us in, and then you let me go first."

"Okay," I said into the dark, hesitating.

He leaned his forehead against mine. "You've got this."

I breathed in the warm, spiced scent of him. "Who or what do you think is in there?"

He drew one of his short swords. "Let's find out."

Then I closed my eyes and summoned my magic. Its primal energy, bolstered by my tunnelling, flowed through my veins like molten lava. Focusing my mind, I extended my senses, reaching out to the elemental forces in the very stones of the dungeon walls and their iron coating.

Gradually, almost imperceptibly at first, the metal trembled, groaning in protest, resisting my efforts. Gritting my teeth, I poured more magic into my efforts, palms flat, fingers pulsing, stretching, hooking, pushing with all my might as I worked to infiltrate the chamber's defences. Blood trickled from my nose from sheer exertion. I felt the tang of it on my tongue. With each passing moment, the pressure mounted, threatening to overwhelm me.

"She's pushing herself too far. Do something, Merlin."

"Listen to the whispers of nature around you," said Merlin. "Let the earth tell you where the chamber is weak."

Determination overrode any sense of caution. With renewed vigour, I channelled every ounce of will into expanding the net of my magic, testing, sensing, and feeling where the dungeon was at its most vulnerable. There it was, a tiny chip in the coating of the floor of the chamber. I pushed harder there, balling up my magic so it was a grenade, a canon, a battering ram, a tidal wave. One last surge of power and the iron coating cracked. It yielded to the force of my magic and exploded inwards with a deafening clamour. Exhilaration whipped through me, and my head spun.

Time stood still.

Deven grabbed both me and Merlin and dragged us back.

The iron-clad walls peeled back like the layers of an

onion, suddenly, almost as if it hadn't been difficult. As if my nose wasn't bleeding and my heart wasn't pounding clean out of my chest. As if it had been easy after all.

My hands still crackled with residual energy as the dust settled, and Deven released the hold on my waist. I gave a tired smile. "I could try banks next."

"I think you'll find as queen you'll have no need for that," said the hare.

Deven ran a thumb under my nose, wiping up the blood. "Can you go on?"

"Yeah."

"I can do this bit without you."

"Not a chance." I crouched down to Merlin. "You know what to do. Circle back here afterwards, just in case we're walking into the lion's den and need you."

"Good luck." He branched off from us, hopping back the way we had come.

Deven's voice was low, barely audible. "Okay. Hurry. We may well have triggered an alarm. Mental shields up."

Clutching his sword, he ventured through the gaping hole I had made. I became Deven's shadow, mere inches from the dull glimmer of his back, taking care to avoid the debris I had caused. Technically, the invisibility spell would protect us enough to confuse any assailant, even if they had a keen nose and teeth eager for flesh.

The chamber was small, perhaps four by four metres, and the air was thick with dust, decay, the putrid smell of human waste and the cloying scent of cigar smoke. Darkness seemed to swallow the feeble light that filtered in from the corridor. We felt our way with careful steps over the wrecked stone and iron. We were too cautious for torchlight or spells to illuminate our path, and our hands splayed out before us lest we stumble and fall or crash into some monstrosity. My ears pricked, straining to pick up on a beast's whimper or the breathing of a prisoner.

The silence was so deep that I thought maybe we'd drown in it and never find our way back.

Goosebumps prickled my skin, but I heard nothing untoward.

Until a thin voice, wrapped in malice and delight, whispered, "I've been waiting for you."

CHAPTER 22

The stranger's laughter wasn't the easy laugh of children in playgrounds or women in the company of beloved friends. It was more pained than that. It was laughter caked with phlegm.

"Marco. Polo. Marco. Polo," he said.

A shiver chased up my spine. He could see us—or sense us—despite the invisibility spell. I spun in the direction of the glowing ember of a cigar, a small point of fiery orange that pierced the darkness like a miniature sun. Too late I realised that there might have been a sensible reason why this prisoner had been condemned to rot in the dungeons. Maybe we shouldn't have forced our way in. Maybe the iron cladding shouldn't have piqued our curiosity.

It should have sent us running.

A growl laced Deven's voice as he lit his torch. "Stay back," he said to me–or the prisoner. He swung the beam of torchlight until it centred on the stranger.

The man sat on a dilapidated mattress and leaned against a putrid wall. His amber eyes resembled the hue of aged whiskey and flickered like candles. His gaunt frame was clad in threadbare grey robes, and it had been some time since he'd had a shower. The stench made my stomach heave. He didn't give the impression of a formidable foe, but Deven let out a string of curses that made me reinforce my mental shields.

Deven's lips parted, his face frozen in disbelief. "It can't be. You died long ago."

"Yet here I am." Blue smoke from his cigar curled around the stranger like a serpent. "Say my name. It's been so long since I have had the pleasure of hearing it."

Deven snarled. "Meet Kaladhar. One of Jalapashu's founding fathers. Don't let him touch you."

I squinted at the stranger, recognising him from one of the pictures in *A History of Jalapashu* that Merlin had stolen for me when I first arrived in the kingdom. He had mere wisps of hair, a wide forehead, deep-set eyes that held a marked sadness, and an impossibly long salt-and-pepper beard that ended in unruly waves at his concave chest. His nails curled at the tips like talons, dirt and grime wedged beneath them. There was no doubt we had found what Menon had been so eager to point us towards.

I did the maths. He definitely should not have been alive.

Deven orbited the room with his torch beam, just briefly, before returning to Kaladhar. He'd been made to live like an animal. There was a basic toilet in the corner, splattered with waste. The iron door was bolted from the outside. A tattered mattress lay on a cot, half chewed by who-knows-what creature. There was no chair or lamp or books. Nothing to while away the time. But even without basic needs, it was the smell that really struck me. Oh god, it reeked. A putrid blend of mildew, mould and tobacco clung to the very walls of the chamber, mingling with the acrid tang of urine and faeces. A rat skittered across the cold stone floor as it searched for remnants of food.

My skin crawled, and my hand hovered at my dagger. *Don't let him touch you.* "What's the nature of your magic?"

Kaladhar's lips spread into a gruesome smile. His teeth were stained a sickly yellow, the enamel corroded and pitted from his tobacco use. "I would rather not say, lest I scare you away."

Every muscle and sinew of Deven's body was on high alert. "He siphons magic. Only shifters are immune."

Kaladhar's tar-coated lungs made him rasp. "I am discovered. I had so wanted to play games."

"We tire of games." The hair on my nape rose. "How can you see us despite our cloaking spell?"

His cigar sizzled. "As the gentleman suggested, I am quite the collector of magic. But I have no reason to use it on you." Then why did I feel the scrape of his nails against my mental shields?

"Disease, not age, has ravaged you. How are you not dead?" Deven's short sword was still drawn as a precaution.

"Magic can warp the natural lifespan, depending on the nature of it."

We had to keep our heads. Why, why had Menon sent us down here? My mind rushed to make the connections. So, the iron coating served as a barrier to contain Kaladhar's abilities, preventing him from sapping magic from those who came into contact with him. Had he initially been imprisoned because he had drained Jalapashans of their magic, or had they feared him being capable of it?

He blew out rings of smoke that made my eyes water. "What stories did they spin about my demise? For all my knowledge, that has eluded me. Did they feed the fervour of gossip-hungry tongues? Spread whispers of sinister plots and clandestine betrayals? Was there talk of arcane curses and vengeful spirits? Was I the villain or the victim of the tragedy? A founding father deserves that much, at least."

"There were conflicting accounts," said Deven. "The first chronicler said you had an encounter with a malevolent flock of sentient seagulls. The second said you ingested a toxic poison, which unleashed a torrent of severe diarrhoea."

Kaladhar's shoulders slumped. "Then the world is as it ever was, and truth is as malleable as clay." He stubbed out his dying cigar on the mattress and lit a new one, and the flare of phosphorus from his match gave his bearded face an eerie glow. A slight breeze flowed into his cell from the tunnel I had excavated, and his crooked nose twitched slightly as he took in the fresher notes, swamped beneath his usual stench, before raising the cigar to his lips.

My eyes narrowed. "Who brings you those?"

"My wife once deemed them a repulsive indulgence. I dare say she had a point. Yet, I find myself unable to part with them. It's not solely the smoky sweetness I rely on or the light they provide in the darkness. They evoke memories of shadowy taverns and hushed confidences from an era when I held sway in this realm. When I wasn't merely a pawn. You might have surmised that smoking so many would put me in a grave." His phlegmy chuckle reverberated around the cell. "It's one of life's little ironies."

"This isn't getting us anywhere. Answer the lady's question, or we're leaving," gritted out Deven.

I shook my head. "It can't have been for nothing."

"You would be wise to heed her counsel." A puff of blue smoke. "I never liked military men. Too solitary and serious. I'd hoped my next visitors would bring the gift of conversation. The quiet sits so heavily. The guard, though dutiful in bringing my meals, is incapable of verbal exchange."

"Praveen, who brings you the cigars?" I repeated, using the first name I remembered from the history textbook.

His unnaturally amber eyes glittered as he looked at me —making me wonder if they'd adapted to the darkness. Making me wonder if he was still a physical threat, given the state of his body. "Perhaps enduring the squalor and solitude for an eternity has been worth it after all. You're quite remarkable."

Deven nudged me towards the exit, not taking his eyes off the sorcerer. "No more."

"Don't go." Kaladhar leaned back his head against the cell. "Perhaps I could have been more candid. Once in a blue moon, I receive visitors other than the guard. Typically, there comes a time in the reign of raja or rani, unless they get themselves killed, when they ask for aid in cementing their power. Relinquishing the crown is not something that the rajas and ranis of Jalapashu readily accept. That's why they haven't allowed me the mercy of death."

"Did Prem bring you the cigars in exchange for your help?" I asked.

His body was crumpled, but his amber eyes held the fierceness of a hunting hawk. "He did."

Deven shot me a glance, moving so close to me now that his thigh was pressed against mine. "Menon said it wasn't about *what* magic Prem has obtained, it was about *how*."

I sucked in my breath. "You're not just a siphoner of magic. You can regift the stolen magic to those who seek it. That's why they keep you in here. That's why Prem Kumar has mind magic."

Deven's curses rung through the air, sharp and biting. His jaw was clenched so tightly, guilt written so large on his face, that my heart ached for him. Prem would be satisfied ruling over a kingdom of puppets, and Kaladhar had given him the power to do it. Yet, it was Deven who blamed himself for his complicity in Prem Kumar's regime.

Kaladhar nodded, and his talons scraped against my mental shields. "I did. He can control the mind of not just one person but an entire kingdom. But I'm not a monster. I only allow them to choose one from my arsenal."

As if limiting the magic gifted made it any better. There were so many in this kingdom who deserved to explore their magic more than Prem Kumar. People who would do good, who had been kept at the lower ranks of this society just because he deemed them unworthy. Not only did he guard the topaz—the precious resource of the gemstones that had already been mined—but he had stooped to such depths to glut himself on even more magic. Not to improve the Jalapashan way of life but to shore up his own self-interest.

Deven's tone was bleak. "So we stop the mind control by killing Prem."

Kaladhar's amber eyes reminded me of a snake's. His words carried the weight of grim revelation. "That would not help those already being controlled. Once engaged, mind control is established, even beyond Prem's death. It needs to be broken before his fate befalls him."

I gave a slow shake of my head. Sweat pooled beneath my leathers and the breastplate. "All this time, you've lived in myth. The myths of the rajas and ranis so anointed by the gods that their powers grew. Yet, no one knew it was you."

Amber eyes warmed. "Say my name. Please."

"Praveen Kaladhar," I said, though maybe he deserved the ignominy for all he had done. But not the degradation. No one deserved decades, perhaps centuries, of degradation. My mind reeled like a kite caught in a sudden downdraft. "Why? You are Prem's captive. Why would you help him? Why would you help any of them?"

His exhale was accompanied by the soft hiss of cigar smoke as it escaped his lips, rising in lazy spirals. "For stories."

I frowned. "For stories?"

"I have been severed from the world, ensnared in this dungeon, and stories brought me..."

Deven's brow furrowed, and his silver scar glinted in the torchlight. "Comfort? Connection?"

"Information." Kaladhar's amber eyes flitted to me, and my fingers flared over my dagger again.

My stomach pitted. "Is it the throne you desire?"

Blue smoke billowed. "No."

"Then have you found the information you need?" I asked.

He gave a casual flick of his cigar, spraying embers on his robes. "I have. It involves you."

Unease rippled through Deven's body. "Speak quickly, or that smoke will leave your body with your final breath."

"Prem Kumar has been very forthcoming. I know about three sisters who came to the kingdom to reclaim their heritage. I know them to be modernisers, truth-seekers, extraordinary witches. Most of all, I know of their bond. And what I've found is that bonds like those, like your parents', Kiya Marlowe, are hard to sever. Especially in a kingdom of magic." His talons scraped against my mental shield. "Where is your eldest sister's urn? Where are Sitara's remains?"

Deven snarled. "Prem had no right to tell you those things."

Fear that tasted like ash on my tongue. "What do you want?"

Kaladhar shifted on his mattress, looking out beyond us to the tunnel. "What I yearn for is respect and release. Do you think you could bestow those gifts on even someone as wretched as me? In return, I will give you a way to overcome Prem Kumar's mind magic. I've spent almost my entire existence in this game of rajas and ranis. I am tired."

"We can't trust him to fulfil a bargain with us." Perspiration gleamed on Deven's forehead. He tensed. "Why haven't you used this opportunity—your cell wide open to the kingdom—to escape? Your magic is likely a match for ours."

"My magic is a match for anyone." The sorcerer's amber gaze took on a hollowness in the torchlight. "Escaping this dungeon is not what I meant by the word *release*. When I was a free man, I siphoned the people's powers, one by one. Some might say this dungeon was punishment enough. But my disease-ridden body has absorbed so much magic that I might live an eternity."

"Praveen," I said, and his eyes jerked to me. "You wish to die."

Another of his cigars burned out. "It has been an age since someone ventured in here with a weapon. They don't know that I cannot die. Neither by an ordinary blade nor ordinary means."

The air was stifling, and my palms clammy. "You want us to kill you."

"Yes." There was such hope in that one word. "I want *you* to kill me. And your sister's ashes are the way to do it. They are still warm?"

I nodded, and the way Deven looked at me—with such sympathy and compassion—was almost my undoing.

"Good. You see, she has not yet fully departed. Call it limbo or unfinished business or the enduring love of a sister. And because she lingers, when you wield the blade, her spirit can take me with her." He rolled a cigar between his fingers almost lovingly as if he knew that the vice was not his to indulge for much longer. "A virtuous spirit and a malign spirit depart together. That way, I can slip the chains of this body and the balance of the world is kept."

My heart wrenched. If Sitara's warm ashes meant that she wasn't gone, it meant she could come back to us. And I wanted her to come back to us so damn much.

Uncertainty tinged Deven's whiskey tone. "You don't have to agree to this. We'll find another way."

A painful choice, Mahi had said. *Your sister is not done with you yet.* "Don't I?"

It's not like we could leave Kaladhar alive to be used and to abuse. He was far too dangerous. If he wanted to die, who were we to deny him that? It meant that future rajas and ranis couldn't cheat the system. They couldn't remain on the throne, pretending they had bested challengers legitimately.

Besides, if Kaladhar gave me the key to stalling Prem Kumar's mind magic, I would have a fighting chance against him.

But what if I was giving up the chance to get Sitara back? What if I could have my sister back in my life, at my side? Her wisdom, her love, her protection. What if that was a possibility? What if life and death weren't finite in Jalapashu but something that could be negotiated, rewound and played again? What if there was this glorious reward to make up for all the heartache and all the sacrifices we had made?

My breath snagged. "Why me? Why do you want me to wield the blade, Praveen?"

"A rani-in-waiting needs to understand violence. Violence against herself and others."

I met his eyes. "Why haven't you tried to siphon my magic?"

"You showed me respect. You said my name." My pulse pounded in my ears as he eased himself off the creaking mattress, shuffled through the bloom of blue fog and extended a taloned hand. I wondered if Kaladhar really was decrepit and what he could do with his magic. "Is our bargain struck?"

"Kiya…" warned Deven, but we both knew there wasn't enough time and that sometimes even mighty generals and the queens they served struck bargains on a wing and a prayer.

His body coiled, and I thought he might slash Kaladhar's throat to prove the validity of the sorcerer's claims. To prove that an ordinary blade couldn't kill him. To prove there was no other way forward except to break my heart.

Until I locked eyes with him. "It's okay."

I swallowed the bubble of guilt and revulsion in my throat and accepted the sorcerer's outstretched hand. An icy chill gripped my spine, even though the air stifled me and I was damp with sweat.

He didn't siphon my magic; he merely folded my hand into his, his touch surprisingly reverent. Even though he hadn't taken from me, something snaked between us—a searing, a binding, an invoking—something I knew would punish me if I broke my promise. "Is it struck?"

Would I be capable of killing a man simply because he asked me to? Was violence where this kingdom eventually led all its rulers? Was it the only way to take the throne and stay on it? I shut down those thoughts, just as I shut down the thoughts of Sitara—for now—and focused on how to thwart the raja. "Yes, Praveen. Our bargain is struck."

Kaladhar shuddered with pleasure rather than regret. "Then you are my end and my salvation."

"Tell me how to take back what you gave to Prem Kumar."

"Listen carefully, rani."

CHAPTER 23

Relief made my bones slack as we left the sorcerer's cell and returned to the tunnels.

Deven remained vigilant, not turning his back on Kaladhar. "We have to lock him in again."

"No." Kaladhar coughed. "You must leave a small hatch open for me. I won't leave until the time is right, but I won't be imprisoned again."

"Kiya–" warned Deven.

"You can't trust someone a little bit. It doesn't work like that."

I raised my hands—ignoring amber eyes looming through curls of smoke—and sealed up the dungeons as best I could, leaving a small section open as requested. Rubble and metal peeled up from the ground, creaking, groaning, straining my magic until my breath came in gasps. When my magic was spent, the seams of the dungeon were not neat: fissures allowed thin streams of light to filter through. But the guard wasn't due to return until the following day and, therefore, we wouldn't be discovered.

Not before our plan had come to fruition.

I didn't collapse the tunnels; we might need them again.

Thoughts reeling, we trudged back the way we came, underneath the palace kitchens and bedrooms and the houses of ordinary people who just wanted to live their lives. The general threw me concerned glances, but we both needed light and oxygen and the sight of a canvas of blues above us to feel human. We made it back to his sister's ranch, a stone and timber structure with a veranda wrapped around its front looking over a clutch of fields and a stable block.

Taking care not to be seen, Deven led me through the fields to the veranda, where he retrieved a hidden key from under a plant pot. The lock clicked, and he let us into the house. He paused in the hallway, with its wooden panelling and muddy boot rack, and released a pent-up breath.

I looked up at him. "What about Merlin?"

"I told him we'd be coming here."

I nodded numbly. He placed a hand on my lower back and steered me into Nisha and Ashwin's living room. Maybe it was the handwoven rug, the colour of the sunset on the floor, the stone fireplace topped with photographs of their cherished son, or the rustic charm of the tapestry on the wall and the cosy sofas. Or maybe it was the quiet desolation of an empty house, the long shadows across empty rooms, the too-plump cushions on the couches and dust motes dancing in the still air.

But something in me broke.

My clothes, armour and weapons dragged me down, suffocating me, and my breath came in quick, thin bursts. Only then did my knees give out. I sank to the rug, uncontrolled and untethered. The landing would have been a hard one had Deven not scooped me up and placed me on the flowery sofa. He removed our weapons and put them on the rustic coffee table, and when he turned around, I was clawing at the straps of my breastplate, my fingers too clumsy to untie the knots.

He stilled my hands and said gruffly, "Let me."

My body gave up its struggle as he worked the straps, pulled the breastplate over my head, and then removed my boots, socks and damp leathers. His mouth was a grim line as I shivered in the cool air of his sister's living room, and he wrapped me in a throw. When the chattering of my teeth continued, he stripped off his own armour and clothes and held me against the beating heart of his chest until my breathing eased at last and the goosebumps dimpling my skin faded. He disappeared for a few minutes then, and when he returned, he brought two mugs of *chai* with him, heaped with sugar, and made me sip from the hot brew until he was satisfied that colour had returned to my face.

He returned my mug to the coffee table and tilted my chin towards him. "I get it. It's too much."

I nodded. I hated the tears that brimmed in my eyes, hated the weakness in me. I hated that a world existed where men imprisoned each other like animals and that I'd agreed to let a man die by my hand. I hated that the fate of the kingdom hung in the balance and that I might get things wrong. Most of all, I hated that Sitara was in limbo, but any reunion—should we achieve that—would be fleeting because of the bargain I'd made.

But it wasn't just hate I felt. My chest ached with love.

I loved that the general didn't flinch from my pain, as though he understood every aspect of my turmoil without me having to voice it. Without telepathy. Without drama. I loved that somehow, during all of this, we'd learned each other's thought patterns, even if we didn't know each other's entire histories. And god, it was a relief to have someone to hold me when I didn't need to explain, persuade, protect or lead.

"For the record, your mind in there…your ability to figure things out and gain his trust. You're incredible, little witch, and I'm not sure you know it." He sat down next to me, muscular thighs on display in his black boxers. He adjusted the throw around us, giving me the lion's share, before tugging me tighter against him, curves against muscle. "I know it was hard. Even though you didn't waiver, it was hard."

"Every step feels like a struggle."

"Do you want sympathy or solutions?"

I exhaled in a whoosh. "Sympathy."

"Then you'll have it."

He hugged me, and the weight of the world melted away. I leaned into his embrace. It was a sanctuary, a cocoon. It was solace from the chaos of the kingdom. He understood the hard choices of this place. He understood sibling love and the need to create a better world. He understood violence and what it did to your soul. That sometimes, it was necessary, but that didn't make it any easier. With him, there was no need for pretence or masks. As his strong arms encircled me, his warmth seeped into my skin, and my muscles relaxed, releasing my gnawing stress.

It was the most radical acceptance I had ever felt.

Acceptance that the general also deserved.

I lifted my head from his shoulder, my words spilling like ink from a broken pen, messy and erratic. "Dev? I saw your face in Kaladhar's cell. You were distraught. No, it was more than that…you looked guilty like Prem's plans are your fault. And I just wanted you to know that it isn't all on you. You're not responsible for what Prem has done. *He* is. That you feel you're responsible shows that you're a good man, but it doesn't make it any more true."

Deven's face shadowed, even there in his sister's home, where he felt comfortable.

Even with our arms wrapped around each other.

I tried again. "No one expects you to be perfect. All those years, you were the buffer… You've already given so much, and you're doing it even now. Don't you see? If you let him make you feel like this, if you let him torment you, he's won. Don't let him win, Dev."

He drew in a shuddering breath. "That's the second time in the past few minutes that you've called me Dev. And as for the other stuff. I can't help what I feel, and yeah, maybe I think I can do more. Maybe this part of my life is the redemption." He pulled me closer, and his inky eyes dropped to my lips. "I like it. The familiarity of you calling me Dev. All these walls I build around myself, and you knock them down with such grace."

"Has anyone else ever called you that?"

"Sure. My family. But they don't make me feel like you do."

"How's that?" I murmured against his mouth.

"Like I want to be a better man. Like you can find out about my past and still see the good in me."

My belly warmed, and I wanted him closer. "I only see good in you."

His jaw tensed, and his words were oh-so-careful. "We've never talked about our future. Not really. Never nailed down the specifics." *Sometimes, I think you could be everything I've been missing. That I've waited a lifetime for*, he had said. And it gutted me that I had shut him down when he'd been ready to talk about it before.

The unspoken question exposed his fragility. Despite the proud tilt of his head and careful wording, he needed the reassurance of knowing what we would be—me and him—when this was all over. His wife's betrayal meant that he hadn't felt secure as a husband, and his cousin's jealousy had compromised his professional standing. Dev's place in the kingdom, though widely known, had been undermined by Prem's whims and his Machiavellian ways.

"I see us together." But I could see in the stillness of his body that he needed more than that.

That it was my turn to expose my heart and make myself vulnerable to him.

I hadn't slowed down enough to imagine the details of what that meant, apart from us being together still, with reams of time to spend together. So I closed my eyes, nestled against the crook of his arm, and let my imagination run wild. A smile curved my lips at the film reel in my mind. He traced lazy circles on my collarbone, but as he heard me speak, his breath hitched, and his hand stalled. Beneath the throw, my nipples peaked through the lace of my bra, eager for his touch. "We wake to streaming sunlight, entwined in each other's limbs. We feed each other morsels from our plates, even in company. I teach you how to get messy using a potter's wheel. We walk hand in hand through the kingdom's markets. I ride your tiger form through the forest. We discuss books late into the night. We invite our family into the palace that is our home. We wear twin crowns on our heads." When I peeled my eyes open, shy and with butterflies darting in my belly, he stared at me with wonder.

"Beautiful." His face crumpled. "But I don't need all that. I don't need status. I just need you."

I was pretty damn sure that both I and the kingdom needed him. "Well, okay. If you don't want to share all that with me, I'll just keep you as my sex toy in the dungeons."

His laughter bubbled up from deep within him, rich and full of warmth. I stared at him because he rarely laughed, and the sound was so joyful that I wanted to remember the exact sound, how he threw back his head, and how his eyes crinkled. When he stopped, heat replaced the amusement in his midnight eyes, and it lit a furnace in me.

I looked at him from beneath my lashes. "Was I brazen to say all of that?"

He dragged a calloused thumb over my bottom lip. "It's refreshing. The women in Jalapashu are less forthright."

"Oh, I've seen them undress you with their eyes."

His lips twitched. "Is that a complaint? Would you prefer them to be more respectful, little witch?"

"They can imagine what the hell they like, as long as it's me you're coming home to."

"I like being off the market." He leaned forward as if he was going to whisper a secret in my ear and, instead, sucked my ear lobe. A moan escaped me when he dipped his tongue in my ear. "In fact, I don't bring any old riffraff to my sister's house. A visit to the ranch means you're very special. Would you like to spend the night here with me, little witch?"

"Yes," I breathed, frustrated at the little touches when I wanted all of him.

He smiled a victor's smile and crossed to the fireplace. With deft hands, like he'd done it a thousand times before in this very room, he threw some logs, scrunched balls of paper and a lit match on the burner. I took in the rippling expanse of his back, covered with his geometric tattoo that marked all the years of his curse, the years it had taken to become himself again. Flames flared to life, bringing additional warmth to the living room. Then he found a stack of throws in a blanket box, laid them on the floor, and beckoned me over. "Take off that bastard's ring and come here."

I set the ring aside and went to him on unsteady feet. "What's this?"

His eyes sparked with mischief. "A seduction."

"Oh." My heartbeat quickened. Two can play at that game, I thought, and let the throw I was holding fall.

His eyes roamed over my face and then my body, and—standing there in my lacy underwear—I almost dove for the throw again. I was sure I was covered in dirt from the tunnels and dungeons, sure that the sorcerer's cigar smoke lingered in my unruly hair, sure that I had smelled better and been more beautiful than that moment. But he didn't look at me like I was a wreck. He looked at me like I was the only star in the night sky. Like I was the answer to his prayers, his muse, or a dream he never wanted to wake up from.

Mouth dry, I drank my fill of his rugged charm. The tousled locks that fell haphazardly across his forehead. His almost straight nose and sensual lips. The broad shoulders and a muscular chest that tapered down to a lean waist. The play of flames danced across his bronzed skin. The boxers that hugged his slim hips and the bulge beneath the line of fabric that I wasn't quite brave enough to look at. The map of scars that marked his body from previous battles. How at ease he was with his body and this moment in time. And the swirling depths of emotion in his eyes.

"Come closer. I need to touch you," he said roughly, not waiting for me to obey.

His hands were gentle on my waist. But I needed him to wipe my mind of the day.

I wrapped my arms around his neck and pressed my softness against his hard planes, and his answering groan of pleasure emboldened me. "Seduction is too slow. I need it harder today."

His eyes darkened with desire and something more tender. Something like understanding. "Okay then, little witch. I'll be rough with you, and I won't stop until you ask me to."

It was like he'd been waiting for permission to devour me all his days.

I gulped, and he covered my mouth with his, and the kiss wasn't gentle. It was a collision of bruised lips and tangling tongues and teeth that nipped and dragged. Our mouths melded together, and I met his unbridled passion with my own, exploring, plundering, dominating. His hands tangled in my hair, and he grew frustrated, pausing to tug out my hair band, raking his fingers through my nape to press me closer and serve the hunger of our kiss.

But it wasn't enough. How could it be enough? He

pushed me down on the throws, and I arched my back as he dipped his head to bite and lick the apex of one breast through the lace of my bra, his tongue swirling over the peak until it strained against the fabric. I scraped my nails down his back, and he laughed huskily as he pulled down the triangle of fabric and took my other breast in his mouth, suckling so hard that I cried out his name, begging for more, begging him to keep stoking the flames of my desire, even as they burned me.

He listened. He listened to my demand for more, to give it to me harder, as he brushed aside my knickers and dipped two fingers into the hot wetness of me, dipping in and out as I writhed on the floor and he took in the view, his eyes hooded, telling me how beautiful I was, how he could feel the velvet core of me. His own arousal was so clearly on display that when I touched him, he cursed and pinned my arms above my head with one hand while working me with the other. And the rhythm, the rhythm of his fingers, the brush of his thumb against the swollen nub, was so skilled, so exquisite, that the world faded into insignificance. Everything faded, all senses except touching and being touched. And there were no thoughts in my head, no thoughts of anyone or anything but him.

When he spun me onto my front, unhooked my bra and peeled my knickers down my thighs at last, I shuddered with relief to have more of him, finally, finally, when the pressure building in me was almost at breaking point, and I needed him so desperately. But he wasn't done playing with me. He dragged up my hips so I was on my knees and administered stinging slaps across my cheeks, once, twice, my name gritting out between his teeth, until my thighs opened up and he entered me from behind, so deep that our groans mirrored each other. He reached over me, squeezing my breasts, kneading them with the possessive pressure I craved, his hand sometimes at the base of my throat, sometimes rolling my nipples with his thumb and forefinger. I ground myself against his hand, against his hardness, shameless, a hussy, telling him how good he felt, how much I needed him. A wild, fierce abandon rocked through me as he pounded into me, flesh into flesh, feeding our need for each other, my body swallowing his, revelling in the fullness of him, until our pleasure ratcheted up like a rocket and spiralled out across the stars, breaking, exploding in a release that sent salty tears down my cheeks.

"I didn't tell you to stop."

He cocked an eyebrow as his hand tightened at my hip. "My mistake. Let me correct that."

I sighed in a haze of bliss. "Just give me a minute."

We lay there awhile, still entwined, until our ragged breaths calmed. He stroked the hair from my face and curled his body around mine. When I twisted my neck to find his lips, his kiss was soft and felt like a promise.

I love you on the tip of my tongue. But our world was so uncertain.

"It's never been like this for me with anyone else."

"Good. The next time other women bring you platters of food, that will give me solace."

He bit back a laugh. "Shall we sleep a while, my love?"

The whiskey rumble of his voice and our exertions lulled me to sleep before I could answer.

CHAPTER 24

I didn't know how long we slept, only that for the first time in days, I didn't have nightmares of strange land-scapes or the withering banyan or eerie figurines. That the sex had short-circuited my troubled subconscious or, more likely, Deven's heartbeat against my ear had steadied my fitful dreamscape, anchoring me to more wholesome rest.

The general's sleep was more fitful. He called out my name in his sleep. One hour, there was a man on the rug next to me and a tiger the next. The shifting didn't phase me, and I soothed him by placing a hand on his rising chest and drifted back to sleep.

When my eyes fluttered open, by the changed light and the position of the dipped sun on the horizon, I guessed it to be early evening. The flames from the log burner danced still, their glow painting Nisha's living room orange. I didn't know at first what had woken me—perhaps the crackle of the fire or my own propensity for light sleep these days—but the room felt different somehow, more crowded, claustro-phobic even. The soft scrape of stone against stone met my ears, followed by the low warning rumble of a tiger.

I sat bolt upright, unnerved but not fearful. Blinking away the remnants of sleep, my gaze swept across the room.

And then, I saw them.

My absconded gargoyles stood a few feet away, and the general—well, he had shifted to his tiger form. His dark gaze was locked onto the motionless gargoyles, sharp canines gleamed in the dim light, and his sleek striped body was coiled and ready to pounce. Each snarl was a warning, but the stone forms of the gargoyles betrayed no emotion. Their stone bodies blended seamlessly with the shadows. That was, with the exception of Harya, who was the only gargoyle in his fleshy grey form and looked distinctly unimpressed.

Despite all odds, Merlin had come through. I hadn't doubted him for a second.

I telegraphed Sindhuja, *Is everything okay at the fortress?*

Of course, mistress, or I would have contacted you as we agreed, she replied.

Be ready, I told her.

"You deserve all the carrots," I murmured to the hare as he hopped to my side. "They come without the raja?"

"They have agreed to listen." Liquid gold eyes glimmered. "Did you find what you needed in the dungeons?"

"We did." I mustered the meagre scraps of my dignity while Deven held the gargoyles at bay, dressed quickly in my leathers and palmed my dagger. Then I walked over to the tiger and ran a tender hand over his head. I swear his snarls became purrs at my touch, but there wasn't time to gawp at him. "I'll talk with you now, Harya."

"You're angry." The lion-maned gargoyle leader shifted uncomfortably. "However, I'm under no obligation to come here despite the hare's diplomatic efforts."

I stared him down, ignoring the silhouettes of the stone forms around us. "But you came nonetheless."

"You woke us from our centuries of sleep. Therefore, I will listen in good faith to what you have to say."

He usually addressed me as *mistress*, and I felt its absence, not because the term itself meant anything to me or I craved respect, but because its absence was the confirmation of our new dynamics. The gargoyles had left. Their voices had vanished from my mind. Sindhuja had confirmed their shifting allegiance. As he stood before me, I could no longer deny it or pretend otherwise.

A tinge of loneliness came over me. "Why did you betray me, Harya?"

He slashed his ridged tail with its pointed arrow tip but took care not to come within range of me lest he provoke the tiger. "The world forgot us when we slept. We existed only as distant villains in the history books of this land. When you woke us, we wanted to be so much more. We had hopes and dreams of our own. I told my brothers to wait awhile. I believed in you, our gargoyle queen. We only had to do our duty, and our time would come."

My breath caught in my throat. "What changed?"

His guttural voice rolled over me. "Our kindnesses changed the people's attitudes to you, but never to us. Even when we did our duty, we were blamed. The breach in the wall wasn't our doing. When one of our own was injured, you sent us away before her last breaths. You rejected us. Undervalued us. Wounded our pride." His voice cracked like dry earth. "The raja pledged to give us the validation we yearn for."

I met his intense eyes, nerves jolting my heart to a frantic rhythm. "But it's not validation you yearn for. It's freedom. And I can both give it and take it away. Because you might have severed our mental connection, but you've forgotten what I can do."

Harya stared at me.

Deven and Merlin flanked me as I opened myself to my power: the spellcasting, the earth manipulation and the giving of life to inert stone. My belief in myself brimmed. I didn't just break soil and rock and metal apart; I could join it. I could heat and meld it, just as I had today with Kaladhar's cell. Without a kiln, without forethought, simply by instinct. As if Jalapashu made me the best version of myself, turning up the dial on my skills, potential and ability to shape the world.

I loosed my magic. Perhaps this is what the seer had been waiting for: this trust in myself. I tugged on the ancient magic inside me that bound me to the gargoyles, the connection that would always be there, even if superficially it seemed gone or silenced.

Slowly, despite the resistance of the inanimate gargoyles, I woke them from inert stone to living flesh. Their voices flooded back into my head—Harya's amongst them—vibrating with confusion, respect and awe. Asking whether I would smash them, crack them, send them into centuries of sleep, make them anew. Gradually, the rough texture of their stony exteriors and the unyielding lines of their features softened. Their rigid poses subtly shifted. As their transformation accelerated, a faint shimmer–like water rippling over stone—danced across their surfaces. Hints of flesh emerged from amidst the stone. Eyes that were lifeless gleamed with awareness.

But I wasn't finished.

As easily as taking a breath, I reversed the process, including Harya this time. Vitality drained from his body and that of his brothers, taking them on the journey to stony sleep. With each passing moment, their movements grew more sluggish, and the lion-maned gargoyle leader's voice called out for mercy.

I stopped, as I had always planned to, and addressed them all. "I'm Vikram Reddy's heir, and Prem Kumar is not. I am the gargoyle queen, and I will command you against your free will if necessary for the good of the people."

Nisha's living room was filled with the faint grinding of

stone as the gargoyles adjusted their positions, filled their cavernous chests with breath and watched me with wary eyes, their claws and teeth and wings a reminder of their warrior natures—a nature they could never use against me.

I paused, remembering Sindhuja's counsel. *Gargoyles might be servile, but we have an internal world, too.* "But I'm more than just the gargoyle queen. This will never be an uneven relationship. I will never desert you, even if your false pride or my lack of attention make you feel that way. Your words live in my mind. I can sense the creaking of your bodies even as I slumber. Do you really think I would neglect you?" I dragged my fingers through Deven's coat, and he gave a rumbling purr. "We found out who breached the wall, and the resistance knows you were faultless. I saved your sister gargoyle. She lives. Stay with me. Rewrite the villainy that haunts your story. Make this kingdom a triumph rather than a tragedy. Repledge your allegiance to me so that together we may unite this kingdom. In return, I offer you your freedom when this is all over. Freedom on the proviso you cause no harm and you return if I need you. Freedom for each of you to pursue your dreams and explore your individuality, just like the people of this place."

Harya's humanoid chest quivered. "Prove it. Prove that Sindhuja lives."

I called for her, and Sindhuja flew into the ranch—through the door the gargoyles had left ajar—and into the living room with her strengthened wings and a halo of daisies resting on her head. Her sleek, scaled fishtail was no longer cracked and peeling. It shimmered like the surface of a tranquil pond under the moon's glow. The gargoyles made space for her at the centre of their group, and she beamed with pride, but there was also a fierceness there, a fierceness that dared them to defy her or me.

She lives. She lives. She lives. Sindhuja, the fishtail gargoyle, lives. Their chorus sounded in my head, and it was a symphony. *Freedom or captivity. Says the gargoyle queen. The queen we deserted. The queen who will never desert us.*

"I wronged you, mistress," said Harya, and when he referred to me as such, I knew I'd won. "Will you forgive me?"

"It's not as easy as that. You almost collapsed our plan." My thoughts whirred, trying to find an advantage in the situation. "You must make it up to me."

His lips pressed together. "There is a tailor at court who was horrified to see us with the raja. He could be an ally."

Lokesh *Saheb*. "Then you will return to the royal palace with the gargoyles and pretend all is as Prem wishes it to be. And you will pass on a discrete message from me to the tailor."

He laid a hand on his chest. "You can rely on me. It will be done, mistress."

"Together, we will trick a raja." I walked towards him and laid a hand on his battle-hardened shoulder. "Just one more thing, Harya. You're no longer the leader of the gargoyles. That honour is now Sindhuja's."

He inclined his head, and his stature seemed to diminish, like a mountain worn down over aeons by the wind and rain. But he joined the rabble around Sindhuja, and any resentment he felt gave way to curiosity.

Behind me, Deven finally shifted back into his human form.

I scooped Merlin into my arms. "Nisha's never going to believe what went down in here."

Deven pulled on his leathers with a grin. "Let's hope she never finds out."

THE NEWLY APPOINTED GARGOYLE LEADER SINDHUJA, THE HARE, Deven and I returned to the fortress as dusk approached. In

Mahi's leaning house, we informed the Council of Rebels about developments: that Kaladhar lived and had been imprisoned through the centuries, that his gift to Prem was not only mind magic but the ability to control an entire kingdom, that Menon's information had given us the key to Prem's downfall. We told them how my magic had heated and moulded the iron of Kaladhar's cell and of the bargains we had struck with him and the gargoyles.

The sorcerer's name sent alarm rippling through the council chamber deep in the bowels of Mahi's house. Warnings came thick and fast from my grandparents and Aanya, although the seer had not focused that kernel of intelligence.

It was the confirmation of her brother's allegiance to us that thinned her breath. Her hands jittered, and her eyes shone with joy for the briefest of seconds before guilt and fear shadowed her eyes. She bided her time, violet third eye peeling open and shutting again, wringing her fingers, thumbing her medallion that was the twin of her brother's, as she waited for the shockwaves about Kaladhar to dwindle, waited to centre us on her brother's fate.

Menon wasn't as dear to us as he was to her.

And it showed.

Deven and I got caught up in the concerns my grandparents and Aanya raised about Kaladhar. They painted a grim portrait of his unscrupulous reputation and the myths that had taken form through the decades, myths so wild and unchecked that the general rolled his eyes.

They told tales of how Kaladhar leeched magic from the powerful and vulnerable alike, with an insatiable thirst and no remorse. He was a master of manipulation and deceit, siphoning magic with ruthless disregard for the consequences. How by the time of his widely recounted death, he had the power to drain the life force of all living beings apart from himself. How he could compel others. How he could control dark entities from other realms. How he could create illusions and craft curses. How he could create pocket dimensions and manipulate a flicker of fire into infernos. How he could absorb the energy of the moon, channel lightening, and alter the flow of time.

Each assertion was more outlandish than the next.

I shook my head, knowing how myths could grow into monsters, and we could rule out half a dozen of their claims by applying the logic of our direct experience with Kaladhar. Irrespective of the range of Kaladhar's magic, a man who hankered after death—and that much I believed was true—had no desire to use it.

Aanya bit her lip. "An armoury of magic, but he convinced you it's death he longs for?"

Deven nodded. "Is it so hard to believe that after a lifetime of pain and causing pain, a man would want to let go?"

Grandfather bristled. "I don't like it."

"Kaladhar's help is the key, Prakash." Sorrow etched deep lines on the seer's face. "It took me too long to see it. But this path. It could work."

I told them about the ingredients needed to nullify Prem's mind magic and my hopes that the royal tailor would administer the potion. I didn't tell them about leaving the hatch to his cell open. I did tell them how we would achieve the release of all the stored magic that would enable Kaladhar's passing. I told them how I was to wield the blade, about the role Sitara's ashes had to play and how, instead of being returned to us, this would seal her fate. I wanted to be a stoic, measured leader, but my composure cracked, exposing the tumultuous sea of my emotions: the longing for Sitara, my urge to prioritise the love of family over the love of the people, the need to be selfish rather than selfless, to break all the rules of religion, biology and morality to bring Sitara back.

The warmth of Deven's hand drifted to my lower back and stayed there as my sister spoke and I tensed.

"You did the right thing," said Leena quietly, not meeting my eyes.

Something snapped in me then. "You want to let her go, and it's not fair. Not fair that you can be okay with that."

Her brown eyes snapped to mine. "So this is what has been bubbling under the surface between you and me. Do you think it's easy for me? Do you think I don't cry myself to sleep at night?" She glanced at Aanya as if the maid had been her lifeline through it all and not me. "It's harder for us than it is for Sitara. Once she passed, she was already not of this world. You saw that. You saw it in her eyes." She sucked in a shaky breath. "So, yes. Yes, I think you did the right thing, and I think our sister, our brilliant, stubborn, ambitious sister, would be thrilled to be part of the birth of a new kingdom. And I think it's a bloody, good way to honour her. And you should stop taking out your grief on me."

Deven's jaw tightened. "Hang on a minute. She's carrying the world."

Leena glared at him. "Sister's fight. Believe me, it's much better than simmering tension."

"I'm sorry," I said miserably.

Nani reached for my hand and Leena's, squeezing each of us. "Everything changes. And eventually, everything ends." There was an infinite sadness in her eyes but a gentleness, too. "But goodbyes can be beautiful, too, if you think of them as a thank you. A reminder of the fragility and grace of life."

"Nothing ever truly ends if you think of nature. Dawn comes after night, and spring after the winter." Leena's expression softened as she looked at me. "She won't ever be truly gone. Not while we're here to remember her."

The knot in my throat was painful. I lifted my chin and gave a watery smile. A whisper of smoky aroma crept up my nostrils. "It's done, then. It's decided."

"Good." Mahi dragged her hands over her face, smudging her kohl-painted brows. "There we can at last turn to my brother. We can't leave him at Prem's court. Not for a second longer. When my gleanings became disorderly, when they didn't come, he risked everything for us. He risked everything for me. Deven, Kiya, please. Help me to save him."

She hadn't ever begged, not even when she found out that Menon was trapped in the labyrinth.

My heart twisted. I opened my mouth to console her, to tell her we'd get him out.

But Grandfather said, "Menon is no fool, Mahi. He knew the risks, and he is formidable enough in his own right as a sorcerer to get himself out of there if he needs to." Beyond his spell craft, it was said he could channel blasts of arcane power, vaporising his nearest foe in an instant. "He knows the palace. He knows Prem's nature. More importantly, he's always known his own mind. If we pull him out now, who's to say we aren't foiling his next move? You haven't trusted him since he returned from the labyrinth. I think it's time you start now."

Aanya gave the seer a comforting smile. "It'll only be a bit longer. You'll see him at the duel tomorrow. And what can happen when the gargoyles are ours? There are others at court and under Prem's control that he can ally with."

Mahi swallowed hard. "A day. We wait a day."

"The separation tears at you, I know," I said. "I can send a message to Menon via the gargoyles. So he knows you're not estranged. So he knows we haven't forgotten him."

"Thank you, Kiya," she said, though we all knew the inadequacy of what I offered, that words across a distance could not nourish an aching heart.

I shared Grandfather's faith. Prem had made a thousand plans, fearing this very moment, but those he assumed were in his pocket—Nitin, the sapling soldier, Menon, Kaladhar and the gargoyles—had broken the strings of his control.

They were ours instead, either rooting for us or crushed beneath our boots.

The general locked eyes with me, and a frisson ran up my spine. We had one last case to make, to a mother and her child, if the spectacle Prem had planned for that day was to turn in our favour.

CHAPTER 25

Deep in the night, I felt a tug on my consciousness: a beckoning to the door.

Deven's arms tightened around me as I rose. "Are you okay?"

I brushed my lips over his palm. "Go back to sleep."

Then I slipped from the circle of his arms, goosebumps pimpling my skin, shrugged on a robe and opened the door. I found the seer on the threshold, her short silver hair mussed with sleep and her violet third eye yawning with the secrets of the cosmos. I quieted the swell of Sindhuja in my mind, asking if I needed aid.

The night air crackled with energy. "Mahi?"

Her words flowed like a river of moonlight, and the crotchety old woman—the one who loved her brother, the general and the kingdom—was submerged beneath the layers of her seer identity. "I've seen the tapestry of destiny laid bare. Tonight, you must go to your studio. And when you are finished, leave the urn amongst your creations. You are the great pottery master's heir, but you are more than him, too. He was the instrument of a deadly queen. You are the product of sisterhood and community. The time has come to prove it."

My breath caught in my throat. "Okay, Mahi. I'll go."

A profound stillness came over her as the violet eye closed and her forehead smoothed. Her otherworldly persona fell away like a cloak. "You offered to send a message to Menon through the gargoyles. This is what I wish him to know. I love him despite the hurts of the past. I missed him every second he was in the labyrinth. I know that he was always drawn to the dark, and he fought it and overcame it because he loves me. And we will spend the rest of our days healing and making up for lost time. Can you tell him that?"

Tears clogged my throat. "I can. I will."

She walked into the night, sadness making her bones slack, and my heart ached to let her go.

I relayed the message through the gargoyle bond, warning Harya to be careful.

With a deep sigh, I changed into comfortable clothing and made my way to the pottery studio, where lights blazed, and the hare sat by the hand-making table as if he'd sensed my impending arrival.

"Mahi gleaned this moment. She said you would come."

"Well, here I am." A pause. "Will this turn the tide?"

"She hopes so. And so do I," said the hare.

The whisper of this future moment had been buried within my soul from when I'd first learned the legend of the great pottery master who'd created the gargoyles. His myth —his history—had lingered in the recesses of my mind, a tantalising echo of what could be.

"Will you tell me if I do anything wrong?"

One sooty ear flopped down. "What can go wrong when you're using your innate talents? It's time for you to stop resisting the call of destiny, Kiya."

He was right. I'd resisted it even as though I'd given the gargoyles new life after centuries of sleep, even as they heeded my commands, as their words loomed in my mind, as I patched up their small and large injuries. It seemed too fanciful, too arrogant to believe I could be his heir, but the whispers in my soul had persisted all the same. I had seen impossible feats since awakening to the existence of magic. I had witnessed Merlin talking and becoming a conduit for our family history, Sitara wielding water as a weapon, men shifting into panthers and tigers, and Leena growing flowers in her palm and turning a man into a tree. The earth itself responded to my will, and doubt still sprung up like weeds in my mind. And it struck me how the future of the kingdom hinged on my actions.

It was cowardice not to live up to my potential.

"Okay, Merlin. I'll try."

I spent a moment with Sitara's warm urn, willing her spirit to be with me. Then I rolled up my sleeves and carried heavy slabs to the making table, each one a blank canvas offering endless possibilities for creation. The rich aroma of the clay filled me with a sense of connection to the natural world. My thoughts drifted momentarily to the great pottery master. Then I pushed him out of my mind because though the past laid the groundwork for creation, art was a deeply personal act, an exploration of the individual and community, and I wanted to forge my own path forward, wanted so desperately for the gargoyles to deliver the hopes of a new kingdom.

With skill and precision, I carved the supple clay, and it seemed to come alive beneath my hands as if I were a choreographer in a dance of creation. With each delicate stroke of my tools against the clay, each crude form shaped and each intricate detail imprinted dictated whether I would succeed. Whether the new gargoyles would be benevolent protectors, guardians of the kingdom, or dangerous monsters wreaking havoc upon those they were meant to safeguard. The questions lingered in my thoughts like shadows, and I prayed. I prayed that they would be good and kind, as well as strong and fierce. The work was honest, and it was brave, and it was healing. My hands moved with purpose, and my brow furrowed in concentration as I wielded my fettling knife and wire tools like extensions of my being. My neck and shoulders grew sore from hours hunched over the making table, from stooping and squinting and kneading. My fingers worked deftly, and my hands tingled with power, coaxing the clay into sinuous curves and fierce visages, forming wings and limbs, talons and teeth.

Next to me, Merlin's bright eyes watched every tweak, every cut. His ears were perked up, and he basked in the creative energy, his movements quickening with anticipation as the process progressed.

I felt it, too: the power of the moment. Magic flowed through me, infusing the gargoyles with a sense of vitality that belied their inert state. Each gargoyle took shape under my hands—rows of them filling quadrants of the studio floor—their forms gradually becoming recognisable shapes. Shapes hewn from my imagination and hopes. Shapes imbued with an aura of ancient mystique. Shapes that seemed to have their own unique personalities, as though their spirits waited within the clay.

Creativity needed to be replenished, yes. But there was always more of it. It was like a river connected to the ocean, and I basked in its power. There was an eagle-like gargoyle amongst my creations, with keen eyes and feathered wings. An owl head with a humanoid body watched us with a serene detachment. A serpent-like gargoyle coiled around itself, with etched scales and fangs bared in a silent hiss. A gargoyle with stag antlers that stretched like branches, with two hooved legs and folded wings. A gargoyle fashioned in the likeness of a dragon, with a reptilian head and claws that glinted like polished steel. A gargoyle with a fleshy humanoid form, ape legs, eyes like voids that absorbed light and wings of inky darkness. And a phoenix gargoyle, its wings set to unfurl in a blaze of fiery feathers, its beak open in a silent cry, ready to rise from the ashes and soar. There were females as well as males. I gave them names, too—Nirantar, Vajra, Agni, Javan, Ulooka, Dhara and on and on—because Sindhuja urged in my mind that it had to be different this time, how the gargoyles were individuals, and it began with naming.

The hours ticked by, and they became more and more, as if I was more than the sum of my parts, as if the earth lent its strength to me, its creative force, a searing connection of the mortal and divine, and I was a vessel through which the magic of creation flowed. When I had finished, the air around us shimmered, and shadows danced around the creations. The studio carried a hint of smoky fragrance. Chest tight, I gazed at the rows upon rows of gargoyles, and they seemed like Frankenstein's monsters. I was scared of what I had done, of the implications of inanimate forms receiving consciousness.

And though there was no room in the kiln for them, that the hours were too short, Merlin and I placed Sitara's warm urn amidst them and went out into the dawn to the sacred tree.

Its once vibrant canopy had withered away, leaving only sparse, desiccated leaves clinging to brittle branches. Its hollow trunk was now riddled with deep cracks, oozing sap-like tears of despair. The roots, once anchored firmly in the earth, now protruded from the ground like fingers desperately clawing the air. Dust and debris littered the ground around it. Deven's soldiers had set up a guardrail, keeping mourners at bay.

The hare's liquid gold eyes glimmered. "I thought it would be here long after my life ended."

I feared one touch would break the tree apart. "Do you think it could be a rebirth?"

"I think it's a dismantling." He scooted closer to me. "What you did in there was magnificent."

Anxiety curled in my belly. "I hope it's enough."

CHAPTER 26

When morning came, we sent word, delivered by Babbu, courtesy of a handwritten note in his crimson beak. He flew above the white-washed royal palace and delivered our missive to the raja's breakfast table as Prem sat on his balcony in a downy robe, with a manservant holding an umbrella above him to prevent the dusting snow from ruining his breakfast of *puris* and pickles.

Prem,
The duel takes place today.
Kiya.

I had written the words in my loopy script with the hint of a smile on my lips. Not because of conceit that I would win—there was a significant chance that I would be felled or at least wounded—but because Prem Kumar was so pompous, he'd clearly take offence that I hadn't used his title. It delighted me to poke at his petty-mindedness.

The sky was still painted in hues of pink and gold when the return message came. Sindhuja alerted me to the lumbering approach of an elephant across the landscape. Two soldiers loyal to the raja sat atop it, and when the wrinkly beast slowed, one clambered down to deliver a ribboned scroll at the gates of the fortress. She brought the scroll to me, and I unwound it to find a message written on gilded ivory paper bearing the royal coat of arms.

We will feast at 6 p.m., then duel.
The presence of every subject is required.
Enjoy your last breaths,
The Raja of Jalapashu

The air thickened around me, and my heartbeat echoed in my ears like the beat of a distant drum. Deven read the message over my shoulder, expression grim. But then we were thrown into preparations, and the fortress became a flurry of activity. Grandfather primed the rebels on the evening ahead, urging great care with shielding. Mahi's restored faith in her brother unleashed further gleanings, finally allowing her to abandon her putrid tea. Nani created the Kaladhar's potion—with the omission of one ingredient —then roamed the fortress, offering wisdom and encouragement to those fretting. Leena and Aanya cared for the children and reiterated to them how to hide when we were gone and what to do in the eventuality that we did not return. Deven headed to the armoury to allocate small, concealable weapons to those who wished to carry one. Merlin and I returned to the weaver's house to check on my creations. They stood forlorn and lifeless at intervals through the pottery studio, and I felt bitterly disappointed then. Disappointed in myself for believing I was Vikram Reddy's heir, that I could make the gargoyles from new, that I'd spent the night wasting clay and not resting in the arms of the man I loved. With a nudge from Merlin—smarting still—I set aside the failure of the gargoyles.

Instead, I got to work and made spell vessels that I prayed would protect us all.

Spells of *abhayam, nidrāṃ dhāvatu* and *tvamapaśya*. Spells of *boe kāṭe, mohitaḥ bhava* and *dhūmrīkṛta kara*. Spells of *andhakāra kara* and *adṛśyatāṁ dadātu*. They demanded fearlessness, unconsciousness and invisibility. They invoked justice, confusion for our foe and darkness. The incantations spilt from my lips in a steady stream, weaving through the air like invisible threads, binding the magic to the vessels I crafted. The studio hummed with feverish energy, the rhythmic splatter of pottery spinning on the wheel filling the air until sweat beaded my brow and my nails and skin were caked with clay. In the corner of the studio, the kiln's fiery maw devoured the vessels one by one. Like Merlin, the kiln was my partner in a delicate dance of creation and transformation. But it was also a merciless judge, its flames capable of consuming even the most carefully crafted spells if they were not imbued with enough power and intent.

When we were finished, there were close to a hundred vessels ready, which Leena, Aanya and I distributed amongst the rebels, prioritising those unable to wield a weapon. Though previous rulers had allowed only a coveted few the chance to access their magic, the people of Jalapashu were no strangers to the mystical energies that permeated their land. I had every faith they'd be able to wield my spells effectively and breathed a sigh of relief, knowing that though we were walking into the belly of the beast, our people would be prepared and able to defend themselves. I caught a subtle trace of a burning scent in the air that smelled like incense sticks or tobacco. A last-ditch attempt at swaying the favour of the gods or living life to the fullest before the final curtain call. We were met with a symphony of thank yous. I didn't quite understand the extent of their awe and gratitude until Aanya explained.

"Don't you see?" Her basket of spell vessels clinked. "For

too long, all but a few have been denied the very essence of our heritage. The magic that courses through our ancestral blood. Giving these away, imbued with your magic, is symbolic of giving us back our birthright. The people are scared, but after these, I'd wager that every single rebel—even those with lingering doubts—will fight for you."

I nodded, biting my lip. There were mere hours before we had to leave. Though terrifying, everything was heading in the right direction. Every decision was calculated, every action deliberate, and it almost felt like we could win. "Are you two scared?"

"I am," said Aanya. "Fear and I are old friends. But I still have my song. And if I have to sing and fight, I will."

Leena gave us a fierce look. "We make sure we get the bastard, and it'll all be worth it. Now, come on. We have to get dressed, and you, my darling sister, have to look the part of a queen."

I returned to my quarters to scrub the clay from my body. Half an hour later, Grandfather summoned the raja's former courtesan, Lata and his former mistress, Sunita—Tanay's mother—to help me dress. I had become so used to the royal tailor poking and prodding me that it took me a moment to feel comfortable. Harya had reported that while he had delivered my message to Lokesh *Saheb,* it was unclear whether he would help our cause or not. My stomach roiled, thinking about how many things could go wrong.

Lata looked around. "Prem likes the trappings of power. He'd never live somewhere like this."

I surfaced from my thoughts with a jolt. "I've always preferred comfort to luxury."

She nodded and began to lay garments on the bed. Years of courtly experiences and the pressure to centre her beauty meant that Lata instinctively knew how to flatter my shape and colouring, how to use winged kohl and a sweep of sea-green eye shadow to accentuate my eyes, and what jewellery would best complement my neckline. Though she had left behind her own belongings when she had fled to the fortress, she flitted from house to house in search of something suitable for me to wear.

As a seamstress, Sunita—like Lata, a beauty in her own right—altered the borrowed clothing to fit me, her skilled hands pinning and adjusting the fabric that hinted at years of expertise. Each careful adjustment transformed the garment, moulding it to my body with quiet determination despite the ticking clock.

"You spoke to Tanay for me?" I asked her. "It's a lot to ask, I know. Kaladhar said his blood must be gladly given. Without it, the potion won't work."

"He'll be here any minute." She removed a pin from her mouth and fixed it in place at my shoulder. "You saved him. How could we say no?"

I squeezed her. "I don't know what to say."

"Just three days ago, he and I would have said no, but you have done in hours what I could not achieve in years. You showed him what his father truly is. A tyrant. I'm grateful."

Lata made one last adjustment to the ribbons of the whalebone corset at my back and brushed a strand of hair from my face. "We are done. There she is, our *queen-in-waiting*. You may look." She turned me to the mirror.

My hazel eyes widened, lashes teased to perfection. The rich blue of my *lehenga* cascaded around me like a river of silk, its embroidered skirt telling stories of the kingdom's craftswomen. The weight of the fabric was a reminder of the gravity of the evening's events. The earthen blouse had a heart-shaped neck, the whalebone corset left me barely enough room to breathe, and the intricate folds of the gauzy scarf pinned to my shoulder served to further restrict my movement. Lata had placed a gold necklace of sapphires around my neck, which cast shimmering reflections across the dark room. My dark wavy hair, usually in a ponytail, had been tamed and sculpted into an elaborate arrangement of braids and twists, adorned with delicate flowers and jewelled pins.

The only concession to comfort was the flat sandals I wore.

In case I had to run.

The women's soft murmurs of encouragement did little to ease my unease. In the mirror before me, I saw not myself but a carefully crafted facade, poised and regal, masking the terror beneath. I was a stranger masquerading in my own skin, discombobulated, until I lifted the heavy skirt to strap my dagger to my thigh, and Sunita handed me spell vessels for the pockets she had sewn.

"We know what it's like to wear masks." Her eyes were like moons. "We know how much you risk for us."

Knuckles rapped the door, and Grandfather entered with Tanay. His hand rested lightly on the boy's shoulder, a gesture of reassurance that a man might show his grandson, miles apart from their interaction when Tanay had thrown a dagger at me. Man and boy looked at me, their eyes wide with wonder.

I glanced at Sunita, and when she nodded, I approached her son. "You're sure about this?"

Eleven years old, with his father's eyes. He had seen too much to retain childish innocence. "He didn't care if I lived or died that night. I wanted to know him. But he…" A sob wrenched from Tanay, and his mother moved to his side, placing a protective arm around him. "Will you hurt him?"

My breath bottled. "I don't know. Maybe. But the potion —your blood—it's to stop his mind magic. So he can't control us or anyone else. Is that okay with you?"

A haunting sadness filled his eyes that seemed to stretch to the depths of the sea. He bit his lip and stretched out his palm. "Take what you need."

I met Grandfather's gaze, and he passed me a small, sterile knife and a glass vial. "It's only a few drops. Ready?"

I crouched before him in my finery and took his upturned hand in mine. His ocean eyes widened as the knife neared, and he winced when I pricked his palm. Tiny beads of crimson welled up from the delicate skin. Carefully, I scooped up the droplets, and his blood pooled in the vial like liquid rubies. I handed back the knife and vial.

Grandfather sealed its precious cargo with a cork stopper, the soft pop echoing in the silence of the room. "I will take this to your grandmother."

Nodding, I pressed a handkerchief Grandfather offered me to Tanay's bleeding palm.

"Thank you, Tanay," I said as the boy stared at the vial and his mother hugged him. "You don't know what this means."

Sunita extracted herself from her son. "This means we stop someone who has had power over us for too long."

The two women dipped to touch my feet in the age-old Indian custom of respect, and I urged them to their feet.

Lata embraced me. "When the night is over, you will be queen, and the raja will be dead."

Then why did I hear the drumbeat of dread in my chest?

I TOOK THE LUXURY OF A FEW MINUTES ALONE TO GROUND myself, and unable to risk ruining my attire with pottery, I unsheathed my thigh dagger and honed its blade on a stone. My movements were precise and focused, but my churning thoughts didn't ease, not even with the chorus of gargoyles in my mind telling me that they were *mine, mine, mine*. That they served the gargoyle queen, that the raja would soon be dead, and that his blood would allow Jalapashu to rise anew. I longed to take off the heavy garments and the pretence so beloved of the raja, get into my armour and get on with the fight. I longed to unleash my magic and exact revenge—no, justice. I longed for Deven's touch, the steady beat of his heart against my ear, his body curled against mine to ground me, to soothe the clop-clop-clop of ever-rising dread and pressure.

Then, suddenly, he was there as if osmosis of thought, the magnet of our longing, had brought him to me. Sensing his presence, glancing up from my task, I found him leaning casually against the door jamb, his eyes fixed on me with such warmth and intensity that my heart skipped, and my fingers stilled on the blade.

He stood tall and regal in a finely tailored *sherwani*, its deep indigo hue complementing the richness of his olive skin. Silver embroidery along the collar and cuffs added a touch of elegance. The fabric draped perfectly over his broad shoulders, chest and thighs, accentuating his muscular frame with understated sophistication. His tousled curls, untamed since he had shed the mantle of Jalapashu's general, were neatly styled and swept back from his forehead in a manner that exuded poise. The stubble on his chiselled jawline added rugged charm—and a hint of rebellion—to his otherwise refined appearance.

He swept his gaze over every inch of me, his voice soft. "You look beautiful."

"So do you," I said, but I couldn't smile, couldn't pretend to be brave.

He closed the door, crossed the room and prised my fingers off the dagger before checking the blade with a satisfied nod. Crouching, he carefully lifted the skirt of my *lehenga* to slide it into the sheath. His lips brushed the soft skin of my inner thigh, and a quiver ran through me before he let the skirt fall into place.

"What if the new gargoyles don't wake? What if we're taking the resistance into this trap, and it all goes wrong?"

"It won't. Whatever Prem has planned, we deal with it." The swirling black depths of his eyes met mine. The dim light filtering through the window cast shadows across him. "I'm not going to let anything happen to you. I won't allow it. Even if we have to leave this place behind."

"You'd do that? You'd leave the people to their fate?"

A breath hissed from his mouth. "I would for you. We fight. But if it comes down to it, we take our family, and we leave." But I knew that duty was imprinted into every bone of his body, that the tattoo on his back was as much a promise to the kingdom as it had been to himself.

"And your magic? Could you live without it?"

"There are more important things than magic." A storm brewed across his face, and he pulled me against him. "Promise me something. My cousin is broken. He feeds off fear. From the moment we step into the palace, he must see you as uncowed, as his equal. We'll walk in with our mental shields up and our heads held high. We go in there… We eat, we dance, we smile, we kiss. We show Prem that nothing in the world can come between us and the future we're willing into existence. It's not just about the deals and bargains we've made, the weapons we've stashed or the spells we've prepared. It's not about how we've armed the women or that we believe in our cause. It's about the energy we exude, the confidence we radiate, as if we hold the universe in the palm of our hands. We show Prem that we're unshakeable and won't yield to his intimidation or manipulation. Every move we make, every glance we share, is a testament to our determination to defy the odds stacked against us. Our aim is to tilt the earth beneath him, to instil doubt in his mind and make him question his abilities. It's a psychological battle as much as a physical one, and we're playing to win on every front. Promise me. Promise me to give yourself the best chance. To not let him get under your skin, but to get under his."

My throat was like sandpaper. "I promise."

I rested my head against his chest, just beneath the hollow of his throat. His sigh echoed through me before he bowed his head to catch my mouth in a kiss, his touch tentative, caressing, as if he was exploring my lips for the first time, learning the shape of them, taking his sweet time.

When he pulled away, my brow furrowed. "Deven? I never asked you. What's your shielding landscape?"

He smiled. "It's a cave in Boundless Bay. It looks like the Amber Hollows, but to me, it's a tiger's den, a lair fortified with stone walls and guarded by fierce tiger spirits."

I glanced at him in shock. "Not the forest? Not Jalapashu, but Boundless Bay? Fortified by stone walls?"

He stumbled awkwardly over his words, and it was so endearing that butterflies darted in my stomach. "Maybe my subconscious has always been waiting for you."

I nodded and reached up to thread my hands through his hair, pulling his lips to mine. This one was deeper, and he groaned in his throat as our tongues tangled. A knock sounded, and he drew away, fixing my smudged lipstick with a careful sweep of his thumb beneath my lower lip before answering the door.

My grandparents stood on the threshold, dressed in their finery, worry making them pale.

"It's time," said Grandfather. "The resistance and the raja wait."

"The new gargoyles?" I asked.

His face tightened. "They remain in the studio where you left them. There are no stirrings."

"Aanya has the finished potion." Nani's mouth parted on an exhale. "What we have planned will be enough. We must have faith in that."

"Aanya knows what to do?" I asked.

"We have been through the plans a hundred times," said Grandfather.

"She is a maid. She is used to being unseen." Nani laid a papery hand on my cheek. "It's you I'm worried about. Be careful, please."

I swallowed the lump in my throat, hating that she knew the pain of partings. "If anything happens to me, you'll look after Leena and Aanya? You'll help them escape and make sure they feel they're not alone as they start their lives together?"

A solemn nod. "I will."

"Grandfather? Release the sapling soldier. He must decide whose side he stands on."

Deven took my hand, and together, we walked into the cold night.

CHAPTER 27

We went into the courtyard, and the people were there en masse. The women wore tie-dye *saris* and cotton skirts that swirled around their ankles, with flowers in their hair that Leena had made, and weapons and spell vessels hidden amongst the folds of fabric. The men, even the aged with bowed backs and thinning hair, had proudly ironed their modest *sherwanis* and had a determined bearing that made me shiver.

"They have faith in you. As do I," murmured Deven as the crowd parted for us.

I gripped his hand tighter. "They're staring at me."

"You have no idea how beautiful you look." Onyx eyes held mine. "They expect a speech."

When we reached the top of the crowd, we turned to face them. Slowly, a fiery sense of justice ignited my core. "Fellow rebels, when we asked if we could hide you away from Jalapashu until this was over, you told us no. Tonight, we run towards danger rather than away from it. We walk as one to the royal palace. It could be that Prem Kumar seeks to change us. That he tries to convince you to back him or choose apathy. That he tells you you'll lose too much if we fight. That it's not worth the sacrifice or the bother. Don't believe him. The loss of hope is more dangerous than a physical blow. Because without hope, there's no resistance. We'll stand our ground. When the night is over, your children won't have to hide anymore. You won't have to fear for their future or your own."

Someone called out. "The fishtail gargoyle remains here, but do the others answer to the raja?"

"If the gargoyles have turned against us, what hope do we have of defending ourselves?" said another. "Was Nitin telling the truth after all?"

"He was not." I dragged in a breath. "The gargoyle host may not stand beside us, but when it counts, they will. I have them in here." I tapped my temple. "They are ours. Tonight, we're no longer pawns in the raja's games of power and control. We are guardians of our own heritage. We are king slayers—" I thought I felt the sacred banyan tree shudder then. "—and the stewards of a brighter tomorrow."

One chant became dozens more. "Victory to the resistance. Victory to our rani."

There were raised fists, palms on hearts, and the folding of hands in prayer, and I didn't know if I could fulfil my promise, didn't know if I could stomach being the reason for bloodshed or worse, didn't know if all the cogs of our plan would come together. But as Deven and the rest of the Council of Rebels lined up with me at the head of the column about to exit the fortress, the weight of sacrifice settled on my shoulders. I was willing to give everything of myself: my magic, my spirit, and my life if it meant securing victory.

With a flick of my wrist and a whisper of magic, the fortress stone door groaned open and our column of rebels filed towards the white-washed palace. We left behind the cries of children, who remained behind under Yuvan, Merlin and Babbu's care. The gunmetal sky hung low overhead, casting a pall over us. Our garments stood out against the drab landscape, and if today was going to be my death day, I was glad that we wore vibrant, joyous colours and not black. The chill in the air nipped at my cheeks and nose, prompting the occasional shiver that made Deven draw me closer to his side, though his coal-dark eyes—and those of his best soldiers—remained fixed forward, scanning for threats.

With each step closer to the palace, anticipation built in the air, electric and palpable. Ahead, the towering domes of the palace loomed, and flags bearing the royal crest—depicting the sacred tree in its former glory—rippled in the wintery breeze, a reminder of the power we had pledged to confront. The raja heralded our arrival with a distant beat of drums. Their staccato rhythm pounded in my chest, driving us towards our destiny, the tempo so fast that fear slipped the noose of my control. I thought of my mother and Sitara, and the winding road that had led us to this point, and about violence and hubris and justice, and whether I was cut out to be queen.

Deven sensed my spiralling emotions. His warm hand curved at my waist, and he murmured *I'm right here*, and *I won't let anything happen to you*, and *we fight this together*.

Then we were there, my heart thundering like the hooves of charging cavalry, my palms clammy as Prem approached, crowned and preening in red and gold like it was his marriage day. He was accompanied by an entourage of his court, foremost amongst them Menon, Nitin, Harya and a silent flock of gargoyles that sowed terror into the hearts of the rebels despite the assurances I had given them.

"Menon!" cried the seer, but her brother's face was strangely vacant, as though his shielding against Prem had been so thorough that his humanity was on ice. She looked at him, broken in sadness.

"Welcome back to the kingdom proper, my traitorous earth witch. I've been waiting for this day. I'm eager to restore order." The raja's glacial eyes crawled over every inch of me. The jewels in my hair, the sweep of my lashes, the swell of my breasts and his ring on my finger. Then, his lip curled at the sight of Sindhuja. "It must have been a disappointment to be left with the weakest gargoyle."

I lifted my chin, my voice cold. "Let's get on with it, shall we?"

His eyes narrowed at the column of rebels behind us. "Where are the children?"

"Out of harm's way." I sucked in a breath as his tiger's claws scraped against my mental shields and prayed that the rebels protected themselves against his probing.

He pivoted towards his entourage with a bemused chuckle. "She insinuates I would hurt them. Can you believe it? That I'd hurt the future of our kingdom."

They tittered on command, no critical thought on display as if it were the most preposterous notion imaginable.

"Come. You are seated at the high table. With me." He gave Deven a dismissive nod and extended his elbow to me with an indulgent smile, but I clung to the general like my very survival depended on it—and it did.

We swept past the raja into the chandelier-lit columned throne room, lined with murals of Jalapashan history. My sandals sank into the thick wool carpet, and my hand closed around the spell vessels in my pockets. The air wafted with the rich aroma of ghee and spices—cumin, coriander and turmeric—mingling with the perfumed jasmine and rose petals and the rich scent of simmering curries. Each table setting was marked with a name plaque in swirling lettering, determining our positions with meticulous precision, making it easier for Aanya to find the royal tailor.

Prem's loyalists were already seated, draped in jewel-toned, sequinned *saris* and brocaded silk *sherwanis*. The clinking of bangles and the jingle of anklets added a musical cadence to the air, complementing the soulful strains of the *sitar* reaching across the throne room from the dais. The tables groaned under the weight of sumptuous dishes: fragrant *biryanis*, spicy *bhajis*, creamy *daals*, simmering *aloo gobi* and *saag paneer*, thick *paratha*, and steaming *naan bread*. On a dessert table, sweet balls of *gulab jamun* and skewers of clementines dipped in cardamom-spiced dark chocolate awaited eager mouths. Yet it all left me cold. The ostentatious, wasteful show compared poorly to Jilu and Radha's offerings at their restaurant and in their fortress cooking: honest cooking imbued with love.

"Can you see Lokesh Saheb?" I murmured.

Deven caught my waist as I stumbled. "Over there. Aanya's already on her way. You really think he'll help?"

"He trusts me. I can convince him to help us. "

"All this time, a telepath at court…"

"That has to stay between you and me, Dev."

"Of course." He blew out his breath. "I don't like how much is riding on this."

A deep sense of unease crept over me as we moved through the room towards the high table. The gazes of the assembled guests were filled with hatred. Their eyes bored into me, dissecting every nuance of my demeanour. I steeled myself against their scrutiny, but it struck me how there was a peculiar rigidity in their movements, a mechanical uniformity in their expressions. Their laughter seemed rehearsed, and their conversations followed a scripted rhythm.

"Keep going," murmured Deven, as repeated phrases looped around us.

A chill ran up my spine. "They're synchronised. Mere shells controlled by Prem."

A vein throbbed in his jaw as he took in faces he'd known all his life. "We help them by sticking to the plan."

I thought I smelt Kaladhar's cloying cigar smoke then. He'd warned us about the raja's manipulative reach—that he could control a whole kingdom—yet I hadn't envisaged the extent to which he would wield this power. I'd expected him to use this corruption of humanity in key moments, not to erase his loyalists' individuality in a single stroke.

Deven led us to our table, and my heart drummed in my throat as our people filed into their seats.

I sat down, and my gaze collided with the tailor, Lokesh *Saheb*, four tables away. His lean frame was clad in a finely tailored velvet coat. A crisp, white shirt and silk cravat peeked out from beneath his coat. His hand rested on the top curve of his feather walking stick, and he took no interest in the food before him. His discerning eyes roamed over me—in them was a hint of curiosity tempered by caution—then he carefully averted his attention, masking his true self with practised ease, before his voice filled my head.

Quite ravishing, even without my expert attention, he said. *Certainly fit to be queen.*

I forced myself to relax, my eyes drifting to the sitar player as we spoke. *I had help from Lata and Sunita.*

Perhaps I should give them a job in my atelier when this is all over. The tailor's tone was tart. *Quite the move, asking your gargoyle to speak with me and then sending the maid to pass me this vial. You know I like a quiet life.*

I know you don't condone how Prem Kumar acts. You kept my secrets and trusted me with yours because I'm your natural ally.

A tired sigh echoed in the halls of my mind. *I should turn you in and protect all that I have built.*

I locked gazes with him, my heart racing. *But you won't. You managed to stay free of his mind control. And it offends you to see your magic, your craft, used so recklessly and cruelly when you've always wielded it with care and respect.*

Surprise flashed across his face. *Yes, Kiya. It does offend me. He has always offended me, but to degrade the very essence of thought, to turn thinking people into fodder to satisfy his hunger for power—it's reprehensible. Unforgivable.*

Then help me. Please. I had to be quick. The raja

approached, surrounded by a whirl of spinning dancers and a trudge of gargoyles. I watched his progression, and Deven squeezed my thigh, urging me to be quick. *The potion Aanya has given you is disguised as perfume. You are the royal tailor. Find a reason to fix his clothing at the high table. Soon. It must be soon. Apply the perfume to Prem's pulse points, and it will be done. He won't be able to control us.*

A long pause stretched out between us as he deliberated, and the dancers spun, and the gargoyles trudged, and the tension in my body ratcheted up. My palms curled around the stem of my glass.

This will not end well for us all, said the tailor. *But it's intoxicating being offered power when I've been powerless for so long. I will help you, Kiya. I like the thought of bearing witness to the end of Prem Kumar's reign and dressing a new regent.*

Relief tingled along my skin and settled in my bones. "He agreed," I said to Deven, and not a moment too soon.

Every pair of eyes turned to Prem, the ones he commanded and the ones he did not, as he reached us and slid into his place at the high table. The seating plan forced key loyalists and rebels together. On the raja's side of the table were Menon, Nitin, the twiddly-moustached sorcerer Bhavesh, the *jhumka* earring sorceress Aarti and Prem's new general, the panther that had pursued us out of the rose garden. Harya kept vigil behind him. On my side of the table were Deven, Leena, Mahi and my grandparents, with Sindhuja standing guard behind us.

Mahi, frumpy in a Punjabi suit which swallowed her frame, reached across the table. "You belong at my side, brother." His eyes flickered with a silent plea I couldn't decipher, and the seer withdrew her hands, bereft.

"Where's Yash?" spat the new general of Jalapashu at Deven. "We didn't find his body."

Deven arched a scarred eyebrow. "You tell me. He got lost under your command."

Prem motioned at a server to heap *biryani, saag paneer* and *raita* onto his plate as his new general bristled. "It's a pity it's come to this. We all could have been the greatest of friends," he said as if he hadn't killed Deven's wife. As if he hadn't ordered Sitara's killing. As if he hadn't coerced me into an engagement with Leena's freedom on the line. As if he hadn't made a thousand cuts, a thousand choices to sever the people's trust and ours.

Sindhuja's ominous creaking reverberated behind me, causing the court poet, who she'd thrown from the fortress, to startle. The lingering fear in his eyes betrayed the lasting impression she had made on him.

I schooled my expression as Lokesh *Saheb* advanced towards us, gliding across the thick carpet with his brightly-feathered walking stick hovering above the ground. Harya moved aside as the tailor hooked his walking stick over his arm and adjusted the already perfectly draped scarf over Prem's red and gold *sherwani*, ensuring that every seam and stitch lay perfectly aligned.

Prem gave a benign smile. "Lokesh is an artist."

"That is because I tend to the whole package. The look, the hair, the scent." With a delicate touch, Lokesh *Saheb* uncapped a bottle of my making. Its matte ceramic surface was adorned with geometric patterns inspired by Deven's back tattoo. A sleek roll-on dispenser sat atop its slender neck. "Do forgive an old man's forgetful brain. I should have applied this perfume in your chambers."

Nani had worked marvels with the *oud*. She had followed Kaladhar's instructions meticulously as she gathered the mandrake root, mugwort, *tulsi*, black cohosh, Angelica root and white sage. Then she added three drops of fresh blood, freely given by a son or daughter of the raja, as per the ritual's requirement. But Nani shrewdly identified vanity as Prem's weakness and his tiger's keen nose as the danger. In making the potion a perfume, she increased our chances of success. So she added agarwood oil to the potion to give the smoky notes of *oud* and included white patchouli, sandalwood and rose essential oils for depth, warmth and complexity. She infused the potion in the light of the early winter moon and decanted it into the vessel I had made.

My court and I held our breaths as the royal tailor dabbed a small amount of the perfume onto his fingertips, then traced a line along Prem's pulse points at his wrist. With each gentle stroke, he infused the air with the scent of *oud*, stepping back only when the last drop of perfume was absorbed into the raja's skin.

"Perfection." Lokesh Saheb capped the perfume and executed a deep bow. *I trust that suffices?*

I'm in your debt. I didn't dare look at him, but my heart bloomed with gratitude.

"I'll keep that." Prem grasped the *oud* bottle, slipped it into his pocket, and turned to speak to me without giving the tailor a second glance as he crossed the floor back to his seat. "Where were we? I forgot to thank you for sending Nitin back to me. It was quite the gesture of generosity." His frigid eyes drifted over Menon. "One that I could never emulate if I discovered treachery. But then you and I aren't cut from quite the same cloth."

Leena side-eyed him, announcing loudly, "Being surrounded by arseholes and marionettes isn't macabre at all."

Prem gave a sly smile. "You noticed my new ability. How astute of you. The gods are smiling on me."

"You're delusional," said Deven, and his eyes narrowed, looking for signs that the potion was taking effect.

"Oh cousin, it's a sign they want me to keep the throne. What you call marionettes can be quite useful. Efficient, obedient, and utterly devoid of troublesome emotions." His entourage mirrored his amusement. But I noted a detachment in his gaze and tension that lingered in the corners of his mouth, as though his puppetry required considerable mental effort, as though beneath his slick façade, there was an undercurrent of frenetic activity. It gave me hope that his control was slipping. That Kaladhar's recipe was in the process of breaking his mind control.

"You surround yourself with sycophants," said Grandfather, eyeing a salt-crusted fish wrapped in a banana leaf that a server placed in front of the raja. "And I am loathe to admit I was one of them."

Completely without irony, the elderly sorceress Aarti threw me a malicious glance, confirming what we knew: Prem's intention was a shaming, a public humiliation, a consolidation of his power so that none would dare challenge him again. "At what hour will you cut down the earth witch, Prem-*ji*? Before desert, I hope."

"I never could stand you," said Nani mildly. Fresh henna covered her roots, like she was battle-ready, in her own way. Like she wouldn't give him the satisfaction of a whiff of fear. Her eyes were clear, and her grip on her cutlery was steady as if her hopes had risen when the royal tailor administered her potion. "I'm not one to toot my own horn, but the quality of your courtiers has deteriorated since our departure, Prem." The omission of the respectful -*ji* did not go unnoticed by the raja.

"In the raja's court, where dark schemes pitch, harmony is restored when he ends the witch," said Nitin.

"Fishtail should have killed him," said Mahi darkly before her attention returned to her brother.

Spotting my lack of appetite, Deven spooned *daal* onto my plate and handed me a slice of *naan* before helping himself. "Eat. You need your strength."

Cobalt eyes sparked with amusement. "My new general doesn't pander to fragility."

Deven's jaw clenched in defiance. "Give it a rest. You'll soon find out she's not fragile."

"Your relationship is." He took his time swallowing a mouthful of curried spinach. "I've been playing so many games with you, and you haven't even realised. All those years, you served me, and I suppressed my jealousy of you. I should have just given my baser instincts free rein."

"Your father should have taken the slipper to you," glowered Grandfather.

"Like yours did to you?" said Bhavesh. "You're still an overbearing old ox."

Prem's lips twitched at their griping. He leaned back in his chair, and his nails were stained with turmeric. "Take your gallant offer to be Kiya's champion in the duel, cousin. I can't tell you how much I enjoyed it when she rejected you. That arse of yours clenched. I bet you went off and had the most spectacular fight about it." He laughed. "Couples should always be supportive of each other. Didn't you tell me that when Roshni was mine? Weren't you rooting for our happiness before you picked up my sloppy seconds? God, you bore me. I can't wait to crush you spiritually and physically. Your fucking idealism makes me sick."

Deven's obsidian gaze snapped to his. "Yeah, well, your nihilism changed my life trajectory as well as yours. But it comes down to one thing, doesn't it, *cousin*? You chase power because you've never found meaning."

Prem retorted, his tone laced with cynicism, "Meaning? What is meaning but a fleeting illusion? Does it clothe you or fill your belly? Does it keep you in royal palaces? Does it give you the power to crush your enemies?" His cobalt eyes held nothing warm, only madness and the joy of cutting deep. "Do you know what's really funny?" His court of sycophants all giggled before the joke had even landed, and his chest swelled. "I struck the law enabling a champion to stand in for their regent years ago."

A muscle flexed in Deven's jaw. "You did what?"

"You didn't think I would shout that little change from

the rooftops? Not when it meant I could watch you squirm. In fact, it was witnessed by our very own Nitin, and he kept it so wonderfully quiet all the days he was in your fortress."

His taunting washed over me, each word a stinging lash against my resolve. With each cruel jibe, frustration rose like a swelling wave. I couldn't understand why the potion hadn't worked yet.

Deven gritted his teeth. "You have hours left, Prem. Not even days. Hours left to play the tyrant."

"No need to be petulant. Kings can shape the entire world to our advantage." He waggled his eyebrows. "And when I gut your beloved—when I get her to gut herself—I will bask in the knowledge you spent your precious time together arguing about me. It's delicious, really. Just as good as the Roshni saga."

Deven snarled. His midnight gaze became twin comets of fury, and he lunged across the table as though he were a cornered beast, newly unleashed. His chair overturned, utensils crashed, and curry spilt as he reached for the collar of Prem's jacket. His muscles rippled, his body braced, and the shift was so close that I could taste it in the bottled breath of those around the high table. He was a moment away from claws and teeth and the ferocious strength of his tiger self. Harya and Prem's new general intercepted, and it required their combined strength to hold Deven back.

Prem brushed himself off and straightened his crooked crown, a cruel smile curving his lips.

I placed a hand on Deven's back, and he froze at my touch. "I promise you will get your chance. Just not now." The fire in his eyes dimmed as he turned to face me. We needed to give the potion time to work. Why wasn't it working? "Dance with me, Deven. What if we don't get a chance to dance again?"

He took a shuddering breath. Then he shook off Harya and the new general, held out his hand and led me to the dance floor as all eyes turned away from the fracas and followed us.

The musicians on the dais eased into a new piece, their *sitars* and *tablas* coming to life with melodies that were haunting—a lamentation rather than a celebration. Under the scrutiny of the loyalists, with shimmering chandeliers overhead, the music took on a life of its own. It reverberated through the throne room, filling every corner. The *tabla* added a rhythmic undercurrent to the song, allowing the strains of the *sitar* to flow freely through the air. Aanya joined them on the dais, and I smiled my gratitude at her. Her notes cascaded like raindrops on a frozen lake, carrying with them her soothing magic. As they played, the melody soared and dipped, and tension eased from my shoulders.

We danced while we waited for the potion to take effect. Deven's hand found my waist, pulling me close as we moved to the rhythm of the music. His touch was firm yet gentle, guiding me with a confidence born of practice. But it was no longer important to me who he'd danced with before, only that he'd chosen me. He'd chosen me in front of all these people, despite his history, despite his broken heart, despite his private nature. Others joined us. My grandparents danced in a formal ballroom style. Nisha and Ashwin, clumsy but determined. Somewhere, Kavita drew laughter for haranguing her husband when he asked her to dance. Aanya garnered gasps and stares when she stepped off the stage and went straight into Leena's embrace on the dance floor, where they swayed, foreheads leaning together. Free, somehow, in the centre of the storm. My hand rested lightly on Deven's shoulder, and I lifted my head to lock eyes with him, and they brimmed with love and longing. We glided across the floor, lost in each other, even though we both knew this was the calm before the storm. That it might all go wrong, and we might not survive. We wrung out that moment of happiness though the spectre of Prem and the potion and the empty throne on the dais loomed. When the music reached its crescendo, Deven spun me around in a graceful arc, and my laughter rang out like a bell in the night.

I wanted the moment to stretch out forever.

But it couldn't because there was always an end.

CHAPTER 28

The music stuttered to a halt as Prem stood. "Enough of this charade."

Deven's arms stiffened around me. "Here it comes. Here's his play."

"You saw what he did," Prem announced to all, jealousy and wrath contorting his face. "The mighty general has fallen from grace. He would break our rules. He would dishonour the terms of the duel."

I looked around for a flicker of awareness amongst the loyalists. Surely they could see through Prem? Surely they understood that he was threatened by Deven. The people's love for Deven made Prem feel small because, even wearing the crown, he couldn't compete. He wanted to sully their regard. Deven had kept hope alive in Jalapashu.

I made to stalk towards him, but Deven gripped my hand, wary. "You said we'd settle this matter without involving the people."

"The rebels aren't my people. They're yours." Claws scraped against my internal landscape, and around us, loyalists snapped into action, and the rebels tore at their scalps, trying desperately to fight Prem's commands. "My cousin won't live to see my victory. My subjects, you will lynch him for raising a hand to your raja."

My chest constricted. *Lynch him?* That was not fucking happening.

Deven's eyes collided with mine, and the hurt in them left me shaken. It was the realisation that no humanity remained in Prem. That his cousin could stoop low enough to raise a hand against him forsaking the bonds of family. That Prem had chosen this road despite Deven standing by him and curbing his worst excesses long after Prem had deserved it. That Prem could command—no, puppet—the people to turn against him, knowing Deven wouldn't truly be able to defend himself because it was one thing felling soldiers during battle but quite another killing the vulnerable. It was indefensible to kill villagers, shopkeepers, farmers, artisans and teachers that he had known and loved, and Deven's honour wouldn't allow it. It was the cruellest death sentence.

Deven turned to me, eyes wild, his tiger demanding release. "The thought of you being hurt sends me to my knees. You're getting out of this. I don't care what happens to me."

"Don't you get it? We save each other. You think I could make it through the duel if anything happened to you?" I grabbed his neck and pulled him down so we were a hair's breadth apart, there, in our glad rags. We'd become part of the raja's performance when, all along, we should have made our own rules. To hell with being safe before I bared my soul to him. "I love you, Dev, and we will have a future."

His lashes swept down, and then he raised his obsidian eyes to mine. "You love me?"

My heart caught in my throat as the people came towards us. "Yes. With all that I am and all that I will be."

He took a shuddering breath and leaned his forehead against mine. "I love you, Kiya. With all that I am."

Then he pulled apart from me, releasing a low warning growl. He was already loosening the ornate top of his *sherwani*, already priming to shift. The mob was upon us seconds later, a cacophony of scorn on their lips: of shame, death, condemnation and unending rage. Men, women and children—nobody on the loyalist side was spared from Prem's puppetry. Their faces contorted with vengeance, and they seized anything within reach to use as makeshift weapons: chairs, plates, knives and spoons. With wild, desperate cries, they lunged towards us, fuelled by pent-up rage and a primal urge to mete out punishment. As if they were extensions of Prem's character. The air rang with the sound of splintering wood and shattering glass, and the swell of violence drowned out all other noise. Drowned out the sound of Leena and Nani's shouts and Aanya's singing. Drowned out the general's urging to get the hell behind him and my clamouring heart.

My thoughts were consumed by the need to shield him from harm at any cost. "We do this together."

He snarled in approval and shifted in a matter of seconds. Golden fur rippled over sinewy muscles, and his teeth gleamed like polished ivory daggers. His tail lashed back and forth in agitation, and he exuded an aura of untamed strength. The ground trembled beneath our feet as I called my magic, and a battle cry erupted from my lips, urging my rebels into action. Urging the gargoyles to join the fight against Prem Kumar.

Adversaries closed in from all sides, loyalists numbering more than the resistance. Cracks spiderwebbed outward from where I stood, fissures erupting in the ground as jagged shards of rock burst forth. But loyalists and rebels were so dispersed that I couldn't hem them in, neither to imprison them nor to keep them safe. So, I began plucking them off one by one, with spells and force and earth magic. The resistance followed my lead, using my spell vials and drawing their concealed weapons to strike down people who had once been their neighbours.

I saw it all happen then. How all our efforts might have been for nothing. How Sitara had died trying to discover this place and how we would die in it. How Leena wouldn't have her happy ending with Aanya, and I wouldn't have mine with Deven. How Nani's heart would be broken all over again. How the people would continue to suffer and Merlin—Merlin was far apart from me at this final moment, and I felt our separation so keenly that my grief was like an anchor dragging me deep into an abyss.

Until Sindhuja's voice broke through the roar in my mind. *Mistress?*

Stand with the resistance. Keep my sister safe. Protect the rebels and refrain from lethal force on the loyalists, I said.

A sudden surge of reinforcements emerged from the shadows. The gargoyles—my gargoyles—came to my aid, and Sindhuja's voice was a roar in my mind as she commanded them. The stalwart guardians of Jalapashu spread across the throne room with a thunderous roar, casting menacing shadows across the room. Some of the gargoyles perched atop the grand chandeliers that hung from the ceiling, their massive forms casting ominous shadows as they surveyed the battlefield below. With a thunderous clap of their wings, they swooped down upon their foes, their blows echoing through the chamber like the tolling of a funeral bell. Chandeliers shook and partially shattered with the force of their flight.

Prem had shifted. His transformation—never before witnessed by the masses in the kingdom—unleashed a wave of terror among the people in that confined space. He prowled towards a group of rebels with predatory grace. He was bulkier than Deven, his pattern of stripes thicker and sparser, and his feral still-blue eyes gleamed with an unholy light as he stalked his prey. A low growl rumbled in his chest as he lunged forward with lightning speed, razor-sharp claws slashing through the air. But Harya intervened, backed by two other gargoyles, using strong legs to propel Prem away, and all at once, he knew. He swung around, his tiger coat heaving with unrestrained seething. The tiger roared loudly enough to shake the heavens, realising that the allegiance of the gargoyles to him had been a lie.

He had been tricked and outmanoeuvred.

The gargoyles were still mine. We had foiled his carefully laid plans.

Despite his best efforts, he couldn't get to us. The trio of gargoyles engaged him on all sides.

Constrain him, but don't harm him. He is mine in duel, as per the laws of this land, I commanded the gargoyles.

The ground quaked beneath me as my magic surged with reckless abandon. I fought beside Deven, commanding the earth to my will, stripping aside the grandeur of the throne room, pulling boulders from beneath us that became projectiles, and calling forth pillars of stone to impede the advance of our enemies. My hair came loose, and strands of it whipped around my face as I moved. The *lehenga* I wore—its whalebone corset impacting the flow of my breath—constrained me, but there wasn't time to stop, wasn't time to think. I could only react. Only rely on my instincts for survival. As my powers surged, so too did the darkness within me, fuelled by the chaos and violence surrounding us. It was a double-edged sword, granting me strength and ferocity but threatening to consume me. My training—not only battle training but my decades of pottery—came to the fore as my hands moved with practised precision, fingers tracing arcane patterns in the air as I called upon the earth. A shroud of dust and debris swirled around me, and Deven stood firm in the vortex of my power. His claws, his teeth and his furious roar challenged anyone who dared to near us, our commitment to protecting each other never wavering.

I'd stop at nothing to ensure his safety, even if it meant facing the darkest depths of my soul.

Prem had soldiers, but half of them had deserted and followed Deven, evening the odds. With regard to civilians, the loyalists were clearly outmatched and ill-prepared compared to our rebels. They had neither the training nor the weapons of the resistance, and their robotic attempts didn't match our righteous passion. It felt good to be on the stronger side, validating our strategy. Throughout the throne room, rebels wielded my spell-infused vessels, launching them like hand grenades amidst the tumult of the room. *Abhayam. Nidrāṃ dhāvatu. Tvamapaśya. Boe kāṭe. Mohitaḥ bhava. Adṛśyatāṃ dadātu.* More and more, until the spells clouded the air and the air thickened with magic. From protective shielding to offensive blasts that scattered loyalists, the spells I had prepared with Merlin flowed through the throne room like a river of light. Loyalists found themselves beset by fear and confusion, their ranks thrown into disarray as they struggled to contend with the spells, as they were harangued into corners, and found blades to their necks or backs or bellies. And when they resisted or when they attacked with renewed ferocity, their blood soaked the ground.

Deven's sinewy muscles rippled beneath the sleek coat of his tattooed fur. He moved with lethal grace, his onyx eyes blazing with a primal ferocity. His movements were swift and precise as he bared his teeth at those who stood against us, his claws swiping out only when necessary. When Nitin came for us, Deven's claws gouged the poet's flesh while I encased the *jhumka* sorceress in a mountain of soil. After every tussle, Deven returned his focus to Prem. But he was thwarted by loyalists, puppets determined to do Prem's bidding. I cursed Kaladhar for the failure of his potion. For our failure to break the raja's mind control. Deven's attackers came thick and fast. We could barely keep up, hampered by our quickly unravelling restraint. The new general of Jalapashu had shifted into a panther and approached with a guttural snarl. The panther leapt into action and met Deven's onslaught with agile grace. Their movements were a blur of motion as they clashed in a deadly dance, claws and teeth meeting in a fury before they circled and pounced again.

As the chaos unfolded around us, I lost myself. I lost my values. At that moment, I didn't care, couldn't care, for anything but the survival of our side. It didn't matter that people were injured or died because every moment we struck out meant that we were alive, that we resisted Prem Kumar's tyranny despite his intent to harm us, to silence us, to enforce his will on us. Once in this very room, when the raja's sorcerers had sent a mist to discover traitors, I had unlocked the doors to allow the people to flee. Now, I barred them with a flick of fingers.

In the midst of the fray, I caught a glimpse of Grandfather, his aged frame standing tall as he shielded Nani from the onslaught. His eyes met mine briefly, and then he drew his sword, calling his own sorcery. Nani was a vision in a silver *sari* beside him, her weathered hands raised and her eyes glowing with ancient wisdom, breathing focused, as she unleashed a torrent of spells that wove through the air like threads of glittering light. She didn't seek to wound, but her fierce and precise spells left her targets reeling as she fought side by side with Grandfather. She stunned the loyalists and froze them in place. *Mohayati* and *Jamāna*. She dazed them and disarmed them. *Avasthiti* and *Nirasta*. She slowed them and repelled them. *Dhīmā* and *Tyakta*.

Mahi's violet eye was wide open, gleaming with an other-worldly light that made even me shiver. Her foresight granted her a keen advantage over those who sought to do us harm and anticipated attacks with uncanny accuracy. She brandished a small dagger with deadly effect, every move-ment purposeful and deliberate, with her brother a statue beside her as though incapable of autonomy over his own body.

Sindhuja stayed close to my sister, and I was fiercely glad. With determination etched upon her beautiful face, Leena called verdant foliage to encircle Aanya like a protective cocoon, but loyalists hacked through. Aanya sang, but it didn't do any good, not against mind control, not when the noise was so deafening and the people had succumbed to their baser instincts. So my sister summoned thick vines and tangled roots to lash out at our adversaries. From the cracks in the stone floor and the crevices in the walls, verdant tendrils emerged, twisting and writhing like serpents as they sought their targets. Thorny embraces bound loyalists in place, and she only showed flashes of deadlier force when Aanya was at risk of harm. With each passing moment, the battlefield became a wild and untamed landscape.

Lata spun into my line of sight, parrying and thrusting with a svelte sword, and Kavita, with rolled-up sleeves, used plates as flying discs. Jilu wrestled with grim finesse, and Radha threw daggers with the same precision with which she cut onions. Nisha had been dancing with Ashwin close to us, and I glimpsed her delivering bare-knuckle punches. One assailant went down, but another came from behind before she was ready. In a flash of movement, Deven sprang into action. His golden fur bristled with determination. With a snarl, he leapt in front of Nisha, his body shielding her from harm. He confronted the assailant, swiping at the loyalist with his powerful claws, sending him stumbling backwards in shock. Growls reverberated through the air, a warning to any who dared to threaten Nisha, and when she had regrouped, he pushed on.

I lost sight of him as the battle raged on—glimpsing only flashes of tattooed golden fur—as I concentrated on what was immediately before my nose. The throne room became a maelstrom of chaos and conflict, with the fate of Jalapashu hanging in the balance. The scent of blood and sweat hung heavy in the air, mingling with the heady aroma of exotic spices and rich foods that had been abandoned in the heat of battle. Broken shards of crystal and porcelain littered the floor, catching the light from the shattered chandeliers and casting fractured rainbows across the room.

There was nothing royal about me now. Jagged tears marred the bodice and skirt of my *lehenga*, revealing glimpses of cut and bruised skin beneath. The hem trailed behind me in tatters, dragging along the bloodstained floor. With wings outstretched and talons bared, my gargoyles soared through the air like avenging angels, sending adversaries to the ground with bone-crushing force. Gone was the semblance of nobility, replaced by the stark reality of war.

The host of gargoyles surged in my head. *We broke our hold. Hurry. Hurry, gargoyle queen. We need our combined strength.*

My head whipped around to locate Prem, my heart a hummingbird in my chest as I summoned a barrage of stones to halt his advance. Dread filled me as I raced towards him, loosing my magic. Though my missiles struck him and drew spots of blood, the earth crumbled beneath his powerful paws as he surged towards his target.

They saw him too late. Husband and wife called their magic, their spells, and pooled their combined strength, but the tiger was already airborne, and their magic stuttered, succumbing to blind panic or diverting to mental shielding, as he seemed to engage his mind magic. They were unable to evade his savage assault. With a snarl of triumph, he pounced on Grandfather and Nani, bringing them crashing to the ground. His bulky form pinned them beneath his weight, saliva dripping from his jagged, browning teeth.

It happened so fast.

Grandfather heaved himself up with superhuman strength, strength grounded in his unending love for Nani, allowing her to scramble backwards. He summoned a shield to protect Nani even as his own strength faltered. Even as Prem clawed open his chest. Grandfather jerked, and his arcane energy crackled and surged, a shimmering barrier of light enveloping Nani in its embrace. I called the earth to cocoon my grandparents, but the tiger was too close, too determined, disregarding any pain of his own in his need to inflict it. He didn't shrink from the blows I directed at him. I was nearly upon them, my dagger drawn, my breath ragged. Prem's cobalt eyes turned to Nani. With a final, defiant gesture, Grandfather channelled his might at the tiger, drawing his attention again in a flare of light and courage. Prem pushed his head through the flare, his skin flaying for the briefest second. Then he sank his teeth into Grandfather's neck and jerked his head to the right. Skin tore. Blood gushed.

I couldn't look. I couldn't look away.

The world went cold and quiet.

Then Nani's anguished cry pierced the air, a soul-wrenching lament for the man who had always put her above all else. A man who had written her love letters, danced with her under moonlit skies and gifted her flowers just because. A man who had praised her cooking and been the father of her child. A man who respected her individuality and their differences. A man, though rigid, who had let her opinion shape his and had held her through their troubles. A man who had looked at her tenderly through the years, grown old with her and given everything for her. A man who had been her first and last kiss. An irreplaceable love. A love that stretched over a lifetime and yet was still too short.

In that moment of devastation, the weight of my choices became heavier than I could bear.

It wasn't supposed to be like this. The people weren't supposed to be fighting each other, relative against relative, friend against friend. Horror washed over me as I looked at Grandfather's body, cradled in Nani's lap, and at my hands covered in blood and dirt. This conflict wasn't of the people's making, and I'd been wrong, so wrong, to walk down this path. It shouldn't have taken lost lives for realisation to dawn.

If I couldn't cut the strings of the marionettes, then I had to separate the people to keep both sides safe.

I unlocked the doors as Prem turned his sights on me, a tiger's smile on his flayed face—a face of nightmares.

Deven came roaring to my side, his fur slick with blood.

There weren't enough gargoyles to get the people to safety, but I had to try before sadness swallowed me whole, before the situation got any worse. I closed down the noise all around me and reached out to the gargoyles. Something new and unfamiliar tingled in my mind. Each gargoyle possessed its own distinct presence, and it was as if my mind had expanded to encompass the stirrings of new energy. New life that brought a rush of warmth and connection.

Take the resistance to the fortress, I commanded as my hazel eyes clashed with Prem's cobalt ones.

There was a rush in my mind, and my eyes widened in astonishment as a multitude of stony grey flesh crashed through the windows of the throne room, materialised in the swirling clouds of spell and joined the gargoyle host.

CHAPTER 29

The gargoyles came, their wings stretched wide, casting dramatic silhouettes across the fractured light of the throne room. Their eyes gleamed with an otherworldly luminance as they surveyed their surroundings.

Though their animated forms looked utterly transformed from the clay state I witnessed in the studio, I recognised them. I recognised them in form—amongst them the eagle-like gargoyle, the owl-headed humanoid, the fanged serpent, the steel-clawed dragon, the ape-legged swell of darkness, the blazing phoenix—and from the way their essence slotted into the landscape of my mind. Nirantar, Vajra, Agni, Javan, Ulooka, Dhara, and more.

Mahi's vision had come true. I was the great pottery master's heir. And maybe, with help from the heat of Sitara's ashes, I had even outdone him. But none of it mattered if I couldn't save the people.

I have sisters. Sindhuja looked around at her kind that now numbered nearly fifty. *And more brothers.*

She rallied them, and the gargoyles hauled rebels from the throne room, two apiece. There were injuries amongst them, and three rebels had lost their lives, but I shut down the emotional part of my brain, telling the gargoyles to bring our dead with us. The loyalists had dead, too. Their bodies littered the floor. A dozen, maybe. I caught the cold, dead eyes of Yash, the sapling soldier. I didn't know if he had chosen a side.

I didn't know who had killed him: our side or theirs.

It happened in a blur, so very fast. One minute, we were on the ground, and the next, Deven had shifted back into his human self. A tiger's roar resounded in our ears as the gargoyles navigated the chaos with unmatched agility. They sought out those in need of salvation amidst the swirling maelstrom and hoisted us into the air.

My magic flowed as I kept the tiger at bay, only just, sweat beading my skin, my chest ashen as though I had been through a fire, and maybe I had. When we were all airborne at last, and the powerful beat of wings filled the evening air —Sindhuja's talons gripping my shoulders, Deven with the phoenix, Leena and Aanya with Harya, Mahi and Menon with the fanged serpent—my eyes snagged on the owl-headed gargoyle Ulooka carrying Nani and my dead grandfather. My heart crumbled like ancient ruins at the sight of them.

The decayed sacred tree loomed up ahead, and its most prominent trunk had split in half as though recoiling from the violence perpetrated against the people.

Finally, with the chill wind rushing against my face, I broke apart.

~

The gargoyles transported their passengers to the courtyard of the fortress and then ascended to the battlements. There, they took up vigil, their watchful gaze sweeping across the kingdom. The resistance lit oil lamps and candles in the courtyard to bring light as though the flickering flames could somehow ignite hope. Though beleaguered and horrified by the demise of the sacred banyan tree, they whispered prayers of gratitude for our escape and stared in wonder at me and the growing battalion of stone guardians. Yuvan, Merlin and Babbu couldn't hold the children back. They spilt out from their hiding places, eyes like saucers, seeking solace and reassurance amidst the chaos.

Merlin had transformed into a jackalope once more, just as he had wanted. Just as he had said, antlers from shimmering ivory crowned his head, perfectly in proportion to his body, as if he had stepped out of a mythical tale. I thought that maybe it hadn't been the labyrinth after all. Maybe his transformation came when the people he loved were in the greatest danger.

The wounded stretched out on cots and blankets in the communal hall, carried in by Ashwin and Deven, who had managed to find some ill-fitting trousers and didn't seem to feel the cold. Whose service to the people superseded his own comfort. Mahi brought out salves and bandages, stopping to place a reverent hand on my shoulder—perhaps for the return of her brother, perhaps for fulfilling my destiny as Vikram Reddy's heir—before she moved away. Stoicism reigned as Leena, and those with capable hands and basic know-how tended to injuries. The smell of herbs and potions hung thick in the air, mingling with the iron tang of blood.

Families reunited and embraced. Nisha, Ashwin and Ishaan. Sunita and Tanay, who wanted to know if the potion had worked. Wanted to know what his father had done and why. Grief bloomed like a black rose for the fallen. For Grandfather, who they had grown to respect. For a farmer called Mansoor and an art teacher called Shanti.

We knew that we wouldn't have long to regroup.

This was a hiatus from battle; the violence would resume.

Prem Kumar would ensure it.

My heart pounded erratically against my ribcage then, and a rising tide of panic swelled within my chest. Suffocation gripped me, and a cold sweat broke out against my brow as though the very air around me had turned thick and heavy, pressing in on me from all sides. My lungs didn't work as they should, my breath hitching, thin and choppy. My hands trembled uncontrollably at my sides, and the world tilted on its axis. So I ran towards my quarters, my vision blurring at the edges, hardly hearing the calls of *Mistress! Mistress!* in my head.

Once inside, I took heaving breaths. A delicate scent of smoke wafted through the air. I stripped off my soiled garments, my skin heavy with blood and grime, struggling with the ties at the back of the corset until strong arms enveloped me from behind, a bare torso against my trembling back.

His whiskey voice anchored me. "Kiya. It's okay, my love."

He undid the ribbons, and I ripped off the corset and sat on the bed in my knickers, head between my knees. His hands rubbed up and down my bare back, and he pushed my damp hair back from my face, extracting the pinned jewels and flowers that nested in it. With each slow, deliberate breath I took, the tightness in my chest gradually loosened, and my heartbeat slowed to a steadier rhythm.

When the earth was solid beneath my feet, I spoke. "I haven't even spoken to Nani yet. I couldn't..."

Midnight eyes grounded me and flicked away for a moment like he'd heard something. "You will."

"He gave his life for her, for me, for what we want to achieve."

"Yes, I think he did." He held my cheek. "You gave the new gargoyles life."

I nodded. "With Sitara's help." I bit my lip. I could still feel his bargain snaking between us, like a bitter residue that coursed through my veins. "But why didn't the potion work? Nani's meticulous. It can't be her fault."

Deven raked a hand through his tousled hair. "I don't know. Let's get dressed and figure it out, little witch. He's…"

"Coming back."

A shuddering sigh. "Yes. He is."

We washed side by side over a basin with washcloths, scrubbing our faces and skin clean—not stopping to clean the grime from our nails when time was short—then put on fresh leathers. He took my hairbrush from me when my fingers fumbled and brushed out the knotted strands before I tied it in a ponytail.

He sniffed the air. "Do you smell that?"

I frowned. "The scent of the battle on our clothes?"

"Must be my imagination."

We had barely finished strapping on our weapons when the gargoyle chorus sounded an alarm in my head. There was a myriad of tones and timbres, each new gargoyle adding its unique resonance to the blend. Their warnings clanged with resolve and urgency. *The battle is on our doorstep, mistress. The raja comes. With soldiers and the people. Synchronised, as though the mind control persists.*

With a sense of grim determination, I steeled myself for the tumultuous storm that was about to descend upon us, praying that we would emerge unscathed. "Dev, we have to protect the people. Prem is here. They are all here."

There was a gentle stirring in the stillness that set my teeth on edge.

We spun towards the faint shuffling, reflexively reaching for our weapons. Then, as if materialising out of a pocket of air, Kaladhar emerged from the shadow and calmly lit a cigar, its embers casting an eerie glow on his gaunt face. He looked taller somehow, as if his dignity had been restored. His back was less bowed, and his beard was trimmed. He had washed, his nails had been cut, and he wore clean robes. His glittering amber eyes held a touch of warmth.

I looked at the sorcerer with wide-eyed incredulity, my skin crawling. "Praveen, how long have you been here?"

Kaladhar's expression was unreadable as he glanced out the window and blew out rings of smoke. "You didn't expect me to disregard that little hatch I requested, did you? If a man is to meet his end, he expects to relish a modicum of freedom beforehand. Bask in the sun's warmth. Feel the caress of the breeze upon his skin. Savour a cup of freshly brewed *chai*. Stand beneath the azure skies. Assess the state of his allies and adversaries."

Deven growled. "You've been around us all this time."

His voice croaked, lungs thick with tar. A hiss of cigar smoke escaped his lips. "Calm yourself. No one caught a glimpse of me. I could have been leagues away. Yet here I am. Because the bargain I made with the gargoyle queen is my release." He took a slow drag of the cigar and looked at it with a sad smile on his twisted lips as he stubbed it out on a plate. Then, he withdrew a polished dagger and a vessel from within his robes. "I took the liberty of collecting my wife's dagger from the palace vaults while you were other-wise engaged this morning. And this, of course, is—"

The raja is almost here. Hurry. Gargoyle queen. Hurry, chanted Sindhuja and her fellow guardians.

I sucked in a breath. I'd recognise the earthy brown urn with its etched swirls of water anywhere. "Sitara's urn."

"Forgive my tardiness. I had to wait patiently for it to cool." Amber eyes glimmered with curiosity. "It remains my pleasure to have met the long-awaited heir of the pottery master. Your gargoyles had quite the awakening."

Deven gritted out his words. "Be quick, Kaladhar. The future of the kingdom depends on it."

The sorcerer seemed oddly at ease as he handed me the dagger and urn. "Then it is time. Let's do this outside, where the ground is fertile. Where the *queen-in-waiting* can awaken the land."

My spine tingled. "That's why the mind control isn't broken yet? Because the bargain isn't yet fulfilled."

Kaladhar nodded. "It will take the spilling of my blood. But magic such as this is complicated. Jalapashu has been deprived of a just ruler for an age. Thus, the potion will only take effect once the land assesses the purity of your intentions. Tell me, gargoyle queen, are you prepared to place yourself in peril for the people, even when your life hangs in the balance?"

My stomach churned as we went outside. The gargoyles were silhouettes against the night sky, their vigil facing outwards as the raja's troops approached. The eyes that were focused on the trudge of boots outside the walls turned to us in confusion at the sight of the stranger. Whispers were all around as we approached the patch of soil beneath the fallen sacred tree. Whispers with the sorcerer's name. Praveen Kaladhar sighed as if he'd never heard sweeter words, as if the falling night and the absent stars were the greatest canvas he had ever seen.

Suddenly, Leena was there, doe eyes focused on the urn I cradled. Two words. A world of meaning. "That's him?"

"Yeah," I said as Kaladhar's lips spread in a gruesome smile at my sister.

"It doesn't have to be you," said Deven as a hush settled over the resistance.

"That was our bargain." Glittering, amber eyes flitted to me as he lowered himself to his knees and offered me his neck. "This position should facilitate matters. But first, you must place the urn on the ground and remove its lid."

"Let me," said Leena, quietly.

We didn't expect to see Sitara again, but we did.

She was mist and shadow. She was our father's heart-shaped face and a mass of midnight hair. She was mossy green eyes, magnolia perfume and a faint tinge of a tangerine shift dress. Her figure was insubstantial because she wasn't entirely present in the physical realm. She was not rage; she was contentment. She was childhood memories and curious intelligence and sisterly affection and arguments over clothes and the most stalwart ally.

"Gods," whispered Leena as my knees almost buckled and my heartbeat raced.

"There is my deliverance," rasped Kaladhar before uttering his final words. "Take my life, *queen-in-waiting*."

I met his eyes, and they were full of joy. I tried not to think. I tried not to feel. There was a swift inhale—mine or Leena's, Deven's, the sorcerer's, the swell of the resistance, I didn't know—as I plunged Praveen Kaladhar's dagger into his heart cavity, felt the resistance and pushed harder before wrenching the dagger out. A crimson bloom spread across his grey robes. His body dropped to the side, his eyes wide open, his mouth curved in bliss. There were cries from rebels and soothing words from Deven or Leena. It all merged in my mind. I stared as a stream of blood soaked into the base of the fallen banyan tree, horror and shock surging through me at my actions. At my easy acquaintance with death. At how wrong it was, even though he had requested it.

Deven peeled my fingers from the hilt of the dagger. "Give it to me, Kiya."

Was it killing a man in cold blood if he had begged you to do it? If you benefited from it and didn't say no? I released my grip, tore my eyes away from what I had done, and turned back to the spectre of our sister. "You opened doors for us, Sitara. I want you here."

"I don't want to live again. I had my adventures. I had my great loves." Her mossy eyes lingered on the two of us. "And that was enough for me. I'm ready to let you go. My body's already gone. It's time. Scatter my ashes in a woodland filled with bluebells. What's left of me will mingle with the plants and soil and fuel the reservoir of life. You'll cry some more tears for me, but the world will keep spinning. And that's how it should be."

"We let you go," said Leena. "But we will always miss you."

My throat burned with tears. "Will we see you again?"

Our oldest sister's mossy eyes shone, and already her hands were rising, cresting a wave, sweeping across the sorcerer's weakening body: her final act of love. She touched her heart, as she had when we were children, to show us she was there for us. "No, but I'm with you. Always. Now, trust that everything will be okay. Win the duel, gargoyle queen. Be well, my sisters. I'm glad we belonged to each other for a while."

With her touch, Kaladhar's body vanished into the fabric of the universe or time or the starless sky.

Sitara disappeared with him. Forever.

As Leena and I held each other, my heart was no longer a welt.

Sitara had left for the last time, but she would be a part of us always. She was free, dispersed across the universe like she wanted to be. We would scatter her ashes amongst bluebells, and the waves of grief would come through the years, but we'd learn to swim with the current.

CHAPTER 30

Rhythmic marching and the clatter of weapons jerked us into action. Rebels clustered tightly in the court-yard, faces pale and tight, as Prem Kumar reached our gates. Every sound was magnified in the stillness of the night. Despite all that we had planned and prepared, I couldn't believe that the hour of the duel was nigh.

While Leena handed Sitara's urn to Yuvan for safekeeping, I gathered the Council of Rebels around me, with one notable omission. Nani's birdlike frame, always so proud and straight-backed, was rounded with grief.

I hugged her, barely holding it together. "I'm so sorry he's gone. I'm so sorry I didn't stop it." I didn't know whether to promise revenge or something more. Something that meant that Grandfather's death wasn't in vain.

"He was so proud of you both. He was convinced you'd inherited his backbone. His need to shape the world." Nani's eyes lifted to mine, though her chin quivered. "Prakash would want us to see this through."

Leena returned, her voice shaky. "Is Prem Kumar's mind control broken?"

I shook my head. "I can still feel Kaladhar's bargain in

my blood. He said the magic is complex. That the land is assessing the purity of my intentions."

"Good. That is good. Do you trust me?" Mahi's face shone like the moon above us. "The strings will be severed when Babbu soars in emerald circles above the battlefield. But we can't wait. If we don't go out there, Prem will breach the fortress walls and loyalists and rebels alike will perish. But if we go outside and brave these next few minutes, we will finish this. And the kingdom can be made anew."

I glanced up at the battlements, where the gargoyle leader stared out. *Show me through your eyes, Sindhuja.*

She opened her senses to me from high on the battlements, the sole gargoyle with whom this was possible, the one with whom I shared the deepest connection. I took in a shuddering breath as the night opened up. Beyond the fortress gates, hundreds of puppeted loyalists held flickering torches aloft. Their vacant eyes were devoid of emotion or individuality. Their bodies were mere vessels manipulated by the raja's dark will. The soldiers—whom Dev cared for and had worked alongside—were pawns in Prem's twisted game of domination. They advanced with battering rams loaded with heavy logs. Siege towers cast long shadows across the landscape, with archers standing ready on elevated platforms, poised to rain death on us. Prem, in his human form, prowled amongst the assembled soldiers and loyalists in loose trousers and a shirt that suggested he intended to shift. His muscles coiled tight with pent-up aggression.

Even in my darkest nightmares, I hadn't envisaged it like this.

I tugged the cord in my mind gently and snapped back to my own perspective like a tether had been released. Disoriented, it took me a moment to connect to the familiar weight of my body and regain my bearings. I sought out Deven, who, in full strategic mode, had flown up to the battlements with Harya for his own review.

He locked eyes with me as he landed in the courtyard once more, then swung around to the people. "Move back!" His lips were set in a thin line of tenacity. "You've played your part in this fight, and we are grateful. Let us handle this next part. Yuvan, Merlin, get them inside. Find cover."

I joined him, gulping as rebels raised their fists in solidarity. "Take care of your loved ones. Stay safe."

The people whispered that I was the great pottery master's heir, the gargoyle queen, their rani, a warrior, a seeker of justice, one of them. They didn't say I was a killer, but that didn't erase the blood on my hands. Didn't tell me if I'd murder two men that day: one who had asked for release and another whose throne I coveted. Didn't tell me if I'd be like the great pottery master of legend, who had stopped her megalomania of his rani by killing her, even though she was about to return his unrequited love for her.

Love couldn't be further from the emotion Prem Kumar inspired in me.

Round and round went my thoughts like a carousel as we coaxed the people to safety. I clenched my fists, knowing loyalists would soon swing the mammoth logs against our walls. I had to keep the people safe, ours and his.

Suddenly, Ishaan slipped his parents' hold and threw his arms around his uncle's legs. "I don't want you to go."

Deven brushed a loving hand over the boy's hair and passed him back to his father, a grave look passing between them. "Even if I promise to play cricket with you tomorrow?"

"Keep my brother safe." Nisha clung to us. "Prem's no cousin of ours. He didn't care if Ishaan lived or died. Our family deserves better. Don't let him take your happiness. I swear, I will come out there myself, Dev."

"She's right, as usual. Give him hell," said Ashwin to Deven. "And ask her."

Ask her? I frowned as Deven clapped his brother-in-law's shoulder and pressed a kiss to his sister's cheek.

Then we jogged over to rejoin the council as the people streamed out of the courtyard and the gargoyles' silhouettes stood firm on the battlements. I looked at them all. My court. My family. There was Leena in a mixture of leathers and armour, Merlin—his ivory antlers a sight to behold—plus Aanya, Nani, Mahi, the parrot on her shoulder, and Menon. Faces grim, weapons sharpened, magic brimming just beneath the surface. I laid a hand on Deven's chest. Through his leathers, his heart was beating with a quiet intensity, a sense of calm amidst the storm.

My chest cracked open with love. "I wouldn't have come so far without each and every one of you. I mean this when I say it. You don't have to come with me."

"Yes, we do," said Leena, as Deven's lips quirked in approval. "We can't fight the duel for you, but you're not alone."

I bit my lip. Even if it was selfish, I desperately wanted them with me. "Okay. But Aanya, I need you inside the walls to keep the people calm." My heart wrenched as she clung to Leena. "I'm sorry. There's no time to argue it. The rest of you, I'll hold out in the duel until the mind control breaks. You keep the loyalists at bay. There'll be no more innocent blood on our hands. They're not the enemy."

Mahi thumbed her topaz medallion. "We can do that. Can't we, brother?"

Menon trembled and gritted out the words with difficulty. "No more innocent blood."

It began.

The thuds of battering rams echoed through the fortress, shaking its foundations. Amidst the swell of rebel cries, I instinctively raised my hands, reinforcing our boundaries with a surge of earth magic. Leena threw up her hands, too, forming a protective barrier that wrapped the walls, inside and out, against the impending assault. Vines of thick ivy sprouted from the cracks in the stone. Vibrant flowers bloomed amidst it, their colourful petals a defiant contrast to the backdrop of war. A reminder that life and love could flourish even in dark times.

We hugged, and I tried not to think about who would live and who would die.

Then, with a shaky intake of breath, I summoned the gargoyles to carry us up to the battlements.

Wind rushed against my face as Sindhuja swept me up from the courtyard. The air was crisp, carrying with it the scent of fear and Leena's flowers. The night sky, bereft of stars, stretched towards the half-abandoned houses of Jala-pashu and the white-washed palace with its ruined throne room. We found our footing on crumbling stone atop walls that groaned with vibrations from the battering rams. I looked down, taking in the challenge of the siege with my own eyes, mouth dry, heart pounding.

Prem Kumar met my eyes, his nostrils flaring.

Destroy their equipment, I relayed to the gargoyles. *Don't harm a hair on the peoples' heads.*

In the blink of an eye, a small battalion of gargoyles under Sindhuja's command swooped down from the battlements, their wings casting shadows across the torchlit battleground. With menacing smiles, the gargoyles plucked squirming loyalists from the siege towers and heaped them unceremoniously on the ground. They tore through wood, wrenching structures apart, until the towers splintered into fragments that littered the ground like fallen giants. Powerful strikes from a trio of stone angels broke apart the stout timbers of the battering rams. Their wheels spun through the night. Shouts rose from loyalists mourning the destruction of their instruments of oppression.

Next to me on the battlements, Mahi and Nani embraced each other in celebration, and Merlin hopped in delirious joy.

With a deep inhale, I asked the gargoyles to take us to ground level.

But the general cupped my chin and turned me to face him, and my stomach somersaulted. *Ask her.*

The moon illuminated his tan skin with silvery light. He cradled my face in his hands, his expression vulnerable. The chiselled lines of his face softened, and his obsidian eyes were the gateway to raw emotion. "I need to say this. Marry me, Kiya. You're the answer to everything I've been looking for. You're my reason to breathe. I can't lose you. Not tonight, not ever. Marry me."

The world fell away. There were only his hands on my face as he searched my expression, wild hope in his eyes. I didn't need to think about it. Safe or not safe, there was only him. "Yes, I'll marry you. I'm yours, Dev."

He crushed me against his chest and caught my lips with his mouth. The kiss was deep and true. It was our first kiss on the beach of the bay and every kiss thereafter. It warmed me and told me the story of who we were and who we could be. It told me he'd burn down the world for me.

Then, we separated, lifted over the walls by the gargoyles, and my heart was a catch in my throat.

We landed in the dirt and debris alongside the rest of our court, with the remnants of the sacred tree at our back, on a hazardous terrain that mirrored the chaos of the conflict. The night pressed in on us, a shroud of darkness that obscured the stars and swallowed the moon. The beat of gargoyle wings filled the air as they returned to the battlements. Then the raja signalled to his loyalists to encircle us. Their eyes were glazed over, their movements unnatural. As they closed in on us, fear clawed at my throat and seeped from the pores of my fellow rebels. All except Deven, who exuded an aura of calm resolve, inky eyes piercing through the darkness.

Even as Prem stalked towards us.

As though the promise of our future was real. God, I wanted it to be real.

"You took my sister and my grandfather." I met Prem's gaze. "I could lay a thousand charges at your door."

"I wouldn't care. Why so sour? Prakash Malini was hardly the model family member." His cobalt eyes glinted with a predatory gleam as he nodded to his new general, who we had dined with hours before. "Go ahead, General."

The new general—limping slightly from his clash with Deven—bowled a sphere towards us.

A sphere pierced by a rod.

I startled, thinking it was a mace or a weapon with a rotating axis. Sindhuja swooped towards us, her wings strong, and Deven snarled as if his tiger had come to the fore. The object hurtled through the air, arcing over the raja and landed at my feet with a thump. It rocked to a standstill, and I stared at it, my synapses refusing to fire, unwilling to acknowledge the evidence of my eyes. Wanting to deny that anyone could be so cruel.

Gasps sounded next to me, and Nani began to pray.

Oh god, oh god. Lokesh *Saheb*.

Bile bubbled up into my throat at the sight of the royal tailor's decapitated head. He'd been impaled through the eye by his feathered walking stick with such force that his eye socket had shattered. His neck was congealed with blood, and his smooth skin was discoloured and frozen in an expression of horror. I closed my eyes as sadness and revulsion threatened to swallow me whole. He'd been so shrewd. So talented and eccentric. So willing to keep my secrets. As a telepath, he would have known in sickening detail what was about to happen to him.

"There's no redeeming you," spat Deven. "Nothing worth saving."

"You're only just realising that now, dear cousin?" Prem sneered. "I'm here to break your world apart."

Every breath felt like a struggle. Did he know? Did he know what the *oud* perfume contained or had he discovered Lokesh *Saheb*'s collusion with me another way? Had it been my fault? My hands fisted at my sides.

I hated him with every fibre of my being.

"You're upset with me, Kiya. Lokesh forced my hand. It's a shame, of course. His skill was undeniable. I'm not sure there'll be another like him. But he couldn't mask his awe when those pesky new gargoyles arrived this evening. I soon realised he wasn't under my control. He'd sided with you. Enough circling, earth witch." Icy eyes flared with savage intent. He called out to the circle of loyalists. "No one intervenes. Not man, woman or gargoyle. Or the duel is forfeit. Of course, my dear people, the rest of these rebels are yours for the taking. I'll reward you generously for every life claimed."

For a moment, I remembered how he had tried to woo me, how he had shown me my mother's picture in the library and told me how his father had wanted to court her, and I thought how we might have been friends if he'd had an ounce of kindness. If he'd not been a man who was wounded by pride. If he'd not hungered for control and supremacy. If he wasn't addicted to the siren call of violence when he didn't get his way. He shifted. His clothes ripped across his broad chest as he went down on all fours. Bones cracked. Fur sprouted. Teeth grew monstrous. And Prem Kumar filled his tiger's skin. His fur bristled with the anticipation of violence. I could almost feel his dark heart pulsing with insatiable blood thirst. I shivered, understanding that he had come as a beast because he was done wheedling and waiting and taunting.

He wanted us on our knees before him with his teeth at our throats.

He didn't just want to see us humbled. He wanted us dead.

I was ready. God, I was ready to take what was his.

CHAPTER 31

I glanced at Deven—in his human form—and at Leena and the rest of my court. Their hopes for me, for the kingdom, radiated from them.

The gargoyle queen stands on the precipice of victory. Her time comes, chanted the chorus of gargoyles in my head.

Magic fizzed in my cells, and my senses sharpened. I wanted to live. I wanted to stop him from harming anyone ever again. I wanted to grow old with my loves. With Deven, Leena, Nani and Merlin. With Deven's loves, too. With Mahi, Nisha, Ashwin and Ishaan. With Jilu, Radha and Yuvan. With the people of this kingdom.

Then the tiger that was Prem charged, and my focus narrowed to him and only him.

He was a blur of motion against the moonlit night. His bulky form cut through the cold air, cobalt eyes fixed on me with feral intensity. He closed the distance between us in seconds, his deadly claws gleaming in the moonlight. With an ear-splitting roar, he launched forward, aiming for my throat.

Resolve burned brightly within me. I stood my ground, sensing the pulse of the earth beneath me, sensing in my bones that it would respond to my call. As I threw my hands up, a wall of dense soil sprung up between us, sending shockwaves through the air with the force of my magic.

Prem skidded to a stop, prowling, cobalt eyes narrowed.

Was there one person in this world that Prem Kumar had treated well, advocated for, or shown kindness to? One person who would stand up for him—without fear or reward —and speak for him?

Then he propelled himself forward again, racing past my defensive wall, sinews rippling beneath his fur. I recentred myself, my gaze locked on Prem as he lunged, jagged teeth bared and claws outstretched. My senses heightened to a razor-sharp edge. With a cold touch of certainty—muscle memory embedded from countless training sessions with Dev—I carved out a dip in the earth with my left hand. Prem's hot, putrid breath skimmed my face as I swerved to the left. He stumbled into the dip, forelegs buckling.

Without missing a beat, I drew my dagger and sliced a shallow cut the length of his body.

His roar slashed against my eardrums, and my heart ricochetted against my chest, but the chill winter air calmed me. My breath formed clouds of mist as the tiger righted himself, and his rage spiralled like a tornado.

I didn't want him to die. Not yet. Not until the strings of the marionettes had been severed.

I trusted Mahi. I really did. We'd been through so much together.

As Prem regrouped, I checked on my court, battling against the shells of the loyalists. The scene distilled into a nanosecond. Deven, in human form, his swords still sheathed, fighting with his fists, showing restraint as we had pledged. Leena, binding her opponents with twisting vines. Merlin, herding and, at times, impaling, men with his jackalope antlers. Nani and Mahi chanting spells that disoriented and confused and sent soldiers to sweet dreams. Menon, on the periphery, pale and trembling, as if he were a ticking timebomb primed by Prem. Sindhuja and a small battalion of gargoyles gripping the most skilled fighters until witchcraft quieted them, keeping them enclosed in stoney wings that couldn't be prised apart, as unforgiving as a jail cell.

The noise and anguish were unrelenting.

Prem was quick to recover, and I braced myself for the impact of his rage. My body already ached from our exertions, already ached from the clashes in the throne room, but I refused to fall prey to self-pity. His claws left deep gouges in the hard-packed ground as he rounded on me, driving me backwards, forcing me to throw outbursts of magic so quickly that the ground erupted with protrusions, and my chest heaved. I dodged his claws and spittle-soaked teeth and retaliated with a barrage of earthy projectiles aimed at his head and flank. I wove spells that left my tongue tangled and throat thick with consonants and vowels. *Tvayā abhimāno nāśaḥ* and *tava atītaṃ bhakṣayatu* and *tvayā hatānāṃ bhayaḥ.* They asked for Prem's vanity to be his downfall, for his past to consume him and for him to be haunted by his killings. I threw anything that came to mind at him. Spells that were familiar and spells that I was certain Merlin sent my way from across the battlefield. My strength waned with each passing moment, my limbs growing sluggish and clumsy.

It would have been easier to be done with it.

To kill him rather than to delay.

He clung to power like it was his lifeline. Like he had nothing else.

He had tricks up his sleeve that we hadn't anticipated. In the space of a breath, Sindhuja allowed me to see through her eyes. How Prem had used mind magic to force Menon to attack Mahi, his sister. How Menon begged Babbu to peck out his eyes, his heart, his brain, to stop himself from hurting her. Menon, who had fought against being remembered as a villain and against mind control. Fishtail showed me their wordless, heart-wrenching goodbye, and the emerald parrot hovered, crimson beak at the ready. How Mahi, beside herself, reached out to snap her beloved parrot's neck. How Leena intervened and turned Menon into a fig tree—there in the middle of the battlefield as chaos reigned all around—to sustain him until we could free his mind. And how Mahi cried tears of relief as the parrot nested on the fig tree's uppermost branch and waited.

Waited for her gleaning to come true.

Then I was back in my own body, reeling.

A cornered animal was a dangerous one. The vibrations of Prem's paws shook the earth. I was tired, so very tired that when he targeted my mind, he broke through the mountainous barriers of my inner landscape. His sinister tendrils found their way to the lawn where I had picnicked with my sisters, where Dad had given us piggyback rides and chased us until we collapsed in giggles. He filled it with his darkness, and I jerked against his intrusion. A misjudged step and his razor-sharp claws raked across my arm, leaving stinging wounds in their wake. Within seconds, he'd met his mark again. I twisted away from his lunge too late, and his teeth gnashed my shoulder, gouging my skin through my leathers. Pain shot through my body. Gritting my teeth against the agony, I created a barrier of solid rock between us.

Somewhere, Deven called my name, his voice growing closer.

The gargoyles clamoured to help. Their chorus rose to a crescendo in my mind. They wanted his blood. Wanted him to swear fealty to me. Wanted to crush him. Wanted his head on a spike.

I told them he was mine even as my lungs burned.

I wouldn't falter. Couldn't falter.

The scent of unearthed soil filled my nostrils. Earth filled with such possibilities that it gave me strength. Prem was deadly, but he was also arrogant. He hadn't realised that all the time he had honed his combat skills, his opponents had gone easy on him, feeding his hubris, pretending to be slower, clumsier, less tactically astute than him. He had expected me to be too weak, too alone, too new to this violent world to pose a threat to him. He thought he could manipulate me. He'd tried it all: false charm, coercion, tricks and grief. But he was his own worst enemy. Dishonesty and fear at the heart of his own rule had rotted his chances of staying on the throne of Jalapashu.

He'd chosen strength and control, rather than softness and trust.

He'd resorted to violence rather than nourishing his humanity.

My gargoyles and I would be the bulwark against his violence for as long as it took. Whatever it took. Even if he flayed my skin and extracted the last thought from my brain, I would stand against him.

Because the people deserved more than he could give them.

Then everything changed. As though I'd sent a prayer into the universe and Sitara and Grandfather had heard. As though the *oud* that Nani had concocted and Lokesh *Saheb* had smeared on the raja's pulse points had finally permeated his bloodstream. As if Kaladhar had met his gods, the scales of his sins had been weighed, and judgment had been passed. As though the land itself had deemed me worthy.

My body stung for the briefest moment as though the bitter bonds of the bargain dissolved. And Babbu soared in circles overhead, his squawking cry a blessed relief, iridescent emerald feathers shimmering against the night sky.

I met Dev's eyes across the newly quiet battlefield. All around him, loyalists blinked or kneaded their temples. They shook off the dense fog of bewitchment, and confusion gave way to clarity.

Prem's mind control had broken. Judging by his roar, he knew it, too.

Exhilaration ran through me like a burst of soda, replenishing my energy. "How about a little chase?"

I darted between jagged rocks, my senses attuned to the rhythm of the earth beneath my feet, taunting the tiger to catch me. At the last minute, I spun, channelling my magic into the ground. The earth rumbled as it ejected a torrent of boulders like a volcanic eruption. My spells streaked through the air like arrows loosed from a bow, aided by jackalope Merlin, who came to my side. *Boe kāṭe* and *piṇḍa* and *mohayati* and more. A heady cocktail of power.

Prem crashed to the ground in a tangle of fur and muscle. He snarled in frustration, but I already twisted my hands like tulips, like a dancer, calling on root and soil to bind him to the ground. His limbs trembled with exertion, and his flank oozed blood. He couldn't muster the strength to rise. Not against the earth itself. It solidified around him, anchoring him to the spot. His cobalt eyes smouldered with hate and defiance.

He roared and demanded me to kill him. To end it.

But there were others he'd wronged more than me.

It was clear who won the duel, even before the people—both inside and outside the fortress—called out *rani, my rani, our rani*. Even before Sindhuja and gargoyles landed in the dirt and debris and bowed deeply before me.

I didn't pity Prem Kumar. I simply walked away.

Others charged forward. The men and women he'd puppeted, released from their bonds, frothed with anger. Liberated from the shackles of Prem's control, they descended upon him like a swarm of angry hornets, their fists and daggers and swords striking him, their words lashing him. Each blow was a cathartic release of the suffering they had endured under his tyrannical rule. They meted out their justice, even after he shifted back into his human form and pleaded for mercy.

Even after he lay battered and broken, and he had breathed his last.

When they were finished, and their fury was spent, I watched with Leena as Deven shifted into his tiger and devoured the remains of the man who had been his cousin, who had broken the bonds of family to claim and conserve his rule as raja. He came to my side, and I ran my hand over his fur, thinking how we hadn't chosen violence, but sometimes it was unavoidable.

As I gazed out into the night, I hardly felt my wounds.

Yellow roses bloomed where we stood, their petals unfolding like the pages of a long-forgotten story. I didn't ask if Leena had made them or whether they were an echo of our mother. Their fragrance wrapped around us like a warm embrace as if to tell us we belonged in Jalapashu.

To tell me I had proven myself worthy of being rani.

When I looked at the sacred banyan tree, new shoots had sprouted.

CHAPTER 32

Our wedding was a simple affair, without extravagant decorations or lavish attire.

We stood in dappled sunlight beneath a dense canopy in the forest where Deven roamed as a tiger. There, Mahi married us next to ancient trees that whispered about past secrets and the promise of the future. We were barefoot, our feet cushioned on moss. I wore a simple white silver-threaded *lehenga* in flowing fabric that caught the breeze. Deven wore a crisp linen shirt and trousers. Leena made garlands of fresh jasmine flowers for us both. We had no desire for jewels; our matching wedding bands were simple gold.

Our only guests were Nisha and her family, daisy-wearing Sindhuja and the Court of Rebels. However, the latter would be dismantled in favour of a larger court, with representation from every part of Jalapashan society.

There were no grand gestures or elaborate rituals. All we needed was each other and our loved ones. When Mahi pronounced us husband and wife, our kiss was tender, and the earth hummed under my feet.

Afterwards, we danced under starry skies, Aanya sang, and our laughter rang out like music.

But life and death were so entwined. There were funerals, too.

More on the loyalist than the rebel side, but we mourned together as one people. Nani, Leena and I said our goodbyes to Grandfather and sprinkled Sitara's ashes amongst bluebell woodlands, just as we had promised. We were grateful for near misses and happy occurrences, for well-laid plans and ideas executed in the heat of war. That meant, for example, that a man could be turned into a fig tree and be reunited with his sister once he was himself again.

Despite the hurt, I believed that the trauma of our battles would fade.

I believed I could be a good, kind queen.

Especially with Deven at my side.

A WEEK LATER, WE WERE CROWNED RANI AND RAJA OF Jalapashu.

It was said that two regents ruling together brought balance to the kingdom.

That we would each bring complementary strengths and perspectives; we wouldn't be corrupted as easily.

On the day of our coronation, the palace grounds came alive with electrifying energy. The kingdom erupted into a riot of colour and sound. Streamers fluttered in the breeze, casting a kaleidoscope of colours against the azure sky. The people dressed in hues of saffron, crimson and emerald. Powder paint adorned the faces of revellers, and they smeared bright hues on each other. Jilu and Radha circulated with trays of sweet *jalebis*, vegetable *samosas*, *pani puri* filled with a spicy chickpea mixture and tangy tamarind sauce.

Dhol players leapt to their rhythm, igniting the crowd. Lata—now studying nursing under Leena—led a troupe of dancers in twirls, anklets jingling with each graceful step. And Merlin, his antlers for now gone, frolicked with Tanay and Ishaan.

No one spoke of Prem Kumar.

I wondered what myths would be written about him, and about me, and about the husband I loved.

I decided that I would write a myth about a brave royal tailor and the clothes he conjured.

CHAPTER 33

Deven put down his book and turned lazily to me. "Come here, wife."

I inched forward into the nook of his arm. Goosebumps sprang up as he trailed a finger from the unsightly healed wound on my shoulder, along the side of my bare breast, down to my waist. "I miss you calling me little witch."

His eyebrow quirked, his silver scar catching the soft spring light. "Oh, I can call you all the names under the sun. Whatever pleases you. Gargoyle queen. Rani. Your Highness. Especially if you make that little moan. You know, the one you make when—"

I swatted him with my pillow, and he laughed with utter freedom as if the other him—the stern general in his cousin's kingdom—had never existed at all. He eyed the fruit platter on the sideboard, where a handful of strawberries and raspberries remained after his deliciously naughty ideas in the bedroom.

My cheeks flushed, and I pushed him towards the shower. "Go on. Otherwise, we'll be late. I'll be there in a minute."

"Fine. But you'll have to make it up to me later. We've earned this rest, Kiya."

"Yes, we have." I sank back onto the pillows as his tattooed back and tanned cheeks disappeared into the bathroom.

The past few months had been heaven. We'd curled up on the sofa together, his feet in my lap, as we read each other passages from our favourite books. He'd wrapped me in a blanket and carried me outside on a moonlit night before pointing out the constellations. We'd cooked our favourite meals together, then run laughing to Biryani Junction in a downpour because Jilu and Radha's cooking was far superior when we'd become distracted and burnt our offerings. I knew now how he took his *chai*: creamy with no sugar, consumed piping hot or not at all. We'd written love letters to each other, heady emotions cloaked in shy words. We'd played cricket with his family and made a mess when I tried to teach him how to use the potter's wheel. We'd spent countless hours exploring each other's bodies, and it still wasn't enough.

The women of the kingdom had accepted me as their rani far sooner than they accepted that Deven was mine.

Dev appeared at the bathroom door, interrupting my reverie. His dark hair was damp, and errant strands clung to his forehead. He leaned casually against the doorframe, his bronzed torso relaxed and glistening with beads of water. He exuded comfort in his own skin. A playful smile tugged at the corners of his lips and widened as my eyes dropped beneath his tapered waistline. "Are you coming, little witch?"

I cast an eye at the clock on our bedside table and grumbled. "Yes, yes. Hold your horses."

Thirty minutes later, we arrived at the sacred banyan tree in the open space where our fortress had stood. The coven's magic had created the fortress that had sheltered the resistance, and it was the coven's magic that dismantled it. I wasn't sad to see the fortress go: it had served its purpose. Though sometimes, in the dead of the night, I dreamed I was still trapped in its mud-caked hallways. Dreamed that a battering ram pounded at our walls.

Until Deven woke me or I nestled against his warm tiger's flank.

With the fortress gone and the weaver family returned to their home, I moved my pottery studio to a room on the ground floor of the white-washed palace. It was strange to live in the palace, with its opulence, secret passageways, and the memories of Prem. I missed our family farmhouse in Boundless Bay. So Deven and I decided to move into his old quarters, which weren't as grand and where elephants roamed in the adjacent gardens.

The council—our voices foremost amongst them—decided the palace shouldn't be solely reserved for grand balls and formal affairs. Instead, we threw open the windows, letting in the fresh air. The palace halls echoed with the laughter of children playing. We opened the throne room to tradesmen on market days during English rains. Families picnicked on the palace lawns. Jalapashans flocked to the library at all hours of the day and night, and Aanya was exploring turning one wing into a new school. Nani had started her therapy circle again in a grand room full of stiff couches and even allowed Merlin to lurk. They'd been getting closer since Grandfather's death, but then, he had a way of mending broken hearts. It wasn't long before he'd add his own confessions to the therapy circle.

For a man who had coveted power for much of his life, Menon had been eager to leave the palace and move into Mahi's leaning house with her. The siblings were making up for lost decades and getting to know each other better. Menon's decision to fight Prem's mind control until his last breath, rather than harm Mahi or derail her dreams of a kinder kingdom, had renewed their relationship.

The gargoyles, too, found new ways of living.

Once, the gargoyles had destroyed the kingdom. Now they had helped to free it.

As the kingdom entered a new era, the gargoyles underwent a transformation of their own. Some—like Harya—longed to seek their dreams and destinies beyond the kingdom. I kept my promise. They spread their wings and disappeared into the sky in search of new adventures. Our connection dimmed until a time when we needed them again, but their presence lingered in the recesses of my mind. Other gargoyles chose to remain in Jalapashu, entering their stony slumber perched on walls and rooftops across the kingdom, becoming fixtures of the landscape.

But Sindhuja stayed, too attached to me and Leena to roam far or to enter her sleep.

The new council had agreed that all Jalapashans, not only the gargoyles, would be free to come and go from the kingdom—as long as they guarded our secrets—or to leave altogether if that is what they desired. Most feared a more porous relationship with the kingdom. They feared the outside world. But others, like Yuvan, would make wonderful explorers. In time, fear would abate, and in the process, they would perhaps win knowledge and openness that would prevent future leaders from curtailing their freedoms as Prem had.

The sky stretched above us in cerulean blue as we gathered for the ceremony. Sindhuja and a handful of gargoyles formed a guard of honour around the sacred tree. New shoots had sprouted with a speed that defied natural law. The people, prone to superstitions, considered the new growth an auspicious sign for the new kingdom. They had gathered at the sacred tree at noon, as requested. Some had brought pieces of ribboned card to tie to the shoots of the banyan tree, imprinted with their deepest wishes for the future and prayers for the earth witch and the tiger general who ushered in a more just era.

We were building a new world.

Our new world treated every citizen equally.

Mahi raised her kohl-painted eyebrows and huffed a sigh when she saw us. "Look at you two. I like T-shirts as much as the next woman, but sometimes you have to look the part."

Deven ran his eyes over my jeans and top combo. "I think my wife looks ravishing."

The seer snorted, but she couldn't hide the gleam of contentment in her eyes. "You've brought out the romantic in him, Kiya. I never thought I'd see it."

"Shall we hurry this along?" asked Leena. "I'm taking Aanya and Nani on a pub crawl in Brighton. Quite frankly, I need a drink after Mahi wrenched the jewels from our bodies."

Mahi pursed her lips as Babbu pecked irritably on her shoulder. "I was very gentle."

Deven's obsidian eyes turned to me. "Are you sure about this?"

I nodded. "I've never been more certain."

The people came to offer us topaz from the now-obsolete Amber Hollows. Faces—all familiar now—made their way to where Merlin presided over a wicker basket, his liquid gold eyes wide with wonder. I went first, placing my topaz jewel inside the basket: first, the fragment that we had mined with Sitara from the Amber Hollows that the seer had hidden in my body, then—to Deven's smirking delight—the ring from my broken engagement with Prem. Deven went next, followed by Leena, Mahi and Menon's medallions, Nani with her own jewel, and Grandfather's. Soon, the people lined up to place their jewels in the basket. Only the luckiest amongst them had been gifted their own topaz by Prem, but the old habits of wanting to please power and my assurances that they would retain their magic meant we had eventually convinced most people to part with the relics.

This was Mahi's gift to me and the kingdom: one last pivotal vision.

The jewels cascaded into the basket. Each gem—a symbol of individual power—was surrendered into the collective pool as a gesture of trust. Trust I hoped we'd earned. That I hoped we deserved. The gems varied in shape and hue, each carrying a hint of its wearer's essence. They clinked against one another, a glittering mosaic. When the last jewel found its place on the heap, I tipped the contents of the wicker basket onto the soil at the base of the newly sprouting banyan tree.

There was a moment of stillness: a collective intake of breath.

I closed my eyes, finding the primal connection to the earth inside myself. A wave of energy surged through me as the land responded to my call. The ground was eager to share its bounty, eager to be renewed. I centred myself, channelling my hands downwards. My magic radiated out from me, making the mountainous heap of topaz glow with ethereal brilliance. Then they split apart: first as shards, then as fine salts. A further burst of magic made them dissolve into the rich soil with a soft hiss. As the last traces of the topaz disappeared into the earth, I sensed the invigorated pulse of the land, the seeping away of corruption, and how magic had been distributed to every corner of it.

The people gasped as, almost immediately, the banyan tree's growth accelerated, new branches reaching skywards. Mahi had seen what came next: how each Jalapashan, when connected to this land, had their own flavour of magic. She had seen how even adults who attended the magic wing of Aanya's new school in the palace would thrive. Her gleanings showed how my choice dismantled some of the power structures in the kingdom and how, with careful treading, we could have both peace and justice.

"This kingdom always had enough magic to sustain us all," I told our people.

The seer's customary gruffness gave way to a radiant smile at her brother.

Deven's hand found mine. "I think that means you're now mine for the day."

As the people of Jalapashu explored their renewed connection to the land, we walked hand in hand to the forest, where he shifted and embraced the wildness within him. He dipped in invitation, belly to the ground, and I approached him slowly, reverently, before climbing onto his back, basking in the velvet texture of his fur. Then he bounded forward, and I held on tight as forest ferns blurred past us and seagulls cried out across the bay.

ACKNOWLEDGEMENTS

Sometimes, I can write stories while interacting with the world. This wasn't that type of book.

It needed me to be quiet for days on end so I could hear its soul. It needed me to cocoon and dip down under blankets and drown out the sounds of the city: revving cars, barking dogs and neighbours taking in their parcels. It was a gift, really, because when I started writing this book, I felt overwhelmed. And when I finished writing the last sentence, I knew myself better. I learned that we can't always be what the world expects us to be or meet the pace we set ourselves. That sometimes it's enough just to be and feel and create and care.

Grateful thanks, first of all, to my readers. Writing is the best job in the world, and you're the reason I can do it.

To my brilliant book team, thank you. To my editors, Trish and Toni, thanks for your patience, dedication, keen eyes and grace when I need it. You bring such ease to the final phases of preparing the manuscript. Fay, your cover art is one of my favourite parts of the process. Thanks for your art, imagination and skill.

Thank you to my beta readers, Debbie and Sherry, who are always willing to read for me at a moment's notice. Your insights shape my stories in profound ways and give me the courage to send them out into the world.

To H, R & N, our children, I'm so proud of you. You will carve your own paths and make your corners of the world special just by being in them. I can't wait to see the magic and the havoc you will wreak.

To Jan, my husband, my favourite person in the entire world, who sees himself in every hero I write, you are my everything. I would give up crowns and kingdoms for you. Thank you, thank you, a thousandfold, for walking through life with me.

SHARE YOUR READER LOVE

I hope you enjoyed *To Trick a Raja*. Please take a few moments to leave a review online. Reviews are so appreciated. They tell authors which stories resonate and help readers discover our work.

If you are a book blogger and would like to feature my books, please get in touch at www.NilluNasser.com.

N. Z. Nasser

xoxo

STAY IN TOUCH & GRAB YOUR SHORT STORY

Come and be part of my tribe and join my facebook reader group at <u>Nasser's Book Nymphs.</u>

To receive the short stories in the Majestic Midlife Witch world and keep up to date with my news, sign up for my fantasy newsletter at <u>www.nillunasser.com</u>.

For a close lens into my world, you can get early access to work-in-progress chapters and other goodies by joining my exclusive community: <u>https://reamstories.com/nznasser.</u>

Here's a coupon for the first time you make a purchase in my online store (it's so pretty!) at <u>www.nillunasser.com</u>: NILLU15.

GARDEN OF INK AND ANCIENT STONE

INK OF THE FAE, BOOK 1

Ysadora is the daughter of a calligrapher in a world where writing has become a lost art. Her elderly father shuns his coveted skill, but she doesn't ask him why. After her mother's disappearance, they shy away from conflict. Each day, they tend to their bookshop. Each night, after her father retires to bed, Ysadora reads from a forbidden shelf in the cellar.

When her father vanishes during a wild winter storm, Ysadora finds spilt indigo ink on the icy ground and a message written in what could only be his hand. A message that tells her to stay away from the dark forest. A message that tells her to run.

Alone and distraught, Ysadora tracks her way into the forest, towards a bewitching land she thought existed only in stories. In the faerie realm, calligraphy skills are not only highly prized but dangerous. Ysadora meets Zephyr, whose cruel allure proves more perilous than any fae magic. If she is to save her father, she might very well lose her heart.

Garden of Ink and Ancient Stone is the first novel in a new romantasy series, Ink of the Fae. If you are a fan of wild worlds, deadly secrets, strong heroines and the swoon-worthy heroes who love them, this book is for you.

ALSO BY N. Z. NASSER

DRUID HEIR

Midlife Dawn, Book 1

Midlife Tremors, Book 2

Midlife News, Book 3

Midlife Drift, Book 4

Midlife Portals, Book 5

Midlife Eclipse, Book 6

Midlife Battle, Book 7

MAJESTIC MIDLIFE WITCH

To Save a Sister, Book 1

To Curse a Rival, Book 2

To Trick a Raja, Book 3

COMING SOON

New series: Ink of the Fae

NEWSLETTER EXCLUSIVES

The Magical Grandmother, Druid Heir Short Story 0.5

A First Date in Paris, Druid Heir Short Story 1.5

Midlife Battle, Druid Heir 7 Bonus Epilogue

To Become a Witch, Majestic Midlife Short Story 0.5

Biryani Junction, a Majestic Midlife Witch Cookbook

ABOUT THE AUTHOR

N. Z. Nasser is a writer of fantasy fiction. Her stories are about women who change the world, filled with magic and rooted in friendship.

A lover of barefoot walks along the beach, she is glad to have left behind her career in the civil service and to never wear heels again. Whether she is writing in her garden office or wrangling laundry, she is happiest with a cup of tea at her side.

She lives in London with her husband, three children, two cats and a fox-mad dog.

www.ingramcontent.com/pod-product-compliance
Lightning Source LLC
Chambersburg PA
CBHW031313210726
48287CB00005B/1529